Praise for *The Make-Up Test*

"Enemies to lovers, set in academia, with the pitfalls of imposter syndrome to navigate? Yes, please! A sweet, fresh spin on how the third time's the charm." —**Jodi Picoult, #1** *New York Times* **bestselling author of** *Wish You Were Here*

"Original, clever, sizzling, *The Make-Up Test* is the perfect mix of unique settings, lovable characters, and the exquisite agony of second-chance romances. It's the grad school, rivals-to-lovers book of my wildest, sexiest dreams! I'll read anything Jenny L. Howe writes!" —**Ali Hazelwood,** *New York Times* **bestselling author of** *The Love Hypothesis*

"*The Make-Up Test* is a charmingly nerdtastic debut from Jenny L. Howe. It's a delightfully sweet second chance, rivals-to-lovers story wrapped up in a cardigan, sprinkled liberally with Beowulf and Chaucer references, and garnished with cat socks." —**Jen DeLuca, author of** *Well Met, Well Played,* **and** *Well Matched*

"Jenny L. Howe's debut novel is heartfelt vulnerability wrapped in a sexy cardigan. . . . Allison and Colin's second chance at love will keep you turning pages, and maybe picking up Chaucer's collected works. *The Make-Up Test* is an A+." —**Denise Williams, author of** *How to Fail at Flirting* **and** *The Fastest Way to Fall*

"This second-chance romance is cozier than one of Colin's cardigans and lovelier than a crisp autumn day. . . . With clever writing that makes her grad-school rivals simmer and spark on the page, Jenny L. Howe has crafted a love story that feels not just swoony and heart-stirring, but achingly [...]

[...]non, bestselling author of *Ex Talk* and *Weather Girl*

"I have lost count of the number of times I went, 'Yes, exactly!' when reading *The Make-Up Test*. It captures all of my frustrations with academia (why *is* Jacques Derrida so impossible?!) so perfectly, but at the same time, it's also a love letter to academia. *The Make-Up Test* has all of the emotions of the roller coaster that's university life woven into its pages. The second-chance romance is a soothing balm to my heart, and the fat representation is exactly what I have longed to see in books. We need more stories like *The Make-Up Test*!"

—**Jesse Q. Sutanto, bestselling author of *Dial A for Aunties***

"*The Make-Up Test* celebrates being who you are and staying true to yourself while also acknowledging that it's incredibly hard when it seems like the world is working against you. A thoroughly enjoyable read from start to finish! A perfect companion read for fans of Ali Hazelwood and Rachel Lynn Solomon."   —**Suzanne Park, author of *So We Meet Again* and *Loathe at First Sight***

"Full of deliciously biting banter, laugh-out-loud observation, and heartbreaking introspection . . . While body positivity, frank conversations about anxiety, and navigating fraught parent-adult child relationships and friendships on the cusp of change are sure to be relatable, it's the bittersweet longing in Allison and Colin's slow-burn exes-to-friends-to-lovers relationship that takes center stage. *The Make-Up Test* is a testament to the risks and rewards of lowering your drawbridge for the one you love. By my troth, if this second-chance debut isn't on your TBR already, fie on you!"   —**Lillie Vale, author of *The Shaadi Set-Up* and *The Decoy Girlfriend***

"Insightful, inclusive, and incredibly fun, *The Make-Up Test* is an absolute delight from beginning to end. Jenny L. Howe is a romance writer to watch."   —**Hannah Whitten, author of *For the Wolf* and *For the Throne***

The Make-Up Test

A NOVEL

JENNY L. HOWE

ST. MARTIN'S
GRIFFIN
NEW YORK

First published in the United States by St. Martin's Griffin, an imprint of St. Martin's Publishing Group

THE MAKE-UP TEST. Copyright © 2022 by Jenny L. Howe. All rights reserved. Printed in the United States of America. For information, address St. Martin's Publishing Group, 120 Broadway, New York, NY 10271.

www.stmartins.com

Designed by Omar Chapa

Library of Congress Cataloging-in-Publication Data

Names: Howe, Jenny L., author.
Title: The make-up test : a novel / Jenny L. Howe.
Description: First edition. | New York : St. Martin's Griffin, 2022.
Identifiers: LCCN 2022010206 | ISBN 9781250837868 (trade paperback) | ISBN 9781250837875 (ebook)
Subjects: LCGFT: Novels. | Romance fiction.
Classification: LCC PS3608.O946 M35 2022 | DDC 813/.6—dc23/eng/20220317
LC record available at https://lccn.loc.gov/2022010206

Our books may be purchased in bulk for promotional, educational, or business use. Please contact your local bookseller or the Macmillan Corporate and Premium Sales Department at 1-800-221-7945, extension 5442, or by email at MacmillanSpecialMarkets@macmillan.com.

First Edition: 2022

10 9 8 7 6 5 4 3 2 1

To my mother, who always told me I could fly.
And to Kevin, who helped me find my wings.

Author's Note

Dear Reader,

First and foremost, I'm so grateful that you are here. Thank you for picking up *The Make-Up Test*. I have written quite a few books before this one, but I could not be happier that *The Make-Up Test* will be my debut. It is full of everything I love (romance, profane cross-stitches, dogs, good friends, good food, knights and other medieval stuff, and BOOKS, SO MANY BOOKS), and I hope it gives you as much joy reading it as it gave me writing it.

The Make-Up Test was born of many things: my love of medieval literature, my time in graduate school, my affinity for second-chance romance and academic rival tropes. But most importantly for me, *The Make-Up Test* is the book that, as a fat woman, I needed most of my life—that, many days even now, I still need. Allison Avery, my main character, is a fat woman, but that is just one small facet of who she is. Her story is not a story of weight loss, or even of learning to love herself for who she is and what she looks like. She already does that. Allison's story is about embracing change and discovering that not only can we change, but so can the people around us. It's about learning to trust herself to love again after her heart has been broken. And it's about being confident enough in herself to go after the things she wants with every bit of energy she has and believing she can achieve them.

The word *fat* does not have to be ugly. But to make that so, we need to disempower it. I believe that stories are such a crucial first step to this. Fat people are more than their bodies. We deserve happily-ever-afters, both romantic and otherwise. I am so thrilled that I get to give Allison one.

While Allison loves herself, she lives in a world that does not love fat bodies, and so *The Make-Up Test* does deal with some heavier issues that might be triggering to some. There is expressed fatphobia by characters and in flashbacks, including by a family member, and the story deals with illness, death, and loss. I hope that I have been able to treat these issues with the care they deserve, and I ask that you take care of yourself while reading.

xoxo,

Jenny L. Howe

The Make-Up Test

Chapter 1

If one more person used the word *hegemonic*, Allison Avery was going to scream.

After almost two full weeks of classes at Claymore University, she should be more adjusted to the quirks of graduate-level literature courses, but it still felt like . . . *a lot.*

Everyone seemed so much older, like Link with his suspenders and bowties themed for every class, and Kara, whose button-downs were so freshly pressed she could roll down a grassy hill and still not have a wrinkle. And they all had laptops (new shiny ones), and were typing away with a gusto Allison couldn't muster while scribbling frantically into her notebook like some kind of Luddite as she missed every other word Professor Behi said.

When Allison had sat through the commencement address at her college graduation in May, listening to some politician whose name she should have known droning on about making the most of every opportunity, she'd let her mind drift to the fall, imagining herself in cute floral dresses, sitting in a snug corner of the library in a worn easy chair, listening raptly to professors wax poetic about Chaucer and Julian of Norwich and Boccaccio. She certainly hadn't planned on being crammed into the same cramped desk/chair combos from undergrad that jabbed at her curves no matter how she angled herself. Nor letting her eyes burn until the wee hours of the morning, trying to make sense of two paragraphs of Jacques Derrida.

And never, ever, *ever* had she expected to be sitting across the discussion circle from Colin Benjamin. Her ex-boyfriend.

Colin, not surprisingly, had been the latest person to cause Allison's brain to pucker by finding a way to work *hegemonic* into a sentence. That was the only reason she was staring at him right now.

He slouched lower in his chair as their professor's gaze shifted to a new raised hand. One of his spindly ankles sat upon his equally spindly knee—there was a reason she used to jokingly call him Ichabod Crane—revealing purple socks with the word *cats!* scrawled around drawings of felines in various stages of stretching and sleeping.

Allison bit the inside of her cheek to keep from reacting. It should be illegal for Colin Benjamin to wear cute socks. Or do anything cute, for that matter. The only adjectives reserved for him should be words like *irritating, maddening, vexatious.*

Behind glasses with thick, maroon frames, his hazel eyes slid toward her, and his hand reached for his dark blond hair. He kept the top long and the sides shaved, and despite all the gel that glued it back from his brow, Allison knew the strands were soft like silk.

The thought turned her stomach. To dismiss it, she thrust her arm into the air.

A smile warmed Professor Behi's face. It sliced a good decade off the age suggested by the thick streaks of gray in her black hair and the crow's feet etched deeply into the skin at the corners of her brown eyes. "Yes, Allison?"

Even from the safety of her desk, Allison's cheeks burned, and her voice turned squeaky. "Professo—er—Isha—" They'd been instructed at orientation to call their professors by their first names. *You're peers now,* the fourth-year graduate student had insisted, proudly, as if to remind everyone what a huge deal it was to be in one of the most prestigious Ph.D. programs in the country. Like Allison could ever forget.

Her mom had framed the acceptance letter and hung it above the fireplace. She made guests stand in front of it and admire the creamy white paper for at least ten seconds, an icon to worship.

But when these "peers" could dismiss students from the program at their discretion, that equality seemed dubious at best. Allison would much rather call them professor and make the power dynamic transparent.

She cleared her throat. "This is probably a dumb question, but if Derrida was so concerned about accessing meaning in a text, why did he go out of his way to make his writing so . . ." Allison clamped down on her bottom lip, trying to figure out the right word. Of course, with twelve other people's eyes on her—including Colin Benjamin's bespectacled gaze—all thought had left her brain. "Impossible," she finally muttered.

Colin lifted his hand to respond. Because of course he did. Colin Benjamin never missed the chance to challenge someone. Or hear the sound of his own voice.

Which, Allison hated to admit, was smooth and low and comforting. He would have made an excellent audio book narrator.

Before Professor Behi could acknowledge him, Ethan Windmore (to herself, Allison referred to him as Ethan Windbag) announced, "You've clearly missed the nuance of his theory."

Though no one said a word, Allison could feel their collective desire to groan. The tension pressed against the dingy windowpanes, thickening the already stuffy air of a muggy September afternoon in New England. After four years as an undergrad at Brown University, Allison should have been used to the fact that autumn didn't properly arrive in Providence, Rhode Island, until November. It made her miss the way the air in Northern Maine grew crisp as soon as school began.

Ethan leaned across his desk, causing his biceps to bulge against his T-shirt. *He should* not *have noticeable biceps,* Allison decided. No one that obnoxious should be allowed such a vanity.

She'd hoped someone might come to her rescue, but the whole

class had become mysteriously enraptured by whatever object was in closest proximity. Link was wiping the screen of his laptop like it was a windshield covered in bug carcasses. Kara smoothed out the faux-wood top of her desk. Alex and Mandy, the two other members of Allison's cohort, both picked at their nails.

Allison *hated* attention. But with three minutes of class left, she was not in the mood for one of Ethan's lectures. "I understand the nuance fine." Lies. Derrida's writing might as well have still been in French for all Allison could grasp of it. But hell would freeze over and pigs would fly and white dudes would admit they're wrong before she'd reveal that she did not comprehend a lick of literary theory. "I guess I'm not impressed by writers who get off on obfuscation."

Ethan gasped. The sound puffed Allison up with pride.

Professor Behi let out a musical laugh. "That seems like a good place to stop for today. Everyone, take Allison's lead and for our next meeting consider why Derrida needs to make his work so"—she tossed Allison a grin—"impossible."

People started to stand and snap shut their laptops, but Professor Behi clapped, returning the room to silence. "For you first-year students, teaching assistant positions have now been assigned. You can find a letter in your department mailbox about the course, your duties, etc. I apologize for the delay. A few last-minute shifts in course offerings resulted in some confusion."

Allison's heart galloped as she packed her bag. Finally, she'd find out if she'd been assigned to Professor Frances's class, British Literature's Greatest Hits: Pre-1800.

With her heart set on a career in medieval literature, a teaching assistantship with Professor Wendy Frances would be the ideal start. The woman was a genius. Her focus on modernizing the oldest of texts drew fire from traditionalists, but Allison knew this was the kind of academic work the world needed. Not criticism so dense it required a dictionary. Professor Frances's work transcended academic lines. People read it for pleasure. And it got them interested in texts that weren't household names. She helped people find themselves in the books Allison loved.

It was exactly what Allison wanted to do. And two flights of stairs up, in the tiny little graduate mailroom within the cramped graduate student lounge, could be an envelope that would set her on that path.

The west stairwell of Haber Hall had no windows, and the lights flickered. A small shiver danced up her back as Allison climbed the steps. At the top of the last flight, she pushed into the brightly painted hallway of the English Department. Unlike the dour gray of the rest of Haber, the third floor was the yellow of a perfect stick of butter, warm and inviting. Colorful posters and pamphlets boasting details for literary conferences and writers' workshops and indie movie releases and book launches speckled the space. Most of the professors' office doors were open and the din of conversation and rapid typing bounced along the worn red rug.

Allison ducked into the grad lounge. An old couch, its brown leather mapped with fault lines, was pushed under the window opposite a small kitchenette, and a random assortment of tables cluttered the center of the room. Along the back wall, rows of mailboxes sat above a countertop that held a printer and a hodgepodge of office supplies, most of which no one had touched since 2006.

Idling in front of the mailboxes was, of course, Colin Benjamin. The recessed lighting overhead turned the gel in his coifed hair to strands of glass as he stared down at a letter in his hands. His tall, gangly form blocked the entire space like he was a grocery shopper who'd stopped his cart in the middle of an aisle to scan the shelves.

The smartest move would be to hang back and wait until he was finished. But waiting required patience, and Allison possessed not one ounce of that. Especially not when she'd been desperate for *weeks* to find out about her TA-ship. She'd spotted the manila envelope peeking from her mail slot as soon as she'd rounded the door. She needed to get her hands on it.

Gritting her teeth, she smoothed down the front of her flowy polka-dotted top and tossed her long brown hair over her shoulder. Then she moved in.

As she inched toward Colin, she took the most subtle deep breath she could manage and held in her gut to ensure she'd fit between him and the counter.

Even growing up in a house where Allison's mother bent over backward to make Allison feel normal and beautiful, it was impossible, as a perpetually plus-sized girl, not to think about those things. Nothing about the world had been built with her body shape in mind, and so every space became a math problem with angles to analyze and equations to work out.

Allison *hated* math.

Thanks to the curse of her father's last name, her mailbox was at the top of the row, forcing her to rise up on her tiptoes to reach the envelope. Even then, leaning forward as far as her short calves would allow, she only managed to snag the corner. The thrill of triumph lasted the one second it took her to realize that, in the process, she'd thrust her ass up against something behind her.

Or, more aptly, someone.

And there was only one someone in this room.

A wail of mortification clawed at her throat as Allison jumped away. She kept backing up until the scratchy, cracked arm of the leather couch jammed into the bend of her knee and pinched her bare legs. The envelope's thick material crinkled loudly against her fingers.

Color flared in Colin's narrow cheeks, and his eyes went wide. Had their unfortunate close encounter of the ass-to-groin kind unearthed the same memory for him as it had for Allison?

Of the first time they'd met? At that party?

The night before classes had started Allison's sophomore year at Brown, she and her best friend, Sophie, had been crushed in the middle of a crowd in some upperclassman's apartment, dancing like their lives depended on it, when someone had pressed up against Allison.

She'd assumed at first they'd bumped into each other, but then seconds passed by and the person didn't move, so Allison had eased her body back and, against her better judgment, let herself grind with this stranger.

Never having been great at impersonal interactions, she only made it about halfway through the song before she glanced back at him.

"I'm Allison," she'd yelled over the music.

"I'm"—his mouth pursed, and his thick blond eyebrows arched over his glasses—"just trying to get by."

It was only then that she'd *really* taken him in, squinting through her haze of alcohol. His arms raised over his head, the discomfort on his face. She'd trapped this poor, unsuspecting guy against the wall. Held him up with her ass.

That was the moment Allison learned embarrassment could be a physical, painful thing.

Over the past few years, she'd tried very hard to forget that night, and the eight months of dating Colin that had followed. But ever since seeing him at Claymore's orientation, it all kept flooding back, uninvited. Every bit of their history, from her horror at discovering two days after that party that he was in her Literary Theory class, to her failed attempts at avoiding him, to their first time getting coffee a week later, to their first kiss a week after that. And all the other firsts, and seconds, and thirds that followed, right up until he unceremoniously dumped her in the middle of spring semester.

They were some of the best and worst moments of her life, and Allison wished she could forget them all.

Colin shifted in front of her, and, to her surprise, a soft smile spread over his face. He almost looked happy to see her. "Oh hey—"

Allison bristled. She was not in the mood for small talk with the guy who'd once broken her heart, especially not when she was holding a piece of paper that could change the course of her whole future.

"Could you not manspread all over the lounge? Other people need to get in here, too." She unwound the red string from the button that held the envelope closed, circling it again and again until it snapped off.

Her tone seemed to amuse him, the right corner of his mouth ticking up higher. Something mischievous sparked in his gaze. "I thought maybe you . . . wanted to dance?"

Allison fought off a squawk of horror. This was *exactly* why she'd been avoiding him since orientation. Maybe to him, their past was a joke, but their breakup had been one of the most painful moments of her life.

Before she could decide how to respond, the trill of a new voice cut through their standoff. "Oh. *Perfect.*"

In the doorway stood a statuesque woman in her late forties. Her ash-blond hair was swept into a messy bun, the shorter strands framing her round face and tangling with her leaf-shaped gold earrings. Her gray-blue eyes were lined with flawless cat's-eye swoops, and she donned that shade of red lipstick that somehow looked good on everyone. Her sensible black sheath dress was adorned with a loose, floral chiffon kimono in shades of blue and yellow, giving her an air of bohemian professionalism that Allison immediately coveted.

Her heart hammered as if she were standing in front of a movie star as Professor Frances glided toward them. "Allison, excellent. I was hoping to see you before our first class on Tuesday."

"*Our* class?" Allison's gaze fell to the unopened envelope in her hand.

"You couldn't possibly think I'd let someone else have you after that writing sample on the similarities between the Wife of Bath and Ursula from *The Little Mermaid*." Professor Frances grinned.

Allison almost squealed. This was *exactly* what she'd been hoping for. The chance to be mentored by the department's most renowned pre–eighteenth century specialist, right from the start of her graduate school career. Maybe if they got along, Professor Frances would choose Allison as her research assistant, invite her on her trips to Europe to examine original copies of some of the oldest works of literature, co-write papers with her. It could all set Allison on track to achieve everything she'd dreamed of from the minute her father laughed at her acceptance to Brown four years ago and asked her how she thought she and her mom were going to pay for it on a waitress's wage. (Sometimes Allison wished her parents had gotten divorced long before her freshman year in college, but without her father's endless negativity motivating her, she might not have been standing here now on the precipice of all her dreams. Lemons, meet lemonade.)

Professor Frances's eyes cut from Allison to Colin, whom Allison had momentarily forgotten existed. She smiled as she spoke eleven words that landed like a bomb on Allison's whole world.

"I'm looking forward to working with both of you this semester."

Chapter 2

Both of you.

Twenty-four hours later, the words still clung to Allison's insides like she used to imagine swallowed chewing gum did when she was a kid.

Not only would she have to see her ex-boyfriend across the room *every week* in all three of her grad classes, but now, as TAs in the same course, she'd have to work with him. That meant being polite and professional, and not ignoring him, no matter how much she might want to.

It was a disaster. A tragedy. A misfortune of Dickensian levels.

Groaning, Allison closed her eyes and tipped her face toward the sun. She'd been hoping that taking her reading outside for the afternoon would help her mood, but she was no closer to being able to concentrate. Just sweatier. Swiping at her damp forehead, she shut the cover of Derrida's *Of Grammatology* and shoved it across the glass table.

"Since when do we abuse books?" Sophie's voice mixed with the creak of the back door as she joined Allison outside. She'd had a dentist appointment that morning, and for Sophie Andrade, any appointment was an excuse for a day off, especially if it was Friday.

"We don't. Except this one." To prove her point, Allison used the end of her pen to push Derrida over the edge of the table. The book hit the ground with a satisfying *thump*.

The noise sent Monty, Allison's seven-month-old Corgi, wriggling like a blender on full blast under Sophie's arm. She'd barely placed him down before he was zooming around the tight circumference of the deck, his nails clicking and clacking against the wooden slats.

"I found that beast trying to use my aunt's pin cushion as a tennis ball." By day, Sophie did data entry, but by night, she was designing her own line of plus-sized clothing, so her room always looked like a crafts store had exploded in it. It was a veritable cornucopia of temptation for a mischievous dog, and Monty had no self-control.

"The one shaped like a tomato?"

"Yup."

Allison sighed. "That's all I need after this week. The ASPCA taking my dog away because he was eating pins."

"I promise, no pins were consumed." Sophie settled into the lounger next to Allison and popped her oversized sunglasses over her face. In her black-and-white-striped romper, she looked ready for a day at the beach. "But didn't you *just* start class? Things can't be that bad already?"

Allison frowned. "Grad school is intense." Sophie hadn't really been around enough lately to observe this.

When they'd moved from their on-campus apartment to this small rental house the day after graduation, Allison had thought it would be like undergrad 2.0. Movie nights and game nights and staying up too late drinking leftover alcohol from parties. Laughing until they couldn't breathe. Everything the same, only better, because there were no more rules and no more homework (for Sophie, at least) to weigh them down.

Instead, there were bills, and chores, and six-in-the-morning alarms. And Sophie had all these new friends at work and designers she'd made contact with filling up whatever free time she had left.

Allison couldn't recall the last time they'd chatted for more than ten minutes.

She scuffed the heel of her sandal against the deck. "There's so much reading to do. And so much your professors already expect you to know. It's like starting a language at the most advanced level. And on top of that, I got assigned my TA position, so now I'm going to have to prep my own recitations, too."

Recitations were smaller discussion sections of ten to fifteen students, which basically meant that Allison had to lead two classes on her own. Never mind that she had to do all of this with Colin hovering everywhere like some kind of malevolent ghost. But she couldn't say that to Sophie. Not yet. She still hadn't figured out how to tell her that Colin was at Claymore.

In her best friend's mind, Allison would always be that girl who went moony every time Colin gifted her a book she'd mentioned wanting to read, every time he sobbed at a movie's happy ending. The girl who, for a time, had insisted that Colin was her "lobster."

Though they'd dated for less than a year, being in college, with only a few hours of their days structured by classes, had allowed Allison and Colin to spend an incredible amount of time together at Brown. Sharing meals and beds and bad days as well as the good ones, witnessing each other's bed head and hangover breath and midnight paper-drafting panic attacks; it had all felt so intimate. And Colin was older and charming and funny, and, sometimes he'd shed his proverbial smart-guy armor, permitting Allison small glimpses of the many other sides to him: the cat lover, the guy afraid of moths and other winged insects (tiny attack planes, he called them), the one who loved his mother and his grandfather so fiercely he might explode from the very force of those feelings.

In the face of all that, no wonder she'd failed to see the worst parts of him, even as Sophie had tried valiantly to point them out.

This was why telling her best friend about Colin's reappearance needed to be carefully planned. It would require time and chocolate and a good sangria. Probably a preset script. None of which Allison had at the moment.

Sophie's eyes widened. "I thought TAing was just showing up for lectures and grading some papers or whatever? You have to run your own class?"

"Yup. I guess Professor Frances likes her graduate students to get a feel for teaching early on, so we do more than most."

Sophie grimaced. "You must know the books, though, right? It's you. You've read everything in existence."

Allison slid the syllabus for British Literature's Greatest Hits out of her notebook and scanned the reading list as if it might have changed since the last time she checked it half an hour ago. *Beowulf.* Chaucer. Malory's *Le Morte d'Arthur* and a handful of other Arthurian romances. *The Faerie Queene.* Shakespeare. *Gulliver's Travels.* She was familiar with everything but a few John Donne poems. (After one attempt at understanding "The Flea," Allison had known she was done with Donne.)

"Most of them."

"There you go. You'll be fine."

Allison shook her head, her stomach tightening. "Reading them isn't the same as studying them. I don't know the common interpretations of *Gulliver's Travels* or the historical influences of Shakespeare. What am I supposed to do if a student asks a question and I don't know the answer?" The thought ramped up her heartbeat enough to leave Allison dizzy.

She didn't know how to be wrong. It was a reality she refused to accept. Not out of pride, but because being right made her smart. And Allison had to be smart.

That adjective had defined her whole identity since her mom had taken her on a trip to visit her cousin at Bates College when Allison was ten. From the minute she'd stepped onto her first college campus, it had felt like home. Like there was a small space in it that was perfectly Allison-sized. Her soulmate wasn't a person—it was a place, a state of mind, a goal—the Academy, academia, the title of professor.

Her father had laughed at her excitement when they'd gotten home. Not in a teasing or affectionate way—Jed Avery was neither of those things—but to cut her down low enough that she'd abandon her dreams before they were fully formed.

He'd gone straight from high school to an electrician's apprenticeship and he made good money, so to his (very narrow, very conservative, very *wrong*) mind, that experience was universal. College was a waste of money. Daycare for young adults so they didn't have to grow up. Over and over he'd promised his daughter that not a cent of his money would pay for college.

For the next eight years, Allison had tried to change his mind by proving how smart she was. She'd won spelling bees and writing contests and academic bowls, earned a 4.0 every quarter (even her awful junior year of high school that had been mostly online due to the pandemic), was awarded scholarships and trophies and plaques. Made high school valedictorian and got accepted to an Ivy League school. And she hadn't stopped after he divorced her mother four years ago, either. Allison still worked herself to the bone at Brown, earning perfect grades (except for that one semester derailed by Colin's assholery) and graduating summa cum laude.

Their entire second-floor hallway at home was a shrine to Allison's academic achievements. And her father, when he'd lived there, never went upstairs.

Her acceptance to Claymore was the first accolade Allison had chosen not to share with him. It was for her, and her alone. But instead of relieving the pressure, it had only been intensified. Allison had to be smart, she had to be the best, she had to be perfect. Because if she wasn't, this all might get pulled out from under her. And if she wasn't excelling at school, if she wasn't the person who'd "read every book in existence," who was she?

She dropped her head to the table. "What if I suck? What if they hate me? What if they boo me out of the room or throw tomatoes and stuff?"

Sophie laughed. "First of all, you aren't Fozzie Bear. You really need to stop streaming those old shows with your mother."

"The Muppets are underappreciated by our generation," Allison muttered into the glass. "Fozzie knows my pain."

"You realize you're identifying with a puppet, right?" When Allison groaned in reply, Sophie's voice softened. "Did you ever boo or hiss at a teacher?"

"Of course not."

"These kids are like three years younger than us. They're not going to be any different than we were in school."

"Yeah but this is *Claymore*. They'll expect a certain level of education. What if I can't give them that?" Allison sat up and dragged a hand through her mussed hair. "I need a WCS."

Allison and Sophie had been playing WCS (Worst-Case Scenarios) since the first week they'd met and Sophie accidentally spilled nail polish all over a pair of her friend's favorite jeans. For both of them, problems were easier to face if they were prepared for the worst possible outcomes.

Monty popped up on the lounger and set himself in Sophie's lap. She stroked his ears, her lips pursed in thought.

"Okay." The chair creaked as she shimmied straighter. "One: they spend the entire fifty minutes on their phones. Two: they challenge everything you say. Three: they refuse to participate in discussions."

Allison flinched with each scenario. Sophie might as well have cracked open her skull and culled them straight from her worst nightmares.

It took her a second to formulate some strategies. "Um . . . ," she mumbled, fiddling with the cover of her notebook. "One: I use Claymore's campus-wide chat app to spam them information on the readings."

"Nice."

"Two: F's for everyone. I'm Oprah but with failing grades." Already, she could feel the tension in her muscles uncoiling. WCS was like a good snowblower after a blizzard. It carved her a path forward through all the static and fog that worry blanketed over her thoughts.

Sophie snorted. "I doubt your professor would go for that, but I love the draconian flair."

"Three: I put them in groups or find a topic they do want to talk about to break the ice."

Sophie's dark curls bounced as she nodded. "See, you've clearly got the instincts. You'll learn the rest."

That was the problem. Allison didn't have time to learn. She needed to already know. "Not before next week."

"Okay, that's it." Sophie jumped to her feet and clapped her hands. "It's almost five o'clock on a Friday and you're way too in your head. We're going out."

"What? Where?"

Her hand shackling Allison's wrist, Sophie tried to pull her to her feet. "My whole office does happy hour at The Cutter downtown. Janie, Brooks, and Sarah will be there. Plus all the hot interns." She wagged her eyebrows salaciously.

Allison scrabbled for her books as if they might save her. "I have like four hundred pages of reading to do. I don't have time for hot interns." Or hangovers. Or staying out too late with Sophie's work friends, who would complain about their co-workers the whole time, making Allison feel more out of the loop the more they tried to include her. Nothing killed gossip like needing to fill in a stranger on ten minutes of backstory.

"Those books have been around over two centuries. They'll survive one more night." Using both hands this time, Sophie hauled Allison out of her chair. "You've barely dated since Colin." From the look on her face, his name might as well have been a large pill she had to swallow dry. "We need to wipe your slate clean."

Allison crossed her arms, a frustrated huff billowing over her lips. "My slate is plenty clean." This was exactly why she could not tell Sophie about Colin being at Claymore. Even as a hypothetical, her hackles rose at the sound of his name like Monty's did when he thought he'd heard an intruder.

Disbelief creased her friend's features. "That's why you find something wrong with every guy that looks at you? Because you're so ready to date?" Shaking her head, Sophie leaned against the deck's rail. Her voice softened as she watched Monty attack a leaf dancing over her feet. "I hate that he hurt you so much you're afraid to let anyone else in."

Allison sputtered. "What? I'm not . . . he's not . . . oh my god, Soph, this has nothing to do with fear. I've got so much going on that I don't have time to date. That's all. At Brown I was focused on getting into grad school. And now that I'm here, I have to excel. It's the only way to ensure I can find a job when I'm done. I can't be distracted by guys and drama and all that."

It was the truth, even if Allison had molded it into a different shape for Sophie's sake.

There'd be plenty of time for dating in a few years, when she was *Professor* Avery. Until then, she didn't plan to let anyone get in the way of her goals. That started with avoiding Sophie's hot interns and any more talk of Colin.

Allison cleared her throat. "What if we have drinks here instead? We could order truffle fries and lettuce wraps and pot stickers from Gatsby's and make our favorite fruity drinks and watch too much of that witches show you love."

Sophie's eyes lit up, happy hour forgotten. Nothing grabbed her attention like sapphic witches. "Can we rewatch the episode where Raven and Natalya make out?"

"Obviously."

Sophie was already listing more episodes as Allison followed her inside. Unlike her original plan, *this* would be a perfect night.

Just like their college days—good food, comfy clothes, and no co-workers or hot interns or Colin Benjamin to force more space between them.

Chapter 3

Nothing summoned graduate students quite like free food.

Which was why Allison, Link, Ethan, and Mandy were crammed around a table in Haber Hall's reading room at nine thirty in the morning.

On the third Tuesday of every month, the English department attempted to entice an audience to their faculty work-in-progress event with the promise of a potluck breakfast, and neither Allison nor her peers had any intention of missing out on home-baked treats.

As they waited for a creative writing professor to begin a presentation on her new book, Allison glanced around, absorbing the room's ambiance. Wood-paneled walls in a soft honey brown framed a mismatched collection of armchairs and sofas. At the back, where she sat, a line of sturdy oak tables boasted green-shaded reading lamps that threw off a soft light the perfect intensity for studying. It was the kind of space where profound ideas were hatched and developed. Where books read a million times became new again.

Mei, the English department's administrator, smiled in greeting as she placed a tray of pastries in front of Allison. Thanks to Allison's slight obsession with properly filling out paperwork, the two of them had talked enough since April to feel like friends.

"You're defending your dissertation next month, right?" Allison asked.

Mei crossed two fingers and waved them in the air. "Here's hoping." During one of their many calls, she'd told Allison about her own experiences at Claymore, pursuing a Ph.D. with two children under the age of three. She'd completed her coursework at half-pace and so her funding had run out as she was starting her dissertation. She'd taken the admin job for more stability (and money) than adjunct teaching could offer.

Allison shook her head. "I have no idea how you manage it all."

"Many calendar apps and very little sleep," Mei quipped.

If she had anything else to add, it never got past her lips because at that moment Colin burst into the room. He made an incredible amount of noise dropping his messenger bag to the floor and pulling out the chair nearest Allison. Its feet screeched against the floor as he sat down.

In the commotion, Mei disappeared to finish setting up. Allison wished she could join her. He'd been here two seconds, and already she'd had more than her fill of Colin Benjamin for the day.

"Oof, it's hot out there," he huffed, fanning himself with the corner of his blue-striped cardigan. He was close enough that his knee knocked against Allison's as he shifted.

And stayed there.

She tensed but refused to pull away. Why should she? Colin had encroached on *her* space. "Maybe don't wear a sweater on a sixty-degree day."

"Cardigans are my look."

Truly. Rare was the day he did not don one. When they'd dated, he'd even sometimes shrugged a sweater on after sex, shuffling around the room naked under its cable knit like it was a bathrobe. He'd admitted once that they made him feel protected. "The world can't touch me," he'd said. "It can't leave a mark." As if wool could be a titanium shield.

They'd broken up before Allison had discovered what kind of scars he was hiding.

A full minute passed, and yet Colin's knee had not moved, no matter how hard she glared at him. His expression was placid enough that she could almost believe he didn't know what was happening.

Almost.

Allison's heart began to do unconscionable things like speed up and skip beats. She crossed her arms over her chest as if that might stop it. She should not have this kind of visceral reaction to Colin. The only part of her body he was allowed control over was her gag reflex.

For a second, she considered the pros and cons of stamping on his foot, before settling on the food as an excuse to angle away. Surveying the tray of pastries, she cursed herself for noticing the slight chill that slipped under her skin at the absence of his touch.

She would *not* let herself be aware of him. She would *not* feel anything about Colin Benjamin. Allison had already learned the hard way that following those paths led to her dreams smoldering in a pile of ash.

She reached for a croissant and tried to lose herself in its buttery goodness.

Colin's hazel eyes followed her movements as she tore off a corner and popped it in her mouth. "Some things never change, huh?"

"What?"

He nodded at her hands, a small smile peeking out of the corners of his mouth. "You and croissants."

Allison dropped the pastry to her napkin, suddenly not hungry at all.

She'd spent her first two weeks in Lit Theory avoiding Colin. It had been clear on the first day of class, when he gawked at her while handing out the syllabus, that he recognized her from that party, and Allison was not interested in reliving one of her most embarrassing moments every time she looked at him. So, she didn't. Instead, she'd created an elaborate schedule where she'd rush into class with less than a minute to spare, and as soon the professor was done, she'd dash back out the door. It was all working splendidly until the day Sophie sent a frantic set of WCS texts, and Allison was so distracted answering them that she walked smack into Colin as they both tried to exit the room.

"We really need to stop meeting this way," he'd said with a grin.

Humiliation slashed heat across Allison's cheeks. "I'm so sorry. I can't believe I did that the other night. I'd had a little too much to drink and—"

He held out a hand to interrupt. "No, I'm sorry," he said. "You ran off before I could say anything."

"I attacked you with my ass," she blurted out.

That was the first time she ever heard Colin laugh. It was neither melodic nor sexy. More like a bird squawking for attention. And it had turned her to mush.

"You didn't attack me," he said. "I was just . . . surprised. And when I'm caught off guard, I tend to put my worst foot forward." His long fingers tapped a tuneless song against his thigh, and he chewed on the inside of his bottom lip for a second, like he was thinking. "Maybe I could . . . take you for coffee? To make up for it?"

Allison was too stunned to do anything but agree.

They went to one of the cafés on campus. It had been prime afternoon-caffeine time, and the line snaked around the circumference of the small building. As they waited, Colin struck up a debate about the top three breakfast pastries. Barely able to stay quiet during Allison's monologue on the perfection of the croissant, he'd done his best to outperform her with a lofty defense of the blueberry muffin. Their little war of words had been silly and fun, and, if Allison was being honest, watching Colin construct an argument had been kind of a turn-on. Before they knew it, hours had passed as they leaned across the table over forgotten mugs of coffee, bickering amicably.

When she'd gotten to Lit Theory two days later, she found a bag with a still-warm croissant sitting on her desk. From across the room,

Colin had flashed her a smile that would have melted metal. After that, a croissant waited on her desk every week for the rest of the semester.

Allison shook her head. She didn't want to dwell on those moments with Colin—the ones that reminded her why she'd fallen for him in the first place. She needed to focus on all the reasons she was glad it was over. Like the obscene volume of his voice, which was bound to summon a series of curious gazes. Their cohort did not know about their history, and Allison wanted to keep it that way.

She shushed him with a flap of her hand.

Colin arched a brow. "Are you ashamed of your love affair with pastry?"

"Please. There's no shame in excellent taste." Allison couldn't stop herself from flipping her hair over her shoulder. It was a reflex born of too many bouts of flirting masked as arguments. "I'd just prefer to eat my croissant, not discuss it with you." She tore off a corner and folded it into her mouth to prove her point.

Colin let loose one of those cacophonous laughs. Allison hated how it made her insides somersault. She couldn't keep talking to him like this. It was too easy to fall back into old habits.

Old feelings.

She turned away, leaning across the table to get the attention of her other classmates. "Who did you all get for your TA assignments?"

Link adjusted his bowtie. "African American Writers with Morgan Sharpe. It's the one I wanted, but it's such bullshit that there aren't more undergrad classes on writers of color here. I can't wait until we get to create our own classes next year. I already have a whole reading list for an Afrofuturism course."

"I demand to sit in on that class," Allison said. Link beamed in response.

"Same," Mandy echoed. "I'm in Children's Fiction with Professor Hasselbach."

Ethan sat back in his chair. "Children's books aren't literature. It's all mooning over vampires and dystopian contests to the death and wizards and cute talking animals. There's no substance." He took a long, slow pull from his protein shake.

Glaring, Mandy tightened her top knot of brown curls like she was preparing for a fight. "Since you clearly only have fourth-hand knowledge of kid lit, I don't think you get to have an opinion."

"Also," Allison piped in, "it's not like those things can't be found in 'serious'"—she used some violent air quotes around the word— "literature. *Dracula*'s got mooning over vampires, there's plenty of kid-on-kid violence in *Lord of the Flies*, *The Lord of the Rings* is full of wizards, and *Animal Farm,* well, it's got all the talking animals you need."

"Yes, but the treatments are entirely different." Ethan tipped his chin, another lecture poised on his lips.

Mandy waved her hand like she could bat him away. "What about you?" she asked Allison. "Who are you working with?"

"Wendy Frances. British Literature's Greatest Hits." Allison cringed when Colin butt in to add, "Me too."

"Does she have two sections?" Link asked.

Allison shook her head. "It's a big class."

More chair-screeching commenced as Colin dragged his seat to the other side of the table to better insert himself into the conversation. "It's going to be awesome. Allison knows everything about medieval lit." He kept his gaze trained on the rest of the group as he said it.

Allison tensed. What was he doing? First the mention of the croissant. Now this. Was he seriously trying to play nice? After everything?

Thankfully, the talk began a moment later, giving her an excuse not to respond.

Though she tried hard to pay attention, her mind spent the next half hour replaying Colin's words. The Colin Benjamin Allison knew was more competitive than an Olympic athlete. He turned everything into a game to be won: grades, writing papers, shopping, you name it. Once he'd challenged her to a race at brushing their teeth when they were late for class. His obsessive need for rivalry had been the cause of their breakup. So what did it mean that he'd just conceded to her, admitted she was better?

Allison fisted her hands in her lap. He had to be messing with her. It was the only explanation.

No way was she letting him get in her head.

As soon as the reading was over, she slid back her chair. "Time for class," she whispered, already on her way to the door. She needed air—and space from Colin—before her first session as a TA.

So of course he followed her into the hallway. "Want some company?"

She absolutely did not. "I was hoping for a few minutes to myself to order my thoughts."

"What thoughts? We're going to be sitting off to the side listening to the lecture."

Allison pursed her lips. "Maybe. But I'd like to make sure I have things to add if Professor Frances wants us to contribute."

A shit-eating grin spread across Colin's face. He always looked like he was fighting to hold back a delicious secret, and that smile only made it worse. It was the natural uptick of his mouth and the perpetual narrowing of his eyes. If only Allison had a permanent marker, she could rearrange his expression. It slid under her skin like a needle and plunged something acidic right into her veins.

When they reached the exit to Haber, he held open the door. Allison crossed her arms and waited for him to pass through first. His gallantry could, as her grandmother used to say, "go fly a kite." She would not fall for this nice-guy routine.

Though he shook his head, Colin obeyed. Of course, that didn't stop him from keeping a hand pressed to one of the glass panels until Allison grabbed the door's handle. She refused to look at him as she passed by.

Instead of taking the long way to Litvak, where British Literature's Greatest Hits was held, she cut through the center of campus, a four-cornered courtyard framed by the library, main administrative building, gym, and student center. Without shade from any trees, the early autumn sun beat down against her face and arms, making her long for the chill of a breeze.

Nestled on the southern border between East Providence and Barrington, Rhode Island, Claymore was a blip of history in the middle of suburbia. Unlike most universities that built up new, futuristic structures among the older campus buildings, whoever designed Claymore's renovations had worked hard to maintain the original Gothic design. Everywhere was ornate stone and high-arched windows and flying buttresses and gargoyles. A wrought-iron fence wreathed with ivy enclosed the school, separating it from the town and further underscoring the stark clash between the campus and the tiny hipster restaurants and SoulCycles and artisan breweries that had infested the blocks around it.

As Allison walked, the early lines of *Beowulf* ran through her head. Most of it was about heroism and masculinity and *blah, blah, blah*—so boring she'd barely been able to come up with some sample lesson plans about the section for her first recitation (which she'd sent to Professor Frances between episodes of Sophie's witchy drama on Friday). Still, she needed something insightful to say. Just in case. She hadn't been lying to Colin about that.

A small stone collided with the back of her calf, pulling her from her thoughts. There, ten paces behind her, was Colin.

She shouldn't have been surprised. Not once had he ever listened to a word she'd said. Like that time she'd come down with an awful flu and asked him for toast and ginger ale. He'd shown up with tomato soup (and zero carbs), insisting it was the more restorative option.

A scream formed at the pit of Allison's stomach, but she maintained her brisk pace. "What are you doing?" she called to him over her shoulder.

"Walking to class."

"I told you I wanted to be alone."

"That's why I'm back here."

Against her will, her steps grew less urgent. "There are easily five different ways to Litvak."

"Yeah but this is the most efficient." Colin grinned. "You know how I love efficiency."

She did. It was his second driving force after winning.

Allison stopped. Her head fell back, and she huffed a breath at the sky. Time to be more direct. "Seriously, Colin. What are you doing here?"

"I told you, walking to class."

She groaned. He was being purposely obtuse. "No. I mean *here,* at Claymore. Aren't you supposed to be at Oxford or Harvard or Stanford or wherever, two years into your deep-dive into the merits of reading science fiction through a Lacanian lens? Isn't that why you left m—"

Allison snapped her mouth shut, hard enough that her bottom lip got caught in her teeth, a shock of copper exploding over her tongue. She concentrated on forcing those thoughts away. The day they'd broken up didn't exist. Neither did the clipped, painful words he'd spoken, nor everything that had happened to get them there. Like a parchment so soaked through with water that its sentences had bled into illegibility, or a document closed without being saved, she'd erased it all from her memories. From her life.

Eagerness pierced his expression. Almost as if he'd been waiting for her to mention their past. "Allison, I—"

"Listen, clearly we're going to have to deal with each other. But there's nothing that says we have to dredge up what happened at Brown." She waved a hand over her shoulder. "It's all ancient history, so let's leave it there. No rearview mirrors. No looking back." With him at Claymore, always there, always looming, it was the only way Allison would be able to continue her forward trajectory. She couldn't hit reverse.

His back straightened, drawing him up to his full height. "Well . . . if that's what you want. . . ."

"It is."

The two of them stood quietly on the sidewalk. Colin stared at her. Allison looked anywhere else.

Discomfort seeped into her skin, and her first thought burst from her mouth to fill the silence. "This isn't going to be like undergrad, you know."

He cocked his head. (Not a gelled hair fell out of place.) "What does that mean?"

At Brown, Colin had been something of an academic superstar. He'd represented the school at numerous conferences, gotten invited to networking events and featured in school promotional material, and had won the Rising Star Award (the university's biggest academic achievement) his senior year. The deans and professors all knew him by name, even if he'd never taken their class. Walking campus with him had been like stepping out with a celebrity. In their Lit Theory course, the teacher had treated Colin like he was the only person there, calling on him first and letting him talk for longer than anyone else.

"In Frances's class, you won't be the smartest or most well-read person in the room."

His face lit up. Nothing made Colin Benjamin glow like the promise of a challenge. "Is that so?"

Allison nodded, sharp and definitive. She jammed her hands on her hips for emphasis. "You can count on it."

"I guess we'll just have to see who's the better TA." All his praise from earlier seemed to be forgotten. He grinned his amused grin. The one that suggested he'd win this round. The same way he'd always won *every* round before.

But not anymore.

Grabbing the strap of her bag in both hands, she did exactly what she'd promised Colin. She sped up her steps and left him behind.

Chapter 4

Allison would be the first to admit she wasn't great at math, but the sea of faces filling the stadium seating of the lecture hall seemed to number well past sixty.

Professor Frances had just finished her lecture on *Beowulf*'s history (the fact that someone had tossed the manuscript out a window during the fire in 1731 was Allison's favorite part), and she flourished an arm toward where Allison and Colin sat in the front corner of the room. Her turquoise bracelets clinked like tiny bells.

"Finally, I wanted to take a moment to introduce you all to your two teaching assistants for the semester: Allison Avery and Colin Benjamin. They'll be leading your recitations and will be a great resource for you as you work on your essays and prepare for exams."

Twice as many eyes as faces swung toward Allison. Heat burst like landmines in her cheeks. Forcing a smile, she clutched her pen until her knuckles blanched.

You need to get used to this, she scolded herself. *You can't teach as a hologram from your bedroom* (but oh imagine the bliss if this was a thing). *People are going to have to look at you.*

She wasn't self-conscious. Allison had lived in her fat body her whole life: it was her, and she was as comfortable in it as she was in a well-worn sweater. But the more attention she got, the more chances for her to look silly or ignorant. To not know the answer.

As if Professor Frances hadn't done enough by drawing everyone's gaze to them, she then upped the ante. "Why don't you both introduce yourselves briefly?"

Allison almost choked swallowing back a laugh. Clearly, their professor had not spent any amount of time with Colin. If she had, she'd know his version of "brief" included a PowerPoint presentation and a ten-minute break for everyone to stretch their legs.

Allison had done a pretty stellar job over the last hour and eight minutes pretending he wasn't sitting beside her, but now his hazel gaze slid to her face, and he arched an eyebrow, asking who would go first.

"Go ahead," she mouthed. Let him set the stage so she could follow and trounce his ass (apparently, when it came to Colin Benjamin, introducing yourself was a competitive sport).

All six feet, three inches of him rose from his chair. "Hey, all," he said, his voice obnoxiously calm. He rounded the table they shared and leaned against the edge.

Directly in front of Allison.

Every pointy, lanky piece of him blocked her view: his razor-edged shoulders, and bony elbows, and straight spine. His flat ass. All places on him she'd touched a million times before.

All places on him she now wanted to stab with something sharp.

"Let's see. What's worth knowing about me?"

"Nothing," Allison mumbled under her breath. Not quietly enough, though, because Colin cast her a glance. The glare of the fluorescent lights obscured the look in his eyes, but that grin of his, the one that promised an anthology full of delicious secrets, spread across his face.

He hooked a thumb over his shoulder. "My friend here says nothing." He chuckled along with the rest of the class.

Friend!? Who was he kidding? That was most assuredly *not* an accurate way to describe how they'd ended things, and anyway, hadn't they *just* discussed that they were going to forget their history?

"Anyyyy-way," he dragged out the word for the extra cute factor.

Allison was in desperate need of a barf bag.

"I got my BA in literature from Brown, and spent the last two years traveling, gaining life experience, figuring things out." As he spoke, he leaned deeper into the table, shoving it against Allison's stomach. "I think my favorite part was my time in London."

With a little hop, he set himself on the tabletop. His ass rested at the edge of her notebook. His whole upper half was in her breathing space, filling her nostrils with the scent of coffee and hair gel and *Colin.*

She coughed loudly.

"I visited Chaucer at Westminster every morning." Except for the slight rise in the volume of his voice, you'd think he hadn't heard her. "Though I haven't decided exactly what my focus will be, I'm definitely going to be a medievalist, which is why I'm so excited to be a part of this course."

Allison had to cough again to cover a squawk of surprise. What the hell?

Colin was a theory bro. When she'd last seen him, he'd been *obsessed* with Lacanian psychoanalysis and Slavoj Žižek, though neither were the trend in lit theory these days. He'd never shown any interest in the medieval period beyond half-heartedly listening to her recount some of the things she'd read for class.

This had to be some kind of ploy. A way to make sure he caught Professor Frances's notice. And their professor was eating it up. Smiling and nodding at every disingenuous word.

Frustration searing her skin, Allison scratched out some ideas in the corner of her notebook, a few tidbits to swing their teacher's attention back her way. Maybe something about the connection between medieval and modern romance to show she was familiar with Professor Frances's research interests?

In front of her, Colin continued to drone on about his favorite texts, all of which (of course) appeared on the syllabus. The guy was the ultimate suck-up. When he started talking about "The Miller's Tale" like he was the Wikipedia page, Allison poked her pen into his spine.

He didn't react, so she jabbed his back harder and more incessantly. They were out of time, and she still hadn't been able to say anything. Normally, that would be fine, but not if it meant she'd be overshadowed by him.

He shimmied his shoulders, finally annoyed enough to acknowledge her. As he shifted, the pen moved with him, sketching a series of erratic black lines over the back of his blue sweater.

Her mouth dropping open, Allison released her pen hastily. It bounced off her open notebook and rolled over the edge of the table. In her irritation, she hadn't realized she'd never retracted the tip. The ink was so dark, and his cardigan so light, it was impossible not to see the scribbles that circled the small of his back. It looked like when Allison's next-door neighbor had written all over the white walls of her house with marker.

But Hannah had been three.

Allison bit her lip to keep from laughing and dug deep inside of herself, searching for the appropriate level of guilt. She'd probably ruined his sweater and it looked expensive.

Yet she only found vindication. It served him right—for not leaving her time to speak, for blocking her from the class, for everything he'd done since the night of that party sophomore year when their paths first crossed. If you really thought about it, every choice Colin had made these past few years had led him to this moment, to this well-earned damage to his wardrobe.

Allison sat back in her chair, satisfaction warming her insides like a shot of whiskey.

With a harried glimpse at the clock, Professor Frances cleared her throat. "Thank you, Colin, for all that insight." She leaned her head to see Allison around him. "We'll make sure that Allison gets to say a few words first thing on Thursday. Sound good?"

Allison nodded. Perfect. She'd have time to plan a perfectly off-the-cuff introduction. And she'd be sure to demonstrate that she understood the definition of *brief.*

Professor Frances dismissed the class, and a handful of students rushed for her desk. Allison crossed her legs, getting comfortable. The three of them had a quick meeting scheduled, but clearly it would be a while before their teacher was ready.

Colin shifted his weight on the table so he could see Allison. "I thought that went well."

"Sure, for those of us who got to say something." She bounced her knee, causing the toe of her crossed leg to bump the table over and over.

"Right. Sorry about that," he said. Then he grinned. *Grinned.* Allison wanted to use his face as a tennis ball. And a frying pan as the racket.

"I hope you accomplished whatever it was you were trying to prove."

"I did, thanks." His voice was placid, but Allison recognized the challenge in his gaze. That familiar glint in his hazel eyes that had been the precursor to every rivalry between them (and some of their best sex). "I wanted to make sure it was clear that both TAs have a background in the field."

Background in the field. Ha! Allison had no doubt that Colin's knowledge of medieval literature extended to whatever he'd been forced to read in high school and college, plus the results of a half-assed Google search.

Before she could test that theory, Professor Frances clapped her hands, stepping down off the dais toward them. "Sorry, sorry, sorry. A lot of students already have thoughts about the materials." She paused at the end of their table. "I know you have your seminar shortly so I won't keep you too long. I merely wanted to check in about your first recitations, in case you had any questions."

Colin flipped open his laptop and clicked on the syllabus. Scrolling through it at a lightning speed that made Allison's head spin, he said, "Take attendance, answer questions, get them talking, right?"

Their professor nodded. "I'd also like you both to offer one to two office hours a week, especially around exam and paper times. You can decide when and where. Let me know once you figure it out and I'll post the hours for students."

She tipped her smile toward Allison. "And while I appreciate the lesson plans you sent over this weekend, Allison, I trust you to decide how to engage your students. You don't have to clear your class activities with me. I see recitation as a place to learn to participate in literary discourse without the pressure of sixty other people watching. Get them looking at the texts, talking about them, and asking questions. Those are your goals. How you get there is up to you. It's a good chance to experiment and learn some things about leading a classroom."

Allison's cheeks burned. Though her face was kind and her voice encouraging, it was hard not to feel like Professor Frances was chastising her for overzealousness. She'd hoped sending her plans would be a sign of her preparedness and professionalism, but maybe Professor Frances wanted someone more laid back.

"If you have any other questions, email me. Otherwise, I look forward to seeing you both on Thursday and hearing about your first set of recitations next week." With that, she disappeared from the room in a cloud of clinking jewelry and floral chiffon.

Colin's gaze was heavy on Allison's face. "What?" she demanded without looking at him. Instead she put serious effort into closing up her notebook, as if she were packaging the Holy Grail.

"You sent her *lesson plans*?"

Allison's jaw tightened. "So?"

"Overachiever much?"

Yanking her bag from its place at her feet, Allison banged it on the table. "There's nothing wrong with being prepared." Out of the corner of her eye, she saw his shit-eating grin on full display. She fought the urge to mock the mess of scribbles on his back. Or to grab her pen and add a few more to his forehead, his chin, his chest.

"What did you send?"

"A debate about *Beowulf*'s monsters. Which was the most monstrous?" Shrugging, she stood and slung her bag over her shoulder. In her mind, she was cavalier. Nonchalant. Apathetic. "I thought it might get them thinking about the themes. And discussions are always easier when you're arguing."

A new smile found Colin's face. Smaller and closed mouth, but somehow brighter. Like he was recalling all their debates, how fun it had been to get worked up with someone else about the books you loved, even if they had all the wrong opinions (Colin had all the wrong opinions, always).

He picked up his laptop and started typing. His long fingers created a melodic rhythm on the chiclet keys. "That's a great idea. I might have to steal it."

His words reminded her of his little speech to the class. "Oh? Like you stole my school? My Ph.D. program? My field of study?"

He flinched as if she'd struck him, and the amusement in his eyes frosted over.

"Since when do you want to focus on medieval literature? What happened to H. G. Wells and Jules Verne and Isaac Asimov?"

He studied the blank surface of the white board. "Plans change."

Allison stepped into his line of sight and crossed her arms. "What changed them?"

He sighed. "You."

His hesitant tone, the tension in his jaw, the way his hands popped opened and closed nervously, it all startled Allison. "What?"

"I thought you didn't want to talk about before?"

She gritted her teeth. "We'll make an exception."

He lifted a shoulder and let it fall, limp. "You remember, you used to go on and on about all the things you read in undergrad. About how funny and brilliant Chaucer was, and how weird Chretien de Troyes's romances were, how amazing it was to read things by women like the Paston sisters at a time when people now believe women had no education or authority or agency. I never forgot any of it." His fidgeting worsened. If it wouldn't have meant them touching, Allison would have reached out to steady him. "I—when I was taking my two gap years before grad school, I picked some of those works up. And you were right. I mean, I read *Troilus and Criseyde* at least three times."

Warmth spread through Allison's limbs. If what he was saying was true, she'd had more of an impact on him when they'd dated than she'd thought.

But bitterness had left her with sharp edges, and she couldn't ignore that he'd spent the last ten minutes purposely trying to outshine her. Just like he had the whole time they'd dated. Right up until he'd ripped that Rising Star Award out from under her.

Allison stalked a few steps closer. He was still sitting on the table, and, for once, they were eye level. She tried not to think of how she was practically standing between his knees. Or how many times they'd made out in that very position. She let her anger explode those thoughts like grenades. "You're really going to get in my way when you know how hard I've worked for this? How much it means for me to study with her? I've been talking about doing *exactly this* for years."

He shook his head. "I've worked hard, too. I *need* this. Getting Professor Frances's attention can open doors. That's sometimes the only way to a tenure-track job these days. And I—" He pursed his lips and considered his words. "I can't step aside and let that opportunity pass."

"Neither can I." Allison refused to blink as she stared him down. Professor Frances might have chosen them both as TAs, but teachers always had their favorites. If Allison stood out, maybe she'd mentor her, help ensure Allison achieved all her goals. That had to be what Colin was aiming for, too.

"I'm not going to hold back. When we were together, all those things we said, what we know about each other, they won't affect me here." She forced herself not to remember how she'd once told him she loved him and how much she'd meant it. Or all the things he'd confided in her about growing up with a teen mom and his close relationship with his grandfather. He would not pollute her goals or reroute her path. Not again. She'd barrel through him like a battering ram on a castle gate if necessary. She hoped her fierce expression illustrated that.

Colin tipped his chin. "There are no rearview mirrors here."

"Good."

He pressed a palm against the table and leaned into it. "May the best man win."

Allison threw her hair over her shoulder and straightened her spine. She smoothed her pencil skirt and striped shell. Unlike negotiating how to exist in the same space as her ex, this was territory she could navigate. Competing with Colin was like breathing.

"I think we're all about done with men winning." She was halfway through the door before she flashed him a smirk. "By the way, you might want to change your sweater before Post-Colonial Lit. It looks like a toddler used you as an easel."

The last thing she saw before she left was Colin walking in circles trying to catch a glimpse of his back, like a dog futilely chasing his tail.

Chapter 5

When they'd dated, Colin had liked to celebrate *everything*. Their first kiss, the first time they had sex, the first time Allison tried his cooking, you name it, and Colin saw it as a reason to splurge on a special dessert or treat themselves to a new book.

It was no surprise, then, that he went all out on their one-month anniversary. Flowers, chocolates, and reservations at this upscale bar-beque place outside of Boston.

What neither of them had known was that it was also the restaurant's monthly line-dancing night, and everyone with a reservation was encouraged to participate as they waited for their food.

The host had set down their menus and pointed to the stage a few feet away, where four or five lines of people—mostly in cowboy boots, jeans, and hats, unlike Allison's tight dress and heels—moved like a flash mob to a honky-tonk song. There was clapping and hooting and a whole lot of foot stamping, the exact opposite of the romantic, candlelit dinner they'd expected.

Allison raised an eyebrow at Colin. She was an okay dancer, but he possessed about as much grace as a drunk flamingo, and the pure fear etched across his face suggested he knew that.

With an exuberant wave, the instructor hailed them, insisting it was the perfect time to "jump on in."

Weighing the potential humiliation of trying to line dance against the current embarrassment of everyone staring at them, Colin and Allison had surrendered and squeezed themselves in at the back of the pack.

The music transitioned into a new song a second later. "This one's called the Cowboy Hustle," the instructor's voice burst through the speakers, "and it's an easy one for any new people out there." She winked at them.

Colin groaned. "What does she know about easy? I bet her feet Cowboy Hustle in her sleep."

Allison gently took his arm. "It's not that complicated, I promise. Here . . ." She slid up next to him so they were hip to hip. "You tap your foot like this." She fanned her right foot in and out twice. He did the same, only to stamp on her in the process.

She choked back a laugh. His face was pinched in a mix of concentration and frustration, and she didn't want to belittle his attempts.

"Now tip your toe back twice," she offered.

"I think it's heel first," he said, squinting at the instructor as she demonstrated again.

"Is it?" With the loud music and the people moving around them, and Colin pressed against her like she was a support beam, Allison couldn't pay attention.

She'd liked him like that: vulnerable, uncertain. Not worried about being the best. It had made her want to pull him into a dark corner and do things to him inappropriate for a restaurant setting. Instead, she settled for a long, deep kiss, not caring if she toppled all the other dancers over in the process.

There was a lot of stumbling and swearing, but eventually they'd figured out the steps, and arms hooked together, they'd danced their way through the rest of the song, laughing the whole time.

They'd had plenty of moments more romantic than that night, but it was one of Allison's favorites, and as she sat on her couch, staring at her Victorian Lit reading, she couldn't seem to stop dwelling on it. Colin Benjamin was a parasite. The more she tried to forget him, the deeper he weaseled his way into her head.

Thankfully, her phone rang a second later, chasing him from her thoughts as her mother's brindle-coated pit bull flashed onto the screen. The dog's tongue lolled from her smiling mouth, the white tips of her ears flapping against her breaths.

Allison answered the video call. "Cleo, tell Mom to press the forward-facing button."

"I did press it." Her mother's voice rose three octaves.

"The one with the arrows in a circle?"

"*Yes.*" Cleo's image shook as her mom moved the phone around. "Press it again."

A sigh buzzed through the phone, and, a second later, the camera blinked, offering Allison a glimpse of her mother.

They could have been twins, except for her mother's blond hair and brown eyes. They had the same round face and apple cheeks, the same slim nose and narrow brow, the same small mouth and closed-lipped smile. Even their skin was the same fair hue, though Allison's mother spent far more time outside than Allison did, so her cheeks had that healthy bronze glow that fled Allison's skin as soon as school began.

Horror settled over her mom's face as she took in Allison's messy bun and loose T-shirt. "Please tell me that's not what you wore for your first day of teaching."

Allison groaned. "First of all, it was *not* my first day of teaching. That's not until Friday. All I did today was sit in the corner of the room and take notes. Secondly, of course this is not what I wore."

"Good, because us pear-shaped gals need to think a little harder about what we wear."

Allison and her mother also shared the same plus-sized body, and the same thyroid condition that meant no matter how healthily they ate, or how hard they worked out, they would always carry fat. Something Allison's father had given them endless grief about, lecturing them on nutrition and taking care of themselves while serving fried chicken and mashed potatoes without a vegetable for dinner, and refusing to let anyone get up until their plates were clear. A real Prince Charming, Jed Avery was.

Allison dug her heel into the carpet, doing her best to channel her frustration into the floor and off her face. "*Ma*. You know I hate that description."

Her mother's brow dipped. "I don't know why. It's accurate and cute."

"It's ridiculous and perpetuates the notion that fat people are obsessed with food."

Allison had once taken stock of every description she could think of for large bodies, and they were pretty much *all* food-related: pear-shaped, apple-shaped, juicy bottom, big melons, etc. It was disgusting. So, until everyone started referring to thin people as "asparagus-shaped," Allison would be *curvy* or *plus-sized*, or if she really wanted to watch people have a shock, *fat*.

Her mother shook her head. "I'm not having this fight again."

"Great. I win."

It was Allison's favorite thing to do, and after her conversation with Colin earlier, she'd been winning all over the place today. She'd been selected for a book giveaway on Twitter, Professor Stanton had raved over Allison's theories about *Things Fall Apart,* and Colin had slouched self-consciously in his seat for the entire two-hour seminar period to hide the pen marks on his sweater. He didn't raise his hand once. Now she'd gotten her mom to concede on her least-favorite word.

Win. Win. Win.

"So, what's going on with you?" Allison asked.

Her mother was one of those people who wouldn't talk about themselves. If Allison didn't ask her point-blank things like "Are you going to the doctor regularly?," "How's your blood pressure?," "Is money tight?," she'd never know anything about her mother's life.

"Oh, you know . . ."

"How's work?"

"Slow. Debbie had to cut some of the girls' shifts because business has been down."

"Let me guess. You gave them yours." Allison's mother would offer her last penny to anyone who asked, even if she needed it more.

Her mom gave her a tight smile. "They're both single moms with small children and no other jobs. I have the baking side gig."

While delicious, the small batches of cupcakes, cookies, and bars she sold to neighbors and occasionally for events were not going to pay the mortgage, and Jed's pathetic excuse for alimony wouldn't close the gap.

Allison did some quick math in her head. Her grad stipend was thirty grand a year. It covered her rent and insurance and other bills and left her only a smidge of pocket money, but if she scraped together all her extra cash for the month and dipped into her meager savings, she might be able to give her mom half the mortgage.

When she offered as much, her mother grimaced. "Honey, I'm *your* mother, not the other way around. It is not your job to pay my bills."

"It is if you can't afford them."

Most of the time, Allison relished being an only child. She liked never having to share her mother or her things and not having any siblings to be compared to (which meant she was always the best). But at times like this, she wished she had someone else to help her shoulder the responsibilities, someone to worry with about their mom alone in that big house with its big bills, refusing to lean on anyone.

"Honey, I'm *fine*. I promise."

Allison's chest felt like someone was standing on it. She pulled Monty into her lap, and raised one of his little paws, waving it at her mom. He'd been a graduation gift, though secretly Allison thought he was more likely a graduation appeasement to make up for the fact that Jed hadn't bothered to show up to see his only child graduate with highest honors from an Ivy League school.

Not that that should be surprising, given that he'd walked out of her high school graduation in the middle of her valedictorian speech to "take a work call."

No matter how low she held her expectations for her father, it gutted her every time he didn't meet them. And he never did.

"Hi, my little Montague," her mom cooed.

"Monterey, Ma. As in the cheese. Monterey Jack."

Her mother frowned. "The *Romeo and Juliet* reference would have been more on brand for you."

"My lifelong obsession with cheese isn't on brand?"

"Cheese is so high in cholesterol."

"Annndddd . . . here we go with the food stuff again." Allison tried her best to avoid it, but food seemed an inevitable part of every conversation with her mother. She was a frequent fad dieter with an inexhaustible love for calorie counters and nutrition labels, while Allison strove for balance but refused to obsess about the numbers. If food became a math problem, she'd be much more likely to become unhealthy about it.

Her mother cocked her head in frustration but didn't push the issue. "Anything else going on at school besides the new class? What about with Sophie?"

For a second, Allison considered telling her mother about Colin. She'd met him twice at Brown while he and Allison were dating, and her mother had always liked him, though she could never remember his name, referring to him as "glasses boy" or "Cody." But if Allison admitted to her mother that Colin was at Claymore and that they shared classes and a TAship, she would ask about him *daily,* and Allison had enough trouble shoving him out of her head as it was.

She opted for "Sophie's good."

"Is she home? Can I say hi?" Her mom treated Sophie like she was her own kid.

"She's out."

"Again?"

Allison shrugged. "She's having dinner downtown."

Her mother's brow furrowed. Somewhere out of sight, Cleo's collar jangled as she shook herself out. "And she didn't invite you?"

Monty squirmed in Allison's lap, channeling her own discomfort. "It's some sort of designers' thing. I'd be bored; she knows that." This was just another of the many pieces of Sophie's life lately where Allison didn't fit. She forced back a sigh. "Besides," she added, "I have a mountain of reading to finish for Victorian Lit tomorrow."

Her mom tugged at the ends of her shoulder-length blond bob. "Honey, don't make your schoolwork a place to hide."

Allison dropped her head back and closed her eyes. "I'm not thirteen anymore. I'm not hiding from the world. Grad school is my *job*. Plus, my classmates and I are getting together this weekend." It wasn't even a lie. They'd planned the gathering weeks ago, after their first class with Professor Behi.

"So you're making friends—"

"Ma."

Her mother raised her hands, dropping her phone in the process. Cleo's big meatball face appeared, hovering above the camera. Then she licked the screen. Everything was a potential snack to that dog.

Her mom shooed her away, and her face filled Allison's phone again. "You have a tendency to get comfortable with things and not branch out. That's all. Same friends, same town, same neighborhood . . ."

"New house, new school, new responsibilities . . ." Allison's heart sang an angry beat. Sophie said the same thing to her a lot, and, quite frankly, it was more than a little irritating. Allison took plenty of risks. Just because they weren't always the ones her mother and friends thought she should take didn't make them any less risky.

Her mother offered a wry smile. "Well, now that I've gotten you sufficiently aggravated, I should probably tell you about your father."

Allison's whole body clenched. "What about Jed?"

"He's got a . . . heart thing."

"What does that mean?"

Her mom's lips disappeared into a straight line for moment before she responded. "He's been to the ER a few times over the last three months because his heart keeps slipping into AFib."

"Like a heart attack?" This news should have summoned some emotion in Allison, but there was only a chilly numbness.

"More like heart failure."

"Is it bad?"

"It's something to keep a close eye on."

Allison's foot ground harder into the carpet. "Why are you telling me this?"

Her mother frowned. "He's your father."

"Only in the most technical of senses."

"Sickness can change that." Her mother spoke the words carefully.

"Fuck that. He doesn't get a pass just because he's sick. How do you know this, anyway?"

Her mom's eyes shifted away from the camera.

Allison groaned. "Are you seriously still talking to him?"

"He calls sometimes—"

"Ma."

"Honey, I know you're an adult now and you've learned a lot about the world but marriage is complicated. Once you've been tied to someone—once you've had a child with them, shared a life—you're tied forever, even if you split."

A million terrible words made their way to Allison's tongue but she swallowed them back. Instead, she and her mother said goodbye with lots of *I love you*s as they blew kisses at each other's dogs.

Allison set her phone on the coffee table and dragged her copy of *Nicholas Nickleby* back across her legs. Monty tackled her hand as she tried to reach for her pencil.

She sighed into the pages. Reminding her mother how little her father cared for either of them was not going to make anyone feel better or change the way Allison's mother handled people. Cassandra Avery would always be too kind, always give away pieces of herself until there was nothing left but dust.

And Allison would keep collecting the dust, keep holding her mom together, because that's what daughters did.

Chapter 6

Recitation for British Literature's Greatest Hits was held in a closet-sized room in the Fyler library.

A conference table that barely fit sixteen chairs clogged most of the space, and their backs and legs knocked against windows and walls as the students settled in. Too many years of school emergency drills made Allison acutely aware of what a deathtrap she'd be stuck in for the next two hours.

Three chairs were still empty, but her phone said it was ten, so she turned to the whiteboard.

Thank god she'd brought her own markers and eraser because the tray stood empty. The room wasn't even equipped for projection. They'd be doing this old school, which, to be honest, Allison rather enjoyed. She was a pen-on-paper, marker-on-board, hard-copies-of-books kind of person. She had an expensive desktop computer for writing and research, but if she could have gotten away with it, she probably would have scribed her papers by hand and used only the library stacks for research. Obviously, that wasn't the way of things these days, but it felt so anachronistic to study medieval literature on the internet. She didn't want to see photos of the Nowell Codex (the manuscript holding the oldest version of *Beowulf*). She wanted to be staring down at it through the glass of the display case at the British Library, wanted to study every burn mark and tear, every ink-scratched thorn and rune.

Of course, whenever she railed about this to Sophie, Sophie liked to point out that by that logic, Allison should be reading by candlelight and using a chamber pot as well.

Even Allison had her limits.

The marker squealed loudly as she wrote her name on the board, cutting through the students' murmurs until the room went silent. When she faced them again, twelve sets of eyes were trained on her. (She'd have to put that trick in her back pocket. Teaching Tip #1: Obnoxious noises get students' attention.)

Heat crept like a colony of ants up the back of Allison's neck. She cleared her throat once, twice, trying to find her voice. There were so many people, and it was getting stuffy, and there wasn't a window to open.

Two weeks ago, she'd been sitting at a desk, watching Professor Behi prepare to start their first class. Now Allison was the one on the other side of the table. How was she supposed to do this? She didn't have any training. And nothing about this moment lined up with the fantasies she'd had in her head. No one was laughing or taking notes. There were no "Aha!" expressions on any of the students' faces. Mostly they all looked bored. A bunch had started scrolling through their phones.

She wasn't some bastion of knowledge here to change these kids' lives. She was a scared twenty-three-year-old who barely understood what it was to be an adult.

No, Allison chastised herself, her hand tightening around her marker. *Don't prove your mom and Sophie right. Show them you can do things that make you uncomfortable.*

Clearing her throat one last time, Allison forced herself to speak. "Hey."

Four students smiled.

She tried again. "How is everyone?"

Some shrugs. A few grumblings of "fine." Then silence.

The weight of it pressed down on Allison, but she forced herself to keep going, even if it felt like she was slogging through tar. Making her way around the circular table, she handed a copy of Professor Frances's recitation policies and a blank piece of construction paper to each student. Once she'd looped back to the front of the room, she asked them to write their names and, if they felt comfortable, their pronouns, on the paper. "So we can make sure we're addressing each other correctly," she explained.

Everyone took the exercise seriously except the boy sitting across from her. He stared Allison down, thick arms crossed over his wide chest, a smirk plastered on his face. He'd pushed his name tag forward as if he wanted to make sure she read it.

Name: Babe

Allison summoned every ounce of confidence she could muster and addressed him. "Write your actual name, please."

"Babe is how I like to be addressed."

Her teeth grinding together, Allison dug a pen out from her purse and rolled it the length of the conference table. It bumped up against his name plate and came to a stop. "Respecting how people choose to identify is something I take seriously. And I expect everyone else to do the same," she said.

After what felt like three hours of silent challenge (though, probably, it was closer to a minute and a half), Mitchell, the guy sitting beside "Babe," grabbed the yellow paper and wrote "Name: Colin Harcourt. Nickname: Cole" across the top.

Of course his name was Colin. Allison fought the urge to yell.

Mitchell shook his head at Cole as he set up the paper in front of him. "Don't be a jackass," he muttered.

Satisfied (and more grateful to Mitchell than she'd ever admit),

Allison turned her attention to the rest of the class. It was a battle not to hold her notes in front of her face and read verbatim from them.

"I really want this to be a space where we can dig into these texts together. I know the language can feel hard, and the structure of the stories is very different from what you see in a modern novel, but once you adjust to these elements, you'll discover that medieval literature and other older works are weird and fun, and explore a lot of the same questions we're still asking today. Plus, without *Beowulf* and Chaucer and Sir Thomas Malory, we wouldn't have *The Lord of the Rings* or *Game of Thrones*. Old English epics and medieval romance set the groundwork for the whole fantasy genre."

Her heart tapped out a wild beat in her chest, but this time, it wasn't due to nerves. For that one moment, Allison felt like an expert, someone who could actually help these students learn about (and, dare she think it, maybe even learn to *like*) these texts.

Unfortunately, that was the one shining moment in an otherwise disastrous first day. Over the next two hours, Allison managed to

1. Call the same student the wrong name three times, even with her name tag in front of her. (Was it Allison's fault if she looked *exactly* like a girl she'd gone to high school with?)

2. Offer a set of discussion questions that prompted absolutely no discussion.

3. Be accused (by Cole, of course) of "spoiling" a thousand-plus-year-old text by mentioning the death of Grendel coming up in their next section of reading.

4. Trip over her own feet while trying to pace at the front of the room.

5. Forget her own copy of *Beowulf* in her car after lecturing the students for five minutes about making sure they had the book with them.

6. Say *fuck* four times.

7. Accidentally wipe the board with the back of her yellow dress when she leaned against it. (She didn't discover this, however, until a student in her second section discreetly pointed it out on her way out of class.)

When everyone had left the room, Allison fell back into her chair. Her stomach was tight and sour, and her body wrenched into knots.

She'd just proven to her students in at least a dozen different ways that she had no idea how to teach. She'd failed. It was a feeling so foreign Allison didn't know how to sit with it. Her skin felt loose from her bones, and everything itched. Dragging her purse into her lap, she clawed through the junk in it (why did she have four tubes of the same lip gloss??), fighting hard to hold back the tears burning her eyes. There was no crying in baseball. Or teaching.

She needed Sophie. This day called for a major WCS list. It would be completely meta: a WCS for a WCS. And once they were done, when they'd envisioned all the scenarios, when they'd revealed every possible monster in the room, the unhinged feeling that had crept into Allison would disappear.

That's how it worked. It was how it had always worked.

But when she found her phone, Allison was met with another WCS.

The worst one of all.

Unknown Number: I hope your first day of recitation went as great as mine!

There was only one other person Allison knew who had his first recitation this week, and though she was loath to admit it, she still recognized his number from when they'd dated.

Fucking Colin Benjamin.

Allison's eyes sunk closed in frustration.

> **Allison Avery:** How did you get this number?

> **Unknown Number:** I took a chance that it hadn't changed since Brown.

> **Unknown Number:** Clearly, I was right.

> **Allison Avery:** It was bound to happen once.

> **Unknown Number:** ☺

Allison dropped her phone on the conference table as if it had burned her and scowled. Emojis were for friends and flirting, not for him.

> **Unknown Number:** So, did you blow all their minds? Are you Superteacher already? 😜

> **Allison Avery:** Why? Did you tank it? 😬

> **Unknown Number:** Don't you wish.

> **Allison Avery:** Like I waste that much time thinking about you.

Of course, that was all she'd done since their fight after Professor Frances's class earlier in the week. Arguing with him was a fucking aphrodisiac and it made Allison want to strangle him.

But it also helped her to forget. And all she wanted right now was to erase the last two hours from her mind. If she didn't have to think about recitation, then she didn't have to remember how badly she'd messed up.

For once, Colin Benjamin could be of some use.

A smile crept its way across her lips as she started typing. She'd show him Superteacher—even if it was fiction.

Allison Avery: Since you asked, my sections were 🔥🔥

Allison Avery: The students were so engaged. They asked a ton of questions.

Allison Avery: We almost ran out of time.

It took him a few minutes to respond. Allison had packed her bag and was halfway down the hall when a new text came through.

Unknown Number: Are you sure that's not because YOU wouldn't stop talking?

Allison Avery: Pssh. We all know that's more likely to be the case in YOUR sections, Captain Longwinded.

Unknown Number: Sorry, Superteacher. My students didn't give me a chance to talk. They were too busy killing it at close reading.

She hadn't asked how his classes went. And she didn't care. Allison would not let him get under her skin. Colin would never get between her and her goals again. She would read every guide to teaching in existence if that was what it took to help her get better. And in the meantime, she'd keep lying.

The sun was weak but persistent as she stepped out of the library and onto the campus's main stretch. She found a stone wall in the shade and sat down to stare at her screen.

Claymore had landscaped right before the start of the semester, and newly churned mulch and fresh blossoms in yellows, pinks, and reds turned the balmy air earthy and fresh. Bees hopped from blossom to blossom behind her, their buzz humming in her ears.

The rocks pressing into Allison's thighs were warm. Though it hurt a little, she leaned into the sensation, like the small burst of pain might clear her head.

For something briefer than a second, she considered jamming her phone in her bag and walking away (both literally and figuratively). Nothing good was waiting at the other end of this chat, while at home, there was Monty and her comfy bed and a night of popcorn and cheesy romcoms.

But if she did that, then Colin might suspect she'd lied. Details were the most important part of any story. She needed to add more to hers.

And oh, she did. Over the course of the next few minutes, she constructed an elaborate tale of complex conversations among her class about what it meant to be a hero. These imaginary students not only offered up a wealth of nuanced definitions of the term, but they brought in an assortment of pop culture examples of heroes and antiheroes from Jon Snow to Deadpool to Mr. Darcy to Maleficent and Elsa from Disney. One student, who had experience with Chaucer from high school, even mentioned the Wife of Bath.

Colin didn't respond again. Not so much as a clapping emoji.

Allison had won.

It should have felt better than it did.

Chapter 7

Allison stared drowsily into her bowl of cereal, wondering if anyone had ever fallen asleep and drowned in a cup of milk.

Seven in the morning was too early to be awake on a Saturday (or any day for that matter). Even Monty was still snoring away upstairs. But after the dream that had shaken her from sleep, there was no way Allison could close her eyes again.

She swirled her Cheerios with her spoon and tried to flush the images from her head. A giant library full of shelves illuminated by old-fashioned gas lanterns, a mysterious mist floating around her bare feet. The beautiful leather-bound edition with the gold lettering she hadn't been able to read as she reached for it.

The book had turned into a hand when her fingers closed around it, and she was pulled through the bookcase as if it were no more than a curtain. On the other side, Colin Benjamin leaned against a white wall in that way he had, the world bending to fit his every point and corner. Even in her dream, his posture sent all of her nerves tingling.

Only when she glanced down did she realize their fingers were laced together. He'd tugged her toward him. His hazel eyes drinking her in, he'd whispered her name like a prayer. Like a beseeching. Like he'd been trapped behind that phantom bookcase for eternity, waiting for her to release him.

This is a bad idea, she'd thought as she stepped toward him.

I should turn and run, she'd insisted as she hooked her free hand into the hem of his oatmeal-colored cardigan.

This will only lead to trouble, she'd understood as his palm settled against her hip.

But that doubt was swiftly smothered by the sheer sense of want that washed over her when her chest met his. The feeling was so intense, so visceral, that it had clung to Allison long after she'd awoken. Even now, as she sat at the kitchen table, her center thrummed with it.

Allison couldn't even escape Colin Benjamin in her dreams.

That wasn't the worst of it, either. Once she was close enough, he'd traced a thumb down her cheek and along her jaw, mapping the curves of her face. Tipping her chin up, he'd whispered her name again. Lower this time. Thick with desire. Anticipation rattled her heart against her ribs and made her lungs heave. Their lips were so close that all Allison would have had to do was ease up on her tiptoes. Every kiss they'd ever shared played back across her mind as she waited, and waited, and waited for him to cross that small distance between them.

And just as he'd leaned forward, her eyes had snapped open.

With a voice loud and graveled with sleep (and other things she refused to acknowledge), Allison had sworn at the ceiling fan.

Who could go back to sleep after that?

Damn her traitorous subconscious. And that stupid text message exchange yesterday. He was too in her head. Too in her *world*.

Allison wasn't supposed to be thinking about Colin Benjamin *at all,* never mind like this. How could she forget their past with her brain reminding her how much she used to love to kiss him? For all his flaws, he'd been an excellent kisser, knowing just when to add pressure or release it, how to sweep his tongue gently across hers.

No. No. No. Allison growled. The sound echoed off the kitchen walls. She would not dwell on Colin's mouth, or his tongue, except to recall every aggravating sentence those two parts of his body had ever produced.

She stabbed her spoon through an oaty O, digging it into the bottom of the bowl for good measure.

Sophie swept into the kitchen as Allison was murdering her second Cheerio. "Oh my god. Is the world ending?" She glanced down at her phone and then back at Allison. Faux surprised creased her face.

"You're hilarious," Allison muttered, shoving a heaping spoonful of cereal into her mouth.

"I didn't think you rose before ten on weekends."

"If I knew I'd be facing the Spanish Inquisition, I wouldn't have bothered."

"No one expects the Spanish Inquisition."

Allison groaned. "And no one needs Monty Python references at seven in the morning."

Sophie shot her a satisfied grin as she grabbed an empty bowl and joined Allison at the table. "Look at all I've taught you." She poured milk into the bowl and then added cereal on top (Sophie did nothing the conventional way, no matter how horrifying). "So, for real, what's with the early rise?"

Allison twirled her spoon through her milk, turning her Cheerios into a whirlpool. Part of her wanted to tell Sophie about her dream, just to speak it out loud. Usually, that stole some of its power. But her best friend considered herself an amateur Freud, and she'd want to interpret its meaning. The last thing Allison needed was to hear Sophie suggest she still had feelings for Colin. And then she'd have to admit why he'd been on her mind, and . . . nope. There was not enough room in Allison's tired head for that.

She settled on the other reason she'd had trouble sleeping. "Teaching didn't go so great."

Sophie waved a hand. "No way. I bet you're being too hard on yourself. No one talks about books the way you do. Remember the guy at that bookstore near my house you schooled on the Middle Ages versus the Renaissance—"

"The early modern period," Allison corrected her.

"Yes. Just like that. They ended up reshelving the whole section. Did I tell you?"

"What?! NO." Allison barked out a laugh. She'd just learned she'd gotten an A– on a paper she'd worked her ass off on and had been feeling pretty spicy that day. "That's exactly the kind of confidence boost I need right now."

Sophie flashed her a grin around her mouthful of Cheerios. "Just think. Soon you'll be inspiring all your students to rearrange their own book shelves."

Allison yawned, and the two of them fell into a comfortable silence. With Monty still asleep, the only sound in the kitchen was their quiet chewing. As she ate, Sophie reached across the table to where she'd left her tablet, revealing a small stack of papers half-shoved under the placemat beneath it. The top one was thick, formal paper with Sophie's credentials listed across the top.

Allison snatched it up, her eyes narrowing. "Why do you have résumés out?" She brandished the paper at Sophie.

Sophie shrugged, her attention on the sketch she was fussing with. "Just giving them a tune-up."

"I thought you were going to go into business for yourself? You know, do the whole trade show thing, not work with a label? You said you didn't want to be held back by other people's visions."

Sophie's olive skin reddened. "I'm just keeping my options open. Maybe it'd be nice to work for a big brand someday. Lead designer and all that. Imagine having all those resources behind me."

"Yeah, *someday*." Allison's knee bounced. She was already rattled, and now her heart had found a new burst of speed. This didn't sound like a résumé tune-up. This sounded like Sophie was actively looking for a job.

"Brooks told me about a few companies in New York and one in Boston that recently put out calls for designers."

Brooks. Of course. Whenever Allison hung out with Sophie and her designer friends, he was always bringing up people Allison didn't know and chortling at their inside jokes. He would be the one encouraging Sophie to apply to jobs whole train rides away.

If Allison and her best friend were growing worlds apart in the same room, what would happen if she moved?

It felt like the floor was dropping out from under her. Pushing out her chair, Allison mumbled, "I should get going. I have an entire, giant Victorian novel to read for class this weekend."

"Wait." Sophie caught her wrist. "No matter where we are, we're always us. You know that, right?" Her dark eyes held Allison hostage. "Besides, I haven't applied anywhere. I'm just assessing my options."

"I know." Allison shook her head. "But I liked our plan. Graduate. Get a place together. Support each other through all the ups and downs as we start our careers and all that."

"We can still do that, even if we're not living in the same place."

She wasn't wrong. Allison let her head fall back. "Sorry. I'm . . . having a morning." She couldn't let Sophie see how much this news had railroaded her. That would only prove her mother right about Allison's fear of change.

More important, like she'd said, she hadn't sent anything out. There was no need for Allison to worry. Not yet, at least.

"It's a big day." Sophie grinned. "You don't usually see the sun until it's reached its peak. This all must be disorienting for you."

Allison offered her both middle fingers, and the two of them fell into a fit of laughter.

Chapter 8

That night, Allison's first-year cohort gathered around Kara's small coffee table.

At orientation, they'd been encouraged to start spending time together. "You'll want critique partners, and writing groups, and someone to call crying the morning of your oral exams when you're convinced you're going to fail. Start building those bonds now," they'd been told. So, while Allison would much rather be at home playing tug-o-war with Monty and hanging out with Sophie (if she was around for once), here she was, participating in what was basically compulsory group bonding.

Ethan Windbag fought a grimace as he stared at Kara. She'd just thrust a tray precariously balancing an army of plastic champagne flutes into his personal space. Each was filled with a bright red concoction.

"Do you have any Scotch?"

"I only bought the fixings for Starburst martinis. The text said it was BYOB otherwise," she reminded him.

"Scotch is not beer."

"But it is *booze*," Allison pointed out as she gently eased one flute off the tray.

"And gross," Mandy added, following Allison's lead. They fist-bumped as Mandy sat back with her drink.

She, Mandy, and Alex were squished on a sofa, the eggshell-colored fabric of which creaked with their every move, while Ethan and Link occupied two red armchairs that looked like they'd been passed down to Kara by her great- (great-, great-, great-, great-) grandmother. The arms had tassels. *Tassels.* Made of gold thread. *Gold. Thread.*

Kara flitted from place to place like a hummingbird turned hostess (in another crisply ironed button-down), and Colin Benjamin lorded over the rest of them from against the fireplace, fiddling with what looked like a crystal cat figurine on the mantel. The way he was lean-ing reminded Allison too much of that dream she'd had this morning, so she'd decided to pretend he wasn't there. Or, if the leaning (which Allison found irrationally sexy) proved to be too much, she'd imagine he was someone else. Hal, one of Kara's non-grad-school friends who'd joined them for the evening. That sounded right. Hal was innocuous and forgettable. Not a boil on the backside of Allison's entire existence.

They'd all been grumbling about their coursework for the last fif-teen minutes, but when Kara (who'd clearly googled "hosting a party" online) had entered the room brandishing her signature cocktail, she'd banned school talk.

Once everyone (except Ethan) had a drink, she set down the tray and clapped her hands. "I thought we could play two truths and a lie. It'll be a fun way to get to know each other."

Allison cringed internally. This was the party equivalent of bringing flashcards on a date. With the exception of family wedding showers, she hadn't played a party game since she was in junior high. Usually alcohol was all the icebreaker anyone needed.

Their host joined Colin at the fireplace. Something about the way she smiled at him twisted Allison's insides like a balloon animal, but he was still so enthralled by the knickknack he didn't notice.

Kara cleared her throat. "I thought we'd make it themed. For added fun." She asked Colin to start, offering him that extra-bright smile again.

Allison studied Kara's smile more closely than she should. Was there something going on between them?

Knocking back a good gulp of her drink, she shook her head. She was being ridiculous. Kara was just intensely attentive. And even if there was more to it, Allison didn't care. Not one bit. Let Colin flirt (or not flirt) with whomever he liked.

He jerked his head up, his eyes wide as he looked at Kara.

"You start," Kara said again. "Two truths and a lie about music."

"Um . . ." He replaced the crystal cat on the mantel as gently as if it were real and scratched at the back of his head. "Okay. Um . . . er . . . One: I've never been to a live concert."

Lie. Allison had attended two with him at the Providence Performing Arts Center. A bunch of folksy rock bands. One had had a washboard player and everything. As a self-proclaimed lover of overplayed Top 40 hits, Allison had been surprised by how much she'd enjoyed herself. She still had songs from some of those folksy bands in her Spotify playlists.

She threw back the other half of her Starburst martini in retaliation against the warm glow overtaking her stomach.

No. More. Reminiscing.

The drink tasted like painstakingly fresh-pressed strawberry and orange juices, the burn of vodka only noticeable at the back of Allison's throat as it swam in her far-too-empty stomach. These martinis were going to be dangerous, she thought as she plucked another one from the tray.

Colin coughed. "Two: I love musical theater."

Truth. Allison didn't let herself think about the time he sang the entire score of *Dear Evan Hansen* to her while she'd lain curled up in his bed nursing murderous menstrual cramps.

"Three: I play the banjo."

Truth. It took all of Allison's self-control not to add *badly* to the end of his sentence. He used to practice in her dorm room while she was trying to study, strumming louder every time she'd beg him to stop.

Kara pointed to Windbag. "Guess." The demand in her voice made this whole thing feel less like a game and more like classroom drills.

Ethan stared at Colin, his face screwed up in thought, his stupidly attractive biceps curling as he tapped a finger to his lips. "Obviously the musical theater one is the lie. Musicals are insipid."

"Oh my god," Allison blurted out. Those two martinis had obliterated her sense of etiquette. "Who was mean to you as a child?"

Ethan's head snapped toward her. "What?"

"How can you not like musicals? *Hamilton. Hadestown. Waitress. Mean Girls. LES MIS.*"

Ethan tipped his chin up. "Hugo's book is far superior."

Allison rolled her eyes (a bad move considering all the alcohol), and the world tipped a little. She braced a hand against the couch. "Hugo's book is overwritten, misogynistic tragedy porn."

"YES." Mandy fist-bumped Allison again, and they broke into a raucous (and riotously off-key) chorus of "Do You Hear the People Sing?"

Allison's heart banged out its own chaotic rhythm, and alcohol pulsed through her veins, draping everything in a hazy gauze. She was having fun, weird throwbacks to junior high and all.

Take that, Mom, she thought smugly. *Look at me enjoying people who aren't my roommate. And with fucking Colin Benjamin right here.*

Colin pulled open his black cardigan to point at the shirt beneath, like Superman revealing the *S* on his suit. But he was the antithesis of Superman, so this display exposed only a black T-shirt with a white silhouette of the Schuyler sisters from *Hamilton.* "I love musical theater," Colin said. "And concerts."

"There's the lie!" Her tan face beaming, Kara pointed to Ethan. "Your turn. Cartoons."

Ethan's brow furrowed. "I have never once watched a cartoon."

Allison dropped her head back against the sofa. This guy was the worst.

"Not even as a kid?" Link asked. He cracked open another of his artisan beers. His dark brown skin had the same dewy brightness from drinking that must be dusting Allison's temples.

"I preferred documentaries."

Allison pondered whether she could make her empty plastic flute into a proper projectile. If only she'd paid more attention in high-school physics . . .

Kara pursed her lips and pulled a sheet of paper out of her pocket. "Hmmm. Okay, how about hobbies?"

Ethan nodded solemnly. As he thought hard about his answers (even striking *The Thinker* pose), Allison made her own list in her head.

1. **Mansplaining women's rights to women.**

2. **Publicly hating everything popular.**

3. **Kicking puppies.**

The real answers turned out to be so much better.

"One," he said dramatically, holding up a finger like they didn't know how to count. "Grammar."

"Wait." Mandy shook her head. "How is grammar a hobby?"

"I like to help people learn it," Ethan replied.

"Like tutoring?" Allison admired Link's attempt to give Ethan the benefit of the doubt.

"Of a kind." He folded his arms over his chest. "I like to help people make their social media posts clearer by pointing out issues with the writing."

Allison was disappointed in herself for not guessing this first.

"Two," Ethan went on. "Dressage."

"The thing with the horses?" Colin asked.

Ethan nodded. He dragged his hand through the strands of long blond hair that had come loose from the knot at the back of his head. "And three." More counting fingers. "I play chess. Extremely well."

Kara turned to Colin. "You guess."

Colin took his glasses off and rubbed his eyes. "It has to be the dressage thing."

Ethan smiled smugly. "Incorrect."

"Then what was the lie?" Allison demanded. He seemed like the kind of person who would treat chess with the gravity of a football fanatic. And Allison knew, deep down in her bones, that the first one was true.

"I play checkers, not chess. It's actually more complicated in its simplicity."

Allison turned to Kara and held up both her empty flutes. "Are there more of these?" If she was going to be forced to bond with Windbag, she needed to be drunker.

By the time she returned with a fresh round of martinis, they'd all learned that Mandy liked to cross-stitch swears onto flowery patterns, Link baked artisanal breads to go with his beers, and Alex crocheted stuffed animals to sell on Etsy. Each fact gave Allison a new appreciation for these people she sat with for hours every week in class. It broadened who they were, made them more than students who seemed older, more intelligent, and worldlier than Allison. They all had things about them to which she could relate.

Allison liked that more than she'd expected.

As she settled back onto the couch, Kara announced it was her turn. "The theme is animals."

Allison took one, then two sips of her martini as she deliberated. It sloshed, sweet like candy, around her teeth and tongue. "Okay." She set the plastic flute on the end table and sat up straighter. "Here we go. I've swum with dolphins twice."

There was her lie. She'd only done it once, when her aunt Janice took Allison and her mother to Hawaii for her mom's fortieth birthday.

"I have a Corgi named Monty." The most important truth.

"A goat once followed me home from a petting zoo."

The moment the words left her mouth, Allison regretted them. Colin would know that was a truth. He'd been there when it happened. *Damnit.*

His eyes fell heavily on her face.

Damnit times two.

Allison refused to look his way, even as her skin warmed beneath the touch of his gaze.

"I'll guess." Kara placed her drink carefully on the mantel. In the time it had taken Allison to drink three martinis, she'd nursed half of one.

She bit her thumbnail as she studied Allison. But before she could respond, Colin did. "You don't have a Corgi."

His voice tugged Allison's attention to him, a puppet on a string. Its tone was raw, scraping, the words coming from deep in the back of his throat. Staring at him now, she saw he hadn't shaved, a light shadow of blond stubble darkening his jaw. It looked good. Exceptionally good.

Suddenly her mind dragged her back to all the times she'd run her hands over those bristly cheeks, felt them scratch against her neck as he nuzzled her close.

Damnit times three. Allison sucked down half her drink, then made a sound like a buzzer as loud as she could, as if that might drown out her thoughts. She needed to get rid of them, somehow. "Wrong," she said.

Kara cleared her throat. "I was thinking it was—"

"What happened to Cleo?" Colin had witnessed a few FaceTimes with Allison's mom back in the day, and pictures of the pit bull had papered her walls all through undergrad.

"Cleo is my mother's dog. Monty is *mine.*"

Allison injected as much force as she could into her words. He needed to stop this line of questioning before people started to realize they knew each other. Having to explain their history to everyone would not keep it in the rearview mirror.

"It's the goat!" Kara called out. "That's the lie." She kept glancing at her watch as if they were about to run off schedule.

Allison welcomed the intrusion. "Nope." She grinned. "I've only swum with dolphins once."

"Okay but seriously." Mandy poked at her leg. "I need to hear more about this goat."

Allison's sophomore year at Brown, the school had brought in a small petting zoo run by a local farm to help with stress management. Colin had offered to take her after he finished a paper, but it took longer than he'd hoped, and by the time they'd arrived at the zoo, the owners were out of feed for the animals. Bummed, Allison had sat in a corner of the fenced-in area, talking to a black-and-white pygmy goat as if it might respond. It had a bell around its neck and liked to kick its legs wildly as it jumped in circles, and Allison had loved him.

Colin had wandered off, and when he returned, he dropped a bag of baby carrots into her lap. "Where did you get this?" she'd asked. He'd given her a wink and one of those mischievous smiles before insisting that he had his ways. With a squeal, she broke a few carrots into small pieces to feed them to her new friend. He'd eaten them right off her palm, and nuzzled her arm gently with his horned forehead to ask for more. She'd obliged, again and again, until a big rush of freshmen who'd just finished up a major bio exam showed up. They were loud and crowded the animals like a group of small children, and it took about two seconds for Allison and Colin to decide to sneak out the back gate.

Well, one of them mustn't have closed it fully (Allison was sure it was Colin, but, not surprisingly, he'd blamed her), and her little black-and-white friend followed them out. They were all the way back at her dorm when she'd heard the distinct tinkle of that bell and spun around to find the goat jumping toward them with his little kicks.

They'd both panicked and charged at the animal at the same time, causing him to bleat and run away. Instead of catching the goat, Allison and Colin crashed into each other. Like something out of an incredibly tropey romcom, they'd ended up on the ground, Colin on top of her, and what started out as an embarrassing laughing fit soon turned into their first kiss (meanwhile, the goat stole the entire bag of carrots, along with Allison's purse, and was found wandering the student commons).

Allison deliberately skipped over Colin and the kiss as she recounted the story for her cohort. Her eyes remained honed on Mandy, and Allison forced a laugh at all the right parts. She shouldn't have needed to fake it. It was a great anecdote. But the way things had ended with Colin draped a dark shroud over that entire year. Allison couldn't think back on any of it without her stomach knotting painfully.

Colin's eyes seared into the back of her neck as he stood, frozen, against the mantel. It was impossible not to wonder what he was thinking. Did that memory jab at him too? Or had he left it behind along with her when he'd graduated?

She flushed with relief when Kara yelled, "Food's ready!," causing everyone to dash for the kitchen.

Allison hung behind, putting as much distance as she could between herself, Colin, and those bittersweet memories.

Allison hadn't realized how much she was craving fresh air until she dragged open the sliding glass door and stepped out onto the balcony. Taking a deep breath, she ignored the acrid scent of exhaust fumes wafting from the street and focused on the coolness of the air in her chest.

Kara's apartment was small enough to make seven people feel like a crowd, and as she'd poured her fifth (and, she swore to herself, final) Starburst martini, Allison had suddenly felt cramped everywhere she went. This happened a lot when she got drunk. As the alcohol turned the world around her fuzzy, she became too aware of her size, of how she fit into spaces. It was like she grew sharper while everything else blurred.

Tugging down the hem of her dress, she lowered herself onto the wooden slats of the balcony and leaned her head against the metal rails. Their cold exterior pricked at the skin of her temple, clearing Allison's thoughts as she watched cars rush by.

She wasn't an introvert. She didn't love being alone. Sometimes, Allison even found the anonymity of huge crowds—like concerts, amusement parks, summer beach days—appealing. It could be nice to be nobody for a few minutes, and, surrounded by so many people, her body shrunk in diameter. It no longer felt as if everyone noticed her simply because she was larger than most.

But more intimate groups, those handfuls of people she knew, were trickier to navigate. You couldn't disappear when everyone knew your name. Never mind negotiating the minefield that was Colin Benjamin on top of that. Allison needed a second to take a breath and just *be*.

She managed two more deep inhales and exhales before she caught the sound of approaching footsteps. A shadow fell over her as the person reached the sliding doors.

Colin rested his head against the screen. "Those martinis have kicked my ass harder than an MMA champion." His voice was quiet, almost swallowed by the city noise.

"I don't understand your sportsball reference."

"There's no ball in mixed martial arts."

Allison threw up her hands. "Semantics."

Colin snorted. "Why are you sitting out here?"

"Air."

"There's a total of like seven people in there." He hooked a thumb over his shoulder toward the apartment.

"And there's four and a half martinis sloshing around in here." Allison pointed at her stomach. "Hence, air."

"Ah." Colin's hazel eyes cut across the balcony. "Room for one more person?"

The darkness that haloed him had soft edges, like the whole world had been painted in watercolors. Allison could feel the alcohol settling deeper into her, turning her limbs loose and her mouth unguarded. "Why?" she asked.

Surprise yanked something between a cough and a laugh from Colin's mouth. "Why do I want to sit with you?"

Allison shrugged, though, in her head, she was screaming the word. *Why. Why. WHY.*

His eyes narrowed behind his glasses. "I needed a break. Despite my extensive collection, I don't know enough about comics to keep up with Alex and Link."

"I don't think anyone does. Not even the writers."

He laughed. Interpreting her response as an invitation, he lowered his long, thin frame to the floor. To accommodate him, Allison had to shift her legs so they hung over the balcony, and Colin did the same. They sat side by side, barely enough space between their arms to claim they weren't touching. Their feet swung in a dissonant rhythm.

The traffic light at the end of the block cycled through one, two, three series of colors. Allison watched them dance: green, yellow, red, green, yellow, red. She swayed a little with the rush of her blood, the spin of her mind from the booze. Her eyelids had started to droop, her head heavy as lead. It had been a smart move to take a ride share rather than drive. She had one of those buzzes that felt thick enough to last for days.

Beside her, Colin shook his head. "Why did you bring up the goat?"

"What?"

"The goat. Before. You said no more digging up the past."

Allison sighed. "I wasn't thinking about our kiss." Lie. "It's just a great story. And perfect for that game. You know how I like to win."

"Do I?"

Allison did her best to glare at him. It was hard to determine how successful she was when she could barely feel her face. "Stop it."

"I'm serious." Colin squared his body so all his attention was honed on her. "How am I supposed to forget the past? What if I . . . I—"

"You just do." Allison raised her shoulders and blew out a breath. "Like this. Watch. You change the subject." Dusting her hands together, she said, "I bet Bo is still thriving." She'd forgotten until this moment that she'd named the goat Bo.

"That creature had no self-preservation skills. He's probably wandered onto a highway by now."

Allison squawked. And, before she could think better of it, she smacked Colin in the arm. It was more solid than she remembered, and her heart hiccupped. His eyes dropped to the exact square of knitted rows she'd touched as if she'd left a mark.

Her pulse throbbed against her wrist. "He managed to secure himself a whole bag of carrots. That seems like excellent self-preservation to me."

"Not if he ate them all at once."

With an amused huff, Allison looked away, her eyes following a car as it pulled a U-turn farther up the road. Bickering with Colin felt both strange and comfortingly familiar. It had been their way, even when they'd been at their best. One of their most fun dates had involved arguing over the best candy at the movie theater long enough to miss their showing. (Colin had insisted it was chocolate-covered raisins. But raisins weren't candy. They were undead grapes.) Allison used to believe that she and Colin challenged each other to be smarter, quicker, better. That was why they'd worked so well. Now she wondered if maybe all the arguing was a sign that they'd been broken from the start.

Mandy's loud laugh echoed from inside the apartment, cutting through Allison's musing. She and Colin shot looks over their shoulders, moving in tandem. The group seemed farther than two rooms away.

"Do you ever . . ." His voice hitched. "Do you ever feel like you don't quite fit here?"

Allison narrowed her eyes at him. "What are you talking about? You're Colin Benjamin. You fit everywhere." It was one of the things she'd always loved most about him, that way he had of settling seamlessly into any situation.

He smiled softly, like he thought she was teasing him. "Seriously though, these past few weeks of grad school have been intense, right?" His eyes traced over her, looking for something in her expression. "At least for me."

"For me, too." The slight wobble in his voice made that fact easier to confess.

"And we . . ." He shook his head, seeming to change direction. "Maybe we could . . . give each other a break? Not help each other, I know that's blasphemy," he said with a smirk. "But maybe we could have a mild truce."

Thanks to the fruity martinis, filterless Allison struck again. "What the fuck is a mild truce?"

He let out one of those fantastically terrible laughs. "One where we agree we are both awesome and don't need to outdo each other. There's no rule that says Frances's class can't have two excellent TAs."

This was a surprise. Colin was rarely so open and direct. The few times when he had been remained some of Allison's strongest memories. Those small, ephemeral peeks he'd offered into other sides of him, like getting to preview the next book in a series before anyone else.

"I suppose it would be nice to put the energy I'd expend trouncing you elsewhere." She flashed him what she hoped was a playful grin. Barely the length between the balcony's bars separated their faces. His breath had a hint of the sweetness from the martinis and that sharp, clean scent of hair gel burned the inside of Allison's nose.

The height of the balcony wasn't helping her dizziness, and, as her stomach swooped, she leaned her head a little farther forward. All the martinis in the world were sloshing around in her skull.

"We might even . . ."

"Yeah?" Colin spoke slow and careful, his usual precision lost. Though she might have been imagining it, it seemed as if he were angling closer to her.

And closer.

And . . .

"We might even be—*oof*." Allison's head slipped from the cold metal bar, cracking her temple against his glasses.

He made a strange noise in his throat, and even from so close up, where they looked as large as planets, and spun just as fast, Allison saw his hazel eyes widen. Her heart stammered in response and, fortified by her drunken state, she said words she didn't think to regret.

"We might even be a good team." Like that time they'd line danced. Or those rare moments back in Lit Theory at Brown where they'd worked together to interpret a text rather than try to prove each other wrong.

She'd never know if Colin heard her.

As if in time with the traffic light, his face blanched green, and a painful gurgle sounded in his throat. He swallowed once, hard, his pointed Adam's apple bobbing.

Allison had enough time to jump to her feet before he vomited all over the balcony. The swift movement sobered her up like all the alcohol had been zapped from her veins. She averted her eyes from the mess beside him and focused on Colin as he groaned.

"I'll go get you some water and . . ." She gestured to the ground. "A bucket, I guess." She was already halfway through the sliding door.

He fumbled around to face her, almost dropping his glasses in the puddle. "You don't have to take care of me."

"Yeah, I do. We have a mild truce now, remember?"

She bent to help him scoot back so his spine was set securely against the glass door. As she turned away, his hand caught hers and squeezed.

The touch couldn't have lasted more than a heartbeat. By the time she glanced back, his fingers were folded in his lap and his head was lolled toward the street. But the feel of his skin on hers warmed her palm the whole way through Kara's apartment, making Allison's own stomach roil.

Already, she was starting to worry that the promise she and Colin had made to each other would be impossible to keep. How could they ever erase their past when it was so tangled with their present?

Chapter 9

Allison's phone buzzed beside her as she stared up at the vaulted ceilings of the Edelman dining hall, puzzling out exactly what she'd tell Professor Frances about her first two weeks of teaching.

Assuming it was Sophie or her mom, she swiped it open without glancing at the notification.

Unknown Number: Running late! Be there soon.

Colin.

Allison probably should have added his name to her contacts, but something about "Unknown Number" appealed to her. It suggested he didn't hold a solid enough place in her world to earn a name. Even if the string of messages they'd shared since Kara's party contradicted that.

Her finger tapped the screen, bringing up a few older texts.

Unknown Number: I can't believe I retched all over Kara's balcony.

Allison Avery: I can't believe you use the word retch.

Unknown Number: Was it as bad as I remember it?

Allison Avery: It was pretty spectacular.

Allison Avery: Technicolor, like Joseph's coat.

Allison Avery: ". . . red and yellow and green and brown . . . scarlet and black and ochre and peach. . . ."

Unknown Number: Stop or I will spew (heave? puke? hurl? barf? are any of these better?) again.

Allison Avery: ". . . and ruby and olive and violet and fawn . . ."

Unknown Number: STOP. PLEEEAAASSEEE.

Allison's heart stuttered, and her insides tightened. The same thing had happened the first time she'd read those messages.

They shouldn't be joking around like this. And Colin should *not* have touched her hand on Kara's balcony the way he had. Truce or no truce, they weren't friends. Or anything else. Every interaction with him was starting to feel too risky, like reopening a wound that hadn't healed.

They needed distance. And space. Six feet and two years of silence between them at all times. Allison muted her phone and placed it upside down on the table. That at least was a start.

She heard the clink of bangle stacks as her professor rounded the table and pulled out the chair across from her. She was much less formal in a pair of dark skinny jeans and a tailored dolman-sleeved top. The lavender fabric was spotted with silver bicycles. On her left arm she wore a woven black leather cuff with an ornate snap and a row of black and white bangles. Her ash-blond hair framed her face in loose waves.

Professor Frances smiled warmly as she sat down. "Allison, thanks for meeting me on such short notice." Her blue eyes scanned the other empty seats. "No Colin yet?"

Allison rested her hand over her phone. She should explain that he'd let her know he was running late. But the competitive part of her resisted. She wasn't his assistant or his secretary. It wasn't her job to make excuses for his whereabouts.

Still, she couldn't stop her mind from drifting back to the look on his face when he'd asked for that truce. His hazel eyes had been so soft and unsure. He'd meant it. And she'd agreed.

Plus, he was right. They didn't need to compete for Professor Frances's approval. She'd chosen them both as her TAs, so she must view them as equally promising scholars.

"My sound was off. Let me see if he reached out." Allison poked around on her phone's screen, pretending to check her messages.

Just as she was about to confirm he was running late, Colin appeared at the table. Sweat stippled his temples and brow, and the lenses of his maroon glasses were fogged. He was breathing raggedly, as if he'd sprinted straight here.

Professor Frances glanced at her watch and then at him. "There you are." There was nothing judgmental in her tone, and she was smiling, but that didn't stop Colin from flinching. Allison would have done the same. Lateness was a mortal sin for overachievers.

"I'm so sorry. My car wouldn't start, and I had to bike here." Colin gulped air as his eyes cut to Allison. "I let Allison know."

"I was just about to tell her." Allison flashed him her phone with his text prominently on display.

His brows arched in surprise, disappearing beneath a tousle of his hair. Without the usual layer of gel, it was loose and messy, basically begging for fingers to get tangled in it.

Damn him for being a hot (in every sense of the word) mess. And for doubting her commitment to their truce. Allison could have easily undermined him just now, but she didn't. It had taken herculean effort and a lot of self-control.

Clearly, she was winning at not competing.

Plus, could she even be sure he would do the same for her? Two years ago, she would have said no with certainty. But this Colin seemed different from the guy she'd known at Brown. Back then, he'd been overconfident and determined to prove to everyone that he was the best at everything. Yet, for all his bluster that first day in Professor Frances's class, the Claymore Colin Benjamin (Colin 2.0, if you would) hesitated before speaking. At Kara's party, he'd wanted to hear what Allison had to say instead of talking over her (at least before he'd yacked everywhere). If she was being honest with herself, *she'd* been the one on competition overdrive these last few weeks.

But none of that matters, she told herself. It couldn't. He was still Colin Benjamin, the guy who'd stolen the Rising Star Award out from under her, then dumped her days later, without so much as an apology. If she wasn't . . . well, *her* . . . that might have marked the end of all her grad school career before it had even started. And he was still the guy currently standing between Allison and everything she wanted.

The reminder burned a hole in her stomach. It was exactly what she needed.

Professor Frances had been digging in her tote bag and finally reemerged, a wallet in hand. "Do we want to talk before or after food?"

"Before," Allison said.

"After," Colin contradicted her.

They glanced at each other, both of their mouths twitching.

Professor Frances observed the food service areas behind her. "Let's get something before the line grows."

The cafeteria was small but well stocked. It had a whole breakfast bar still active as well as a deli station, pasta station, salad bar, and daily entrée, which looked like some sort of chicken in cream sauce. Allison swerved by without stopping. Breakfast was always her first choice, no matter the time of day.

Ordering a waffle piled high with strawberries and cream, turkey bacon, and a kale smoothie, she leaned against her tray, her eyes straying toward the drink kiosk. Colin and Professor Frances both pumped coffee into their reusable mugs. She was too far away to read their lips, but Colin said something, and the two of them laughed.

Allison's hands turned to fists at her sides. He was doing that thing again, flipping his charisma on like a flashlight. Whomever he pointed it at would be caught in his spell. That's probably what he'd done in his recitations, too. He didn't need any knowledge of medieval lit. All he had to do was smile and crack a joke and his students would love him.

Doing her best to keep her tray steady, Allison stomped back to her seat. Professor Frances had invited them to lunch to discuss their teaching. That meant Allison was going to have to sit here and listen to how amazingly well Colin's classes were going. And then, against her better judgment, she was going to have to lie. Again. Or risk exposing that she was a terrible teacher. And no pact, mild or otherwise, would force Allison to show that kind of weakness.

Not to Wendy Frances.

And certainly not to Colin.

By the time they'd returned to the table, Allison had sawed her entire waffle into individual squares. On each, she'd piled one strawberry and a dollop of whipped cream. The uniformity was comforting. There was control in it. Order. The world on Allison's plate made sense in a way her real one never would, especially with Colin around, stirring up endless chaos.

As an undergrad student, whenever Allison had felt uncertain about how to interpret a text, she'd approach her confusion head-on by participating first in class. The things that made her anxious were always easier to handle if she didn't let them balloon out of control. She figured it couldn't hurt to try that method here. "Professor Frances," she said as soon as her teacher sat down.

"Call me Wendy."

"Wendy. Sorry." Damnit. Would she ever get the etiquette here right? "After a conversation I had with my recitation groups, I've been thinking a lot about Grendel's mother, and the significance of the primary female character in *Beowulf* being both a monster and a mother. So often, mothers are characterized as monsters in medieval and early modern texts, and even the medical literature makes their bodies sound unnatural."

Wendy's expression brightened. "Your students are already interested in Grendel's mother?"

Allison nodded. She might as well have gotten herself a shovel for how heavily she was piling it on. "They were all so engaged, they'd read ahead and had a ton of thoughts." *Lies. Lies. Lies.*

"That's impressive. They must have felt incredibly comfortable to take a risk and talk about a part of the text I haven't reviewed with them yet."

Colin observed their conversation quietly, a wide smile slowly unfurling on his face. He looked . . . well, shit . . . he looked proud of Allison. As if he'd expected nothing less from her. She was pummeled by a wave of contradictory emotions: shame for lying, regret for competing when she shouldn't be, and something a little too close to affection for her liking.

Wendy moved her gaze to him. "What about you, Colin? How did recitations go this week?"

"Not as great as Allison's, clearly," he said with a wink. (Seriously, a *wink*. Allison wanted to spear a piece of her waffle and fling it at him. Square between the lenses of his glasses.) "But I thought my students did a good job of asking questions about the reading and adjusting to the format of recitations."

Nodding thoughtfully, Professor Frances—no, *Wendy*; Allison had to start learning to think of her that way—prodded them to share some specific moments from their sections. Allison did her best to let Colin take the lead so she could avoid digging herself a deeper pit of deception, but it was impossible to listen to the sincerity with which he recounted his students' thoughts and questions without feeling the need to make herself shine a little brighter.

Once they'd both had a chance to speak, Wendy clasped her hands in front of her and sat up a little straighter. "I hope that you both know how thrilled I am to work with you," she said. "And how impressed I am with the progress you've already made with your students."

Allison shifted, guilt creeping like spiders across her shoulders. Imagine how unimpressed Wendy would be if she'd witnessed Allison's actual first few days of teaching.

"I wish I could say that I'd asked for this lunch solely to talk about pedagogy. Unfortunately, I have a bit of regrettable news."

Allison's muscles were instantly in knots. When she glanced at Colin, he was staring back at her, his eyes full of questions. Was Wendy about to drop one of them as a TA? Had she been assigned too many by accident? Who would she pick? And what would Allison do if it wasn't her?

"I'm afraid I won't be able to take you both on as advisees as I'd originally hoped." Wendy pushed her tray aside to lean toward them. "I take my advising responsibilities seriously, and with new graduate students, it's so important to be present. When we accepted two medieval studies students this year, I thought I'd have the time. But now my research funding and my sabbatical have come through together, and I won't be able to give you both the attention you deserve."

This couldn't be happening. Allison wrung her hands in her lap hard enough to squeeze the blood from her knuckles. Working with Wendy Frances had been her entire motivation for applying to Claymore. What was she supposed to do if that wasn't an option?

Beside her, Colin nodded stonily, his arms crossed. His left cheek worked as he worried it between his teeth.

"What happens to the person who's not chosen?" Allison asked.

"I will, of course, help them find a suitable adviser and support them in any way I can."

Allison had been working toward this her entire life. She couldn't just pick a new area of study like a game of eeny, meeny, miny, mo. "Can you be a medievalist without an adviser in the field?"

"We will find a way to make it work," Wendy promised.

Colin cleared his throat, the first noise he'd made in a while. "I appreciate your generosity and would be thrilled to work with you, no matter the capacity."

If shooting venom from one's eyes was possible, Allison was doing it to Colin at this very moment. What happened to not trying to one-up each other? His obnoxiously even-keeled response had made Allison look like a petulant child. She fought back a scowl as she mumbled, "Same."

Wendy raised her mug of coffee to her lips and blew lightly on it, sending a ghost of steam across the table. "I know this is inconvenient and I am truly sorry for it. My hope is to use the semester to get to know you both so I can make an informed decision, but I promise no matter what happens, you will get the best guidance and preparation possible, so don't let that be a worry."

"When will you decide?" Colin asked.

"Before Thanksgiving break."

Two months. Allison braced herself. She had sixty days to ensure that Wendy chose her. When their eyes met, she saw the same thought reflected at her in Colin's steely gaze.

"Let's put this aside for now. As best you can, I'd like you to push this whole thing from your minds and focus on your coursework and your recitations."

Allison and Colin maintained their stare as Wendy lowered her head to take a dainty bite of the cream-sauced chicken on her plate. Allison sat so straight it felt as if her spine might bend in the wrong direction. Colin's slim shoulders were curved toward his ears, his sharp jaw pulled tight. Their expressions said everything their mouths couldn't. Whatever truce they'd cultivated over the past few days was now over.

It was every woman for herself. Allison would win this advisee position, even if she had to ram straight through Colin to get it.

Chapter 10

Halfway through Allison's first semester at Brown, her Introduction to Literary Studies professor had set a flyer on her desk.

The paper had been thick and cream in color, the letters embossed in gold. It had looked more like a wedding invitation than an academic announcement: something special, distinctive, important. Allison's hands had begun to sweat as she gripped it between her fingers.

At the top it read *Brown University's Rising Star Award*. Below that was a call for "all students, sophomores through seniors, interested in pursuing advanced degrees, with a focus on joining the academy." It might as well have been addressed directly to her. Allison, even as an eighteen-year-old, had known a life in academia was what she wanted.

Her teacher tapped the center of the sheet, a smile lighting up her face. "Keep this on your radar," she'd said. "I think you'll be a shoo-in." Allison couldn't help but notice that she didn't give a copy to anyone else in the room.

She tucked the sheet carefully into her binder and, when she got back to her dorm, pinned it to her aspirations board. For the rest of the year, she read it over every morning, memorizing the requirements. Tucking the honors that came along with it deep into her heart.

Each year, the recipient of the Rising Star traveled to the Undergraduate Scholars Symposium as Brown's representative to present a paper that was then published in the Symposium's academic journal. Those two things alone would have been enough to catapult Allison onto the acceptance list of any grad school she applied to, but there was also a ten-thousand-dollar cash prize. Jed had just moved out, and the divorce lawyer was costing Allison's mother a fortune. Ten thousand dollars would have offered them both some breathing room. And it would have saved Allison from needing to find a job on campus, allowing her to channel all her energy into her academics.

It was everything she could ever hope for rolled up into one perfect accolade.

As soon as sophomore year arrived, Allison dug into the application. The process was intense, requiring not only a personal statement and a sample essay, but an original piece of writing on that year's topic. Between January and March, she did little besides write, revise, and obsessively review her materials. She was behind in all her classes, but confident she'd catch back up once her application was submitted.

From the beginning of their relationship, Colin had shown no interest in the award, a fact so surprising that Allison was still asking him about it a week before the deadline.

They'd been sitting in the dining hall, both still groggy from too little sleep, and he'd waved one of his long hands over his plate of toast as he shook his head, adamant. "The last thing I need after drafting ten Ph.D. program applications is another demanding submissions process. This one's all yours."

As if to prove he meant it, he became an unwavering pillar of support in those final days, providing endless rounds of feedback on Allison's materials, taking charge of late-night snack and coffee runs, and offering her a comfortable (yet bony) shoulder to nap on. For once, they'd really felt like a team committed to the same goal: her success.

Allison had never been so confident as she was when she'd hit send on that application. It represented her best writing and, even more important, her best thinking. Her reading of Beatrice from Dante's *Paradiso* was definitely a graduate-level analysis. As a college sophomore.

What was she, if not a Rising Star?

The day the recipient and runner-up were announced was more stressful for her than college decision day. Her future, her dreams, seemed to totter on the tip of a blade. What would happen if she didn't win? If she didn't have the publication to lean on? If she didn't get the money to help her mom? This award seemed like the most perfect path—maybe the only path—forward for her.

In the end, Allison's name had, indeed, appeared on the announcement. But in second place.

Above it sat the recipient of that year's award.

Colin Benjamin.

He'd never intended to get out of her way. Instead, he'd been an iceberg lying in wait for the *Titanic* to smack into it.

And now he was doing it again.

That was all Allison could think as she sat in British Literature's Greatest Hits the day after their lunch with Wendy. For the second time, Colin was scheming to steal something from her that he hadn't worked for and didn't deserve. Anger churned like an acidic pit at Allison's center.

Beside her, Colin scratched notes into his book like he was etching them in stone. More than once, the margins of his anthology tore under the force of his pen. No wonder all the books he'd borrowed from Allison when they were dating came back looking like they'd survived an apocalypse. He had no respect for Johannes Gutenberg's legacy.

Scritch. Scritch. Scritch. The sound crawled its way up her spine like slowly creeping fingers.

Scooting her chair farther down the table, she whisper-hissed, "Where's your laptop?"

Colin's eyes scanned the stanzas of *Beowulf* lying open in front of him. "I like writing directly next to the passages when we're analyzing texts."

Allison's books were too marked up with her own ideas to add anything new during class. Course notes required their own binder. Which was preferable, honestly. She liked to preserve her interpretations separately to ensure her arguments were original. But perhaps Colin didn't read closely enough to spark his own analyses. The thought puffed up her proverbial feathers. Yet another reason why she was bound to win the advisee position.

On the dais across from them, Wendy glanced at her watch. "We have about twenty minutes left, and I've done enough talking for the day. I want to hear from you all." She flourished her hands toward the students, her bangles (pink and gold today) singing.

Allison cast her eyes out over the stadium seating. More of the students' faces were familiar thanks to her recitations, and everyone she recognized sat as silently here as they had each Friday in her class. Maybe she wasn't the cause after all (or at least not entirely).

Another ten seconds of quiet passed, then she raised her hand. Time to show Wendy her initiative (and gain herself a few extra points in that *win* column).

Her professor smiled at Allison and nodded.

"I've been really struck by the various ways that the author locates both Grendel and his mother outside the world of men through their descriptions." Allison flipped through the pages of her book, searching for a solid passage. "Of course, the most obvious example is the fact that Beowulf and the Geats have to leave Hrothgar's hall to find Grendel's mother. She's literally *outside*. To me, this clearly shows how invested the text is in establishing normative definitions of masculinity."

Out of the corner of her eye, Allison noticed students take up pens and start writing. Others had flipped open their laptops and were typing. Her heart leaped. No one had ever taken notes on what she was saying before (not even in her recitations). Pride beat through her veins, hot like a sunbeam.

That heat fizzled a second later when Colin cleared his throat and thrust his own hand into the air. His book was splayed open and pressed to his chest like he was trying to contain himself, even as he leaned forward over their table to make sure Wendy could see him.

"Yes, Colin?" There was a hint of amusement in their professor's voice. Most likely because he was two seconds from gnawing on the edge of his book like an overenthusiastic puppy (Allison had enough bite marks on her class texts from Monty to know this was a thing).

"Allison's right, but I do think it's more important to consider the differences between Grendel and his mother and how they're treated by the text, rather than what they show us collectively."

Allison wanted to bash him in the face with the heaviest object she could find, which would probably be his own ego. But if she showed her irritation, he'd know he'd gotten under her skin by contradicting her. She wouldn't give him the satisfaction. "You do, huh?" She offered him a razor-sharp grin.

He echoed her smile as he relaxed against his chair. "I noticed that while Grendel tends to be described in terms that can be attributed to humans, Grendel's mother is often called a thing? A creature? It reminded me of what you were saying yesterday about mothers' bodies in these literary works being wrong or unnatural."

Hearing him build off her ideas set Allison's heart racing. Did he not realize that he was giving her further credit? She straightened her shoulders and snuck a glance at the room. Everyone was watching them. And not in frustration or boredom. Students were still taking notes, and some even mirrored Colin, leaning into their desks. They'd all walk out of here with *her* ideas in their heads.

This was what she wanted from her recitations. If only she didn't need Colin to get her here. She didn't want to need Colin for anything.

She cleared her throat. It was still her they were listening to. She needed to remember that. "The discourse around mothers' bodies is important, but I don't think it's as relevant to this poem, since the author doesn't seem to care much about women."

He held up a hand. "If I could play devil's advocate—"

One of those words was accurate, and it wasn't *advocate*. "When don't you?" Allison challenged.

His face lit up as if she'd told him how good he looked. "What if the poem cares too much about women? What if the author feels the need to vilify Grendel's mother more because a woman with power is too troubling?"

Bastard. It was a good point.

Wendy stepped out from behind her desk and gathered everyone's attention before Allison could find a way to undercut his reading.

"And that," their professor said with a smile, "is what we call a discussion. This is the kind of work I want to see you doing"—she raised her arms to indicate the whole class—"in your recitations, and here, when we have the chance."

Allison shifted her focus to her notebook, jotting down a bunch of ideas she'd had as she and Colin argued. Heat flooded her skin, and her heart thrummed like she'd completed a hard run. Part of her wished they could have pushed the discussion further. Even if it was Colin at the other end, challenging her ideas, it had been . . . well . . . exciting . . . to dig into literature she cared about this much. Allison took part in plenty of conversations in Post-Colonial Lit, and Victorian Families, and Literary Theory, but it wasn't the same because the books in those courses didn't burrow into her psyche the way the ones in her own field did. Did she have ideas about those books? Sure. But they left her as soon as she didn't need them anymore.

That wasn't true of medieval lit. Grendel and Grendel's mother and all those lines in the text she'd referenced had made her yell out loud while she was reading, and they'd stick with her long after the class had moved on to Chaucer and Gower and Shakespeare.

Wendy dismissed everyone, inviting the usual ruckus as students packed up. Allison followed suit, standing to put her bag on the table.

Colin watched her with those keen hazel eyes. "That was awesome."

Suddenly, Allison's bag was in need of extreme organization. Move the folders this way, the notebook that way. Try the pens in another pocket. Anything to ignore the twinge his gaze summoned to her insides. "Yes. You did an excellent job building off thoughts I'd already had. Bravo."

"What?" She glanced up in time to see his jaw drop open. She hoped a fly would buzz in. Maybe hammer him in the throat or box with his uvula. "Did you not see what we just did?" He waved a hand at the empty seats behind them. "They were enthralled. *We* did that together by exploring some stuff you'd overlooked."

Allison's notebook hit the table with a loud slap. "First of all"— taking a move from Ethan Windbag, she held up a finger, counting along with her points—"I did not overlook anything. You didn't give me a chance to finish my thought before you butt in."

"Yeah but—"

She glowered at him, and his mouth snapped closed, almost as if she'd done it herself.

"Secondly"—two fingers in the air this time—"*we* didn't do anything. You tried to show me up and you failed." Sure, feeling like a real teacher for a minute had been great, but this teamwork stuff was absurd. He hadn't done any of this for her. He never did anything for her. The Rising Star debacle proved that. "We both know that that truce of ours died the second Wendy said she could only take one of us on as her advisee, so let's not pretend there's anything else going on here."

Colin sighed loud enough to quiet her. "Can I talk now?"

She folded her arms. "Maybe."

Behind Allison, a throat cleared. "Everything okay over here?" Wendy asked carefully.

Allison turned, her expression more rictus than smile. "Absolutely." She tossed a look at Colin. "Just finishing up our discussion from class. We had a few things we . . . um . . . needed to clarify."

"Well, I'm glad to see you building a camaraderie rather than a competition." Wendy's voice was full of subtext. "I really am grateful to have you both here. That discussion was fantastic and did a great job of modeling what participation and conversation in a lit class can look like. Maybe next time, turn the discussion to the students and see if you can pull them into the debate?"

Translation: stop your performative bullshit.

Allison and Colin nodded in unison.

"Great." She clapped her hands. "One more thing before we go. Friday afternoon there's a lecture at RISD on medieval architecture. Since you both have a vested interest in this period, I thought we could all attend."

"I'm done with recitation at noon," Allison said.

"I'm free all day," Colin noted.

"Perfect. The talk isn't until two. We can grab lunch first. Maybe off-campus for a change."

Once they'd both agreed, their professor hooked her purse over her shoulder and slipped from the room, leaving Allison and Colin in a silence thick as mud.

Allison was snapping closed her tote bag when he cleared his throat.

"I wasn't—" His words halted abruptly enough to pull her gaze to his face. His fingers danced against the table like he was playing a piano. "I wasn't trying to undermine you."

"Sure." Allison tried to remain frosty as she shrugged, but the hesitation in his voice was quickly melting that resolve.

He always did this. Seeped into her cracks and split her open. She folded her arms as if they could keep him out.

Sighing, Colin dragged a hand through his gelled coif of hair and then hefted his bag off the table. "I know it's easier for you to see me as a villain after . . ." He waved a hand. "Well . . . everything. And I get it. I just wish . . ." He shook his head.

"What?" Allison couldn't keep the word on her tongue. Without realizing it, she'd slid a step forward. It felt like they were standing on the precipice of something, dangerously close to an unforgiving edge. Tilt the wrong way and they'd both fall.

A second later, Colin pushed them over.

His eyes skimmed her face, soft as the brush of a fingertip, even as his mouth was a hard line. "You're right. It's the past. No rearview mirrors."

Except everything about his tone suggested the opposite.

Chapter 11

Allison,

Your mother tells me you're back in school. Something about an advanced degree? It didn't make much sense to me, but then, you know my thoughts on college.

Work's been the same. Busy. Paula is doing well, though we decided that living together really didn't work for us so she's back at her own place. I know your mother told you about my heart thing, but it's not something to worry about. Just a blip in the system. She's making a big deal out of nothing as usual.

Good luck with the school stuff. If we don't talk before then, let me know if you're going to come by for Thanksgiving so I can plan accordingly. The last thing I need is to buy extra food for nothing. We know you have a hearty appetite.

Jed

Allison paced the room, her phone gripped in her white-knuckled hand. This was the third time she'd read Jed's email since she'd received it an hour ago, but instead of calming her down, she frothed over with anger each time she scanned it.

Never mind his dismissal of her biggest achievement—getting into a top Ph.D. program with the very scholar she wanted to study under—he hadn't asked how she was. Instead, he'd insulted her mother, diminished her goals, and, to add insult to injury, called her a glutton. All in the span of three paragraphs. That had to be some kind of record.

Monty danced at Allison's feet, trying to keep up with her brisk steps. When she pivoted suddenly, she almost squished his paw, and he yelped and scurried under the bed. Seeing him cowering beneath her duvet cover, his tall ears flat, Allison burst into tears.

Fuck Jed for doing this to her. Again.

He was her father. He was supposed to be supportive. He should be building Allison up, making her feel strong and powerful and capable. He was supposed to be a model for her future partner. Except Jed was nothing but a big warning sign, screaming in neon: *Issues Ahead.* Allison was so tired of it.

Kneeling on the carpet, she coaxed Monty into her arms and stormed down the hall. She needed Sophie. And a WCS. Anything to stop crying.

Her father shouldn't get her tears. He didn't deserve them. Someday, she'd stop giving them to him.

Though the door was open, Allison knocked. Sophie invited her in, her voice muffled around the three pins in her mouth. In front of her, the bottom half of a dress form was draped in silky black fabric. The silver threads woven through it caught the light from her desk lamp, glistening like stars in a night's sky.

Her curly black hair was bunched at the top of her head with two colored pencils, a scarf tied around it to keep her bangs back. She'd cut the neck off an old Batman T-shirt so it slipped off her shoulder, 1980s style, and her gray leggings had latticework snaking from ankle to thigh. Only Sophie could look so cool in her loungewear.

"What's up?" At the sound of Sophie's voice, Monty wriggled out of Allison's arms and dove into the closest pile of fabric. He turned in endless circles until he was nested in navy-and-white-striped cotton, near enough to lick Sophie's ankle. She absentmindedly patted his head.

"I need a WCS list for never talking to my father again." Allison plopped into the oversized armchair beside the door.

"Uh-oh." Stabbing her needles into the heart of her mannequin, Sophie sat back, giving Allison her full attention.

"Yup." Allison lobbed her phone across the room.

It was barely in her hands before Sophie was reading. With each word, her copper-colored eyes narrowed further. "Is he fucking serious? Two lines about that ottoman with a mouth, Paula, and you get nothing? Not one question about you?"

"Hence the WCS." Allison's cheeks stung from the tears drying on her face. She swiped at them with her knuckles. Even if everything else was changing between them, Sophie was *always* on Allison's side when it came to Jed.

"Girl, he needs more than a WCS."

Allison cocked her head. On the floor, Monty did the same, as if he were part of the conversation. "What would that even be?"

"I don't know but this assbag needs it." Sophie scrolled through the email again, her head ticking more violently with each flick of her finger. "One: he doesn't walk you down the aisle at your wedding."

"Fuck that. I'm not someone's property. I'll be giving myself away whether I still talk to him or not."

A sketchbook lay on the floor by Allison's feet, open to a drawing of a midi dress with a modified sailor neckline that exposed the shoulders. Allison picked up the sketchbook and flipped through the other images. Sophie was so talented. And she always imagined her styles on plus-sized bodies. As a fat woman herself, she understood the struggle to find comfortable, stylish clothes in the world they lived in. She wanted to design for the bodies that were afterthoughts. Her ultimate goal was to team up with disabled, genderqueer, and trans designers to create a totally inclusive line of clothing.

Allison held up the sketchpad and nodded to the dress form. "It looks like your designs are coming along?" She hated how long it had been since the last time she'd asked. She supported her best friend. She wanted her fashion dreams to come true. Allison just wished those same dreams weren't what was pulling Sophie away from her. Why couldn't they both get everything they wanted and stay here? Together?

Sophie hooked a thumb at her closet door. "Progress has been made." Three garments hung along the outside. One was the sailor dress from the sketchpad. The other two were jackets, a military style peacoat and a plaid blazer with patched elbows.

"Whoa." Allison stepped over Monty and several other islands of fabric on her way to take a closer look.

Sophie liked to say she thrived in chaos. She'd done her best to remain relatively neat while she and Allison had shared a room (neat meaning keeping her explosions of fabric, colored pencils, paper, and sewing tools contained to her half of the dorm room), but now, in a space completely her own, she'd embraced the term *mess* fully as a concept and a lifestyle.

Allison passed the soft fabric of the sailor dress between her fingers. "What happens now?"

"I finish my sample pieces and hopefully get them into the next trade show in New York to find some buyers."

Allison's eyes widened. "That's a huge step."

Sophie nodded. "You like that one, huh?"

"It's gorgeous." The fabric was so soft it must have felt like wearing a summer rainstorm.

"Good. Because you were my inspiration."

"What?" Allison spun around. "You look at me and think sailor?"

Sophie laughed. "No. I look at you and think classic with a touch of risk."

Allison's cheeks flushed. It was always such a shock to see the versions of herself that emerged through other people's eyes. Nothing about her style or her life felt risky. Wasn't that what her mother meant by being too comfortable with the familiar?

Still, she smiled. "Ohhhh. I like that."

Sophie laughed. "Of course you do. Now sit down and stop changing the subject. We have two scenarios left for Jed."

Sighing, Allison maneuvered her way back to the chair. She wasn't even fully in her seat when Sophie said, "Two: he'll probably cut you out of his will, and we know how cheap that man is, so he must have money to spare."

"I don't need his money. Mom and I are doing fine."

"Cassandra will probably be mad at you. You know how weird she is about you having a relationship with your father."

"I don't have a plan for that one," Allison muttered.

Being an adult was supposed to mean steering your own ship, acting independently of the people who raised you. So then why, with the exception of graduate school, did every decision Allison made feel infected by one (or both) of her parents?

Sophie scooped Monty into her lap and stroked his head. "Listen. I know I'm like the last person to give advice on this, since my family is disgustingly functional, but I don't think anyone could blame you for not responding. Or ever reaching out to him again."

Allison dropped her head back with a groan. "That doesn't seem like enough. He'll probably forget we haven't spoken. I want him to know I'm upset." Her fingers dug at the chair's arms. "No. Not upset. *Mad.*"

Now that she'd said it out loud, she felt the truth of it. Most of her life, Allison had dealt with her father by minimizing contact. If she didn't see him or talk to him, he couldn't harp on her weight or remind her what a waste of money her private schools were. He couldn't degrade her life choices if she didn't tell him about them.

She'd learned these tactics from her mom, whose whole adult life had revolved around deescalating Jed and his insults.

But all that did was protect him. And the last thing he deserved was protection.

"What do you want to do, then?" Sophie asked. She tossed Allison her phone.

Allison opened it and tapped back into the email.

"I think I need to respond and tell him exactly how I feel."

Chapter 12

A spicy aroma burned pleasantly in Allison's nose as she pulled open the door of the Thai restaurant.

Even though she was already late, she stopped and inhaled, letting the air linger in her lungs for five beats before breathing out again. She felt her heart begin to slow. The last thing she needed was to show up frazzled to this lunch with Wendy and Colin.

For the last few days, Allison hadn't been able to think about anything but that email from her father, and it had thrown her completely off balance. She was behind on all her course work, and her latest set of recitations had gone more abysmally than the first few. She needed to write Jed back, to close that door like she'd told Sophie she would, but she had no idea what to say.

How the hell was Allison supposed to excel in the present and secure her future when her past wouldn't stop barging in to ruin everything?

As if on cue, her eyes settled on the most troublesome piece of her history sitting at a table for four near the front window. Sunlight feathered his features, drawing out the golden hue in his bronze hair and the smattering of freckles across his cheeks and nose. Once, Colin had let Allison connect them using a light shade of eyeliner. They'd been loopy from finals stress and lying awake in her bed too late at night. His head was in her lap and she'd been lazily tracing shapes across his cheeks with a finger.

"I wonder if they make anything?" she'd mused.

He'd murmured noncommittally, already half asleep.

"Like constellations."

"Find out," he'd mumbled.

She wasn't sure what he'd expected her to do, but his eyes had shot open and alert when she returned with her eyeliner.

"It washes off," she'd promised.

On his left cheek, she'd found an hourglass. On his right, a heart.

They'd stood side by side in front of the mirror above her dresser as Colin inspected her work. His fingers played lightly over the drawings, though his eyes, the yellow-green of leaves ready for autumn, had been pinned to her. "Time and love," he'd whispered. She'd smiled.

In that moment, they'd thought they had plenty of both.

Now, though, Allison knew it was the opposite. Each second together had been ticking them closer to Colin snapping them in half.

She swallowed hard against the lump forming in her throat. The more determined Allison was to forget her past with Colin, the more stubbornly it clung to her.

Dragging her hands over her face, she squared her shoulders and stalked across the restaurant.

Eyes on the prize, Avery.

Right now, her life was about that advisee position. Nothing else. She opened two imaginary boxes in her mind. Into one, she threw Colin, slamming the lid and shoving the box on the highest shelf. She tossed Jed in the other and put it aside to deal with later.

Compartmentalizing was a gift. And the only reason she was able to force an easy smile onto her face as she pulled out the chair across from Colin.

His eyes tracked her movements. "I was starting to wonder if you were going to come."

"Why? I'm not *that* late." Allison would have dragged herself here bleeding if it had come to that. No way would she gift Colin an entire afternoon alone with their professor.

"You didn't see Wendy's email?"

Allison shook her head. "I've been in recitation all morning."

He flipped over his phone, his finger brushing up and down the screen. "She had a cat emergency and isn't coming. She wants us to go without her."

Allison grabbed for her own phone. He had to be joking. The universe was not this cruel. Yet there it was, at the top of her inbox: a brief but apologetic email from Wendy encouraging Allison and Colin to attend the lecture and "report back on the interesting bits."

Her first instinct was to bolt—she could not spend an entire afternoon alone with Colin Fucking Benjamin, like they were on a date or something—but knowing him, he would go to this lecture without her and send Wendy a fifty-page report. Letting him look more dedicated than her was not an option.

While she continued to white knuckle her phone with one hand, she flipped open her menu with the other. Colin had been observing her closely, and his posture relaxed when he saw her studying the entrees.

"I was going to order for us, but I wasn't sure . . ." His voice trailed off the same way it had the other day after Wendy's class. Uncertain and nervous.

Allison hated how the tone flipped her stomach. This new version of Colin was like an alchemical bomb to her body. Why was vulnerability in him so damn alluring? What she needed was one of his shit-eating grins or for him to give her a good ol' "but actually" followed by a healthy dose of mansplaining. That would reset her equilibrium to "push Colin Benjamin off a steep cliff" mode.

She gulped down two large sips of water. "Sure of what?"

His fingers tapped the edge of the table. "I didn't know if shrimp pad thai was still your go-to?"

There'd been a Thai restaurant the two of them had frequented when they were dating, and Allison *always* chose the pad thai. Once you found a dish you liked, why branch out? That only led to regrets. Meal FOMO, as it were.

But, small as it might be, ordering her favorite meal would be admitting that she hadn't changed. Allison needed Colin to know she wasn't the same girl he'd treated so heartlessly two years ago. She needed to remind herself of that, too.

"I'm into drunken noodles these days," she announced, reading off the first thing she saw on the menu.

Colin raised an eyebrow. "You like the heat now, huh?"

There was a playfulness to his voice that Allison hadn't expected, and she couldn't help but respond to it, that constant urge to pull where he pushed getting the better of her. "You have no idea."

He narrowed his eyes devilishly.

Fire burned in her cheeks. She tried to hide it beneath her long hair as she studied the menu like it was a GRE practice test. She couldn't do this with him. Flirt. Make allusions to sex like it was still on the table. As if their past didn't exist.

As if it didn't hover over their present, ready to strike again.

Allison cleared her throat, her eyes searching the table for a safer topic. A paperback book sat beside his arm, a spoon jammed in the pages to save his place. *Perfect.*

"What's this?" she asked, reaching for it.

The corners of the faded cover curled inward, and the spine was bent enough from repeated use to obscure the title. It reminded her of her old copies of *The Hunger Games* series, so well-loved the glue from the spine had given way. She bet the pages crunched rather than whispered and that it smelled like time and ink and old paper.

The light dimmed in his eyes as Colin trapped the cover beneath his palm. He drew the book into his lap like something precious. "It's my grandfather's copy of *Sir Gawain and the Green Knight*. He loves this stuff."

"You're reading ahead?" It wouldn't surprise her.

"No. Just trying to feel closer to him."

Colin had grown up with his grandfather and his mom. After having him at seventeen, his mother had put herself through college while working full-time, leaving Colin with his grandpa after school and on the weekends. He used to love to regale Allison with stories of the mayhem the two of them would cause: almost sawing down the big maple tree in the backyard trying to build a fort, racing to see who could read books faster until they both had splitting headaches, experimenting with whatever food was in the kitchen like they were on some chaotic reality TV show. Colin and his grandfather were the best of friends, same as Allison and her mom.

Family trauma had a way of doing that. Bonding you firmly to the person who seemed most safe. Least likely to disappear.

The times Colin had confided in her about his family had been some of the moments where Allison had felt closest to him. Maybe that's why she asked, "Is everything okay?"

He ran a finger over the book in his lap. "He's . . ." If, a second ago, his face had been an open window, now it was shuttered. Locked from the inside. "He's just getting old," he muttered.

The server appeared a moment later to take their order. While Allison bit the bullet and took her chance on drunken noodles with beef, she discovered that Colin's eating habits had not changed. As always, he ordered three appetizers in place of an entrée. He claimed he liked the variety, but Allison had spent enough time with him to recognize that he was a picky eater, and appetizers tended to be safer.

Plus, he was always willing to share, making this his least obnoxious quirk. She smiled as he handed off his menu, glad for this small sense of familiarity not tinged with the bitterness of their breakup.

His cheeks reddened, and he began mopping up the condensation from his water glass with meticulous attention, as if it were a matter of national security. "How was recitation?"

Allison's muscles yanked taut. Both sections had been a disaster. Again, no one had volunteered to talk and, though Allison had a lecture prepared for this inevitability, she kept losing her train of thought because she was so distracted by that email from her father. She was pretty sure the only thing that anyone learned today was that she had no idea what she was doing.

On top of that, Cole had made it a point to stop by her desk on the way out to inform her how much fun his friends were having in *Colin's* recitation. "They say he's really funny and smart and gets the whole class talking." His tone was completely disinterested, like he'd been commenting on the weather, but every syllable was a stake hammered deeper into Allison's heart.

She waited, hoping Colin might derail the conversation to echo Cole's report, but for once, he seemed more interested in her than the sound of his own voice.

Leave it to him to become considerate when it was least convenient.

Allison tried to relax against her seat. "It was fantastic. They couldn't stop talking about Grendel's mother. I think every student said at least one thing. I even made a few jokes. And, afterward, two students stopped by to tell me our recitation was their favorite class."

With every word, her insides slithered into a tighter knot. Her lies just kept growing, more out of control than Pinocchio's nose. She couldn't seem to stop herself. Even if it meant stealing Colin's moments and making them hers.

The right corner of his mouth tipped up into a grin. "Whoa. Superteacher for sure, then."

Allison shrugged, her fingers crushing into the hem of her skirt. She didn't want to keep talking about this. There was a tenderness to Colin's expression that chiseled her lies into pointed blades. She couldn't wield them anymore today. Not with Jed weighing so heavily on her mind, and Colin so determined to resurrect these things she'd once loved about him.

Her eyes cut to the window. Across the street was a small independent movie theater. The big black letters crammed into its tiny marquee read

Double Feature Friday

JEEPERS CREEPERS

JEEPERS CREEPERS 2

"Oh my god." She bumped the windowpane with her finger, pointing at the sign.

Colin followed her movements and groaned.

Allison couldn't help it. She burst out laughing. Then she broke her own no-past rule. "Remember when we saw the second one?"

Colin scratched at the back of his neck, his expression sheepish. "Yeah . . . but we aren't supposed to be remembering things."

She ignored him. "You *sobbed* at the end. So hard. You used all my napkins."

"Yeah."

"It was a horror movie."

"Movies just . . ." Colin blew out a loud sigh. "They always wrap up so easily. Everything fixed and perfect."

Allison crossed her arms and sat back. "More than half the cast was dead at the end of that movie. The body count was like thirteen."

"Yeah, but the monster gets caught. There's a clear ending. Things get resolved."

Horror movies were famous for doing the opposite of that, but Allison refrained from correcting him. She was not Ethan Windbag. She would not "well, actually" Colin, especially not when he was on the verge of sharing something he'd refused to talk about two years ago.

"You don't like happy endings?"

He pulled off his glasses and scrubbed at his eyes. His narrow shoulders bent inward. "I think the problem is more that I like them too much. No one gets that in real life."

Something in his tone tugged at Allison's center. "I feel like that's the point, though? Did you ever read 'Cinderella' by Anne Sexton? At the end, she talks about how happy endings aren't life. That happily-ever-after doesn't leave room for living. Life keeps going. Keeps changing. I always loved that. This idea that the true happy ending is the one that doesn't stop."

Colin's mouth thinned. He folded his napkin into his lap, once, twice, three times. "People deserve happy endings and not enough get them. That's all I mean."

The arrival of their food put an end to the conversation. Allison watched Colin organize his plates of appetizers, disappointed that she hadn't been able to press him further. Though she hated to admit it, she'd wanted to hear what he meant by that last comment. Who didn't get the happy ending they deserved?

He couldn't be talking about them, right?

Thankfully, the delicious scents coming from her plate offered a welcome distraction. Grabbing her fork, Allison dug in and quickly discovered she'd made an excellent choice. The drunken noodles' sauce had that perfect balance of heat, sweet, and salt; the flat noodles were tender; and there were so many vegetables (including those little baby corns she loved).

With her second bite, she accidentally groaned with pleasure, and Colin's head jerked up. "You sure seem to be enjoying that meal you say you eat all the time."

"Shut up."

Colin snorted. Then he reached across the table to set a spring roll on her plate.

Allison's gaze jumped from her dish to his face. "What are you doing?" He might as well have grabbed her hand and pressed it to his mouth given the way her heart was thumping.

"You love spring rolls."

She did. So much. And when they'd dated, he'd never given her one unless she'd asked.

Allison's bones felt like they were crumbling. *This* was what she couldn't do. This was why they needed distance, why they shouldn't be out sharing a meal like it was a date and laughing over old times like they were pleasant memories. Spending time with Colin was quicksand. A riptide. A tornado. It would swallow her up. And take everything Allison wanted, everything she'd worked for, and dash it to pieces.

It was easier—*safer*—for her heart (and her future) if Colin remained a villain. Otherwise, she risked a repeat of sophomore year. Except, at Claymore, there were no second chances.

"Colin."

He sighed. In his fingers, he spun a cup of plum sauce. "I know. We can't go back." When he glanced up, his eyes snagged hers. Their table was small enough that they had to concentrate to keep their knees from bumping, and so close, Allison could see every glint of bronze and green in his irises. A cache of coins and emeralds. A trap like dead man's treasure. "But sometimes, I"—he was whispering, and she had to lean in to hear him—"I wish we could go forward instead."

So do I.

The silent words were a blast to her chest. Allison couldn't want this. She needed to go. Without guards, a thick titanium wall, and at least three sets of hazmat suits between them, Colin was a danger to be around.

Glancing at her phone, she decided on her typical escape hatch for bad dates and other social emergencies. Swiping open a three-day-old text from Sophie, she muttered, "Shit. Sophie needs me. I have to go."

"What?" Colin gaped up at her.

She dug in her purse for some cash and tossed it on the table. "Help yourself to my leftovers." She'd barely had three bites.

"What about the talk?"

"You go." With that, she left.

As it turned out, a positive side effect of that horrible lunch with Colin was that Allison's desire not to think about him outweighed her wish to avoid her father and his email.

Her entire drive home, she'd had to actively work to keep Colin's words out of her head. Like a game of Whac-A-Mole, they kept popping up, forcing her to punch them down again.

I wish we could go forward.

People deserve happy endings.

No. No. NO. She shoved each memory away. What was he doing? Was he angling for them to get back together? Did he not remember how much they'd argued? Or the way things had ended? How he'd dumped her without warning?

They were done. There was nothing left between them except Wendy's class. And the advisee position over which they were competing.

As Allison mounted the stairs to her room, she whipped her phone out of her pocket and brought up Jed's email. She needed something big to squash these Colin thoughts.

She read her father's dismissive words once, and then twice, letting the anger boil into her veins. Sitting at her desk, Allison folded her legs beneath her on her chair and summoned her monitor's glow. No more agonizing over this. Jed deserved anything she had to say to him.

"Whatever you write, you send," she told herself. She needed to resolve *one* thing today. It wasn't going to be teaching and clearly wasn't going to be Colin, so her father would have to do.

Monty gave a growl of agreement from her feet, where he wrestled with one of his bones.

Pulling her keyboard toward her, Allison pressed a breath between her teeth and started typing. Each letter clacked louder as her fingers found them.

Jed,

I know talking hasn't really been our thing, but if I am being honest, that last email you sent hurt. It seems like all the life choices I've made disappoint you. Even if you don't care about college, I do, and I wish that was enough to make you try. This is my dream, and I'm doing it, and I've gotten this far with absolutely no help or support from you. Why do you think I would need any now?

And for the record, this degree won't cost me or Ma a penny. The school's paying ME to be here.

After a lot of thought, I've decided that I won't be coming to Thanksgiving with you and Paula. I also won't be writing for a while. Part of me feels like when you left Ma, you left me too, but that can't be true, because you were never really there to begin with. You've never been a part of my life.

Maybe someday I will feel differently. But for now, I want space. That way you can make your choices and I can make mine and neither of us has to feel bad about it.

Take care,

Allison

Chapter 13

Another Saturday. Another night of mandatory bonding.

This time, Allison's first-year cohort was having drinks and appetizers on the back deck of Mandy's ranch-style house in Pawtucket. Roomy enough to fit two sets of tables and chairs and an outdoor sectional, the structure overlooked an in-ground pool that Mandy explained had just been closed for winter.

In his typical crass fashion, Ethan asked, "How do you afford this?"

"It was my parents' house. I grew up here. They gave it to me when I graduated from Columbia and they retired to a new place in Florida." Mandy cast a wistful glance over the expansive backyard. "I know it's a lot of house for one person. But my sister comes to crash with me when she's on break or needs to escape dorm life, and I love it too much to get rid of it. I can imagine raising my own family here, you know?" She laughed, as if the idea was a fantastic punchline to a joke. "Someday. Assuming I survive grad school."

After that (probably to avoid further interrogation) she herded them all inside to, as she put it, "get the festivities started."

Beyond the sliding glass doors stretched the hallway that led to three bedrooms. It was a veritable tribute to Mandy's cross-stitching.

Wooden hoops in an array of sizes lined the pale blue wall in a zigzag, each boasting a beautiful floral design. And the more intricate the pattern, the more profane the words. The messages ranged from the simple *Eat a Dick* in a Shakespearean flourish, to the delightful *I do not spew profanities, I enunciate them clearly like a fucking lady*. But Allison's favorite hung at the hallway's end, centered on an otherwise blank wall. Small violets and peonies had been sewn into four corners, creating a square within the circular frame. At the center was an elaborately rendered Coach purse, and around it, in lettering that matched the brand, were the words *Don't Be an Assbag*.

Allison moved closer to admire it. "You have to teach me how to do this," she said to Mandy.

Mandy's coffee-colored eyes brightened. "It's actually pretty simple to pick up."

"Maybe if you're a crafty type. I can barely use a coloring book. And knitting made me want to impale myself with the needles."

"Smaller needles with cross-stitch."

They both laughed.

"What's so funny over here?" Colin's face appeared over Mandy's shoulder.

Allison worked up a sweat suppressing a sigh. She'd been doing her best to avoid him since she'd arrived, but he kept popping up and trying to talk to her. Like she hadn't made it very clear at lunch yesterday that the conversation he'd been trying to have was done. Over. Never happening to begin with. They were *not* moving forward, whatever the hell that meant.

She ducked away before he could try to broach the subject again.

And if she happened to put a little swish in her step, it was only right since she was wearing her favorite pair of skinny jeans. (It was Allison's deepest belief that plus-sized women looked just as good in skinny jeans as everyone else, and people would have to pry her seven pairs out of her cold, dead hands before she'd stop wearing them.)

Everyone else had wandered back into the kitchen to grab an-

other round of drinks. Allison fished her third raspberry cider from the
fridge, promising herself it would be her last. There would be no repeat
instances of alcohol-induced heart-to-hearts with Colin like at Kara's
party. Only distance and Olympic-caliber avoidance.

Reemerging from the hall, Mandy beckoned them all to the living
room. The space took up most of the front of the house, with a series of
bay windows overlooking the street. The couch, loveseat, coffee table,
and armchair were pushed up against the cream walls, and, in the
center of the room, dining chairs clustered around television trays, two
chairs per tray. Each tray held a noise contraption: a squeaky toy, a bike
horn, or a baby rattle. Leaning up beneath the flat-screen TV mounted
on the east-facing wall was a white board.

Mandy grinned. "Welcome to trivia night."

Apparently, Kara had started a trend, and every gathering would
include an activity.

Alex thrust his old-fashioned in the air. The russet-toned bourbon
sloshed as ice clinked against the sides. "I call Link as my partner."

"Sorry. I already created the teams," Mandy said. "That way no
one gets picked last. I still have nightmares about that from gym class."
She pointed to the tray table with the black-and-white squeaky cow.
"Kara and Link. You're Team Cow." Next she gestured to the center
table with a rattle in the form of Captain America's shield. "Alex and
Ethan are Team Marvel."

Allison swallowed a groan. Mandy was clearly an agent of the
universe, intent upon forcing Allison and Colin together. Angling the
bottle to her lips, she took the longest pull of cider she could manage
without choking, then dropped into one of the two open chairs. She
picked up the bike horn and gave its red bulbous end a good honk.

"That makes us Team Horn." She aimed it at Colin and honked it
again, compressing the rubber ball slowly and methodically for max-
imum annoyance.

He cringed and snatched it from her. "You can't be trusted with
this."

Narrowing her eyes, Allison slugged more cider. Forget the original plan. She would need to be very, very drunk if she was going to have to be on the same team as Colin Benjamin.

Mandy clapped her hands. "Let's get started, folks. I have takeout scheduled to arrive in an hour and a half, which should give us enough time for a good game. I'll be your host tonight, Mandy Garcia." She curtsied, though she was wearing high-waisted jeans and a cropped yellow-and-white-striped top. The thick black hair piled on her head bobbed in its top knot. "The rules are simple. I'll read a question. You'll have a minute to confer with your partner. Use the noise-maker when you think you have the answer. One point per question. First team to twenty-five wins."

"What do we win?" Ethan asked.

Mandy's small mouth twisted with glee. "It's a surprise."

Win. Allison's favorite word. Taking one last gulp, she set her cider out of the way and folded her legs beneath her, ready for action. "I'm going to stomp the floor with you," she whispered to Colin. Competitiveness: the perfect antithesis to awkward, quasi-romantic half-confessions.

Judging by the way Colin's eyes narrowed and the corners of his mouth perked up, he agreed. "Not if you're already squashed under my boot."

Allison sneered. He never wore boots. Only beat-up Chucks and Doc Martens oxfords, like he wanted to join a nineties grunge band. At Brown, he'd bought her a pair of red-and-white sneakers like she should emulate his style. She fought off a shudder.

Mandy put a hand to her mouth conspiratorially and whispered, "You guys are on the same team."

"Only in the most technical of senses," Allison pointed out.

As if to prove her point, Colin set the horn in his lap instead of on the table.

"I'm not reaching for that there."

"Good. I wasn't in the mood to fend you off, anyway." His eyes studied the empty columns on the white board like it held all the answers.

"Put the horn on the table."

"No thanks."

Mandy cleared her throat to get their attention. "We're going to start with some easy stuff. You know, to warm up," she said. Then she proceeded to rattle off a series of questions that only people in a literature Ph.D. program would deem easy. Colin got each one right, never bothering to consult Allison.

After his third correct answer, he shined that shit-eating grin her way. "Pssst. You're not stomping me too hard here."

Allison refused to take the bait. Sitting back in her chair, she crossed her legs and organized her expression into something bored. "Your vice grip on that horn suggests you know exactly what would happen if you gave me half a chance."

He snorted. "When have you *ever* beat me at trivia?"

Never. They used to go to the events hosted by Brown twice a month, and he'd answer every question like he was a walking Google browser.

Allison's coolness faltered. There he went, bringing up their past again, like it was a compulsion he couldn't control. "I wouldn't know, since this is our first time playing." Subtext choked her voice. Under the table, she swung at his leg with her ankle boot, satisfaction trilling through her veins when she connected.

Setting the horn on the table, he rubbed at his shin. His gaze dodged hers with the intensity of a third grader running from whomever was "it" in tag. "Let's see who the better player is, then."

Mandy called out the next question. "What is the technical term for the hashtag symbol?"

Allison was the *queen* of arcane facts. She squealed (out loud) as she dove for the horn. But at the same time her fingers crushed its rubber nose, Colin's hand encircled hers. They both squeezed with all their might. *Honk. Honk. Honnnnkkkkkk.*

Mandy nodded at them. "Team Horn, again."

"This is bullshit," Ethan yelled.

Over him, Colin hollered, "Pound sign," while Allison said, "Octothorp."

Mandy arched an eyebrow. "Which answer are you going with?"

"Pound sign," Colin insisted.

Allison jerked in her chair to face him. "Like hell we are. I know, one hundred and fifty percent, that I'm right."

"That's not an actual percentage."

She glowered. "Do you subsist off technicalities?"

His fingers tensed over her hand as he laughed. Only then did Allison realize that neither of them had let go of the horn (or each other).

Still, she maintained her grip. How else was she going to ensure she won?

"It's definitely the pound sign," Colin said. "That's what it was called on landlines."

"But that's not the technical name." Allison had to bite her tongue to keep from reminding him that she googled punctuation facts for fun. He used to mock her mercilessly for it. Instead, she pinned him with her gaze. "Trust me on this." Her voice had a (wholly unintentional) sultry tone.

Colin's mouth swept up. "What do I get when you're wrong?"

"Whatever you want, because I won't be."

His grin widened, igniting that clever glint in his eyes. It did something to her insides that Allison refused to acknowledge.

With a wink (a fucking *wink*), he turned back to their host and said, "We'll go with octothorp."

"Correct." Mandy slashed another line in their column.

Allison tipped her chin in triumph, then yanked her hand from beneath his before Colin misread it as anything more than competitive thoughtlessness.

For the next half hour, Mandy fired questions at them. The other two teams managed to squeeze in a few responses, but Colin and Alli-

son were almost always quickest to the draw with their horn and very
rarely wrong. They fumbled a few sportsball questions and didn't even
try to answer the ones about cooking (Allison had long ago made a
pact with Sophie that she would do dishes if Sophie dealt with the
meals), and somehow, neither Allison nor Colin knew anything about
Restoration comedy. But otherwise, they dominated.

Colin continued their rivalry, diving for the horn, smirking every
time he answered first, but the tension in it was gone. And he kept
filling their silences in ways he'd never bothered to before. Quietly
mocking Ethan, congratulating Allison, commenting on the various
mundanities of Mandy's house (Allison had no idea what chair rails
were but he mentioned them twice). Multiple times, his foot tapped
hers under the table, and his fingers accidentally found the soft skin of
her wrist. And he was staring at her, his eyes warm and wide, as depth-
less as a murky lake. At some point, that same energy that had crackled
in the air between them yesterday before Allison fled had returned. It
was as if they couldn't help but gravitate back toward each other, their
connection natural and magnetic and impossible to control.

Allison didn't know how to break it. But she needed to.

The prizes from the trivia game turned out to be cross-stitches. Allison chose an intricate floral design with *I am a delicate fucking flower*
stitched in loopy cursive beneath it. Colin took one with an image of
an adorable smiling whale, water shooting from its blow hole. Above
it simple lettering read *blow me*.

Dropping onto a loveseat beneath the window, Allison pulled her
phone from her pocket. A photo of Monty, upside down and dead
asleep with a bone hanging out of his mouth, filled her screen.

With no one else around to show it to, she flashed the phone at
Colin. "Look at this goofball."

He joined her for a better look. The couch had more than enough
space for both of them, and yet his hip pressed into hers. She scooted
toward the arm, but her jeans kept sliding across the leather until she
was jammed against Colin again. Whoever dreamed up leather sofas

should be drawn and quartered, she decided. Her muscles ached as she held her frame awkwardly to force some space between them.

"Is this the famous Corgi?"

"Yup. That's Monty. Sophie's hanging out with him tonight."

"You still live with Sophie?"

Allison nodded.

Without her phone tethering them, they both readjusted, Colin perching himself on the arm, his spindly knees propped under his elbows. Allison let out a slow breath. Though barely any part of them had touched, it felt as if he'd been lying on top of her.

"I wish I'd kept in touch with more people from Brown." He smoothed a finger over the cream-colored stitching of the fabric. "We all sort of drifted off after graduation."

"Well, you were doing all that traveling."

"Sure." Something stony hardened his smile. Perhaps those European adventures he'd bragged about hadn't been as grand as he'd let on. "It would have been nice to have people to catch up with, though."

"If it helps," Allison said, "Sophie's never home. She's got this new, awesome life." She wrung her hands. "Sometimes it feels like there's no room for me in it."

She wanted to believe she'd admitted that only to one-up his confession, but it had been the look in his eyes that had done it. Their gentleness coaxed words from her lips like the Pied Piper lured rats and children with his instrument.

He tapped her hip with his toe. "Hey, you've got a pretty awesome new life, too. I know we don't know each other well"—he winked (another *fucking* wink, was he serious?)—"but something tells me you never used to go out on Saturday nights unless you were dragged by one of your friends. And yet here you are. Of your own free will."

"I'm pretty sure these gatherings are compulsory." She grinned, hoping it hid how much the truth of his words hurt. She didn't want to be seen that way, as a hermit content to never venture into the world.

But she liked what she had. Her life made sense. "I just don't understand why things have to change."

Colin rocked his empty glass at her. "Time for a refill." He knocked a hand on her knee as he stood. "You know, just because things look different doesn't mean they're gone."

As she watched his lanky form duck into the kitchen, Allison wondered if he might be talking about more than her friendships.

Chapter 14

"I can't wait until we start teaching first-year English and have our own offices," Link said, wrinkling his nose. "This place smells like week-old burritos."

"I found the culprit." Colin tapped the trash can in the far corner of the study room with his toe.

Holding her breath, Allison grabbed the edge of the gray plastic bin and dropped it outside the door. She didn't dare glance inside.

"We're still going to be dealing with other people's . . . smells," Ethan pointed out as he kicked closed the door. "It's not like we won't be doubling and tripling up."

Colin shrugged. "The devil you know."

It was Tuesday evening and the four of them were meeting up to finalize their presentation for Literary Theory next week. The irony of the fact that she'd been paired with three men (one of them the biggest theory dudebro on campus) to introduce feminist theory had not been lost on Allison.

Once they'd installed themselves around the square table at the center of the room, Allison unfolded a handout from her binder and smoothed it across the chipped Formica. "Okay. It looks like we have twenty minutes to do two things: define feminist theory and identify points of controversy within it."

"Honestly, this is so simple it's a joke." Ethan hadn't bothered unpacking his bag. The only things in front of him were his water bottle and his phone, which he scrolled through without looking up. "Feminist theory is hardly sophisticated, which is probably why so many people gravitate toward it." He shook a fist idly in the air. "Women rock. Woo."

"Wow." Allison glanced at Colin and Link, failing to suppress the scorn in her voice or her face. "Looks like Ethan doesn't need us for this."

He lifted his broad shoulders in a shrug. "She said it. Not me." Then he yawned. *Yawned.*

"What's your brilliant plan, then? I doubt Behi is going to accept 'Woo, women rock' as our presentation." She pantomimed his earlier gesture with as much vitriol as she could muster.

"We talk about Butler, Irigaray, De Beauvoir, done."

"Dude," Link said, shaking his head, "that list's a little bald, don't you think?"

"What about Roxane Gay, Kimberlé Crenshaw, Julia Serano?" Allison counted each one off on her fingers.

"We're doing race theory later. And queer theory too." He shot a look at Link, the one gay, Black man in the room.

Link deserved a Nobel Peace Prize for not punching Ethan in his already crooked nose. Allison wouldn't have been able to restrain herself if he'd looked at her with that much subtext.

She banged her palm flat against the table to get his attention through the titanium-thick exoskeleton that was his ego. "First of all, you might want to check your white masculinity. It's leaking all over the place in here. Secondly, obviously Butler and Irigaray and De Beauvoir are important, but you can't talk about feminism without considering the importance of intersectionality."

Ethan lifted his hands off the table. "Why do you care? You have no interest in the complexities of theory anyway. You're all into literature."

"The point of *literary* theory is to apply it to *literary* works," Colin said. "No?"

"For a literature person, maybe." Every time Ethan said the word *literature* it sounded more grotesque. As if he'd eaten something rotten and accidentally swallowed it. "I'm more interested in pure theory. In its many intricacies."

"But isn't that exactly what someone like Roxane Gay is exploring?" Allison asked.

Ethan rolled his eyes. "You only want to talk about Gay because she writes on fatness."

Allison had to sit on her hands to keep from doing something she'd regret. "What does *that* mean?"

Ethan looked at her blandly. "Well, you're f—"

"You're absolutely *not* going to finish that sentence." Colin was on his feet, his hands balled against the tabletop. His height drowned Ethan and his indolent expression in shadow.

Allison rested her hand on Colin's arm to ease him back down. His eyes were wild as they searched her face, making her heart hammer. She'd never seen him react so forcefully to . . . well . . . anything before.

The last time someone had insulted Allison's weight in his presence, Colin had shrunk from the confrontation like a withering flower. They'd been waiting to be seated at their favorite diner near Brown, and some guy had shoved by her with a loud, not at all subtle, "Move it, fatty."

Allison responded by noting his (obviously) small manhood, causing him to spin around, his face the color of a tomato. "What?" he'd demanded.

She'd cocked her head. "It sucks to have someone comment on your body uninvited, doesn't it?"

Before she got to hear his retort, Colin dragged her out the door, its chime yelling in her ears. With wide eyes, his hands fisted, he'd said, "You have to ignore shit like that. Reacting only leads to more trouble. I was bullied enough as a kid to learn that the hard way."

"I have to do no such thing. I'm not going to hide from people like I'm not allowed to exist in the world the way I am," she'd said.

Allison was no damsel in distress. She didn't need a guy to defend her. But seeing Colin cower at the thought of speaking up had left her stomach thick and sour with disappointment. He was usually the first person to offer an opinion. Why hadn't he wanted to support her?

Now, though, Allison could hardly keep him in his seat.

She turned her attention to Ethan. "I'm fat? That's what you were going to say, right?" She kept her voice mild. This guy would not be gifted the satisfaction of her anger.

He lifted his shoulder again. Somehow, he managed to seem even more cavalier.

Link and Colin both sputtered in protest, but Allison shook her head. *Fat* was only an ugly word if you let it be.

Though her knees felt weak, and a primal scream burrowed its way through her belly, she regarded Ethan placidly. "Yes. I do appreciate that Gay will engage with the lived experience of fatness as part of her feminism. But more importantly, writers like her elucidate the limits of white feminism. Feminism *has* to include women of color, queer women, and transgender women." She pushed back her chair, letting it shriek loudly against the faux wood of the floor. "You three can do whatever you want for this presentation. I'm going to end it by talking about Gay, Crenshaw, and Serano."

That meant potentially forfeiting twenty percent of her grade, but even for the most overachieving overachiever, such a fate was more palatable to Allison than one more second attempting to analyze feminism with a misogynistic asshole.

Hooking her bag over her shoulder, she stalked from the room. No matter how much she accepted—no, embraced—her fatness, it never felt good when someone weaponized that word. And over her dead body would she participate in Ethan's cishet-white-dude worldview.

So close to dinnertime, the library was quiet, allowing Allison to find a corner tucked away under a window. Blinking back tears she pretended weren't there, she heaved her copy of *The Riverside Chaucer* onto the table. Along with the presentation in Behi's class, Allison had been tasked by Wendy to lead a short discussion in lecture on a few lines of "The Knight's Tale." She'd warned both Allison and Colin that she'd expect them to do a few of these as a precursor to their big lectures before Thanksgiving break. It seemed a safe bet that their performances would be factors in her final decision about her newest advisee, so Allison was determined to make each minute she had the floor in British Literature's Greatest Hits count.

She'd just found the lines she wanted to work with when her phone dinged with a message.

Unknown Number: Did you leave?

Allison Avery: No. I'm around the corner near the window.

Why had she told him that?

Every day, things with Colin became a little muddier. Since Mandy's party, he'd sat next to Allison in every class, and his chair in Wendy's lecture seemed to inch closer to Allison's every meeting. Last Thursday, their elbows had butt against each other the whole class, and neither of them had moved. He was texting her regularly too, and once, in a fit of panic, she'd reached out to him when she overheard Sophie on the phone doing what sounded like an interview. It had been like a reflex, her fingers finding his number, typing out a message. As if he'd always been her emotional support contact. The text was halfway through the ether before she'd realized what she'd done.

Things had become so easy, so—dare she say it—friendly, that she often forgot she was supposed to be avoiding him. He was standing between her and another once-in-a-lifetime opportunity. Letting herself grow close to him (again) was only going to drill the pain deeper if she lost. It could be sophomore year 2.0, but with greater consequences. And yet, knowing all that, she couldn't seem to keep away.

The moment she set her phone back on the table, it rang. Ducking sheepishly like she would be chastised by the empty chairs around her, Allison swiped open the call. "I said I was around the corner."

"Allison?"

Oops. "Hey, Mom. You got my text about rescheduling our Face-Time, right? I have a presentation I have to prep. I'm actually still at the library."

"This can't wait."

Allison's back straightened. "What's wrong?" WCS after WCS crowded her head.

1. Her mom was sick.

2. Her mom couldn't pay the bills and was losing the house.

3. Her mom had lost her job.

Colin rounded the corner, his lips poised in a half-smile, but he snapped them shut when he saw her expression and sat down silently across from her.

"Your father and I talked today."

Allison placed a hand over her mouth to stop the groan rising up her throat. The email she'd sent to Jed had had exactly the effect she'd wanted. He hadn't written back, nor had he crossed Allison's mind since she hit send over two weeks ago.

"Mom, I can't do this right now."

"Allison, he told me about that email. How could you send such a thing?"

"How could—how could *I*—" Allison crumpled the sheet of

notebook paper in front of her in her fist. Its edges dug at her palm in an almost satisfying way. "Did he happen to mention the one he sent me? Where he didn't once ask how I was and called me fat?"

Her tendency toward impulsiveness meant the words were out of Allison's mouth before she remembered Colin was sitting there. He was doing his best to feign obliviousness, his face buried in his phone, AirPods tucked in his ears, but she saw the furrow in his brow and the tension in his neck, revealing how hard he was exerting himself not to look up.

Her mother's sigh bashed against her eardrums. "You know how he is."

"I do. And I don't have to put up with it."

"He's your father."

"I know, Mom." Allison set her empty hand flat on the table, but it continued to tremble.

She couldn't do this anymore. No matter how much Allison loved her mother, she couldn't keep Jed in her life for her. Her voice shook as hard as her hands when she spoke again. "And if you have some kind of bond with him that overrides all the horrible ways he's treated you, then so be it. But . . ." Allison closed her eyes, concentrating on finding the right words, on forming each syllable precisely on her tongue. She was afraid they wouldn't fit through her lips otherwise.

Cool skin pressed over her hand. Her eyes flew open to find Colin's fingers sheltering hers. Her heart squeezed. She couldn't remember the last time he'd comforted her. If he ever had. And his expression wasn't composed to offer advice or explain how he knew exactly how she felt in this moment; it was soft, caring. As if he recognized a source of pain he couldn't challenge or surpass.

"But," she repeated. "He's my father. I have to decide what that means for me. And right now, I can't handle his half-assed attempts at being in my life. They hurt too much." She sounded so strained, so close to an edge she didn't want to fall over, that she didn't recognize her own voice.

Colin rounded the table and folded himself noiselessly into the chair beside her. He slid closer, until the corners of their seats kissed. His long legs were propped on either side of her chair. For someone so thin, Colin could take up an incredible amount of space, and his presence cocooned Allison in a way she wished she hated.

A single tear slipped past her defenses, the hot streak burning down her cheek. She raised her knuckles to catch it, but Colin's hand was there first, his thumb gently blotting the wetness.

"You don't know how much longer he'll be around," her mother said.

Sniffling, Allison sat back, her spine a hammer against the seat. "He said you're blowing his heart stuff out of proportion."

"And he never takes things seriously." Her mother exhaled sharply. "I know he hasn't been the best father." A scoff tore from Allison's lips. Her mom ignored it. "But you don't want to have regrets. When he's gone—"

"I'm not the one who'll have regrets." Another tear betrayed Allison, breaking away from her lashes. "I shouldn't have to let him hurt me just because he's my parent, Ma."

"I think you're wrong about this."

"And I think *you're* wrong about this. I'm not sixteen anymore. You can't force me to sit across from him at a dinner table simply because you say so."

Her mom went silent. Each of her breaths crackled against the phone line. Colin didn't move a muscle, as if he'd glimpsed Medusa and turned to stone.

"I didn't raise you to be unforgiving," her mother whispered.

"But you raised me to be strong and stand up for myself."

"Allison—"

"I'm sorry, Ma, but I can't discuss this right now. I've got a ton of work to do. I'll talk to you later, okay?"

"I'm really disappointed in the choice you're making."

"I know." Allison's heart felt like it had been skewered and torn from her ribcage. She could be seventy years old, and she'd still be devoured by guilt when it came to her mother. But somewhere beneath all that, she knew she was making the right decision.

Sometimes, the right choice hurt far worse than the wrong one.

"Tell Cleo I said hi, okay?" With that, Allison hung up and dropped her phone on the table. As soon as it left her hand, she gave in to the sob shoving at her chest.

Colin's lips were a tight line. His hands waved about, lost birds uncertain where to go.

Her mother and Ethan had drained all the fight from her. There was nothing left to stop Allison from dropping her forehead to Colin's chest. Nothing to warn her against knotting her hands into his shirt hem. The rise and fall of his breaths lulled her like the rhythm of a rocking chair. One of his hands smoothed her dark hair while the other settled on her lower back. Her tears soaked the front of his T-shirt.

She gave herself two minutes. One-hundred-and-twenty seconds, each one counted down by the tick of Colin's watch. Then she sat up and swiped her face.

Sniffing, she pointed at the dark blue spot on his chest. "I drowned Aquaman."

He glanced down at his shirt. "Irony."

They both laughed, and it felt to Allison like a deep breath after staying too long underwater.

"Sorry to make such a scene," she mumbled.

He shook his head. "Do you want to talk about it?" His hands flexed as if he was fighting the urge to reach for her.

Colin knew about Jed. One night not long after they'd started dating, they'd been in his room, tangled in each other with a rerun of *Friends* (another of her mother's favorites that had haunted Allison's childhood) streaming in the background, when Allison had caught sight of Monica Gellar's fat suit. Straddling Colin with her bra straps by her elbows and her pants unzipped, she'd launched into a ten-minute tirade about representations of fatness in popular culture that had eventually led to a confession about how awful Jed had been about her weight (and everything else), and how hard it was to have her mother pushing her to have a relationship with him, as if none of his hurtful words mattered.

Not to be outdone (of course), Colin had then shared how, because of him, his mother had never gotten to go to law school or become a law professor, which had been her dream, and how his grandfather had given up on retiring early to support them. Colin had promised them that he'd be the professor instead. It was the only thing he thought about most days. Making it up to them for choosing him.

Clearly, Colin understood family pressures, but there wasn't anything to say. Allison had told her mother and Jed what she'd needed. And even if she *had* wanted to talk, it couldn't be to Colin. They couldn't grow closer. Too much was at stake if they imploded a second time.

Pushing her chair a few inches to the left, she placed her Chaucer textbook on the table. Jabbing her finger at the book hard enough to hurt, she said, "I want to talk about this."

She pretended not to see the disappointment in Colin's eyes as they dipped to the open page.

Chapter 15

Allison let herself fall into the rhythm of the iambic pentameter as she stood before the class, hitting each of the hard vowels and consonants that gave Middle English its Germanic sound with as much gusto as she dared.

"O deere cosyn Palamon," quod he,
"Thyn is the victorie of this aventure.
Ful blisfully in prison maistow dure—
In prison? Certes nay, but in paradys!"

By the time she reached that last hard vowel with para-*dees*, her jaw ached from nervous tension.

Raising her eyes to the room, she took a breath, the air crackling against the silence. Clothes rustled softly as some of the students shifted in their seats, and the keys on a few laptops clacked.

This was it. Her chance to prove to Wendy that somewhere inside of Allison was the teacher she pretended to be every time the word *recitation* was mentioned.

Her gaze skirted to Colin, who gave her a thumbs-up. Before Wendy had called her to the lecture podium, he'd scrawled some affirmations on the top corner of Allison's presentation notes. Goofy things like *You're going to slay this* and *Don't let this be a knightmare.* Who knew bad puns could be a balm to one's anxiety?

Colin, apparently.

Returning his smile with a small one of her own, Allison rolled back her shoulders and shifted her attention to the class.

"I chose this passage," she said, "because of the language. In the face of Arcite's love for Emily, words start to lose their meaning. Being free from his prison becomes a prison unto itself because he'll be separated from the sight of her. Meanwhile, he views his cousin, still locked in the tower above Emily's garden, as not only free, but in paradise. This is a subtle way in which Chaucer's narrator depicts love, and the women who incite this love, as dangerous and unsettling." She cast a glance over the faces before her. "Do you see anything else in this passage that might support my ideas? Any lines, or even words?"

Whole minutes ticked by without a response. Sweat gathered at her temples and soaked the backs of her knees. If she moved from behind the lectern, everyone would see it raining down her calves.

Clearly, Allison would never be good at this. She'd led herself down the wrong career path. How naïve to believe her dreams from elementary school were sound life goals.

She settled her finger on the second line of the passage, ready to start talking if no one else would. But then she saw a hand rising slowly from one of the top rows. She recognized this student. Jackie DeLuca, from her second section of recitation. As she called on her, Allison's muscles liquefied with relief.

Jackie pushed a blond curl out of her face. " 'Ful blisfully in prison maistow dure—' " She stumbled over the language, but each syllable was a symphony to Allison's ears. "Everything seems wrong in this sentence. I thought 'dure' meant, like . . . 'endure,' which sounds like suffering and seems to relate to prison. But 'ful blisfully' sounds like a pleasant thing. It reminded me of what you were saying. Meaning stops . . . I don't know . . . meaning anything?"

Allison beamed, blinking away a rogue tear that had smuggled its way into her lashes. "That is a *great* example. There are so many contradictions in this line, right?"

More hands blurred the air, and soon the class was analyzing lines not only from the passage Allison had introduced, but other parts of the text as well. Wendy even offered one. Allison's heart took up too much space in her chest, and it was a battle to keep the grin off her face. *This* was what she'd dreamed about when she'd imagined herself as a professor: students alert, active, stumbling over each other to suggest examples. Her body buzzed warm, electric.

At the first lull in the conversation, Colin raised his hand.

Allison immediately stiffened, and a sharp response rushed to her tongue.

She bit it back. Her reaction wasn't fair. Lately, there'd been an unspoken ceasefire between them. Though there'd been no changes to the advisee situation, he'd grown more supportive, enthusiastic about understanding and developing her ideas, as if, together, they could unearth the most profound reading of any text. Even this morning, when she'd commented on his need for a translation to read Chaucer, Colin had laughed it off, recognizing the remark as the reflex that it was, competition so natural to Allison that it wasn't always intentional.

"Yes, Colin?" She did her best to smooth the edge from her voice.

He ran his fingers over the stanzas in his text. "That's really how you read this section?" His eyes were soft when they rose from the page to her face. Nothing about his tone suggested a challenge. Rather, he seemed curious.

Where was this going? "It is."

"You think Chaucer's that much of a cynic about love?"

"No, I think he's a realist. Love can pummel you." Colin had taught her that. Allison wished she'd learned it from Chaucer first. It would have saved her a world of hurt. "That's pretty much what 'The Knight's Tale' is about."

His brow furrowing, Colin pulled his glasses from his face to wipe the lenses. Everything about his body language looked poised to disagree, but Wendy had returned to her spot on the dais.

"These are some great points," she said, drawing the class's attention to her. "Let's all thank Allison for a fantastic discussion and some excellent practice in close reading."

With a nod, Allison gathered her materials and returned to her seat. Colin's gaze swept over her face, but she avoided it. She'd finally had a good day of teaching, and she wanted to bask in that, not get drawn into some philosophical debate about the definition of love or Chaucer's feminism. Thankfully, Wendy seemed to have one more thing to cover before she ended class, which meant Allison was free for a few more minutes.

Their teacher gathered a packet of papers in her arms and started handing them out to the students. When she returned to her desk, she propped a copy of a black-and-white book on the podium. Allison's eyes zeroed in on the title.

The Mabinogion.

"My next project is going to be to look closely at Welsh Arthurian myth," Wendy explained. "I'm really interested in exploring how some of the more modern, more recognizable legends around Arthur have come to be by considering where they started. To that end, I've recently gotten the permissions necessary to view, in person, the manuscript of 'The White Book of Rhydderch,' a part of this"—she pointed to the book—"at the National Library of Wales, and my grant funding for the trip has been approved. I have spots available for a few research assistants, and I'm hoping that some will be undergraduate students."

Her professor's voice grew distant and fuzzy beneath the rush of Allison's pulse in her ears. A research trip. To *Wales*. She'd see a medieval manuscript in the proverbial flesh. Words scribed almost a millennium ago, sitting there right before her eyes.

Allison needed to be one of those research assistants. But she wasn't familiar with *The Mabinogion*. If Wendy asked them to contribute, she'd have nothing to say, nothing to show she deserved a spot on that trip. A more horrifying thought stole into her mind. What if Colin *did?*

Without her phone, which was in her bag under her chair, Allison had no way to plan for this most WCS of WCSs.

Her eyes fell on Colin's laptop, sitting beside her elbow. A shiny chrome-and-black solution to her problem. While he watched Wendy speak, his fingers white-knuckling a pen with the same intensity Allison felt, she dragged the machine closer.

"Can I borrow this?" she whispered, already typing.

He glanced at her blankly for a second, then his brows jut together, realization settling into his features. "Actually . . ." The rest of his sentence was lost to his concentration as he wove his hands under and through Allison's to reach the keyboard.

It had small, chiclet keys, the touchpad hardly the size of a sticky note. As they wrestled for control, their knuckles and thumbs and elbows bumped and brushed. Allison ignored the tiny fires bursting to life all over her skin. She cared only about finding some factoid about this text that would ingratiate her to Wendy.

Colin angled his pointy frame in front of the screen, blocking her the same way he had that first day in class. For a moment, she considered grabbing her pen and committing a second act of fashion vandalism, but chose decisive action instead. Jamming her shoulder against his to push him aside, she crammed her face before the screen, and, for good measure, threw her long hair over her shoulder to obscure his vision. With the few seconds that bought her, she took control of the search bar.

Their cheeks skimmed together as Colin pressed forward to see the browser. His long leg stretched out under her knee, and every time he shifted, his pants tickled the sensitive skin there.

Allison intensified their war for the keyboard to keep her mind from cataloging all the ways his body was currently tangled with hers. As they both tried to type at once, their thumbs prodded the track pad, and, when Colin clicked the next search result, an ad window popped up as the website began to load.

A deep moan of satisfaction exploded from his speakers at full volume. Allison and Colin froze, their faces twin flames of embarrassment. A commercial for a porn site filled the screen with writhing limbs and close-ups of plump, parted lips and the curves of cleavage and asses. Bad music mixed with guttural screams of "yes, yes, yes" and overexaggerated groans of pleasure engulfed them.

The entire class went quiet, and, as the ad played on a loop, each iteration seemed to grow louder and louder. Performative sex in surround sound.

"Oh my god, turn it off," Allison hissed. Why did her every moment in Colin's presence result in chaos? Her fingers fumbled with the touchpad while Colin's flapped around her. His cheeks were the color of her favorite red pen.

When Allison finally closed the window, the sudden, blissful silence summoned a sigh from her lips. The relief of it left her giddy, and she fell into a fit of helpless laughter. What else could she do after loudly streaming porn in the middle of a class?

A second later, everyone else joined in.

Her sides aching, Allison hugged herself. Colin's chair was still pressed up against hers, and she whispered, "We're a menace," as she dropped her forehead to his shoulder. The potent blend of adrenaline and glee swimming in her veins filled her head like alcohol, not leaving her room to weigh the consequences.

"Or maybe we're magic."

His breath flit through her hair, no more solid than the brush of a dandelion tuft. The catch in his voice plucked at something raw and open in Allison, a part of herself she hadn't let anyone near since their breakup. Her arms tightened around her waist.

When he turned to face their professor, she wished she didn't notice how carefully he moved, like he didn't want to shake Allison away.

"We must have dismantled the pop-up blocker. I'm *so* sorry," he said to Wendy.

She grinned. "I think Chaucer would have appreciated it."

Sitting up, Allison reclaimed some distance from Colin. "Or asked you to increase the volume," she joked.

That elicited another chorus of chuckles.

In its wake, Wendy dismissed the class. She was still smiling when she joined her TAs at their table. "That was an adventure. You two are quite the team."

Allison and Colin shared a glance that lingered a little too long, but neither of them replied.

"Again," Allison repeated instead. "We're so sorry. We were both trying to pull up information on *The Mabinogion,* and a little too much button mashing ensued."

"It's fine. A little levity is always a good addition to a lesson." Wendy displayed her copy of the book. "Have either of you read it?" she asked.

Allison waited until Colin shook his head to do the same.

Their professor blew out a breath. Her pinched brow caused Allison's muscles to bunch. More bad news? Were no grad students allowed on her trip? Or had she already chosen more advanced ones?

"It's a truly fascinating piece of literature, and the manuscript is quite something to see. I wish I had more funding." Wendy pressed a palm to the table, her bracelets clacking as they slid down her arm. "As much as I would love to—"

"You can't take us," Colin concluded.

She shook her head. "I can't take both of you," she clarified. "Which pains me a great deal."

Her words were like a set of cymbals crashing between Allison's ears. "Who . . . will go with you?"

"My advisee. I try to co-write at least one paper with each grad student I advise, and this trip is the perfect opportunity."

Allison crushed her fingers around her knees. A publication with someone as renowned as Wendy Frances was the chance of a lifetime.

This was the Rising Star Award all over again. Only there was so much more for Allison to lose this time. The advisee position, the trip, and the paper it would produce could all help Allison secure one of the precariously few tenure-track jobs in medieval literature that might be available when she finished her degree.

She needed this.

She *deserved* it.

And no one, especially not Colin Benjamin, was going to take it from her.

Whatever affection Allison had accidentally cultivated for him these past few weeks fell away like autumn leaves from a dead tree. She pinned him with her gaze, ready to fight for this mentorship, no matter what it took. She suspected, by the time this was over, any speck of goodwill left between them would be obliterated.

Wendy rapped her knuckles against the table. "I recommend giving it a read when you have some time. And again, please try not to let these things overwhelm you. The beauty of Claymore is that opportunities abound. No matter whom I pick, you'll each get plenty more."

Allison studied Colin as he watched their teacher leave the room. His mouth was pulled tight, the muscles in his jaw working against taut skin. "Wow."

"You're done with this now, right?"

Colin finally looked at her. "What?"

"You can't possibly think, after what happened at Brown—*no, what you *did* at Brown*—that it's okay to compete with me for this." Allison shoved to her feet.

Pain creased his face. "Allison." He had the audacity to reach for her. She slid around the table. "I have to," he whispered.

Her eyes seared into his. Every part of her felt ablaze. It was happening again. She'd tried to do everything different this time, and yet here she was, caught in some cruel time loop that would never let her loose. Never let her win. Sophomore year endlessly dragging her back. Beating her down.

"No, you don't."

"Allison," he said carefully.

"Oh, fuck you." The words rushed from her like a breath.

Colin reared back, acting for all the world like she'd tossed a pot of scalding water at him.

It took incredible self-control not to bash him in the face with her anthology as she packed it in her bag. One of her notebooks bent awkwardly against the spine, and something else deeper in the crevices tore. None of it mattered.

Anger beat through her forcefully enough to make her sick as she stalked from the lecture hall.

After the Rising Star announcement, Allison didn't leave her room for two days. Colin called, he tried to visit, he slipped notes under her door, but she refused to talk to him. She was mad, yes, "fit to be tied," as her grandmother would say, but she'd also been so defeated. She'd never lost anything before, especially not something for which she'd worked this hard. She'd had no idea how to sit with those feelings of failure. Everything seemed pointless. Without the Rising Star, it felt as if Allison would never achieve her dreams. And to have Colin be the one who'd taken them from her had only sharpened the knife.

Now he was twisting that same blade deep into her back. Making sure it stuck for good this time.

In her rush to leave, she'd turned the wrong way out of the classroom and trapped herself in an alcove. And there he was, right behind her. Always there. A shadow she couldn't shake. She pressed her spine to the wall. This time she'd be the one leaning.

Only the bastard took her cue and angled himself against the window, resting on the sill. He'd pushed up the sleeves of his gray cardigan, accentuating the line of muscle in his slim forearms, and his posture seemed to broaden his shoulders. Sunlight sliced russet streaks into his blond hair and drew gold sparks through his green eyes.

Fuck the sun. Fuck nature. Where was a washed-out fluorescent lightbulb when Allison needed one?

His eyes dipped over her. "You need to understand."

"I don't need to understand anything. You stole the one thing I wanted at Brown. Now you're going to try to do it again."

Sighing, he scrubbed at his forehead with the heels of his hand. "Has it ever occurred to you that I might have needed the Rising Star? That I might *need* this?"

"You were practically a celebrity at that school. Everyone loved you. You had the best recommendations, top scores, a department-chair approved sample essay. Like hell, you needed the Rising Star." She hiked her bag higher on her arm and stepped away from the wall. Her gaze grabbed his like it had hands. She wished a look alone could bruise. Mangle. Scar. "And you don't need this advisee position or this trip. It's just another chance to feed your ego. Another trophy for your wall. By this time next year, some new 'huge' thing will have caught your eye, and you'll leave medieval lit behind. Like it never mattered."

The same way he'd left her.

"Allison."

"No." She raised a hand. "I'm done here. *We're* done here."

Allison would not relive what happened at Brown. She would break the time loop. She'd find a different ending.

No. Fuck that. She'd *make* one.

Chapter 16

Colin broke up with Allison to the jaunty tune of "Jingle Bell Rock."

It had been late March, but the Christmas Diner embraced its name and celebrated the holiday year-round. Tinsel and ornaments were strung from the ceiling and glittered from every window frame, hot chocolate and gingerbread cookies were always on the menu, and every booth boasted its own tiny Christmas tree while festive music blared nonstop from the speakers.

Usually, Allison loved the kitsch of it all—the winter holidays were her favorite, and let's be honest, some of those songs were bangers—but on that day, a little over a week after Colin had stolen the Rising Star Award right out of her hands, she'd found the garishness repulsive. Or maybe it was just the sight of Colin striding toward her.

She hadn't seen him since the night before the announcement. They'd been up late at his apartment, hands wandering all over each other as they pretended to study for midterms. Cocooned in the quiet of his room, her fingers teasing the skin of his hip bone under his maroon cardigan, his palm easing across her stomach and drifting toward her breasts, everything had felt warm. Comfortable. Safe. He'd been so supportive of her as she'd worked on the application, and even after it was done, he was more complimentary and attentive than ever. As if something significant had shifted between them. Allowed them to grow closer.

Now she saw those days for what they were. A lie. The realization cast Colin's stark frame in a harsh light, so he looked cold, calculating, the planes of his face edged like blades as he crossed the final squares of black-and-white linoleum between them.

Even the small smile he offered her as he slid into the opposite side of the booth seemed empty. A chill chased up Allison's back.

He noted her shiver and immediately began shrugging out of his charcoal cardigan. "Are you cold?"

She waved him off. She didn't want anything of his touching her until she got some answers. She barely let him finish ordering (buffalo chicken nachos, their usual, as if this was a normal afternoon) before she spat out, "What happened to not applying for the Rising Star?" The harshness in her voice clashed with the jolly chorus demanding that they all dance and prance in Jingle Bell Square.

Colin flinched. "I didn't plan on it." Leaning forward, he rested his bony elbows on the edge of the table and wrapped both hands around his glass of water. "My adviser insisted. She said it would be a good way to seal the deal on my Ph.D. application." His movements were methodical, almost robotic, as he brought the cup to his lips and took a long sip. "You know how competitive the good programs are."

All those words and not one apology. Allison folded her arms over her chest. Could he really think he was blameless here? "And you didn't think you should tell me?"

His lips pursed. "It was a last-minute thing. And I never thought I'd win."

Lies. Colin didn't do anything unless he was sure he'd win. "Or were you more afraid that I might?"

It was the only explanation she'd could fathom. If she'd won, it would have upset their equilibrium. She'd have something Colin didn't. That would never have sat well with him.

"What does that mean?"

"We all know Colin Benjamin doesn't like to be outshined." There was venom on Allison's tongue. She wasn't sure what she'd expected from this conversation, but given all those times he'd tried to contact her, she'd expected him to grovel or at least offer an explanation that would fix things between them. Instead, he seemed resigned. Detached. Like he had nothing invested in this discussion.

Or in *them.*

Her fear of that stung enough to make her defensive.

He held still except to raise the water glass to his lips once more. Allison longed for the erratic flurry of his hands. Some sign that he was nervous or hurting. Anything. "I don't know what you want from me, Allison," he said.

"An apology? A promise it won't happen again? Some reason that would make this all okay?" She was practically begging him for something he should have offered willingly. To ease her own anxiety, she reached forward and twirled the straw in her cup.

Colin shifted stiffly, then cleared his throat. "Listen."

The straw bent between Allison's suddenly cramped fingers.

"These past few days gave me a lot of time to think."

The plastic snapped in half, and a sharp corner sliced through her knuckle. Allison's nerves were too raw from his tone, his words, to notice. She could be run over by a truck in this booth and she probably wouldn't feel it.

"This whole Rising Star thing made me face something I hadn't wanted to. I almost didn't apply for it because of you"—he cleared his throat again when Allison balked—"because of *us,*" he clarified. "What if I hadn't? And then I didn't win?"

Allison shook her head. She had no idea what he was getting at, but it didn't sound like anything she'd asked for.

"The Rising Star, that's not even the biggest decision I need to make this year. Huge things are coming up for me. Important things. Life-changing things." His hazel eyes were steady. He'd practiced this. Which meant he'd thought about it long enough to draft a script. "My

life's about to start for real, you know? I can't be held back by anything. I have to make the right choices for me. Only me."

Allison's heart cracked. Here she was believing they were growing
closer, when, actually, Colin had been planning to tear them apart.

He didn't wait for her to respond before he said the handful of
words that cleaved her world in two.

"I need to make those choices on my own," he said. "I need to be
on my own. Alone."

Allison had thought this was a fight, something for them to work
through, to grow from.

To Colin, it was an end.

On his own. Alone.

Those were the last words they spoke to each other until Claymore's orientation two years later. Because that day, after he'd broken
her heart, Allison gave him exactly what he wanted.

Rising without a word, she turned from him and headed for the
door.

Chapter 17

"Who's the handsomest boy? Who?" Allison cooed at Monty over the blast of her music.

She straightened his bowtie, awed he wasn't nipping at it the way he did everything else. As soon as she let go, he pranced from one end of the bed to the other, paws kicked out high in front of him, as if he knew exactly how dapper he looked.

Allison faced herself in the mirror. Navy swing dress with small crochet detailing on the cap sleeves, a cream cardigan, brown knee-length boots, the crescent-moon pendant necklace Sophie had gifted her last Christmas. Hair swept up in a messy bun it had taken her half an hour to perfect, and small moon-shaped studs in her ears. A dab of mascara and a mulberry lip, as if she'd just sipped a glass of red wine.

Any other day, the stylish girl reflected back at her would have had her high on confidence, but that fight with Colin yesterday and her PMDD had teamed up to drag her down. Her hair was too flat. The cap sleeves accentuated the flab on her arms (hence the cardigan). The jersey cotton fabric of her dress clung to every lump in her mid-section. Her bra was giving her uniboob. Her thighs looked like blocks of cellulite. She almost wished for her period so the body dysmorphia and spiraling thoughts that accompanied her PMS would dissipate.

It was a wish she knew she'd regret as soon as her first cramps ripped through her insides.

Having a menstruating body was a real amusement park of misery sometimes.

Shaking her head, Allison crossed the room to clean up her desk. She plopped pens back into their assigned mugs (the good gel ones got the Schuyler sisters cup, the rest a plain-old floral design), straightened stacks of papers, and piled her library books in alphabetical order. Then she adjusted Mandy's cross-stitch above her monitor. Who knew why she was cleaning when no one would be coming upstairs, but Allison couldn't stop fidgeting.

Beside her mouse sat her own cross-stitch project. Mandy had brought the supplies to class last week, and Allison could not have been more grateful. She'd spent most of last night stabbing a needle through holes in the hatched fabric, imagining it was Colin's face. It had been rather cathartic. And a lot less bloody.

She couldn't wait to show Mandy her progress when she and the rest of their cohort arrived.

It was the second weekend in October, Allison's designated week to host their gathering, and, for the sake of spontaneity (and also because Link had plans on Saturday), they'd opted for a Friday night meet-up instead. Despite her best efforts at apathy, she'd purchased far too many frozen appetizers, made two signature cocktails, and concocted a complicated murder mystery game based on famous unsolved cases she'd found online. Clearly, her need to be the best extended far beyond her academic life.

Hooking Monty under her arm, Allison snapped off her speaker and grabbed her index cards (ten, scribbled front and back with notes for the game). As she set the Corgi down on the hallway runner, she noticed that Sophie's door was closed, with a sign reading *Please Stay Out* swinging from a pushpin. This was regular party protocol for them (Allison's sign, of course, read *Abandon All Hope, Ye Who Enter Here*), but it seemed extreme for only six guests. Hopefully, Colin would not show his face. For too many reasons to count, he was the last thing Allison wanted to deal with tonight.

Her stomach lurched at the thought of his name. Wendy's news about the Wales trip had dredged up so many bad feelings from Allison's past—how she hadn't been good enough to earn the Rising Star, how she hadn't been worth holding on to when Colin graduated, how she'd weighed him down. The depression she'd fallen into when she hadn't been able to get her grades back up and almost failed two classes. Those oppressive thoughts squashed whatever self-confidence she'd gained from her presentation, and holding her two sections of recitation today had been brutal. Every time she'd spoken, Allison had been sure doubt clouded her students' gazes, and only a few of them had bothered to take any notes.

Ugh. She needed a drink. *Pronto.*

More music drifted up the stairs, and the front door opened and closed twice in a row, inciting a small yip from Monty before he bounded his way toward the foyer.

Allison jumped. Was everyone early? It was barely seven. A half hour ahead of schedule seemed outlandish, even for her herd of nerds.

She scooped Monty off the floor as the front door swung open again. Irritation twitched in her veins as she rallied a smile. Who walks into a house without being invited? What kind of reverse vampires was she going to school with?

Turns out, the tall guy staring down at her was less Transylvanian and more modern Viking. His sun-streaked hair was secured at the nape of his neck with an elastic, and he wore distressed jeans with a loose white linen shirt that laced up over his otherwise bare chest, the three-quarter-length sleeves straining against his biceps. Something that reminded Allison of a Wiccan symbol hung on a silver chain around his neck and leather cuffs braced both his arms. A shadow of blond stubble outlined his jaw. Really, all he needed was an ax to complete the look.

"Hey," he greeted her. Then, still filling the doorway (and welcoming in the chilly night air), he yelled Sophie's name so loudly the sylla-bles rumbled through Allison's body. Under each of his burly arms he hefted a twelve-pack of Bud Light.

Sophie burst from the kitchen, her face flushed.

"Eric!" she yelled (because, if his name wasn't Leif, it *had* to be Eric). "Thank god. We were running out of alcohol." She yanked at the front of her halter jumpsuit. Her C-cups often tried to escape her bra when she was drunk. Her free hand gripped a plastic wineglass brimming with a candy-pink liquid that resembled too closely the watermelon sangria Allison had toiled over all afternoon.

She hugged Monty to her chest. "Who's running out of what alcohol?"

"Allison has emerged!" Sophie threw up her arms. Her pink drink sloshed over her shoulder as she pulled Allison into a hug. "I was afraid you were going to hide in your room all night," she slurred. Her exaggerated movements wreaked havoc on her neckline, and this time Allison had to grab her top and haul it up. Viking man licked his lips as if she'd done something hot, and Allison fought the urge to hurl all over his shiny black boots. She got a sick sense of satisfaction at the idea that his loose laces would be dragged right through it.

Turning Sophie around, she focused on tightening her friend's straps. Allison had never understood how Sophie could date the most amazing women, but the most Neanderthal dudes. Her last girlfriend had been a *poet*. Leif Erickson here drank fucking Bud Light.

And why was he at the house anyway?

Sophie nodded toward the kitchen. "Everyone's in there."

"Everyone?"

"Janie, Sarah, and Brooks, and like ten of their friends from work. I guess Eric's got some of his buddies on the way."

"Great. The IQ level in the place will drop by twenty."

Sophie smirked. "Listen, we're going to need some kind of enter-tainment. We've already burned through all your supplies."

Allison's mouth fell open. "All of it?" The ingredients for the sangrias had easily cost her eighty bucks, never mind all the food.

"There were only a few tiny pitchers and it was *sooooooo* good."

Monty began to squirm against Allison's tightening grip. "That was for tonight." How was she going to host the best gathering without a signature cocktail? Mandy still waxed poetic about Kara's Starburst martinis.

"Yeah, for our party!" Sophie tossed up her hands, almost clocking the Viking. He set his Bud Light down on the stairs so he could wrap his arms around her waist.

She tapped the side of his face but otherwise ignored his nuzzles. "I'm so glad you suggested it. It's been way too long since we've done something like this."

There'd been a handful of parties at the beginning of the summer, but they'd been *Sophie's*, full of her fellow designers and co-workers.

Tonight was for Allison. It was supposed to be an intimate gathering of her peers, not some rager. "I said I was having people over."

Sophie's eyebrows quirked. "Right. I figured I would, too. The more the merrier, right?"

Wrong. So, so wrong. There was nothing merry about any of this. Allison's murder mystery wasn't suited for more than eight people, and, even if it were, Sophie's friends were stylish and sophisticated. They wouldn't be into a DIY party game, and, anyway, Allison had no interest in performing it for what would no doubt be a hostile audience.

She shook her head. "Sure. Right."

Sophie's eyes narrowed. "No. I know that tone. What?"

It wasn't worth arguing about while drunk. The conversation would go nowhere, Sophie would cry, and then not remember a thing the next morning.

"I'd just been saving that sangria and the food for my friends from school, that's all," Allison explained.

"It's fine." Sophie grinned, slapping the Viking's arm. "Eric brought beer. And we can order pizza."

Allison nearly cracked a grin as she imagined herself offering Link, the king of artisan brewing, a Bud Light. But that tiny drop of humor quickly soured.

First her fight with her mother. Then the Wales trip. Now her carefully planned gathering was ruined. Tightening her jaw, she turned to Eric. "Can I get a few of those?" Time to obliterate this disaster of a week.

He popped the box open and offered it. "They're warm." Allison was pretty sure his eyes skated over her own set of D-cups as she reached in.

"I do not give a shit."

"Hard-core."

"You know it." As if she needed validation from the Nordic equivalent of a caveman.

Rolling four beers out of the box, Allison stuffed one in each of her pockets and another under her arm. The fourth she cracked open with one hand and guzzled without taking a breath. She did her best to ignore its yeasty taste, which reminded her of how the kitchen smelled whenever Sophie made bread.

She slammed the empty can on the end table, earning another appreciative mumble from the Viking. Without hesitating, she cracked open beer number two and pounded it back. It was going to take an ocean of this garbage to snuff out her anger.

Sophie took her arm, her brow furrowed. "Slow down there. We've got all night."

"I'm good," Allison lied.

A tepid stream of amber liquid slipped from the corner of her mouth onto her dress as she chugged. The stain it left behind was the exact shape of Colin's big, dumb head.

How fitting, Allison mused as she popped the tab on her third drink.

If anyone in Allison's cohort was disappointed by her party, she never would have known it.

As more people arrived, they grabbed whatever drinks and snacks were available and settled right into chatting with the rest of the guests. The last time Allison saw Mandy, she was actively flirting with one of the Viking's friends. Everyone else had joined Sophie and the designers in the living room to watch some terrible reality TV.

Allison was the one being antisocial. For the last half hour, she'd been sitting outside on the front stoop under the pretense of giving Monty, who had become extremely overstimulated by all the people, some much needed quiet time.

But really, she was fuming and drinking, two of her favorite pastimes, especially when done in tandem.

Despite all her planning and careful thinking and rethinking, this entire week had gone off the rails. Every one of Allison's sound decisions seemed to summon some sort of chaos. Deciding to cut ties with Jed had led to Allison's mom not calling her for days. All her preparations for this party led to its ruin and to a not-so-subtle reminder of how far apart Sophie and Allison were growing. And well, Colin was . . . Colin. Of course he'd taken a bulldozer to her week. That's what he did.

Allison cracked open her sixth Bud Light and tossed it back. Imagine what tonight could have been if Sophie hadn't railroaded everything. Right now, Allison would be guiding a group of stumped academics through one of the hardest murder mystery games she'd ever seen, like some film noir ringleader. They'd all be laughing and yelling and drunk on delicious sangria, and, on Tuesday, Colin would have had to hear all about it from the outside. It would have been delightful. And one more point in Allison's win column.

Instead, she was outside without a jacket or leggings in forty-degree weather and only had Bud Lights to warm her insides. She'd considered more than once going back in, but every time her feet refused to cooperate. Her frustration had built up around her like a wall, thick as concrete and steel and pushing everyone away. If she went back in the house to find herself on the outskirts of her own party, it would break

her. Without Sophie to walk Allison through a set of WCS about anxiety and party etiquette, it was easier not to try. Nothing she avoided
could hurt her.

Still, when another round of laughter seeped through the open
window, it stabbed like a stake in Allison's heart.

There was only one thing to do. She popped open another beer. At
this point, she'd more than bypassed buzzed and was full-on drunk,
which meant the Bud Lights no longer tasted like anything (yay!) but
her stomach was a nauseous pit (boo!). She gulped, doing her best not to
let the liquid touch her tongue. More slid down her chin than her throat.

Like the lady she was, she used the back of her sweater to wipe
her face and neck. Somewhere in her, Allison knew she'd regret that
choice in the morning, but the cloud of beer foaming her brain didn't
let her care.

Monty growled, and his long tail curled up in attention. Putting
more tension on his leash, Allison let her gaze follow the dog's down
the sidewalk as she took another slug of beer.

Most of it ended up soaking the front of her dress. Her drink never
reached her lips.

Less than a block away, Colin stood in the dusky light thrown by
the nearest streetlamp, his height rivaling his shadow. His phone sat
in his long fingers like a compass, but he was staring straight at her.

Just what this night needed: Colin Benjamin. Her hand squeezed
the empty beer can until it crumpled against her palm.

He approached her, stepping so close that only a slab of concrete
remained between him and Monty. The dog still watched him keenly,
but his tail had begun to wag. The traitor.

Allison crossed her arms. "Why are you here?" She glanced up
at the window, hoping no one was looking outside. This was *not* the
time for Sophie to discover that Colin was back in her life. Allison did
not have the bandwidth to deal with that, especially not while drunk.
Besides, she had every intention of doing her damnedest to push him
right back out, so it would be a non-issue.

"It's our weekly meet-up."

Allison rolled her eyes. "You were uninvited."

His head tipped to the side. "When?"

"When you decided to try to fuck up my life again by going after this Wales trip."

Link's distinctive laugh wafted through the window, drawing Colin's eyes to the house. "What are you doing out here if they're all in there?"

"Monty and I are getting some fresh air." Allison snapped the tab on her beer. At some point, she'd have to go inside for more. Or, perhaps, she'd continue her hermitage and order some cider from Büzer instead. It cost an arm and a leg, but you couldn't put a price on proper misanthropy.

"Can I join you?" Colin nodded to the steps.

"No."

"Allison."

"I have this alone thing down to a science."

"Allison."

"Colin."

"I've been trying to text you all day."

Hence the reason Allison had muted her phone hours ago.

She cocked her head. It made the whole world tilt. "Did it ever occur to you that I might not want to talk to you?" She let her eyes rise to his face, but it was hard to focus on anything beyond his lips. They were pursed and red like fruit punch, and her drunken mind kept trying to remind her what they'd felt like on her skin all those years ago.

Butterflies. Feathers. Flower petals. Silk. Soft and teasing things that sent a swarm of chills up her back.

"I can explain."

"I don't care." Allison didn't want to hear his rationales about why this situation was different from the Rising Star or why he deserved a chance as much as she did. That award had meant everything to her, and he hadn't needed it, and he'd competed against her anyway, just to win. Just to further bolster his already massive ego. Now the stakes were even higher—this was her career, her future. Years of her life she'd dedicated to learning as much as possible about her field of study. And he was ready to take it all from her again.

How had she ever thought he cared about her?

He dared to cross that last square of sidewalk. Allison was low enough on the stoop that he towered over her, and for one of the few times in her life, she felt small.

She hated it. Grabbing the top step with her hands, she clumsily scooted up the porch. Monty extended his leash to weave himself through Colin's legs.

"I know what this all must look like to you—"

Allison dropped her head back and groaned loudly. He'd stand here all night, all semester if necessary. That's how dedicated Colin was to getting the last word. The quicker she let him get this over with, the quicker she could get back to her Colin-free existence.

She fished her phone out of her pocket. "I'm going to need a lot more alcohol for this."

She was already making a mental Büzer list as she turned on the screen. The crowd of notifications staring up at her smacked Allison like a bucket full of freezing water. In the blink of an eye, the world went from fuzzy to crystal clear.

There were five missed calls, one voicemail, and seven texts. All from her mother, whom she hadn't heard from since Tuesday. The texts read CALL ME NOW.

Colin had stopped mid-wherever-he-was in his rant and gaped at her. "Are you okay? You're white as a sheet."

Allison hushed him, her hands shaking as she dialed her mother's number.

She picked up on the first ring. "Allison."

"Mom, what's wrong?"

"I'm at the hospital. You need to get here."

Allison's heart jammed into her throat, and she swallowed hard, trying not to choke. "Why? What's wrong? Are you—"

"It's your father."

The words were yet another bucket of water, this one icing Allison over. "You scared the shit out of me. I thought *you* were sick."

Her mother had said Jed had been to the hospital with AFib a number of times. Allison had looked it up after their fight. While it was technically considered heart failure, it was manageable and people could live a long time with it. There was no need for this level of drama.

The alcohol still in her system had Allison prepared to say just that, but then her mother went on. "It's bad, honey. He's not even conscious."

Her fingers white-knuckled, Allison tucked the phone closer to her ear and glanced up at Colin. His lips were pressed together, his hands flapping around him in duress, but he didn't approach her.

"You should come," her mother said. "Now. He might not make it through the night."

Every part of Allison was frozen, but beneath it, something lanced, painful and sharp. She nodded uselessly. "I'll figure it out."

A couple of beeps and a muffled voice broke through the line before her mom spoke again. "Honey, I have to go. We're at Northern Light." Then a soft click and a buzz of silence displaced her mother's voice.

Allison's phone tumbled to her lap. She pressed a hand to her mouth. Her stomach roiled, all the beer in her burning like lava.

"My father . . . he's had a heart attack or something. I've got to go." She had to say it out loud to make it real. And Colin was the only one close enough to hear it.

She swayed as she hurried to her feet. When Colin caught her elbow in his hand, she ripped it back. The force sent her tumbling to her knees on the porch with a grunt. A bunch of her empty Bud Light cans clattered away from her.

"How many of those have you had?" he asked.

"Don't even start." Allison had to get home to her mom. She didn't have time for a lecture. When she stood again, she succeeded at remaining upright. Only to have to swallow one, two, three gags.

Colin's hawk eyes caught every moment. He glanced toward the house. "Someone will take you. Sophie? Maybe someone from our group?"

Allison shook her head. "They've all been drinking for hours, and I need to get home now." She would never actually get behind the wheel, drunk as she was, but she hated to let Colin gain any ground.

"Allison."

Bending slowly, one arm out to steady herself, she snatched her phone from the step below her. "There's a bus or a ride share, I'm sure." That felt like less of a concession. She jabbed at the screen with trembling fingers.

"Don't you live in Northern Maine? It would be astronomical."

Her head snapped up. "I have to go *now*, Colin. My mother said he might die. I don't have time to brainstorm options with you."

He sighed. His breath sliced the air, sharp and certain. "Let's go."

"Excuse me?"

"I'm driving."

"Stonington's like four hours away."

He scooped Monty into his arms. "Who else is going to take you?"

He was her only option. She hated him for that. And even more for being right. "This doesn't make everything okay."

"I'm well aware." He smoothed Monty's ears with impossibly gentle fingers. Allison hated those fingers. And wanted them to hold her at the same time.

Not waiting for her answer, Colin started walking. His strides were long and urgent. He was taking this seriously.

Allison hated him for that, too. And hated herself for needing everything he was giving her. She stumbled along in his wake, refusing to let go of Monty's leash. "Then why are you doing this?"

Colin glanced back over his shoulder. His mouth was a line of worry, his hazel eyes wide. "Because I'm not the monster you want me to be."

Chapter 18

There were some situations not even donuts could fix.

The dozen sitting on the dashboard of Colin's old Honda Civic were a testament to how hard he was trying to prove this theory wrong.

Allison nibbled on a vanilla-glazed brioche as she pressed herself into the passenger side door. The car was so tiny it was hard to put space between them. And she needed space, because it didn't matter that he was driving her drunk ass from Rhode Island to Maine in the middle of the night. Helping her because it was, morally speaking, the right thing to do would not simply erase everything else he'd done.

"Donuts are the best pre-hangover food, am I right?" His eyes cut from the stretch of empty highway to her face. They'd only been on the road for half an hour but it felt like an eternity.

"Nope. Bagel sandwiches." Allison stared through the windshield, watching the headlights slice at the dark.

"You should have ordered one, then."

She scowled. "I didn't want anything. It's you who ordered the smorgasbord." She flicked a hand toward the box of donuts.

"You have to eat something."

"Okay, Dad."

As soon as the word was out of her mouth, Allison regretted it, flinching at the feel of that one syllable on her lips. She'd never called Jed "Dad" that she could remember, and now . . . well, she might not have the opportunity. Stomach twisting, she glanced down at the phone in her lap. Nothing from her mother.

Hopefully that meant Allison still had time.

Colin's eyes on her face were too keen, too prying. If it wouldn't have led to their inevitable death via fiery car crash, she would have knocked his glasses from his nose.

"Allison," he said gently.

The softness in his voice hurt. With every part of her full of cracks, it was exactly the tone she needed, and Allison hated wanting it. She wasn't that girl who fell apart in emergencies. When Sophie's grandmother had lost her battle with cancer junior year, Allison had been her rock. She'd kept her best friend afloat. Now she was drowning, with only Colin to pull her up.

She didn't want to cling to him.

"What?" she snapped.

"You smell like a brewery."

The statement was so frank, so absurd that a laugh burst from Allison's mouth. "Thanks," she coughed out.

"A bad one that the board of health is about to close." His eyes were on the road but his lips twitched toward a grin.

"I get it."

"Just like . . . really? Bud Light?"

Allison spun toward him, forgetting all about her carefully crafted distance. Without considering the ramifications (like that he was driving, and donuts were precious and delicious), she tossed her glazed donut at his face. It hit him smack on the cheek, the sugary fried dough clinging to his stubble for a moment before sliding (achingly slowly) down his face and into his lap. It was like something out of a cartoon. Another laugh broke from her, the relief of letting it loose almost painful.

"That is brazen violence against donuts," he muttered as he plucked the pastry off his lap and crammed the entire thing in his mouth.

Allison crossed her arms. "Stop alcohol-shaming me, then."

"I merely thought our tastes were supposed to improve with age."

"Oh my god. I did not seek out the Bud Light. I'd made these amazing sangrias and then Sophie and her friends polished them all off in like two minutes, so I had no choice but to drink the cheap beer."

"I would have abstained."

Allison cocked her head, deliberately and (she hoped) bitingly. "Well, I was pissed at someone and needed to drown the anger."

"Monty?" Colin gestured his head toward the sleeping puppy in the backseat.

"Nope, someone else in this car."

"You really shouldn't harbor anger toward yourself—" Her glare was enough to silence him. Colin sighed. "Are you going to let me talk now?"

Allison flourished her hands at the car's interior. "It's not like I have much else going on." Leaning forward, she snuck open the donut box and grabbed a chocolate frosted. Her stomach protested, but Allison took a big bite and swallowed it, washing it down with a swig from a bottle of water (one of five) Colin had also purchased. He was right. She couldn't show up at the hospital drunk.

He snuck a quick glance at her before pinning his attention to the road. "I'm sorry you feel like—"

"Nope," Allison bit out around the heap of frosting filling her cheeks.

Colin's mouth fell open like a fish's. "I haven't finished a full sentence. How are you already disagreeing?"

"You're apologizing wrong."

Who knew his mouth could open even wider? Allison had the urge to shove something disgusting into it.

"How can you apologize wrong?"

Allison crossed her arms. "It is *super* passive-aggressive to apologize for my feelings rather than what you did that might have summoned said feelings."

His sigh was as beleaguered as they come. "Point taken."

"Try again."

He smacked his lips, mulling over his words "I'm sorry I'm competing with you again for something you care a lot about." He shrugged, the movement sagging, defeated. "I'm still learning how to consider other people in my choices."

When he didn't say anything else for a full minute, Allison poked his arm. "I hope you don't think you're done." Acknowledging that his choices impacted her was barely a start. She licked her fingers, one by one, relishing the ganache, then popped the last piece of pastry in her mouth. *Do your work, donut,* she prayed. *Sober me up.*

His jaw tightened, the muscles of his face rippling under the tension. "I'm not. I just . . . it's complicated, and I don't know how to explain myself without disclosing stuff I'm not proud of."

Pursing her lips, Allison sat back against the seat. It was hard to imagine that he had any secrets *that* embarrassing, but then again, wasn't she the one who'd been lying to him about how well her recitations were going? Competition with an ex did weird things to people.

COLIN BENJAMIN'S WCS

1. **He hasn't been keeping up with the reading.**

2. **He is worse at translating Middle English than he has let on.**

3. **He secretly paid his way into the program, Hollywood-celebrity style.**

Colin cleared his throat. Not in the I'm-about-to-patronize-the-crap-out-of-you way, but more nervously, like a cough that wasn't fully realized. "So I didn't . . ." His knuckles whitened as he clenched his hands on the steering wheel. "I didn't really take two gap years."

"What does that mean?"

"I went to the UK for a week the summer I graduated, but other than that, I was back living with my granddad and working as a mail clerk at his old firm."

"There's nothing wrong with taking time off to work." Allison chose her words carefully. Even without understanding what he was trying to tell her, she recognized a minefield when she wandered into one. "Did you defer your acceptances? Is that why you're starting at Claymore now?"

His body tensed. "I wish."

Allison waited for him to go on. The endless stretches of dark highway and the white numbers of the car's clock ticked off the minutes: one, two, three. Finally, she huffed a breath. "I love a good mystery as much as the next girl, but can you stop being so cryptic?"

His fingers extended and contracted against the steering wheel. "I had to take two gap years because I didn't get accepted to any Ph.D. programs." He flinched with each word as if they physically hurt.

Maybe they did. Allison couldn't wrap her head around such a fate. She'd gotten into three of the eight programs to which she'd applied, and those stats had felt dismal.

Her mind whirled. He'd broken up with her—and thrown everything in her life into upheaval—because he didn't want to be tied down when his life truly began. Allison had always assumed he'd gotten into a number of places and that's why he'd been so adamant she couldn't be part of the decision. "Did you know, when you ended things with us, that you weren't going anywhere?"

"I thought we weren't talking about the past."

"Colin." His name sliced from her lips like a shard of glass. Though it had been over two years, his answer to this question felt pivotal. She needed to know if he'd taken everything from her—the Rising Star, her confidence, *them*—for nothing.

"Yes."

Who knew one word could cut a person in half? Allison choked. "What the actual fuck? Were you tired of me and you thought saying you didn't want me to burden your future plans would hurt less?"

"No." He released one hand from the steering wheel long enough to scrub his face.

"Then *what*?"

"I couldn't . . ." He exhaled loudly. "I couldn't tell you I was a failure."

Of all the things she'd expected him to say, it had not been this. "I wouldn't have cared."

"It wasn't about you."

"Now I'm even more confused."

His long fingers fished his coffee cup from the holder, and he brought it to his lips. The bitter aroma filled the car as he sipped. Allison struggled not to cringe. He'd never taken his coffee with enough cream or sugar. If it didn't taste like warm ice cream, it wasn't worth drinking.

Blond eyelashes long and light as moth wings fluttered against his glasses' lenses as he blinked.

"Remember when you presented that paper at Brown's undergrad conference?"

She nodded.

Though Allison had spent the weeks before the event sick to her stomach at the idea of standing up and reading her work in front of a big crowd of strangers, that conference had, in the end, been the thing that crystalized her resolve about pursuing a Ph.D. It had been the first moment where she truly saw herself as a scholar, and after answering a handful of questions about her analysis of consent in *Troilus and Criseyde* with a deftness she had not thought she possessed, Allison found herself hungry for more.

Colin had been there, sitting in the front row, one ankle crossed over one knee so his socks were visible (orange with black cats arching their backs). The whole time she'd read, he'd nodded along, as if he were hearing these ideas for the first time, not the tenth. But it was the expression on his face that Allison remembered most. Beaming, like he'd never been so proud of anyone in his life. When she'd joined him after her panel was over, he'd wrapped her in his arms and whispered, "You were brilliant" into her ear, his voice husky in a way she'd never heard before. Back then, she'd been so mesmerized by his intelligence that hearing him call her brilliant was a thrill. But it was more than that. It had felt like he'd suddenly spotted this facet of herself that Allison had been afraid no one would ever notice.

Colin scratched the back of his neck. "I'd always known you were smart, and capable, and driven. But that was the day I realized that you were going to do this thing we both wanted. No question. Ph.D. program, tenure-track job, all of it. So, when I didn't get in anywhere . . . when that future looked a lot farther away for me, I . . . just . . . I couldn't lose at everything."

Allison narrowed her eyes. "It wasn't a contest."

"Come on. Everything was a contest between us back then."

That had been his fault, not hers. "Is that why you went for the Rising Star?"

"I thought, if I won, one of the schools would reconsider." He sighed. "They didn't."

"Your adviser didn't suggest that you do it?"

He shook his head.

"And you'd already been rejected everywhere?"

A nod.

"So you ruined my hard work, then broke my heart, to preserve your ego?" Allison's voice was as dull and worn down as she felt.

Cringing, he loosened his hold on the steering wheel to run a hand over his face again. "That's the thing. The breaking your heart part . . . I did that *for* you."

Allison couldn't hold back her stunned squawk. These were some serious mental gymnastics. She folded her arms. "You broke up with me for me? I'm not quite sure how that works."

"I wanted to make sure you won."

He was speaking in code. Allison wanted to shake the truth out of him. Or maybe she just wanted to shake him so she'd stop feeling the flutters that kept invading her heart every time his voice hitched or his eyes skittered around as errantly as his nervous hands usually did. "Won *what*?"

"Everything. I wanted you to have everything." He shook his head. "No, I wanted you to *get* everything. To take it the way you ought to. The way you deserved. And I was afraid . . . I was afraid you couldn't do that with me hanging around. That maybe all this failure of mine was contagious. I didn't want to infect you."

Allison's breath caught in her throat. This whole time he'd been afraid he'd hold *her* back? How was that possible? It didn't make sense with everything she thought she knew about Colin Benjamin. Everything she thought she understood about that afternoon at the Christmas Diner. "Colin—"

"I figured, junior year, free of me, free of everything, you'd be able to apply to the Rising Star again and win for sure."

Allison snapped her fists into her lap, the anger his earlier words had numbed seeping back in. "Yeah, well, I didn't."

Surprise, and something softer, flared in his gaze. "Why?"

"I just didn't." The loss to him and the breakup that had followed in its wake had wounded her enough to make her not want to try, but she couldn't tell him that. Or wouldn't, at least.

He seemed to sense her guardedness. "If it helps, the year after graduation, I applied to another round of schools. And, again, I didn't get in anywhere. Not even Brown."

"Wow." Two rounds of rejection had to be brutal.

"Yeah." Colin shrugged. "When I reached out to one of the schools for feedback, the department chair said my application was too passé. It looked like every other application from a white, straight, middle-class dude—my words, not hers. My grades and scores and recommendations were good, my writing sample and letter were fine, but nothing made me stand out. And genre fiction is becoming too popular a field these days." He bit his lip and swallowed, his Adam's apple bobbing violently. Constructive feedback was never easy, but especially not when your confidence was high. And back then, Colin's had been as high as the moon. He must have felt so lost.

Sympathy tugged at Allison. She wished she could swat it away, but it spread, like maggots. Like rot. Like an infection she knew would have no cure.

Colin cleared his throat. "My aunt is practically famous in the world of college admissions, and she offered to throw some of her weight around to get one of those rejections revoked—"

Allison grimaced. "What's up, white privilege."

"Exactly. I told her no. If I couldn't get in on my own, what was the point? It didn't mean anything. But it was clear I had to do something different because my application wasn't making me stand out. I had to reimagine myself as a student. Start from scratch. And, for a long time, the realization left me rudderless. Thankfully, though, Granddad's house is full of books."

Beneath the tension in his face, a brightness sparked. "He's a carpenter by trade, but a historian at heart. His house is basically a library. Full of all these beautiful mahogany shelves he built himself. And every one is crammed from end to end with hardback books. Granddad does not believe in softcovers."

"A wise man, indeed," Allison quipped.

"And there are globes and maps everywhere, and reproductions of historical artifacts. He even has a suit of armor."

Allison's medievalist heart leaped. It was her dream to one day possess one of those, tucked into a corner of her office. She'd call it something absurdly mundane like Steve or Ethel.

"His name is Ned." Colin cracked a grin.

Damnit. It was perfect. "Is Ned what inspired this sudden passion for medieval lit?"

Colin's besieged breath suggested he'd caught her sarcasm. "The first text I took from his shelves was Layamon's *Brut*. Granddad found me buried in it one day and dug out Geoffrey of Monmouth's *The History of the Kings of Britain*, insisting I start there instead. The more I read, the more time we spent talking. He loved the parts about King Arthur best. It fascinated him that this renowned fictional character could have had a real-life equivalent. So I introduced him—and myself—to all those Arthurian romances you used to go on about. Remember, you were taking that class?"

Allison nodded. "King Arthur in Fiction and Film." That course was to blame for her infatuation with all things chivalric. "And I remember you endlessly dismissing them as the pedestrian origins to Tolkien's masterpieces. Which for the record, isn't even accurate since Tolkien—"

"Studied Old English, not medieval lit, I know." Colin rubbed at the stubble on his jaw. "I'm sorry I didn't give you more credit back then." His eyes skimmed her face. "I get it now," he said softly. "Granddad read Malory at least four times. All the discussions we had made me think, 'Wait, maybe this is my field.' I'd certainly logged enough hours thinking about medieval lit thanks to him, and it felt right to study something that mattered to the people that mattered to me." A muscle feathered in his jaw.

Allison's stomach dipped like they'd crested the tallest incline on a rollercoaster. "People?"

"Granddad, obviously, but you, too." Colin whispered the words to the windshield. "I wasn't lying when I said you inspired me."

"Okay." With her heart banging in her chest and drowning out her thoughts, it was the only thing Allison could think to say.

Colin shook his head as if clearing out cobwebs. His gaze honed more intently on the road. "I wrote a fifteen-page writing sample on Malory's construction of Arthur, and crafted an entirely new statement of purpose. And I tried again." His hands strangled the steering wheel. "All rejections, again—"

"Except Claymore."

"Except Claymore." His throat bobbed against a swallow. It looked hard enough to be painful. "Someone on the grad committee there saw something in me, for once."

He dragged his fingers through his hair. The day's allotment of gel was long gone, and it fell in soft strands around his eyes and ears. Allison had to sit on her hands to keep from brushing it back. From getting lost in its silky texture.

Damn his hair and his arms and his perpetual need to lean against things. It was as if Allison was cursed to always be drawn in by them.

"So all this time, you've been trying to prove yourself?"

"Maybe. I mean, I'm not really a medievalist, right? Not the way you are. And this is it. The only school that wanted me. That's why I can't turn away from this mentorship. From the research trip. This is my one shot."

He didn't have to explain what he meant. Colin's need to prove to his mother and grandfather that their sacrifices for him were worth it had always spoken loudly to Allison. It echoed her desire to show Jed she hadn't needed everything he wasn't willing to sacrifice.

They were the same, in that way and so many others.

Thinking of Jed caused another grip of panic to squeeze her heart, and Allison let her head fall back against the seat. She was too tired to be angry at Colin *and* worried about her father. She lowered her window slightly, letting cool air fan her feelings as it dried the perspiration at her temples.

Colin had told her something scary, something she would have been loath to admit to anyone if it had happened to her. Never had he made himself so vulnerable to her before. Maybe she should do the same. Admit her lies about how her teaching was going and release that burden from her chest.

But then he cleared his throat. Its distinct hint of condescension raised Allison's hackles and swept any thoughts of confession from her mind.

"You know, I'm still thinking about your reading of that passage

from 'The Knight's Tale.' I believe you're interpreting it all wrong."
Apparently, they were shifting back to familiar territory: Colin disagreeing with every word she said.

Allison rolled her eyes. "I picked up on that, yes."

He pressed his lips together as the palm of his left hand trailed
restlessly up and down the curve of the steering wheel. "I think there's
something more complicated going on there. I think the Knight, or
Chaucer, is exploring, or possibly even celebrating, the messiness of
love, not criticizing it. Love's confusing, and unpredictable. It ebbs and
flows. You can think you're over it, and then all of a sudden, *wham,*
your world's upside down. Heaven is hell and hell heaven. *Paradys* is a
prison and vice versa."

His voice was too solemn, his face too drawn and tight. Allison's
heart was too wild in her chest. But she was too drained, and the night
stretched out ahead of them too long, for her to try to work out what
it all meant. "Maybe you're right," she conceded.

"Yeah?"

She pressed her elbow into the armrest, and her upper arm
brushed against his. "You're better at this medieval lit stuff than you
think, Colin. So, could you please, *please,* stop using me to prove that
to yourself?"

Colin held up a pinky, his eyes not straying from the road.
"Promise."

She hooked her finger in his.

Neither of them let go.

Chapter 19

Silence settled over the car as the clock crept past midnight.

Allison and Colin had exchanged small talk for a while but now they were both watching the darkness skim by. A show tunes playlist hummed softly in the background.

Allison stared down at their hands. Their pinkies were still interlocked. She had no idea what it meant, but she knew she didn't want to let go. In some ways, his hand felt like the only thing keeping her in this moment.

Her finger tightened around his. In less than an hour, she'd be at the hospital. What was she supposed to do? To say? Of course, she hadn't hesitated to come when her mother told her what happened, but her feelings toward Jed hadn't changed. He was a lousy father and he'd been awful to Allison for too long. She didn't want him in her life right now. But she didn't wish him dead either.

It was an impossible situation. Maybe that was why Allison found herself adjusting her hand so not only her pinky, but all her fingers nestled into the crooks between Colin's. His skin was always cool, but somehow it warmed her as their palms pressed together.

She saw the surprised twitch of his head toward her, but she kept her eyes glued to the road.

"You doing okay?" he asked softly.

"I think the donuts and water helped."

"I didn't mean physically."

Allison exhaled, letting the air hiss between her teeth. "No, I'm not okay."

"Want to talk about it?" He gave her hand a squeeze.

"I don't know what to say."

"Don't think. Just let loose whatever's on your mind. That's what my therapist has me do when I'm feeling super emotional."

"You see a shrink?" As usual, the words had more control over her mouth than Allison did.

Colin snorted. "Jack would say that he does not have the right degrees to properly be called a 'shrink,' but yes. I started seeing him this summer after Granddad's dementia got bad enough that we had to move him to a facility."

"Dementia?" Had this been what he'd meant when he said his grandfather was getting old? Allison's heart dropped. "I'm so sorry."

Colin's smile was sad. "He got the diagnosis years ago, but for so long it was mild. Sometimes he couldn't think of the right word for something or he'd forget what he'd done an hour ago, things like that. Even the first year I lived with him after graduation, it wasn't too bad. I had to keep more of an eye on him at night because the confusion often set in after dinner. Sundown syndrome, they call it." He sniffed and blinked hard. "But last winter, things declined fast. That's when we knew he couldn't live at home anymore."

Allison rested her free hand over Colin's knuckles. The gesture seemed more helpful than any words she could think of.

"He doesn't always know who I am. But he never forgets the books. He says at least one lucid thing about the medieval period every time I see him." A small smile struggled across Colin's mouth. "The nurses say it's the visits, they help, so my aunt, my mom, and I try to make sure one of us goes to see him every day."

Allison tightened her grip on his hand. "I'm sure even on the bad days, somewhere inside him, he knows you're there."

"Maybe. Dementia can eat away at a person until nothing of them is left." Colin worked his mouth, up and down, up and down, as if the tension made it ache. Or maybe it was the words that came out of his mouth next. "Sometimes I wonder if I'm doing it more for me than for him."

"What do you mean?"

Colin squinted at the road. His eyes shined a little too glossy behind his glasses, and he used his knee to steer for a quick moment as he swiped at them with his knuckle. Allison loosened her fingers in case he wanted to let go, but he only reaffirmed his grip, pulling their clasped hands into his lap as if to protect them.

"For the guilt, you know? So, when he's gone, I can feel better knowing I went to see him, even if it didn't do anything for him at all."

The words pierced Allison. Too real. Too true. Like hearing your native language spoken amid a sea of foreign words.

Was that what this trip was about for her, too? Was she trying to assuage her own guilt? Because not seeing her father when he was this ill would be awful. Right? Her mother would certainly think so. And Allison didn't want to be perceived as awful. Nor did she wish to feel that way about herself.

How selfish was *that*?

"I get that. Too much."

For a second, she considered having Colin turn the car around. But she swallowed back the urge. It was late, and they were both exhausted, and having him drive her all this way for nothing seemed unfair.

She smoothed the hem of her dress against her knees. She should have changed before she left. Or packed a bag. Who knew what kind of rejected outfits she had waiting for her at her mom's house.

"Yeah?" Colin's thumb drew down the heel of Allison's palm so gently her body trilled.

"That's probably exactly why we're in this car right now. Guilt. Because I don't want to be that person who doesn't go visit their sick father." Allison dropped her head back against the headrest. "But if I'm being honest, he doesn't deserve this. He doesn't deserve me leaving my own party, or rushing four hours to his side in the middle of the night, or me having to ask my friend to drive me because I'm too drunk from said party—"

"Your friend?" It came out like a croak. As if that was the last word he'd expected to hear from her lips.

Allison glanced at their hands, still clutched in his lap. "Are we not friends?"

"I hope we are." He gave her a small smile, encouraging her to go on.

"A few weeks ago, I emailed my father and told him I didn't want him in my life right now."

"Wow. That's intense."

"Yeah. And my feelings on that haven't changed."

Colin chewed on his bottom lip for a moment. "I remember you telling me back at Brown that he was pretty terrible."

Allison nodded. "After he moved out, he disappeared from my life. Now and then, he'd pop up with a phone call or an email or an occasional holiday visit and, every time, he'd do something upsetting. In the last email I got from him, he said he needed to know if I was coming for Thanksgiving now so he could properly shop since . . . and I quote, 'We know you have a hearty appetite.'"

"Are you fucking kidding me?" The car swerved a little.

Allison grabbed the armrest. "Nope. That was what prompted my decision to cut him out of my life. I like who I am, and I like how I look, and I don't need that shit. Mom wasn't too happy about it, which is what that call was about, the other day at the library."

Colin bobbed his head, putting the pieces together.

"She laid all this guilt on me. So, is that why I ran off tonight? To make *her* happy? To make the guilt go away? I don't want him dead, obviously, but I don't really want him in my life either, heart attack or not, so what am I doing?"

The squeeze of Colin's hand comforted like a hug. Allison wanted to fold into its embrace. "You're doing the best you can."

"I guess." Allison closed her eyes, willing her mind vacant.

If only there were a fast-forward button for life, so she could rush past these next few days and all their unknowns. Would Jed live? What would he say to her when he woke up? How pissed would her mother be? How would Allison react? What would all this change, if anything? Right now, her life felt like an episode of a TV show you hate but have to endure to enjoy the better ones. Or better yet, those opening pages of *The Fellowship of the Ring* that review hobbit lineage ad nauseam.

But to hurry past this was to sprint through whatever was happening in Colin's car. It would mean erasing the tingle that burst through Allison's skin with each movement of his fingers against hers. She wouldn't get to feel that soaring sensation as her heart leaped in her chest at his stolen glances. She'd miss the slight tremor in his hand against hers.

Allison wanted all that. Not only to experience it, but to *relish* it. She wanted to swim in these feelings like a pool of gold.

Though a few hours ago he would have been her last choice, she was glad Colin was the one driving her to Maine. Not simply because it was the right thing to do, or because he wasn't a monster, as he'd claimed. She wanted it to be him because something had persisted between them. Something a bad breakup and two years of silence hadn't been able to erase. Something Allison hadn't been able to shake all this time, no matter how much she tried.

Lost in a fog of grief and fear, she no longer had the energy to lie to herself.

Colin Benjamin wasn't her nemesis. He wasn't her rival. He wasn't even her friend.

He was something more.

Either the Bud Lights hadn't entirely left Allison's system or she was more emotionally exhausted than she'd realized, because closing her eyes to think had rapidly resulted in her passing out until Colin gently tapped her elbow what felt like seconds (but turned out to be about forty minutes) later.

Allison blinked awake to find herself staring at her childhood home. Even in the dark, the cornflower-blue door shined like a beacon beneath the outdoor lamp.

Everything about the house was big but aging. Its natural wood shingles had been faded to gray by the ocean water that slapped against the coastline a few blocks away, and the sprawling white deck where Allison would sit outside and read all summer from sunup until the mosquitos swarmed at dusk was chipped and crooked.

Her heart swelled. Her house was a welcome sight: familiar, well-worn, that place where she would always be safe.

It took Colin three jokes about her sleeping—apparently, she sounded like a zombie with a deviated septum—and three attempts at attaching Monty's leash as he lazily rolled around on his back, before they got him in the house. After settling the puppy in Allison's old room and checking on Cleo, they'd rushed the last few miles to the hospital.

Now they sat in the Honda outside the visitor's entrance to Northern Light, the idling engine a low growl against the cold night air.

Though she should be thinking only about hurrying to Jed's side, her mind was muddled with a million other thoughts. Like how Colin managed, bleary-eyed and sans hair gel, to still look so good. The harsh light thrown by the security lamps beside the front doors cut his already angular face into sharp relief, making his cheekbones and jaw seem to be etched out of smooth, pale stone. Freckles she'd forgotten about dotted his brow and trailed from underneath the glasses perched on his pin-straight nose. Where sometimes his frame appeared knobby and awkward, the moonlight and the darkness (and probably Allison's hormones and lingering buzz) painted him as elegant, refined, a stoic elven figure striding out of a fantasy wood to inhabit the car.

There were so many things she should be saying to him. Like *Thank you for the ride,* or *I appreciate you doing this for me,* or *Are you going to be okay to get back to Providence?*

But all she could think about was him with his grandfather (in Allison's head they were both in oversized cardigans under smoking jackets, sitting beside a blazing fireplace, satin slippers adorning their feet as Ned, the armored knight, stood sentinel) arguing about her favorite texts. Every time, her heart lost its way. Battered right out of her chest.

She stared quietly at him, wondering what would make him take her hand again. As if her silence could keep them frozen here, stop time from marching forward.

Colin broke that spell. "Do you want me to come with you?"

The Colin Benjamin she'd once known would never have made such an offer, and she nearly took him up on it. But instead she shook her head. "I'll be okay. Mom's here." She wrung her hands in her lap to stop thinking about holding his. He needed to go home and get back to his life, and she needed distance to remember why he was a thorn in her side, not a rose in her hand. No longer denying her feelings toward him didn't change the fact that he was still a threat to Wendy's advisee position and the spot on her research trip.

"Do you want me to wait? Give you a ride home?"

"Colin." Allison held his gaze. "You've done enough. Thank you. Get yourself home. Or you can crash at my mom's if you're too tired?" She started to fumble in her pocket for the keys.

He shook his head. "I'm fine." He placed his hand over hers to still her movements. "But I want to make sure you are too."

I'm not, Allison thought to herself. "I am," she said out loud.

He picked up her phone from where it lay on the dashboard. "You have my number, right? You didn't delete it?"

"I do."

"Are you sure? I don't see it?" His finger scrolled over the screen. Allison needed to put a security code on that thing.

"Try . . . Unknown Number." Her cheeks found heat in the cold night air.

His brow furrowed, Colin kept searching, then abruptly stopped. And barked out one of those amazingly unattractive laughs.

She shrugged. "You can change it if you want."

"No way." He tossed her a wide grin, a hint of mischief playing at its edges. Its roguishness did unmentionable things to her insides. "This is way better. The anonymity is ironically more personal."

"Give me that." She went to snatch the phone from his hands, but instead her fingers closed around his, the silicon case pressed like a chaperone between their palms.

This touch felt different than earlier. His skin had an unexpected warmth, like his fingers and knuckles were blushing, and his pulse skipped beneath her thumb where it settled on the inside of his wrist. Allison's entire body thrummed in time with it.

They were both leaning in, squaring off the way they always did, but the energy between them was charged with something new. Less sharp and more . . . wild . . . his breath hot on her cold cheeks, her long hair dusting the skin of his forearm.

Allison needed to get out of this car, or take her phone away, or at least sit back against the seat, but he was like a laser beam from one of those old sci-fi books, and she was caught in him, unable to move, to think, to do anything except be this close.

His hazel eyes swept over her face, keen as ever, cataloging every blink, every twitch, every deep inhale. She smelled like old beer and had bags under her eyes and stale donut on her breath, and yet none of that stopped his tongue slipping from his mouth to moisten his lips.

They were sitting outside a hospital. Jed was in there unconscious, his heart failing. Her mother was waiting for her. Yet Allison was entirely preoccupied by Colin's mouth. She was horrible. Maybe he was her punishment for being the worst daughter at the most inopportune moment.

After far too much mental and physical effort, she detached her phone from his hands and pushed open the car door. The frigid air was a balm to her hot flesh. "I should go. Thank you again." She meant it, even if it was all she could give him.

Before she pulled herself from the vehicle, Colin said her name. His voice hitched, tender and graveled, like he was speaking a spell or a sacred word. No one else said it that way, transforming three syllables into something worthy of reverence. Something special.

As if *she* were something special.

Every part of Allison stuttered.

For someone who could often barely function without considering (and planning for) every worst-case scenario, she could also be oddly impulsive.

Which explained why, instead of getting out of the car, instead of calling her mother to let her know she'd arrived, instead of waving, clearing her throat, having any kind of mundane, rational response, Allison cupped Colin's cheek in her hand. His stubble scraped against her palm as he turned his face into it to press a light kiss to her skin.

"Colin?" Her voice had gone husky, her throat full of sandpaper. Was she really doing this? Right here? Right now? With her father in the hospital and her mother waiting for her? With everything she already knew about Colin Benjamin and his tendency to crack her heart in two? What if she didn't survive it this time? What if it ruined all her plans for herself?

Colin took her hand in his and gently exposed her inner wrist. His head dipped low. Allison shuddered as his lips met the tiny crescent scar beside her paths of veins. His mouth was everything soft, so light against that sensitive patch of skin it was hard to be sure it was real.

When he lifted his head to peer at her, his gaze was full of fire. It ignited something in Allison too.

The two of them crashed together.

It had been over two years since the last time Allison had kissed Colin, and every one of those moments was tainted by the way things had ended between them. And yet, she'd expected this first kiss to be familiar. Like an old book she hadn't read in a while, the story returning as she followed it again.

Instead, their kiss had the electricity of something new and surprising, and a little bit forbidden. His mouth was hungry and urgent on hers, his hands tangled in her loose waves. The collar of his T-shirt was balled in Allison's fist. If only he'd get closer, press himself against her. He tasted like powdered donut and smelled of coffee and hair gel, and it was like kissing a stranger Allison had been dreaming about for too long.

She pulled away, breathing raggedly. Her heart pounded. Her lungs begged for air.

Colin's mouth moved silently for a moment before her name left his lips.

"I have to go," she replied.

Then she threw herself from the car and slammed the door before she could add another to the pile of mistakes she'd made tonight.

Chapter 20

Allison found hospitals unsettling enough by day. In the middle of the night, they bordered on creepy.

A chill snuck up her spine as she maneuvered her way through empty, antiseptic hallways toward the ICU. Nurses smiled somberly behind surgical masks as she passed, and Allison almost reached into her purse for her own out of habit. (Since the pandemic, everyone she knew carried one with them just in case, like a scar lingering behind from those awful years.)

At the sterile-white doors to the intensive-care unit, Allison gave her name over the speaker and waited to be let in.

A buzzer cawed like the one on her washer and dryer back in Providence, and the doors swung open. Inside, the lights were bright, shining like spotlights on the square, white nurses' station at the center of the room. All around the periphery, darkened rooms hid behind glass sliding doors dressed with clipboards and white lettering. Machines beeped from every corner, an electronic symphony, and as the doors eased shut behind Allison, an alarm screamed from a nearby room. She jumped to the side as a grave-faced nurse rushed by.

A thirty-something blond woman sitting behind the desk glanced up with tired eyes. "Who are you looking for?"

"My father."

The woman's mouth tightened, but her voice remained calm. "Name?"

"Allison."

A loud breath left the woman's lips, and she stood up, her eyes closed. "Your father's name, honey."

Allison's hands shook at her sides, and she gripped the strap of her purse to steady herself. Under this woman's no-nonsense gaze, she felt small and childish, like a five-year-old lost somewhere she didn't belong.

"Jed. Jed Avery," she stuttered.

The nurse smiled. "You're Cassandra's daughter. I should have known. You two could be twins."

Allison twisted her mouth into something vaguely friendly.

"Second door to the right."

Thanking her, Allison took a hesitant step forward. Suddenly, she wished the nurse had been more interested in talking. Anything to give Allison time to determine how to handle whatever came next.

But after five slow steps, she was standing in front of the glass door. Through its thick cream curtain, she spotted a prostrate form on the bed and the silhouette of someone in a chair beside it that could only be her mother.

The glass swooshed open, sensing her presence, and she forced herself to walk in.

Though average-sized in height and weight, Jed and his uninvited opinions had always taken up so much space in Allison's life that he'd seemed extra-large. But in that hospital bed, with its white sheets and flat pillow, monitors flanking his shoulders and wires crawling across and beneath the sheets, his face pale, his mouth slack around a breathing tube, he looked powerless. Decrepit. Feeble. Incapable of the pain he'd caused Allison over the years.

A sob lurched from her mouth.

Her mom was cradling one of Jed's hands in both of hers, her head ducked over his fingers. At the wretched sound Allison made, her gaze jerked toward her daughter.

"You're here." She set Jed's hand against the sheet gently, as if this man, who had been so cruel to them both, were suddenly wrought of thin, fragile glass. Allison fought the urge to throw something and watch him shatter into pieces.

For the hundredth time since she'd gotten in Colin's car, she wondered what she was doing here.

Her mother folded her into a hug, pressing her daughter's head to her shoulder. "I'm glad you came," she whispered, "even if you smell like you've been swimming in a keg."

How many showers and gallons of perfume would Allison need to wash the shame of those Bud Lights from her skin? "We were having a party."

Her mom held her at arm's length. "You didn't drive here, did you?"

"I got a ride."

"Of course. Of course." She set her arm around Allison's shoulder. Her free hand smoothed a few of her flyaway waves. "You've always been a smart girl."

If, at the nurse's station, Allison had felt childish and small in all the wrong ways, now it seemed right. With her mother's arm around her, it was okay to be afraid. To not know what to do or how to feel or what came next. Her mom would take care of all that. She always did, no matter how old Allison was. You were never truly an adult when your mom was around.

Allison's eyes strayed back to her father's bed. "How's he . . . I mean, what's happening?"

"He was awake a little while ago but his heart rate was outrageously high." Her mother nodded toward a monitor above the left side of his bed. "They put him out while they try to get his rhythm steady."

The green numbers on the monitor pulsed: *140, 142, 139.*

"What's his heart rate supposed to be?" It felt like one of those things Allison was supposed to know now that she wasn't a kid anymore, like a normal blood pressure, or her blood type, or what to do when one of your parents was sick.

"Between sixty and a hundred when resting. It was almost two hundred when they brought him in."

"Oh my god."

Her mom kissed her temple. "I know."

"It's better then?" She gestured at the monitor. *142, 141, 141, 140, 142.*

"Better, yes, but still not good."

142, 143, 140.

"What are they doing to fix it?" Allison was surprised by the ferocity of her own question. She hadn't thought she cared enough to know. Sick or not, Jed was still Jed. But standing here in front of him, watching one machine track his irregular heartbeat while another monitored his oxygen levels, and needles pumped medicine and fluids into his veins, she found herself desperate for the details.

"They've tried some meds. Tomorrow they might have to shock it into rhythm—"

"Like with those paddles on TV shows?"

Her mother nodded.

Allison's hand pressed to her mouth. "Oh my god."

"It's more routine than it sounds." She squeezed Allison a little closer.

"And if that doesn't work?"

"They have more invasive things they can try."

That word rolled around her brain. *Invasive.* Intrusive. Dangerous. What if they had to cut him open? How was she supposed to handle that in this weird emotional purgatory she'd been cast into? Where was Virgil to guide her way?

"Oh sweetie." Her mother pulled Allison more snuggly to her side.

"There's nothing we can do at this point except be here. Doctor Friedman seems optimistic the shock will work."

"And until then?"

Her mom mussed Allison's hair and straightened the shoulders of her dress. "Until then, I'll leave you with your father for a quick minute and then we'll get you home. You look exhausted."

"I just got here."

"And you'll be close if he needs you. But there's not much to be done at almost two in the morning while he's knocked out."

With a final kiss to Allison's temple, her mother ducked out of the room, abandoning her daughter to a quiet broken only by the steady hum of machines.

Allison's eyes shifted to her father and the wires and tubes tracing up and around his body. Somehow, attached to someone she knew, the equipment looked alien and threatening. Her fingers itched to tear at the wires and break the monitors.

Instead, she held herself perfectly still. Refusing to blink, she let her mind map her father in that bed, bearing witness to his illness. Preparing for whatever happened next. Though her tongue was heavy with words, none of them were meant to be whispered in the dark. They were words for screaming throats raw, for being muddled by tears. They demanded to be heard, to be taken in, to be reckoned with. When Allison finally spoke, Jed would be fully conscious.

Which was why, when her mother returned ten minutes later, Allison had still not said a thing.

"Promise me you'll sleep when you get home," her mom said, patting Allison's hand, hooked in the crook of her elbow.

Now that the anticipation of seeing Jed had passed, exhaustion had slammed into her. "That is a promise I can keep," she mumbled through a yawn.

They exited the elevator onto the main floor, their steps in tandem, the way their lives had always been. Though Allison hadn't lived at home regularly in almost five years, they were still a team, a unit, the two of them permanently intertwined.

The hallway leading to the lobby was dim and empty, their foot-steps' echoes hammering the silence.

"After I drop you off, I'm going to head back here. I'll call you if anything changes, but his heart rate is slowing enough that I think he is out of the most dangerous territory."

Allison nodded. Relief, regret, and apathy had formed a painful knot in her chest. Her mother would expect her to return to the hospi-tal in a few hours, and on Sunday and Monday too, playing the dutiful daughter. But if Jed was going to be fine, then Allison was ready to leave. She couldn't pretend the last twenty-three years of her life hadn't happened because Jed's heart had decided to briefly malfunction.

The café and gift shop came into view as they rounded the corner, metal grates blocking the entrances. Across the way marched rows and rows of beige chairs flanked by coffee vending machines and end tables balancing stacks of magazines waiting for a new round of people to distract.

Only one wasn't vacant, the occupant slouched near the exit with a cell phone angled close to his face. Its blue light painted the maroon frames of his glasses a searing red, and his knobby ankle, crossed over an equally knobby knee to expose a pair of white, cat-print socks, bounced nervously.

Allison's heart froze. She'd been upstairs with her mother for at least an hour. Why was he still here? "Colin?"

In a blur, he was on his feet. "Hey."

"What are you doing here?"

He smiled sheepishly. "I wanted to see how your father was."

"I told you I'd let you know—"

He raised a finger to quiet her. "That's the thing, you actually didn't. You dove from the car"—he smacked his lips nervously, his gaze hopping to her mom at Allison's shoulder—"after . . . you know . . . we got here."

Thankfully, he didn't mention their kiss. Obviously, it had been nothing but a knee-jerk response to a lethal combination of acute stress and too many bad beers, and Allison lacked the mental fortitude to explain that to her mother right now.

Her mother. She spun around. "Mom, you remember—"

Her hand was already reaching for Colin's. "Cody!"

"Colin."

"Right. Glasses boy."

Allison shook her head. "Sure."

She arched an eyebrow in apology, but Colin was too focused on her mother to notice. "I'll happily answer to any and all of that."

"Then I'm henceforth calling you Cody," Allison declared.

He waved a hand. "Only your mom gets to give me pet names."

Did it count as murder if a person was stabbed in a hospital? They'd probably save him in time, right? Allison considered doing a quick WCS for ending Colin right here in the lobby of Northern Light, but her mother interrupted her list.

"Is this your ride?"

"Yup."

"I didn't know you two were in contact again." She was addressing Allison, but still held Colin's hand. Apparently, this was some sort of quirk with Avery women.

"Colin's in my program at Claymore."

Amusement flooded her mother's face. "How serendipitous."

"How indeed," Allison muttered.

Colin's gaze snagged hers. "Do you have a way home? I could drop you off." Having finally extracted himself from her mother, he rested a shoulder against the doorway, his frame loose and relaxed in that way that made Allison's heart dance against her will.

Damn him and his leaning to the ninth ring of hell.

"What a gentleman." Her mom smiled. "This saves me a ride."

"Perfect." Colin straightened and stepped to Allison's side. "I can drop you off, then head home myself."

Her mother balked. "Where's home?"

"Outside Providence."

"Nope." She shook her head. "You're not driving four hours at two in the morning. I'm sure Allison will appreciate the company, since I'll mostly be here."

Allison ignored the implications of this invitation to focus on her mother. "What about work?"

"It's my weekend off." Her mom's wide smile couldn't conceal the lie. Weekends promised the best tips, and she needed the money. She never took off a weekend.

"I'll visit him tomorrow, Ma. You go to work." The words burned as they fell from Allison's lips.

Her mother swallowed her in a hug. "How about if you go to sleep for now and we'll fight about this in the morning?"

Conceding was only a step away from acquiescence but Allison was too tired. "Fine," she muttered.

With one more tight hug, her mom headed back toward the elevator, calling over her shoulder about extra bedding in the closet and English muffins in the freezer.

Which left Allison alone to face the idea of Colin in her house. Overnight. After they'd just kissed.

Suddenly, Jed was no longer the only one with a racing heart.

Chapter 21

The night Allison first had sex with Colin could have been ripped from the pages of a movie script.

There were rose petals and soft candlelight and a fancy hotel room in Newport and they'd been in their formal wear after a posh Christmas party thrown by the father of one of Colin's roommates.

The hotel's balcony overlooked the ocean, and Allison could still remember the feel of the winter air pinching her cheeks and slicing across her bare shoulders as she stared out at the shoreline, smeared silver with moonlight, and the white-frothed waves dancing beyond it.

When Colin had joined her outside, he rested his back against the glass door and pulled her close, his mouth angling over hers. His hands grasped Allison's waist, his leg nudging hers apart, while she clutched at the ends of his unwound tie to draw him in. For what felt like ages, they'd remained on the small balcony, each kiss longer and deeper, each touch more urgent.

They took their time that night, learning each other's bodies slowly and thoroughly. Allison hadn't been a virgin, but when Colin kissed her out of her dress, sliding his mouth down every inch of her body until she lay before him in nothing but her red silk panties and the heat tinting her cheeks a similar shade, when he pulled those panties down and settled his mouth between her legs, it had been a first for her.

Allison rubbed at her temples with the heel of her hands, trying to chase the memory off. Ever since she'd kissed Colin outside the hospital, she couldn't stop thinking about all the other times they'd kissed. And everything else they'd done.

And what that might feel like now, after all this time.

This was so bad. She was in her childhood home. Her estranged father was in the hospital. It was late. She should be going to bed, not sitting in her living room thinking about sex with Colin. He was the guy who'd broken her heart. Who'd once almost upended her academic plans. And who now stood in the way of everything she wanted all over again. The last thing she needed to do was sleep with him.

What had happened in his car was a fluke. End of story.

Allison cast her gaze around for a distraction. Something to clear her head. On the bottom shelf of the coffee table, under some old photo albums and her mother's endless stacks of crossword puzzles, the box of her old Scrabble game peeked out.

Perfect. A way to occupy her mind *and* kick Colin's ass. A twofer.

He was sitting on the floor in front of the couch, still wiping his face from the exuberant welcome he'd received from Monty and Cleo. Allison dropped the box in front of him, the tiles inside rattling.

He arched an eyebrow. "I'm not sure Scrabble is a three-o'clock-in-the-morning game."

"Scrabble is an all-the-time game." Allison grinned. "Unless you're afraid I'll win."

"I fear nothing." He removed the box top and set it aside with care, as if the split corners might cause the cardboard to disintegrate.

Settling across from him, Allison began to shake the lettered tiles out of their velvet pouch while Colin got out the board and the tile holders. One of his knees was bent to cradle his elbow, his other long leg stretched out. The toes of his white cat socks wiggled in the periphery of Allison's vision.

She nodded at his foot. "Did you ever get that cat?"

"Huh?"

"You always used to say the first thing you were going to do after graduation was get a cat. Preferably an orange one."

His hand stopped fiddling with the tile holder as he looked up at her. There was something delicate in his gaze that made Allison's heart flutter. "I can't believe you remember that."

She remembered everything, as if their entire history had been carved into her bones.

She shrugged. "I thought it was cute."

"Thought?"

She rolled her eyes.

"His name's Captain Pepper Jack." Colin tugged his phone from his pocket.

"Excuse me?"

Fussing at the screen with his index finger, he turned it her way, revealing a photo of a tubby orange tabby with one eye sewn closed. "I stopped by a shelter right after graduation and adopted him."

"You did?" Allison didn't know why she was whispering. Or why her body suddenly felt so disjointed.

"It was the only good decision I made that semester."

His voice was too soft, and his words too full of meaning. Allison focused on alphabetizing her tiles. "So, Captain Jack, huh?"

"Allison—"

No. She refused to hear whatever had caused his voice catch that way, whatever had summoned the slight tremble to his fingers. "Is that for the one eye?" She switched the *G* and *I* in her row of letters. She suddenly couldn't seem to recall which came first.

A few of Colin's tiles clacked, and he sighed, but when he answered, most of the heaviness had left his voice. "Captain for the one eye. Pepper Jack because it's the best cheese."

Her gaze flew to his face. In college, half their relationship had revolved around arguing over what to eat because Colin couldn't consume dairy and Allison perpetually craved pizza and grilled cheese. "You're lactose intolerant. You despise cheese."

"I have since discovered Lactaid, the ambrosia of the gods."

She took in this fact, clinging to it hard. It was easier to digest than everything they'd purposely *not* said a moment ago. Or, more aptly, that she wouldn't let him say. "I don't know if you've been a true cheese lover long enough to be naming pets after it. You're practically an amateur."

He laughed. "I'm honestly surprised you *haven't* named a pet after a cheese."

She flourished a hand at the puppy snoozing on the couch behind him. "Meet Monterey Jack."

He glanced over at Monty. "Ah, yes, the second-best Jack."

He was goading her. Allison jabbed her finger against the star at the center of the board. "Stop procrastinating. Let's commence with this linguistic massacre." She shot him her most cutthroat grin. "I'll even let you go first."

Shaking his head, Colin tapped at his glasses as he studied his tiles. He kept the rack close to his body, like he thought Allison might cheat.

As if she'd need to.

After what felt like three years, he chose some letters, then placed each one on the board with a methodical precision that made Allison twitch.

R
E
G
R
E
T
S

Sixteen points. Plus fifty more for using all his tiles. She wanted to comment on his need to show off, but her heart was racing too hard.

Allison concentrated on her own breathing (in and out, in and out) as she positioned her letters horizontally from his *T.*

O
U
G
H

It was the best combination given how he'd started the board, and a double-word space brought her to eighteen points. But now it looked like some kind of response to a question he might or might not have been asking. She watched him study his tiles, her body ticking like a clock.

He was so focused on creating a word that it was impossible to read anything else in his face. Their breaths (and the dogs' snores) were the only sounds in the room. Allison had to shove her hands under her legs to hide their shaking as Colin picked up a few tiles, only to rearrange them on the holder.

She let her eyes sink closed and tried to recalibrate. They were playing a game, not passing clandestine messages like members of the Knights Templar. Still, she couldn't help but feel that whatever he placed down on that board next would change everything.

Anticipation rocketed through her, buzzing in her veins as he reached forward with his letters.

L
E
A
R

Allison's stomach dropped, and her eyes burned from staring at the ivory-colored tiles. Of course he wasn't using Scrabble to confess his feelings. Nothing that had happened tonight proved anything except that Colin Benjamin had become a better person over the last few years.

Reaching deep into herself, Allison recaptured her competitive spirit and shook her head at him. "L-E-A-R is not a word."

"Sure, it is. It's a look you give someone." He cocked an eyebrow and hitched up one corner of his mouth. "Like this."

She rolled her eyes, giving the gesture an extra dose of derision. "That's L-E-*E*-R."

"Oh. Right." Colin crossed his arms. His teeth fussed with his bottom lip, and it took everything in Allison not to remember how his mouth had felt on hers earlier. "Obviously, I meant Lear, as in King Lear."

"Nope. Even if you weren't lying, there are no proper nouns in Scrabble."

"Not even for the Bard himself?"

"Not even for him."

Colin gaped at her. "What kind of lit student are you?"

"The kind that knows the real rules for Scrabble." One by one, Allison lined her thumb and index finger up behind the last three letters and flicked them at him. "Try. It. Again." It was satisfying to bombard him with something, the same way he'd inadvertently overwhelmed her with feelings.

The first two tiles landed in his lap, perfectly aimed. The *A,* however, flew wild and bounced off the corner of his chin.

He yelped in surprise, his hand cupping his face.

"Shit." Believe it or not, Allison hadn't meant to do that.

He grimaced. "Next time we play this game, I'm wearing armor."

"I guess I'm still a little competitive."

"Try a lot," he mumbled.

Allison couldn't deny it. She didn't even try. "I'm sorry. That seems to be my default setting for dealing with you." Reaching across the board, she brushed her fingers across his jaw. It wasn't bleeding or anything (not that she could have done much if it was); she just . . . wanted to touch him. And didn't think to stop herself. The tickle of his stubble against the pad of her index finger sent a thrill up her spine.

He held incredibly still, like Allison's hand was a butterfly that might flee if he moved. Neither of them breathed for a full minute.

When Allison pulled her hand back to her lap, the air around them was thick and charged, like those heady seconds before a lightning storm.

"I'll try again." This time, he gathered three tiles, cradling them in his palm as if they were precious. With a deliberateness that belied his always fiddling fingers, Colin ordered them along the board.

Each plastic piece clicked sharply, sending a jolt through Allison's heart.

K
I
S
S

Chapter 22

Not everyone would look at Colin Benjamin and swoon.

He was tall and lanky and full of sharp angles like an isosceles triangle, and he wore nerdy shirts and ill-fitting cardigan sweaters and spent an awful lot of time coifing his hair so that it lay perfectly. But from the moment Allison had (mortifyingly) pressed her ass into him at that party she'd been mesmerized by his long, trim muscles and the sharpness to his face that made him resemble some kind of Fae prince.

She stared at that face now as her heart slammed against her chest. In her hand, she rolled a *Y* tile and an *S* tile round and round.

They'd already kissed tonight, but using those letters to spell out *yes* felt much more definitive. A choice rather than a whim. Allison's pulse sang in her ears, and her skin had gone clammy, but none of that stopped her from putting the pieces down.

With each movement, she mirrored Colin's careful precision from earlier, as she laid down her own tiles now.

Y
E
S

She meant every letter of it.

The tiles flew across the carpet as Colin scattered the board. He moved toward her on his knees, stopping just shy of physical contact. Then he hovered over her, his hands braced to the floor so close Allison could practically feel them on her skin. Though he said nothing, the look on his face was as expressive as any poetry.

He wanted this. He wanted *her*.

Her whole life, Allison had been a collector of words. Her freshman year in high school, she'd started a word wall, where she papered every spare inch of space in her bedroom with sticky notes displaying the new terms she discovered as she read. To this day, when she wrote papers, she'd craft every sentence, revising it one, two, three times before moving on, certain the perfect combination of words existed to manifest her ideas on the page.

But as Allison and Colin drank each other in, neither moving except for the rise and fall of their chests, the world gone silent around them, she realized some words had meanings that defied articulation. Ache, she knew now, was a sensation, one that mere letters or strings of phrases could never adequately encapsulate.

It swelled in her chest until it might crack her open. Until she couldn't swallow back the small moan of relief as Colin mercifully closed the space between them, his mouth pressing to hers.

Allison bunched the sides of his cardigan in her hands and pulled him toward her, its buttons digging into her palm. His lips were soft and yielding, and they still held some of the sweetness from the donuts they'd polished off earlier. As her mouth opened to his, Colin's smell filled her senses, smothering everything around them so there was only him, him, him.

When they pulled apart, it was with ragged breaths. Desire shook Allison's frame like a shot of adrenaline, and the space between them, barely the length of her arms, felt cavernous.

"What are we doing?"

His question was a snowstorm in July, a shock to Allison's system. She didn't want to talk or have to make sense of this. She wasn't sure she could. If she pushed too hard, asked too many questions, the night was likely to crumble to dust in her hands.

She climbed to her feet and strode to the couch the dogs had not yet commandeered, putting some distance between them.

"I don't know. Why are you here?" she asked. "Why did you drive me home?"

If anything was to blame for what was happening, it was all that uninterrupted time in the car. All those windows into him that had been thrown open, forcing her to confront the new sides of Colin Benjamin she'd been trying hard to ignore all these weeks. If he was the same old Colin, it made sense to resist these . . . *things* . . . she was feeling. But if he'd changed . . . what if he'd changed?

Allison shook her head, dispersing those thoughts.

He blew out a breath. "I couldn't let you go through this alone."

"Why?"

"Because . . ." His long fingers clawed through his unkempt hair, and he began to pace in front of her.

Allison wanted nothing more than to be the one combing back those silky strands. Tugging them between her fingers. She wrung her hands in her lap. "Because no one else could? Because it was the right thing to do?"

He stopped and faced her. "Because it's you." Behind his maroon-framed glasses, his gaze was firm. Certain. He knew what he was doing. What he was saying. "Allison . . ." He lowered himself onto the other end of the couch. "I think about you constantly."

Her heart lost its rhythm. She couldn't seem to stop herself from confessing, "I think about you, too."

Colin reached for her hand. "I don't mean I think about how I'm going to trounce you in class or win this mentorship or prove I'm the most medieval of medievalists." His thumb traced a line of heat up the inside of her wrist. "I think about how much I want to thread my fingers through your hair. And about every look you give me, unpacking it to see if there might be more than animosity in it. I think about the endless string of brilliant things you say, and about how it used to feel to hold you, to kiss you, to do *this*"—he lifted their hands—"and how I fucked that all up. And more than anything else, I think about how much I lost when I broke up with you. How much more I would gain if we found a way back to each other now."

The couch beneath Allison was worn, full of lumps and crevices from the weekend watch-a-thons and Thursday-night reality-TV binges Allison and her mom had shared for years. To sit on it was to immediately sink down to the springs. And yet, each of Colin's words piled onto Allison until she felt herself dip lower. Until she wasn't sure she'd find her way back out.

"What do you mean?"

Colin's eyes drifted closed. "If you'd told me two years ago that you'd only be smarter and more articulate and more beautiful now, I wouldn't have thought it possible. But every day, you manage to say something that . . ." He flicked his free hand beside his temple, mimicking his mind exploding.

Allison's heart drilled against her chest. He really had been confessing his regrets on that Scrabble board. "And you want that?"

His eyes stole her gaze. "Yes."

He's not the same, she told herself. *I'm not the same. That means the outcome won't be, either.*

She was probably fooling herself. She should have created twenty-five different sets of WCS lists before ever stepping into that car with Colin tonight. But Allison was exhausted, and she wanted this badly enough not to question it.

Sliding his glasses from his face, she set them on the end table and snaked her arms around his neck. He yielded to her gentle tug, kneeling over her as she lay back against the arm of the couch.

His lips seemed to search hers. Gone was his confidence, his ego, displaced by a timid sort of wanting that made Allison bolder. It was her mouth that opened to let in a soft sweep of his tongue. It was her hands that first crawled up the back of his cardigan and the T-shirt beneath to explore the smooth skin and sharp points of his back, the small patches of hair on his stomach and chest.

When her fingers started to tease at the waistband of his jeans, he jerked back with an urgency that sent her blood pumping. His chest heaved up and down, matching the thrum at Allison's center, as he wrestled with the hem of his shirt.

He seemed to forget all about his baggy wool cardigan, trying to pull his T-shirt up by the waist, and ended up a tangled mess. With everything bunched around his head, he stumbled off the couch, knocked into the coffee table, and fell flat on his ass.

"Well, this is awkward," came his muffled voice through the layers of fabric.

Allison howled with laughter. "That was hot."

It might have been a joke, but there was a kernel of truth within it. Allison was drunk on this clumsy, vulnerable version of Colin. It felt safe to be close to him, to open up in the same way.

"A little help?" he whined.

She rose from the couch and, dragging Colin to his feet, tugged his sweater down rather than off. The dogs were still sleeping on the other couch, and if Cleo had taught Allison anything in high school, it was that dogs would inevitably participate in some coitus interruptus at precisely the wrong moment. She nodded toward the stairs. "We should probably take this elsewhere."

Colin's eyes were round and dark, his pupils dilated like a starless night. His voice was graveled and thick as he urged her to lead the way.

They barely made it to the second floor before he leaned Allison against the wall, pressing a hungry kiss to her lips. His tall, thin body curved around her, as if she were a magnetic force pulling him in, and his warm hands skimmed up the back of her legs. As they brushed against the lacy edge of her underwear, Allison angled herself more tightly against him, until she could feel his hardness press into her hip. She couldn't fight back the sigh it summoned.

Fumbling toward her old bedroom, they bumped one, then two, of her accolades off the award wall. Allison thought she heard a frame crack under Colin's foot but lust fogged her brain too heavily to care. She pulled him through the door with the *Ssshhhh Allison's Library* sign from fifth grade plastered at the center, all the while shucking his cardigan and yanking his T-shirt up and over his head.

His shoulders were pale and smooth with more freckles than Allison remembered. She ran her hands over them as if to emboss them on her palms.

Dropping onto the edge of the tiny twin mattress, Colin trailed a path of gentle kisses down her jaw as his hand slipped up her dress to skim lightly over the fabric of her bra.

Allison's heart hammered, and her body pulsed with want, but somewhere beneath all that, she was nervous. Like everything else with them, his touch felt both familiar and strange, threatening paths they'd already tread while offering brand new journeys yet to come.

He could hurt her again. But they could also become so much more than they were before, their past like a shadow shrinking in the sun.

She wanted the chance to be what she'd once pretended they were. And she wanted this. Colin's long fingers finding the most sensitive parts of her. His soft lips exploring her skin like it was a thing to be worshipped.

She leaned back to look him in the face as he eased her sweater off her arms.

"Hi," he whispered.

"Hi." The word was barely a rush of breath on her lips.

"Okay?" he asked, starting to bunch the hem of her dress in his hands. Allison nodded, no more room in her for words. The fabric was soft jersey cotton and with each inch Colin crept it up her body, her skin tingled. By the time it was a puddle on the floor, she felt seconds from exploding.

Caging his neck between her arms, she kissed him deeply as she joined him on the bed, locking her legs on either side of his hips. His fingers hooked in the lace corners of her panties, tugging at them like an obstacle he needed removed. Allison ground against him in response. She was too aware of the countless layers acting as a barrier between them. Those panties. His jeans. Whatever was beneath his jeans. Her hands dropped to his belt, fussing with the buckle.

He cupped her face and drew her mouth to his. His kiss was as slow and deep as her body's rhythm in his lap. His free hand popped the hooks on her bra, and Allison's senses heightened as the cool air touched her chest.

Her desire burned like a fever, rocketing through her body and taking control of it. The sounds of Colin's buckle falling aside and his zipper lowering were a kind of release, surging through her, reminding her of what was to come.

"Let me get a condom," he huffed as their mouths fell apart, both of them heaving breaths. They rocked together one more time, achingly slow, before Allison moved aside to let him stand. The two seconds it took him to shed his pants and retrieve the condom felt like an eternity to her lust-addled brain.

He kissed her again as he climbed back onto the bed. With his mouth open and his tongue moving across hers, his hands eased Allison's underwear from her hips. She scrambled to help him. Never had she so urgently needed to be naked, to let someone have access to all of her.

Propping himself up on one arm, he trailed a finger along the curve of her jaw, down her neck, over the slope of her breasts. Though she moaned, practically begging him to deepen the touch, his hand continued its travel, roaming across her stomach, exploring her thighs, its feathered brush never quite finding the spot between her legs, no matter how she writhed. The whole time, he held eye contact, as if he enjoyed watching her want him.

But now was not the time for teasing. Allison needed him to fill her up, to press against all the parts of her that thrummed and set them free.

She drew his face to hers, doing her best to convey this through her kiss. Their mouths danced the way their words always did, back-and-forth, back-and-forth, neither willing to relent, until Allison urged him onto his back and straddled him.

They both groaned when he was fully inside her.

His mouth found the shell of her ear as they began to move against each other, and he whispered her name in that reverent way.

Allison put a finger to his lips. If there was ever a time for Colin Benjamin to shut up, it was now.

They were chest to chest, his hands in her hair, then guiding her hips, then teasing her breasts. Every touch was a little explosion, fueling the heat that built and built at her center.

Allison's fingers dragged up his back, and she burrowed her face into his neck. They'd had sex plenty of times when they were dating, and it had always been good, but it never felt like this. Like he'd found somewhere in her she hadn't known existed.

Hugging him close, she lost herself first in the tangle of their bodies and the growls rumbling from his lips. Then to the orgasm that followed minutes later, so intense it felt as if she would break in two.

Chapter 23

Thanks to Cleo's love of squirrel watching, the blinds in Allison's childhood bedroom had a dog-shaped hole in the corner, and the morning sun blazed through it, urging her awake.

Groaning, she turned away from where her head had been pillowed against Colin's bare chest and started to rise from the mattress.

"Nooo," he moaned. His arm wrapped around her waist and coaxed her more tightly to him. "Stay." There was a sleepy rasp in his voice that warmed her center.

Allison let him hold her. At some point, they'd had the wherewithal to get dressed (Colin in his cat boxers, Allison in a baggy T-shirt and some underwear), but with his warm breath dancing through her messy hair and his fingers burrowing beneath her shirt to stroke her stomach, she felt every bit as close to him as she had during sex.

Ever since she'd lost her virginity in high school, sex had been one of those things that made Allison feel too *in* her body. No matter how much she loved herself, it was hard to chase off worries about her size when someone's hands and mouth were all over her, or when she remembered how rare it was to see a shape like hers viewed as beautiful or attractive. Was he comparing her to thinner girls? Did her waist, her ass, her chest feel wrong in his hands? Was she not enough? Too much? Sometimes, those thoughts grew so big they crowded her head, making climaxing impossible.

Yet with Colin, in this bed, as the sun had crept over the horizon, there'd been only him and her, and the feel of being tangled up in each other again. Letting go had been as easy, as natural, as breathing.

His lips brushed her shoulder with a softness that sent a shiver through Allison's limbs. "I'm glad last night wasn't a dream."

Her heart fluttered. "Me, too."

Gentle fingers tucked her waves behind her ear as Colin's mouth traced a path up her neck to her lips. They'd just sunk into a slow, deep kiss when Monty let out a bark from the floor below.

With a pained sigh, Allison broke off their embrace and slid out of the bed. So much for round two.

Colin rose to join her, but she waved him back down. "I'm going to let the dogs out." She threw the blanket over his head. It was barely eight in the morning. No sense in them both losing out on more sleep.

On her way out the door, Allison grabbed Colin's cardigan from the floor and shrugged it on. Maine was too damn cold until the sun found its proper place in the sky. Mumbling obscenities, she pulled the edges of the sweater tightly across her chest and tucked her hands into the too-long cuffs. Somehow, the brown and tan knit had absorbed the smell of his hair gel, and Allison inhaled deeply.

The dogs' excited greetings were cut short the moment she opened the door to the backyard. In an instant, Cleo was on the lawn doing her business, Monty zooming in circles around her.

Allison poured herself a glass of orange juice and, grabbing her phone, settled down at the breakfast bar. Under a bunch of mailers piled on the counter peeked out two bills with LATE NOTICE stamped in red across the front. They might as well have painted it across her mother's head like a scarlet letter. Why companies needed to publicly shame people for having money issues baffled Allison. It wouldn't do anything to help them get their payments more swiftly.

She ground her teeth as she ripped the envelopes open. The first one was a two-hundred-dollar credit card bill, the other an electric bill that was three months behind. Picking up her phone, Allison swiped away a pile of text messages and opened her banking app. With a few quick key strokes, she'd paid both bills and set up some automatic payments so her mom wouldn't have to worry about them for a while. She'd have to be careful with her spending—no more five-dollar smoothies every time she went to campus and definitely no pricey dinners out—but she could swing it. And even if she couldn't, she'd do it solely so her mom could worry a little less.

Stuffing the bills at the bottom of the recycling, Allison opened her messages. One was from her mother, a few hours ago, letting her know that things were the same with Jed. A handful of others were from Sophie. It had taken her until three in the morning to realize Allison was gone. Her stomach twisted at that, but she did her best to shrug it off. They'd all been drunk. It was surely an honest oversight.

Mandy had sent the last few messages. There were three, one every hour since six this morning, as if she were keeping a close eye on her phone.

Allison sent the same reply to everyone but her mother.

> Allison Avery: Hey! I am so so sorry for disappearing. My mom called saying that my father was in the hospital and I just panicked and left.

She'd barely brought her glass of juice to her lips before the responses started flying in.

> Sophie Andrade: OMG. Are you okay? Why didn't you call me? How did you get home? What can I do?

> Allison Avery: I'm exhausted but okay. He had some kind of heart attack or heart failure. He's doing better now, I guess.

The easiest way out of this would be to ignore her question about how Allison got home. But as Allison thought of Colin's long frame draped across her twin bed, she couldn't bring herself to do it. Last night felt like some kind of monumental shift. She didn't want to start this brand new . . . whatever it was . . . with secrets and lies.

And especially not to Sophie. Keeping things from her best friend wasn't doing anything to help Allison mend the rift she felt spreading between them.

Allison Avery: Colin drove me home.

Sophie Andrade: Colin who?

Allison Avery: Colin Benjamin

Sophie Andrade: Since when are you back in contact with him? Did he reach out? When???

Allison Avery: He's in my program at Claymore.

Ellipses.
Ellipses.
Ellipses.
Allison braced for the novel-sized rant Sophie was drafting, but when her message came through, it was only a few words.

Sophie Andrade: Why didn't you tell me?

Because I didn't think you'd care. Allison's heart hammered against her ribs. It was a simple answer, and yet so complicated at the same time.

She was still staring blankly at Sophie's last text when the phone rang in her hand. The screen read "The Cross-stitch Queen."

Mandy.

She thought about Colin again. Her heart sped up, and a flush stole into her cheeks as a few images from the night before popped into her head. How could she explain him—or what had happened between them—in a few texts to someone who only knew Colin 1.0?

But with Mandy, there was nothing to hide. Nothing that needed explanation. There was no Colin except 2.0 with her.

Clearing her message app, Allison hit the green button and said hello.

"Your dad. Allison. I'm so sorry. What can I do?"

As she busied herself making some English muffins, Allison explained what had happened. She even filled Mandy in on a little of their history.

"So, wait. How did you get home? You were pretty smashed when I last saw you."

Allison took a deep breath. And a giant leap. She didn't know yet what she and Colin were, but she didn't want to pretend it hadn't happened.

"Colin drove me," she admitted.

"Oh, did he now?" Allison could practically see her friend's knowing grin, even through the phone.

Chapter 24

Jed's new hospital room was larger than the one in the ICU, yet with him alert and staring at her, it felt as if there was barely enough space for Allison to breathe.

Gripping the strap of her purse as an anchor, she did her best to mask the deep, calming breath she pressed from her chest.

"Where's your mother?" Jed asked gruffly.

"Working a half shift." The verbal feats Allison had had to perform to get her mother to agree to go to the diner for the afternoon were virtually Olympian. She'd pleaded and reasoned and finally, when all that had failed, had admitted to finding the late bills and paying them. Allison didn't care about the money; when her mother inevitably tried to pay her back, she'd refuse it. But her mom needed to detach herself from the bedside of a man who would never have shown this much care for her.

"So, I'm going to be alone all day?" Jed scratched at his salt-and-pepper beard.

Anger boiled Allison's blood. How was it that yesterday she was ready to cry over this man? "Are you alone right now?" She watched the heart rate monitor, letting its spiky rhythm ease her own pulse: *120, 117, 119.*

Her father's eyes found the ceiling. "No." He spat out the word like a petulant child who refused to admit he was wrong.

Allison moved deeper into the room. Draping her coat over one of the guest chairs, she sat gingerly at its edge, still gripping her purse as if she might flee at any minute. "You know you're not her responsibility, right? You left her."

As much as Allison had welcomed her parents' much-needed divorce, she hated that, in the end, it had been Jed, not her mother, who had left. And, in what would be a surprise to no one, he'd done it for another woman. A thin one, whose wiry adult son worked at his electrical company. From what Allison could piece together, that's how her father had met Paula. She'd brought cookies to the office or some other equally antiquated domestic gesture, and Jed had slept with her for months before he bothered to end things with his wife.

The monitor beside his bed beeped, its numbers rising: *135, 131, 132.*

"Where is Paula anyway?"

"Home." Groaning, her father dug his head deeper into the flat hospital pillow. If Allison were her mother, she would already be searching for a new one. Instead, she was wondering how to come by a flatter and less comfortable replacement. Maybe some sheets made out of the hair shirts medieval monks used for penance, to boot. Good bedding should be a luxury available only to the pure of heart.

"Figures." Paula was not exactly attentive.

137. 135. 138. The heart monitor jumped with Jed's temper. "Don't start." He jabbed a finger at her. Tubes stretched from his wrists to the IVs behind him like external veins, and Allison had to fend off a shudder.

"Has she come at all?"

Jed grabbed the TV remote and turned up the volume. "She's called," he yelled over the noise.

Allison snatched it back and snapped off the TV. She'd never met a man more infantile than the one who'd supplied half her DNA and, considering that most guys acted like five-year-olds on a daily basis, that was saying something. "She should be here."

When he left them for Paula, Jed should have become her responsibility. But somehow, she seemed to appear only for the good times, especially if they involved Jed's bank account. Junior year, while Allison and her mom were taking out student loans to pay for Brown, Jed had given Paula's son, Shawn, the down payment for a house. Granted, Allison had never wanted her father's money—that would have meant conceding to his way of things—but it was a particular kind of wound to watch him shower someone else with it. Most days, it felt like Jed viewed Shawn as more his child than Allison ever was.

So why was she here instead of them? Her mother's extreme-sports version of generosity had clearly rubbed off on Allison.

"I'm surprised *you're* here," Jed said. Her father's blue eyes, the same shape and shade as her own, narrowed at her. "After that fit you pulled in your last email."

Allison drew in a breath through her nose so sharply it hurt. *Fit.* The word weaseled its way under her skin. Jed subscribed heavily to the very Victorian notion that all women were, at their core, on the brink of hysteria. Any display of emotion, be it rage or laughter or tears, was evidence of how overly emotional both Allison and her mother were, and, in Jed's mind, emotion immediately discredited whatever they might be saying, no matter how valid.

Not today, though. Allison was too hungover, too tired, and too . . . well . . . happy (thanks to Colin) to participate in her father's toxic masculinity. And that meant not taking the bait. Because Jed understood Allison's worldview enough (or at least the strawman version his right-wing media fed him) to use words like *fit* on purpose to ensure she had one, thereby reconfirming his misogyny. Wasn't confirmation bias grand?

"You had a heart attack. Of course I'm here." She said the words as matter-of-factly as she might read a passage aloud during Literary Theory.

"I had heart *failure*," he corrected her.

Allison swallowed a scream of frustration. Sometimes talking to her father was like asking a hamster to run the opposite way on its wheel. "You realize that sounds worse, right?"

"It's not. My heart was out of rhythm. It's fine."

135, 139, 137. Allison pointed at the monitor behind him. "It's still out of rhythm."

He waved her off. "It's better. They'll shock me later and it will be fine."

"Mom said you could have had a stroke."

"Your mother ex—"

"The doctor said it, too."

"The doctor's overreacting. She's like all those others back when that flu was around. Being too careful and turning everyone's life upside down in the process." He shook his head, his dark hair shaggy against his ears. His beard had been going gray for ages, but the silvering around his temples was new. Some of the skin on his arms, covered in tattoos from his military days, had gone loose, like he'd lost weight. He looked every bit as sick as he swore he wasn't.

"It's your life. Shouldn't we be careful?"

"Stop. I just want to go home and have a beer and watch the game."

Allison sighed. "You're probably not going to be able to have beer anymore—"

Her father threw up a hand. It shook with a palsy she'd never seen before. That couldn't be good for an electrician. His eyes watched the tremors for a moment as if surprised by them as well. Then he slammed the hand down against his leg. "No."

"Jed—"

"You're the last person to talk to me about diet." He gave her that same look he used to at meals when he handed her a plate. The one that said he found everything about her existence detestable.

Allison had expected at least one comment on her body, but anticipating a blow never made it hurt less. "I'm not the one in the hospital with heart failure—"

"No. If you're going to insist on sitting here, talk about something else."

Insist on sitting here. As if she were an imposition. As if her body, which he hated so much, was filling too much space. Allison stared at her father. She could have a hundred mouths and not be capable of screaming enough to release her frustration.

"What do *you* want to talk about?"

The age lines in his brow deepened. "You still haven't explained why you're here."

"You're *sick.* I'm your *daughter.*" Irritation seeped into her voice. It tasted bitter, like too much ginger on her tongue. "I thought you'd want me here."

He shrugged. *Shrugged.*

Why wasn't she enough, or too much, or whatever it was about her that made him care so little? Her bones felt broken with the weight of it. Or maybe it was that she was shrinking. Because sitting in that chair beside him, clutching her purse to her lap, her eyes wide on Jed's bland face, Allison could have been a toddler lost at the mall.

She couldn't swallow it back anymore, all these things she was feeling. "Why don't you care about me?"

"Allison, don't start." Jed reached for the remote again, but she batted it away.

"Don't start what? Don't start saying how I feel? How you've *made* me feel for the last twenty-three years of my life?"

Pushing a rough breath from his nose, Jed groaned. "Ah yes. You've had such a tough life. What with the roof over your head, and clothes on your body, and all the food"—he gestured at her in a way that said *look at all that food*—"on your table."

Allison wanted to erupt like a volcano, or maybe to turn him into a tree, like Nimue had done to Merlin, to punish him for his entire existence. But Jed didn't respond to emotion. She tried derision instead.

"Congratulations on fulfilling the bare minimum of parenting. Wait here while I get you your participation trophy."

"I'm not sure what you want from me."

She closed her eyes. In her head, she saw her father's heart rate monitor perform its endless dance: *132, 139, 134.* "To care. About anything," she whispered. Then her eyes snapped open. She was tired of holding things in, tired of lying, of pretending. She'd finally stopped with Colin, and look at where that had led her. Maybe it was time to stop with Jed, too. In person, not a faceless email.

"I want you to care that I'm in an important Ph.D. program, that I'm going to be a college professor someday, that I'm doing *exactly* what I promised you and Mom I would. Not everybody does that. Not everybody is able to grasp their dreams in the palm of their hand and make them real. Some people try, so so hard, and all they end up with is dust. But I'm doing it. Me, your daughter. I want you to care about that."

Allison was on her feet, gripping the end of her father's hospital bed as if that would somehow make him look her in the eye. He picked at his nails instead. His mouth moved like he wanted to say something, but he didn't.

"I want you to care about how much you've hurt me."

At that, Jed balked. "How have I hurt you? I gave you a good life."

Allison had never known that rage could be painful, but her bones seemed to crack. "Mom gave me a good life. You tried to make me hate myself."

Jed's lips thinned. "You're having a fit again."

"This is not a fit. It's the truth. Do you know what it was like to live with you? The constant remarks about my weight? The diet printouts everywhere? The way you'd buy junk food and stock the house with snacks and then shame me for eating what was available? The way you brushed aside everything I cared about?" Her fingers ached from their grip on the bed frame. "I guess I should thank you, since your disinterest motivated me. But there's always been this part of me that was empty, a hole I couldn't fill because it was yours."

Sometimes, when she was feeling especially self-reflective, Allison wondered if her lack of relationships over the last few years had less to do with Colin, and more to do with Jed. Or at least with the scars he'd left her. When Colin broke up with her, it had activated something left festering from her father. This idea that she wasn't enough, that she wasn't worth the hassle of holding on to. How many guys had she pushed away after one date, one hookup? Allison had convinced herself none of them were right for her, but maybe she was too afraid she wasn't right for them. That there were too many holes in her for her to fit anywhere.

Even when she'd tried to cut Jed from her life, he'd clung like barnacles. Like mold. Like the errant pen strokes on illuminated manuscripts that left permanent imperfections.

Her father stared at her. He lifted his hand, and for a blip of time, Allison thought he was going to reach for her, but all he did was grab the TV remote. "I don't know what you expect me to say."

Allison threw up her hands. She felt hollow. Maybe, now that she'd said everything she'd been holding in for years, this feeling would be permanent. Maybe she'd never feel full again.

The thought was exhausting, and when she heaved a labored breath, the fight left with it. Jed was an insurmountable rock. A surface with no pores. He'd never let her words in. If Colin had shown Allison that people can change, her father was a reminder that this wasn't true for everyone. Some people were born etched in stone.

She dropped her hands to her sides, her pulse throbbing in her fingers. "I want you to say that you hear me. That you understand. That you're sorry."

His mouth was a tight, unmoving line. His heart rate followed it. *130, 130, 129. 128.*

"I want you to say you love me, Dad." Her voice was frail and that last word didn't quite form on her lips. It was like something in another language, the meaning of which she couldn't quite grasp. If she still had her word wall, it would be underlined in question marks.

And yet, he said nothing. Just looked at her, like he didn't understand its meaning, either.

A moment later, his doctor swooped in, her perfume sharp and citrus against Allison's runny nose. She hadn't realized she was crying until Dr. Friedman put a hand on Allison's shoulder and said, "No need for tears. He's going to recover. The meds have been doing a good job lowering his heart rate and all his labs look good. A little shock this afternoon and then everything should be ticking at the right speed."

Allison nodded as she swiped her wet cheeks. Dr. Friedman's words were a relief, but probably not in the way she'd intended.

If Jed was going to be fine, then there was no need for Allison to stay.

As the doctor left the room, Allison looked Jed in his blue eyes. The only thing they truly shared. "I'm done here," she said. Then she left the room and her father behind.

Chapter 25

If, on Friday, Allison's ride to Maine with Colin had felt like an eternity, their drive home Sunday morning passed in the blink of an eye.

He'd pulled his Honda into the driveway of her house in Providence a good ten minutes ago, and the two of them were still sitting silently, staring out the windshield. Against the gray clouds and black shutters, the house's paint gleamed a frosty white.

Though the car was warm, Allison hugged her arms around herself. She didn't want to get out.

The last few days, she and Colin had existed in another world. Just the two of them and the dogs, sheltered from the cold Maine air and the stress of Allison's family drama by her beloved childhood home. After she'd left Jed (and endured an endlessly circuitous conversation with her mother about why Allison was leaving), she'd returned to discover Colin had ordered Chinese food and unearthed every streaming film based on medieval texts he could find. Somewhere between the egg rolls and a horrific attempt at adapting *The Decameron* into a sexcapade (which starred none other than the guy who'd botched Anakin Skywalker in the *Star Wars* prequels, a fact about which Colin did not know how to shut up), Allison broke down about her encounter with her father at the hospital. The whole time, Colin quietly held her hand, swiping away rogue tears that snuck down her face as she recounted how apathetic Jed had been.

Confiding in Colin opened up something in Allison, and, after that, she couldn't seem to stop touching him, or leaning into his side, or putting her head in his lap as they battle-quoted *Monty Python and the Holy Grail* in bad British accents.

Later, they'd ended up entwined once more between the sheets of Allison's old twin bed, then in her very pink shower stall, and finally, at two o'clock in the morning, when Monty whined to go out, up against the back door of the house. A blush crept into Allison's cheeks merely thinking about it.

But now that they were back, the real world was about to encroach on their perfect little bubble. Allison and Colin were still in the same grad program, they were still competing for the same advisee position and research trip, and Allison still hadn't explained him to Sophie.

She had no idea how she was supposed to handle any of this when she didn't know what she and Colin *were*. Had this weekend simply been a retreat to the past? A one-weekend stand? Or did he want this to be more? Did *she*? (Yes, the answer was yes, even if Allison refused to admit that out loud until Colin did.)

She had no answers. It was not a position she enjoyed. For all the confessions and kissing and sex that had happened over the last few days, there had been very little time dedicated to figuring anything out.

Colin let out a rough cough, drawing her out of her thoughts. "Now what?" His voice was barely audible over the chug of the heating vents.

"Huh?" Allison's heart stuttered. Maybe she wasn't the only one wondering where they stood.

"Are you . . . going inside?"

Never mind.

Her hands grabbed the door handle. Half to hold herself steady and half to . . . well . . . get out.

"Or—"

She jerked toward him. "Or?"

Smiling, Colin reached for her. "I'm going to visit my granddad. You could come." Her heart flipped as he threaded their fingers together and raised her knuckles to his lips. "Then we don't have to say goodbye just yet."

She angled toward his touch. "What about Monty?" The puppy snoozed quietly in the back seat.

Colin shrugged. "He loves dogs."

Everything but Allison's rampant heartbeat stilled. His words were like a rope thrown to her as she dangled off a cliff. Colin's grandfather was so important to him. Taking her to meet him meant something.

She nodded.

It was a step toward an answer. One that Allison hoped for more than she wanted to admit.

Ahead of Allison, Monty's tail wagged, shaking his small loaf of a body under Colin's arm. They'd paused outside of room 135, and Colin wiped his palm against his jeans before knocking.

A voice brittle with age invited them in. As Colin peeked his head around the door, the same voice announced, "Look, Janey, the prodigal grandson returns."

Colin shook his head. A good-natured grin filled his face. "I was here two days ago."

"Too long. Too long," the old man replied.

Colin cast a glance at Allison as he took her hand and led her into the room. "A good day," he mouthed.

His grandfather's living quarters were the size of a hotel room, one half dedicated to a sleeping area, the other holding a sofa and a leather lounger aimed at a flat-screen TV on the wall. A shield with a coat of arms was mounted over the bed and a map of England hung above the dresser. Large sections of the country were colored red, bisected throughout by spots of blue, especially around the western edge.

Allison recognized the pattern. It was a representation of Lancaster and York territories during the War of the Roses.

Colin hadn't been joking about his grandfather's penchant for medieval history. Or books for that matter. They were stacked in piles everywhere, on the floor, the nightstands, the dresser. The sharp corners of a few poked out from the half-closed closet like they were chancing an escape.

This old man had not yet spoken a word to her, and Allison already loved him.

His frame challenged Colin's for the title of most spindly ever, hardly taking up any room in the reclining seat. Short silver-gray hair stuck up at all angles on the top of his head as if he were endlessly running his fingers through it, and his cheeks were sunken and sallow. Yet the smile he offered was as bright and charming as his grandson's.

"Aunt Jane," Colin greeted the woman perched on the sofa. She looked to be in her mid-to-late forties, grave in expression, and stylish but subdued in attire. She tucked strands of her sleek, auburn bob behind her ear as her nephew leaned down to kiss her cheek.

With a start, Allison realized she recognized the woman from Claymore's promotional materials. The Dean of the Graduate School of Arts and Sciences: Jane Evans.

Her fingers sunk into the hem of her sweater. *This* was Colin's aunt? The one who'd been ready to play a rousing game of Wheel of Nepotism for him? She worked at Claymore? Was their program the one she would have snuck Colin into?

No wonder he'd been so tight-lipped about it. As unfair as it was, Allison's brain was already devising a million scenarios where Jane forced her nephew's way into the grad school without his knowledge or consent. Imagine what Ethan Windbag would do with that kind of information. He'd have Colin in the stocks out on the quad, regardless of how much Colin deserved to be in this program.

Allison was thankful when Colin's grandfather asked, "Who's this young lady?," interrupting her thoughts. She moved closer to Colin and stretched out her hand. "I'm Allison."

"And this"—Colin tipped his hip so the puppy in his arms was on full display—"is Monty." He then quickly introduced his grandfather and aunt as "Granddad and Jane."

The old man huffed. "I don't get a name?"

Colin laughed. "My apologies. Allison, this is Charlie."

But Charlie was too distracted by Monty to hear the correction. His narrow face puckered as he cooed and smacked out loud kisses. "Who's a good boy?" His voice was high-pitched in that way everyone addressed dogs and babies. "Is it you? Can it be you?" The Corgi was slathering Charlie's face with licks before Colin's grandfather had him fully in his lap.

"So how do you two know each other?" Jane motioned for them to sit on the couch.

Allison took the cushion beside her, Colin balancing on the arm.

"We went to Brown together," Allison said. "And now we're in the same cohort at Claymore."

Jane's brown eyes sparked. "Allison . . . Avery?"

Allison nodded, though her thoughts began to race.

A WCS FOR WHEN YOUR ACADEMIC DEAN RECOGNIZES YOU BARELY SIX WEEKS INTO CLASSES

1. The administration had her on some secret watch list because of internet searches she'd done on campus.

2. She had mistakenly been admitted to the program and no one had figured out how to tell her.

3. One of her recitation students had taken their complaints about her teaching to the administration.

She found herself panicking at the thought of that last one until Aunt Jane said, "Wendy Frances *raves* about you," causing Allison's heart to race for an entirely new reason.

"She does?" Allison and Colin asked in unison. He'd been holding her hand, but now it felt more like he was crushing it.

Jane's bob feathered in time with her nod. "She's so impressed by the knowledge of the field you already have and by your analytical skills. She believes you've got a great career ahead of you."

Allison was falling. Down and down and down. Chasing Alice into Wonderland.

Could everything she wanted—that she'd worked so hard for— already be within reach? Even after only half a semester, could Wendy see Allison's potential?

No. Fuck that. Not her potential. Her *value*. She believed Allison could have a career in academia. That Allison-shaped hole in her field existed. She simply had to step into it.

Pride warmed her face as she glanced back at Colin. His smile was plastic.

Hearing that your professor was raving about your direct competition had to be about as enjoyable as a colonoscopy. She bumped his knee. "You know, Colin is Wendy's teaching assistant, too. And his students love him."

Jane's face lit up. "Do they now?"

Allison nodded. "One of my own students stopped me after class the other day to tell me how much his friend loves Colin's recitation."

Fighting the cringe off her face took concerted effort. Allison had basically just admitted that her teaching was so bad her students had to compliment other people in her stead.

If Colin realized that, his expression didn't show it. It was open and gentle and uncertain, and it made her heart squeeze. "Really?" His thumb grazed the inside of her wrist, the touch so soft it almost hurt.

"Really." She could hardly get the word out.

His shoulders relaxed, and he leaned back into the couch cushion.

"I bet it was that discussion questions activity I tried. They seemed to love that one."

"The what?"

"My students were having trouble talking about *Beowulf* because they were worried they didn't understand it. So, a few weeks back, I asked them to write down every question they had about the poem, no matter how stupid they were afraid it was. Then I read them all anonymously. Starting with my own—'Why is there only one creature like Grendel?'" He smiled sheepishly. "It seemed to break the tension. Ever since, they're much more willing to ask whatever questions they have."

"Wow." Something thick clogged Allison's throat. She struggled to even come up with discussion questions, never mind finding good ways to use them. How did he do this?

And why couldn't she?

"I can share my write-up of the activity if you want." His face was bright, eager. It tightened the knot in her stomach.

"Luckily, my students don't seem to be afraid to ask questions. Most of the time they have so many, we can't get anything else done." God, she couldn't seem to stop lying about teaching. Even if it meant making Colin look bad in front of his aunt. She tried to smile as she backpedaled. "But thanks. It sounds fantastic."

Beside her, Jane clapped her hands. "I always knew you'd be an excellent teacher, Colin."

"Yes, yes, yes!" Charlie rotated Monty in his lap so he could better pet the dog's ears. "Allison, this boy taught me so much when we were living together. All about the French Arthurian romances and the Vulgate Cycle and the Lancelot tales." He had eyes the same color as Colin's, though they were much smaller in size and closer together on his face, and they gleamed with every word. "He's a bastion of knowledge. And those facts never leave him. Like he's the Tower of London." There was so much admiration in his voice that it caught in the back of his throat. Charlie coughed to clear it, apologizing to Monty with each jerk of his body.

"Dad," Jane piped in. "Remember when he was little and he used to give us lessons after Sunday dinner?"

"Wait, *what?*" Allison's hands fisted in delight. Embarrassing childhood stories were the best ammunition.

Colin groaned, trying to block her ears. She swatted him away.

"I had this old blackboard in my study," Charlie said. "It was on rollers and that boy would wheel it out every Sunday night, positioning it at the head of the dinner table. Then he'd teach us about something he read that week."

"He had these little bottle-cap glasses that never stayed on his face, and a pointer," Jane added.

Charlie's eyes crinkled against the widest of smiles. "And he'd rap it against the board"—he flicked his hand to demonstrate—"*tap, tap, tap*, and clear his throat, like some salty old schoolmaster."

Allison glanced back at Colin, her lips flattened together and her eyebrows arched high. His face was practically the color of his glasses. "I hope your methods have improved," she joked.

That got a laugh out of everyone, including Colin, who rested his head against Allison's temple as if she might hide him from the memory.

It was so easy to picture, this little Colin Benjamin, puffed up by his own knowledge, demanding the attention of his adult pupils. But as the image warmed Allison's heart, it also opened a crack right down the center.

Because that was the other thing about their cozy Maine bubble. There'd been no talk of school. Wendy's class and her advisee position and their grad careers had felt a million miles away. A problem for some alternate version of them.

But as Jane extracted her phone from her purse and asked Colin if she could share his lesson plan at her next faculty-development workshop, she ushered those realities back into the room. They haunted its corners like phantoms, cooling Allison's skin.

Her eyes strayed to the clock on Charlie's wall. "I should get home," she said abruptly, rising to her feet.

As much as she didn't want to face Sophie, Allison wanted to listen to more celebration of Colin's teaching skills even less.

It didn't matter how good it had felt to be close to him this weekend. Or how much he'd helped her. Colin wanted that mentorship with Wendy every bit as much as Allison did, and, if she wasn't careful, he could very well snatch it right from her fingers.

Chapter 26

MOM: Went back to see your father after you left. Just got home.
They did that shock procedure and everything is looking good.

MOM: *MOM has sent you a picture*

MOM: Do you see the color in his cheeks?

MOM: And he's bugging the nurses for a hot dog. Ha. Back to himself
for sure!

Allison frowned. Colin had dropped her off hours ago, and she'd been
staring at the pages of an article on Victorian childhood ever since. She
couldn't seem to absorb a word of it. There were too many thoughts
buzzing in her head about Colin and the mentorship and Sophie and
what Allison was supposed to do about any of it.

And her mother's endless texts were *not* helping.

She didn't want updates on Jed. After their conversation yesterday
at the hospital, she was done. She wouldn't cater to someone who'd
caused her so much pain. It didn't matter if he was her father.

Not that her mom was willing to hear that.

With a sigh, Allison tossed her phone in her desk drawer and slammed it shut. This was no time to resume the merry-go-round of guilt. She needed to get into the Homework Zone and that required silence.

So, of course, Sophie knocked on the door a second later. Her stack of dark curls greeted Allison first as she peeked her apple-cheeked face into the doorway. "You're back."

"I am."

"Do you have a second to chat?" Her hand spun around the door-knob like she was polishing it.

Allison didn't (or, more accurately, didn't *want* to) but she couldn't keep avoiding this conversation.

Sophie's cinnamon-scented perfume filled the air as she crossed the room and dropped onto Allison's bed. She hooked her heels onto the rungs and hugged Allison's donut pillow to her chest, the same way she had at Brown every time they had a roommate heart-to-heart.

Some of the brittleness in Allison's muscles softened. From the first day that she'd sat behind Sophie in English, they'd clicked. She still vividly remembered the initial words her soon-to-be best friend spoke to her: "That shirt is killer." No one had ever complimented Allison's clothes before.

The two of them understood each other perfectly. They were brain twins. Why had Allison been so certain that would change if other things did? Sophie was still Sophie, even from a distance.

"What's the news on Jed?" Sophie rested her chin into the edge of the donut. Allison tried not to notice that it was a chocolate frosted with sprinkles, the same kind she'd eaten on her ride with Colin on Friday.

Allison shrugged. Which felt four different kinds of wrong given the circumstances, but it was how she felt. Apathetic, detached, indifferent. "I guess he's fine? They did some kind of procedure today where they shocked his heart back into rhythm and, according to my mother, he's doing much better."

"It must have been weird, after everything, seeing him."

"I kind of"—Allison's eyes drifted to the ceiling—"had it out with him. Or as much as you can have it out with someone when they don't give a shit about what you're saying."

"Are you serious?"

"He told me I was being dramatic."

Sophie huffed a loud breath between her teeth. "I *hate* that word."

"Yup." If only Dante were still alive to create a nice nook for it at the center of hell. "I want nothing to do with him. Even if my mother keeps sending me updates like I signed up for a listserv." Her hands were trembling a little, and Allison jammed them under her thighs. Of all the weird emotions to feel in this moment, she was *nervous*. As if Sophie might judge her.

"For what it's worth, I think you're making the right choice."

Her words were a breath of fresh air. Allison inhaled deeply, taking them in. "It feels fundamentally wrong to disown a parent. Like it's a mortal sin. He's my *father*."

"And he's a son of a bitch. Just because they gave birth to us doesn't give our parents free rein to abuse us. And that's exactly what he's done to you forever. All that stuff with your weight and the food and the way he dismisses all your achievements, that's abuse. Something doesn't have to leave bruises to hurt."

Allison cringed. *Abuse* had such a strong connotation to it. She didn't like to imagine herself as someone who could be abused. But that was bullshit. The idea that this only happened to certain kinds of people was victim blaming. More patriarchal assholery that had slipped beneath her skin without Allison realizing it. She made a mental note to read a new feminist theory book this week.

Sophie squeezed the sides of the donut until it looked more like a cruller. "You're going to kill me for saying this, but sometimes I wonder if there isn't a direct line of connection between Jed and Colin."

Allison jolted. "Colin is *not* my father."

"Maybe not, but he could be so full of himself sometimes. Remember how, every time we'd watch a mystery or thriller, he'd try to guess what happened and blame bad writing when he was wrong?" In a fit of gesticulation, the donut pillow tumbled from Sophie's hands to the floor, prompting Monty to dive into its hollow center and immediately fall asleep. "Or the way he used to correct us whenever we used *fewer* or *less* wrong, like he was fucking Stannis Baratheon."

Allison had no defense for that one. Colin 1.0's admiration for one of *Game of Thrones'* worst characters had always been a bone of contention between them. He and Ethan Windbag would probably have been the best of friends, rescuing the internet from grammar mistakes one pedantic comment at a time.

"Or what about the way he would edit your lit theory papers with a red pen instead of just giving you feedback." Sophie shook her head.

"He's changed." What drew Allison to Colin 2.0 were all the things he'd lacked before: empathy, vulnerability, a willingness to let someone else sway his views. Three years ago, he probably would have tried to tell Allison how to deal with her father rather than offering her a space to talk, as he had this weekend. He was like an old house that had been gutted for renovations: the same on the outside, but almost unrecognizable within.

Sophie's mouth thinned. "That's hard to believe when you've been hiding your relationship from me."

"I wasn't hiding it. We had sex like four hours before I told you we were together." *And I don't even know if we really are together,* Allison reminded herself.

"Yeah, but he's been in your program for like two months now." Her friend's words were pointed.

Allison's stomach clenched. It felt so much worse hearing it out loud. She'd spent all this time keeping secrets from Sophie, holding in feelings she could have been working through out loud. And why? Because she was afraid that Sophie had changed too much? She hated the idea that her mother was right about Allison's penchant for the familiar. "For most of that time, there was nothing happening. We were arguing, or ignoring each other. I literally ran away from him at orientation."

Sophie cracked a grin. "Smooth."

"As always." Allison sketched a small bow from her chair. "I tripped over the curb in the process."

Sophie snorted, but the amusement quickly faded from her coffee-colored eyes. "What about school?"

"What about it?" Tension snapped through Allison's shoulders.

"After he stole the Rising Star from you, you fell apart. You stopped caring about anything. You barely finished your classes. And you were so convinced that you were never going to get into grad school just because you didn't win. If your mom and I hadn't convinced you to retake everything over the summer, you might not be here now."

Allison dug her toes into the shaggy pile of her carpet, her eyes darting from Sophie's face. Over the last few years, she'd done her best to forget the aftermath of Colin breaking up with her, letting her anger at him burn the rest of those memories out. She'd felt like such a failure. She'd held everything she'd wanted in her hands, only to open her palms to the wind and let it all blow away. That feeling had gnawed away at her insides until Allison couldn't handle the smallest bit of feedback without falling apart.

She'd never admitted it to anyone, but she'd started a new word wall that summer, hiding it along the side of her dorm bed. Every word a synonym for failure.

She gripped the seat of her chair in crushing fingers. "I got over all that." She wasn't that girl anymore. And Colin wasn't the guy who had made her that way.

Sophie's lips quirked. "But now you're in this big important program. Your career is on the line. If he messes with your focus—"

"He won't."

Sophie's face was etched with disbelief.

"I won't let myself fall apart like that again. I'm stronger now," Allison clarified.

Sophie didn't look finished but something in Allison's expression seemed to make her think twice. "Why didn't you tell me?" she asked instead.

Allison sighed. *Here we go.* She tugged her long hair over her shoulder and twisted it around her fingers. Time to get everything out in the open. At least, it would be one less boulder weighing her down.

Though she wanted to look anywhere else, she forced herself to maintain eye contact with Sophie. "I didn't think you'd care."

Sophie flinched. "What?"

"You're never around, and when you are, you're buried in your sketches and your fabrics. We barely see each other, never mind hang out. I thought, when we signed the lease on this place, that nothing would change. It would be just like Brown."

"Allison." Sophie's brown eyes were wide. "We're not in college anymore." Her tone was too careful. "Our schedules are polar opposites. I'm gone all day, and you're in class or studying all afternoon and evening. We don't have free time the way we used to."

"I know. I'm not stupid."

"Then what's with this 'I wouldn't care' stuff?"

Allison's finger twisted more tightly in her waves. "It just feels like your new life is more important than our old one."

Anger was not the expression she expected to see flit across her friend's face. But there it was, contorting Sophie's cheeks and darkening her gaze. "I'm not the only one who's not here, Allison."

"What?"

"All your hangouts with your classmates and your study sessions and lectures and whatever? You think I don't worry that I'm losing my best friend to people who understand her better than I do?"

It felt as if Allison's chair dropped out from under her. "Impossible. You're my brain twin. My better half. You get what this"—Allison gestured toward her body—"is like." Before meeting Sophie, Allison had never had anyone in her life who understood being plus-sized besides her mom. Having a friend truly share your lived experience was a gift. It made the world a hell of a lot less lonely.

"Still. They know all those million-dollar words that come out of your mouth. And they love books the way that you do and have read the same stuff." Sophie held up a hand to quiet her protestations. "And even if that wasn't the case, you can't begrudge me a life and a career because you're afraid of change. Providence is not a fashion town. I can't get a proper internship here. I need to go to trade shows. I might need to take a job somewhere else. That has to be okay. I can't fuck up my future because I'm afraid to hurt your feelings." Sophie pushed to her feet and stooped to give Monty a pat on the head. "Especially if you're going to hide things from me."

The words hit Allison hard. "I wasn't," she lied. It was too natural a reflex these days. "I won't. Not anymore."

As Sophie eased into the hallway, a sad smile tipped over her face. "I just don't understand why you'd do this to yourself again. That's all. There's so much more at stake."

She was gone before Allison could respond.

Chapter 27

Allison scanned Wendy's email for the fifth time since she'd sat down, as if the words might have rearranged themselves in her absence.

She'd been doing the same thing over and over since the email had arrived the previous afternoon.

Their professor had scheduled their big presentations for British Literature's Greatest Hits. In three weeks, Allison would have to prove to Wendy, the class, Colin, and—most importantly, herself—that she could present a lecture and engage students.

Murmurs drifted toward her from the hall's stadium seating, a reminder that she had an audience. She set her phone down and schooled her face into a neutral expression.

At least she was going second. That would give her an extra weekend to prepare. And the chance to make adjustments to her own presentation based on how well Colin's went.

She had the upper hand. She'd be fine. Great, even.

When they'd been on the phone last night, Allison had made sure Colin felt that confidence. "I'm going to totally out-lecture you," she'd insisted. The laugh he barked through the phone had caused Allison's ears to ring.

Then, with a voice sultry and warm like a good cup of cocoa, he'd whispered, "I guess we'll have to see." The soft click as he'd hung up had coaxed a shiver through her.

If he was trying to use the fact that they were hooking up to throw Allison off balance, it was working. She'd spent a good hour afterward dogged by sleep as she tried to chase off the mental image of Colin leaning languidly against his bedroom wall as he whispered into the phone.

Damn him.

Shaking her head, Allison watched the clock tick over from 10:55 to 10:56. At the front of the room, Wendy's podium still stood empty. Colin's chair beside Allison remained so as well.

Where were they? Like a reflex, she began churning out scenarios involving Colin and Wendy bonding without her. She wrung her hands beneath the table. Clearly, this whole dating-while-rivals thing would be a thorny briar patch to navigate.

Eyes fell upon her as the students waited, expectant, some of them with bags in their laps, ready to jet. Cole had put his coat back on.

Maybe Allison should dismiss them. That would be the best way to avoid a black-plague-ravages-medieval-Europe-level disaster. What was she going to do with a room full of sixty students when she couldn't teach fifteen? And she didn't have any material prepared.

10:59.

She cleared her throat, ready to set them free. They'd probably like her better for it. And what were student evaluations, if not a popularity contest? Even as the biggest of overachievers, who had always been deeply invested in her own education, Allison used to give higher scores to the professors she found funny or nice, regardless of whether they challenged her or helped her learn.

That settled it. Free period for everyone.

As she pushed to her feet, a few strokes of her handwriting from her open notebook caught her gaze. She'd filled pages with ideas about "The Wife of Bath's Tale" (their reading for the day) and its potential feminism. The sparkles from the purple gel pen (Allison believed deeply that girliness had its own sense of power and was not mutually exclusive from feminism) winked at her under the fluorescent lights.

She might not have a prepared lecture, but she had plenty to say. And, in its most literal sense, as a teaching assistant, her job was to assist with the teaching. What was more assisting than taking over the class if Professor Frances couldn't be here? It would be a disservice to herself and the students to take the easy way out.

Straightening her shoulders, she did her best to act like the empty dais was not a surprise. "Okay. Well, um, everyone, take out your anthologies and spend a few minutes reviewing the reading for today. Find, like, five lines you think are significant." That would buy her a few minutes to gather her thoughts.

Her anthology hit the table with a *thud* she hoped sounded imposing, and not like it had slipped from her trembling hands.

One of the most interesting things about "The Wife of Bath's Tale" was the way in which they spoke to each other around the idea of women and knowledge. Allison could focus on that and, maybe, pull in "The Tale of Melibee" as a contrast. "Melibee" wasn't an assigned text, but that meant Allison could teach the students something new. Maybe Wendy would be impressed.

There. She had a plan. Swallowing back the bile clawing its way up her stomach, she prepared to address the class. *You can do this,* she told herself. *You WILL do this.*

She never got the chance to find out if that was true.

Colin came skidding through the doorway, his bright blue cardigan a blur against the white walls. His Chucks squealed loud enough on the linoleum to grab the room's attention.

"I'm here, I'm here," he announced. He set his hands on his knees and heaved a breath, then smoothed his hair back. Not that any of it had moved. "I just got off a call with Professor Frances. Unfortunately, she's quite under the weather, so Allison and I will be handling class today."

Their eyes met. Behind his loose composure, panic flashed. Seeing it helped to calm Allison's own. Something about being afraid with someone else always made it easier. That's why the buddy system existed.

Besides, Colin didn't know it, but Allison already had a plan. And plans made everything manageable.

"All right." She clapped her hands. "You heard Colin. Everyone get into groups of four and, um, do the following." Grabbing her squeakiest dry erase marker from her bag, Allison approached the white board and jotted out instructions to help them compare the Wife of Bath's tale with her prologue.

She faced the room again. "You have twenty minutes. Go."

As if she were some sort of conductor, a cacophony of voices and movements burst to life at the wave of her hand. Pride filled her chest.

Stepping down from the podium, Allison joined Colin at their table. He was staring down at her anthology, comparing it with her open notes. He'd jammed his hands on his hips so his elbows jutted out, a pair of bony wings.

As soon as he sensed her presence, he slid closer so their arms pressed together, as if he couldn't help but touch her. Allison's face grew hot. She bent toward the open page so her hair would shield her from the students.

"Good call on the group work," he said. "And the questions."

She shrugged. "I just mimicked what Wendy does when we start a new text. And group work is always effective in recitation."

Colin scratched his chin, his eyes on the book. "I should try that more often. They talk so much I worry there wouldn't be time." His tone was not the least bit boastful, but it still skewered Allison's middle.

She pretended to study the lines of the poem. "So, Wendy called you?" she asked casually. *Don't ask why. Don't ask why.* "How come?"

Her mouth knew no authority but its own.

Colin arched an eyebrow. "You mean why did she call me instead of you?" Allison cringed, but his mischievous smile was front and center. He pulled off his glasses and wiped the lenses on the hem of his "Gotham Is for Villains" T-shirt (the boy had no DC/Marvel loyalty; it was gross). "She didn't specifically seek me out. She called the main office while I was in there and Mei handed me the phone."

The tension strung through Allison's muscles eased. He could have lied and lorded it over her forever, yet he'd put her feelings before winning. Heat burned her cheeks, and she pressed her arm more firmly into his. "Admit it," she teased. "You were hanging around the office, hoping she'd call."

With a glance over his shoulder at the class, Colin dipped his head toward hers. "I only do that for you." His breath was feather-soft as it brushed over the shell of her ear. Then, as quickly as he was there, he was gone, pacing the front of the room with her book cradled in his arms.

Allison's head spun with his sudden absence, and her body blazed. She needed to sit down, but her chair felt too far away, so she dragged herself onto the tabletop.

She swore some of the students were staring at her, like they could see the throb of her pulse in her veins. She needed to get her head back on track. They were leading a class here. *Find some damned decorum, Avery.*

"So." Her voice cracked, forcing her to clear her throat to cover it. "I'm assuming Wendy gave you instructions?"

Colin laughed. "She said, and I quote, 'You two have got this.'"

"Shit." Allison bit her lip.

Colin's hazel eyes caught the movement. Slowly, they traced the curve of her mouth. "I know you have a plan."

"I do not." *Lies.*

Though at this particular moment, that plan involved letting him kiss her up against the whiteboard until she forgot her own name.

God. No wonder people warned against dating co-workers. This was torture.

Straightening her shirt, Allison gave her side a small pinch. They needed to get their TA hats on right now. And secure them there. With cement, if need be. (Or, perhaps, Colin's strong-hold hair gel.) Her future in the program depended on it.

He crossed his arms, hugging her book to his chest. "You *always* have a plan. Let's hear it."

It took Allison another moment to fully banish all thoughts of last weekend from her mind. Then, with a sharp breath through her teeth, she straightened her spine and nodded toward the board.

"I thought we could organize the class around the last question."

Colin flipped through her notebook. "I like it."

"Then if we have time, we can show them some lines from 'The Tale of Melibee.'" She stopped herself from explaining why. This thing between them was never going to work if she couldn't turn the rivalry off, which meant she had to stop constantly trying to prove she was smarter and more knowledgeable.

He froze. "The what?"

"'The Tale of Melibee'? One of the tales from Chaucer? The character?" Colin's face was blank. "His response to 'Sir Thopas'?"

He shook his head.

"Have you never read *The Canterbury Tales* all the way through?" That was practically a felony for a medievalist.

"Not all of it."

She tried her best to force the judgment out of her voice when she said, "I guess I'll handle that part."

He frowned. "You'll have to."

She rose to her feet and ran her hand over his arm. She hoped the contact conveyed everything she couldn't. "Why don't you get them started?"

"Yeah?" His face was so uncertain when he glanced down at her that it was criminal she couldn't press a kiss to his lips. Her body felt full of hands, all of them reaching for him.

He cleared his throat. "Maybe I could pull up a few examples from church writings to compare with how the Wife of Bath uses religion—Charlie went through a bit of a Christian history phase too, so I have some experience with that."

"That sounds great. We can use the examples as a jumping off point and then dig into the other ways that she establishes her authority."

For the next few minutes, Allison constructed a loose outline while Colin got the projector working and displayed a passage from some church father Allison had never heard of.

When he asked the class to end their group work, it took about three seconds for him to have their undivided attention. As if he'd cast some kind of spell.

Sitting back in her chair, Allison did her best to observe Colin not as a rival, but as a colleague. Someone from whom she could learn something. He was smooth, pacing the podium with languid grace, and every third word wasn't *um, like,* or *sort of* (which seemed to be the main components of Allison's vocabulary whenever she was in front of a classroom). It was as if he'd written out an entire script beforehand and memorized it.

Apparently, he'd even learned something about brevity since their first day in class, because his lecture only lasted about ten minutes before he cast his gaze to Allison and said, "This is, of course, only one kind of authority the Wife exhibits in the prologue. What are some others?"

Damn him. It was a perfect segue, deserving of an EGOT, a Michelin star, a Pulitzer.

Rising to take his place by the podium, Allison felt her heart hiccup when she turned and saw all the hands in the air.

Chapter 28

"When Katie in the back row made that comment about how the story focuses on the value of women's experience . . ." Colin lolled his head along the top of the cushions of Allison's couch in a daze.

After their incredible team-teaching session, Allison had decided it was time for him to sleepover at her place. She figured if Sophie was forced to interact with him, her friend would see how much he'd changed. And Allison needed Sophie to get on board with Colin. For whatever reason, it felt like the key to fixing everything between them.

But when they'd gotten back to Allison's that night, it was empty. Sophie had left a note on the refrigerator whiteboard that she was crashing at the Viking's. If she wasn't already practically a ghost, Allison would have been convinced her best friend was avoiding her.

But at least this meant some uninterrupted alone time with Colin. Thanks to all the clandestine touches and subtle flirting in class today, Allison's hormones were completely revved up.

The way his finger was tracing lazy circles around her kneecap was not helping matters. Lately, he reached for her out of instinct. Like she was a natural part of him. Like they were books in the same series that fit perfectly together on a shelf.

Allison felt him smile as she nuzzled her face into his neck and pressed a light kiss to his jaw. She seemed to touch him just as easily.

"It took everything in me not to cheer."

"Actually, you did a little whoop," she pointed out.

He grimaced. "You caught that?"

"Everyone caught it. But it's a whoop-worthy moment when a student reaches a conclusion on their own."

"YES." He tilted his head to look at her. The softness in his face melted all its sharp angles. (And Allison's heart, too.) She moved forward to kiss him, their mouths joining deep and slow. His hand glided up her back to anchor her to him. It would have been incredibly romantic were Monty not between them, taking turns licking their necks.

Laughing, Allison sat back. "We should deal with dinner."

Colin's eyes lit up. "Let's cook."

"Uh, that is not one of my skills."

He winked (his damned winks were as absurd as all his leaning). "But it's one of mine."

In ten minutes, he'd rifled through every shelf in Allison's kitchen, pantry, and fridge, and had rustled up the ingredients for carbonara. They marched along the small counter like an army ready for battle.

"We have pasta," Allison said as she watched Colin create mounds of flour on the granite and hollow out little craters in the center.

"The fresh stuff is so much better." He cracked an egg into one of the holes and began to swirl it with a fork, being careful to keep the hill of flour from toppling over. "Come help."

"Pass." Allison's skills in the kitchen included burning toast and soup, as well as causing cereal to go soggy too quickly.

One of Colin's floured hands tugged her gently to the counter. A cuff of white powder remained around her wrist in its wake as he situated himself behind her. Resting his chin to her temple, he guided her hands, showing her how to swirl the egg to grab a little more flour every time. Once it had turned into a paste-like consistency, he used her hands to work the dough. Allison was trying to pay attention but with his hips locked solidly against hers, the slow rocking motion they made as they rolled the dough this way and that was distracting (to say the least). Her whole body tingled with want.

She faced him, her mucked-up hands clutching the hem of his shirt. She needed him closer, as many parts of his body as possible jammed up against hers.

He was brushing a few strands of her long bangs out of her face when Allison's phone let out a wail, and the two jumped apart.

"Leave it." Allison's fingers snatched for his shirt again, but he'd already crossed the kitchen to check the caller ID.

He shoved up his glasses with the back of his hand. "It's your mom."

"My hands are gross. I'll call her back." This was no time for a Jed update or a guilt trip. Not when Allison ached to have Colin's spindly frame mashed against her.

He grinned. "Or I could just answer."

"Wait, no—"

"Hey, Mrs. Av—"

Damnit.

"Right, sorry. Cassandra." Colin hooked the phone between his shoulder and his cheek and ran his hands under the faucet. "She's right here, but we're in the middle of making fresh pa—"

Whatever Allison's mother said sent Colin's head snapping back with a laugh. "No, for real. Who would have imagined? She's catching on, though."

Allison crossed her arms, giving Colin her most impatient glare. She was *not* okay with them bonding over her less-than-stellar cooking skills.

He offered her a sheepish grin. "Do you want me to give her a message?" Allison caught snippets of her mother's voice between Colin's nods. "Yep. Okay. Got it. I'll make sure she calls you back when she's not elbow-deep in flour and egg."

As he ended the call, Allison returned to the pasta dough and began kneading it like bread. "I can't believe you answered that."

"Whoa. Whoa." He rushed over and placed his hands over hers to stop their motion. "That pasta is going to be the consistency of car tires if you keep that up. I'll take it from here." With a spin like they were waltzing, he moved her from her spot. "I thought you and your mother were tight?" His hands fluttered around the counter like neurotic butterflies that had just discovered their purpose.

Shrugging, Allison pulled herself up on a clean bit of counter space. "We are."

"Then why wouldn't you want to talk to her?"

She grabbed a small piece of discarded dough and balled it between her fingers. "Because all she wants to talk about lately is Jed." She tossed the dough at the sink. It hit the metal basin with an echoing *thunk*. "I need a break."

"Ah. Fair enough."

When she threw the next dough ball, her aim went wild, and it bounced off Colin's temple, knocking his glasses askew. In the fit of laughter that erupted from her, she banged her own head against the cabinet.

Colin adjusted his glasses, failing to fight off a grin. "I should have learned by now not to be anywhere near you and projectiles. I'm pretty sure I still have a scar from that Scrabble tile."

Allison turned to the consistency of warm, melted chocolate at the mention of that night. It had been almost a week, but the memories of his hands all over her, their bodies tangled together, were vivid enough to give her goose bumps. She wanted a reenactment. An adaptation. A reimagining.

Sliding a little closer, she rested a hand on his arm. He'd shucked his cardigan hours ago, and the sleeves of his plaid shirt were rolled up to his elbows. The pads of her fingers brushed along the muscles in his forearm. Allison's voice was husky and low as she insisted, "My target was the sink, I swear."

"Your athletic skills are subpar."

"I should try again. Practice makes perfect." She smirked, pretending to aim at him this time, but Colin surprised her with a soft kiss. While she sunk into him, he wrestled the last of the dough away and lobbed it into the open trash bin.

"You play dirty," Allison mumbled as they separated.

A shit-eating grin quirked his lips. "I'll show you just how dirty later."

To save face, she rolled her eyes (no one should fall for a line that corny), but Allison's insides sparked. It was absurd how badly she wanted this man covered in flour with negligible flirting skills.

She cleared her throat. "Have you figured out what you're going to present on for Wendy's class?" They'd never get dinner done if she didn't change the subject.

Colin had shifted his attention back to the pasta but his hands lay flat against the counter. "Why? Have you?" he asked.

Obviously. Allison had a new notebook upstairs with three pages worth of thoughts scribbled in it.

"I want to discuss the disruptive nature of beauty in chivalric texts." She'd been developing this idea since her senior year at Brown, when she'd taken a course in medieval French romance. It fit perfectly with what she saw happening in "The Knight's Tale," and gave her a chance to delve a little deeper into her theory. She might already be on her way to a dissertation topic, years before she needed to be.

"Think about it. The excessive beauty of the main female character is always to blame for what happens to the knight that saves her." The buzz of a good analysis bounced through her body, making her fidget. It was the same spike in adrenaline she got from a good scare. Or a truly spectacular kiss. "In other words, beauty's a beast." She grinned at her own pun.

"Wow." Colin's eyes had lost some of their focus. "You've got your entire argument worked out."

"You don't?" How had he not been thinking about this all semester? She needed to teach him the value of a good plan.

"I have some ideas, but I'm not sure what to pick."

"Let's hear them." Allison straightened herself on the counter.

He hesitated for a moment, unsure, but then huffed out a breath. "Okay. Idea one. Masculinity and knighthood—heroic or toxic?"

Allison waved a hand, flicking the words away. "Been done a million times."

"Right." Colin pulled a mound of pasta dough toward him, his movements clipped and quick as he rolled it out.

She watched him, eyes narrowed. Even if he wasn't widely read in the field, he had to know how passé that idea was. More than enough white dudes had already written books on the white dudes in medieval romances. "What's number two?" She gave him a gentle nudge, relieved when he didn't jerk away.

"The relationship between magic and religion."

"What about it?"

"They seem similar somehow?"

"That's not much of a thesis."

His jaw tightened. "I guess."

His knife strokes were heavy as he slit the flat dough into strips. The blade scraped against the counter with a shriek even Allison knew wasn't good for the surface or the knife's edge. "Clearly, I don't have anything," he muttered.

She caught his arm, holding him still. "You said you had three."

"The last one sucks, too."

"Tell me."

Pulling from her hand, he busied himself at the sink. "Eroticism in the age before pornography."

"Oh." Her eyes widened. "I like that."

Colin still wasn't smiling, but something hopeful eclipsed his gaze. "I thought it might be interesting to discuss how sex is described in Chaucer. Medieval lit, hot or not? Something like that."

Allison brushed some flour off her leggings. "Have you read much about this stuff?"

"Not yet. Why?"

"So . . . eroticism was different back then. Most scholars see it playing out in the mystical texts more than romance and popular literature."

"It's not worth pursuing, then?" There was too much brittleness in his voice.

Allison touched his elbow. "I'm not saying that at all. It's a fascinating approach. You just might be leaning hard on the texts rather than research to support your interpretation." She gave his arm a little shake. "Plus, think of the fun you can have."

"What do you mean?"

"All the puns!" She lowered her lashes and did her best to make her voice sultry. "His mighty weapon stood tall. The knight brandished his sword." She made an obscene gesture to get her point across. "His pole was long and stiff, prepared for the next joust with his mistress." Allison wagged her eyebrows, barely able to contain the giggles bubbling up her throat.

Colin didn't laugh. Instead, he stared, his hands frozen to the countertop. "Wow. Okay. So you *do* think my topic is ridiculous."

"What? No." Allison gaped at him. "I was just being funny."

"At the expense of my ideas. When you know that I'm not as good at this stuff as you are."

Allison reared back. That was the last thought on her mind. "I don't think that."

"You don't need to keep parading around how much more you know about medieval lit." He was back at the sink, hefting the full pot of water to the stove with tight shoulders. "I get it. Trust me."

She'd never done that. Or . . . if she had, it was only because he'd tried to cut her down first. Allison almost accused him of rubbing his teaching skills in her face, but then remembered she wasn't supposed to be having trouble in that area. "I wasn't parading or mocking anything," she mumbled instead.

When Colin returned to collect the pasta, Allison rested her palm over his knuckles. He stilled beneath her touch.

Working side by side with him today in Wendy's class had been great. When he was around, Allison always thought harder, clearer, more deeply.

But she loved them like this more, the way they were in quiet spaces. Easy, comfortable, the world molded to fit just them. Alone with Colin (2.0), Allison could breathe, her lungs fully expanding. She wasn't too much. Or not enough.

She was just right.

But those two versions of them couldn't exist in tandem. They couldn't be rivals and be together. Otherwise, both were likely to break.

"Should we not . . . ." Allison pressed a breath between her teeth. "Should we not talk about Wendy's class anymore? All this arguing and insecurity and trying to one up each other feels too much like how we used to be. And I like this"—she pointed between them—"so much better."

Back at Brown, Colin used to make Allison feel small. Most of the time, he treated her as his greatest opponent rather than someone he cherished. But since their trip to Maine (and, really, even before that), it was more like she was the Enide to his Erec. He'd fight anyone to prove how much she mattered.

That was worth protecting. Maybe even at the cost of winning. . . .

Colin pursed his lips. His nervous hands fiddled with the arms of his glasses, even as his gaze was so intense it pinned Allison in place. "I do, too."

"It's agreed, then," she said.

He nodded.

"Good." Allison's smile was sheepish. "Just . . . though. One last thing."

"What?" he groaned.

"Do the eroticism topic."

"Yeah?"

The tension around them thinned as he whispered the word. It was as if they'd found the threads that held them at bay and had snipped them clean in two.

Setting down his knife, Colin moved in front of her. His hands smeared wet dough across her shirt as they slipped around her waist. Allison's knees fell open to draw him closer.

"I'll need to do some research." The words were in his throat. Graveled with want.

Allison's legs hooked to his hips. "Consider me an open book."

Chapter 29

With only two weeks until their big presentations in Wendy's class and her regular coursework getting more demanding than ever, there'd been little time for Allison to hang out with Colin or her Claymore cohort. They'd even had to cancel Saturday's compulsory bonding at Ethan's (a fact about which no one was complaining) because of a big annotated bibliography due in Victorian Families.

A handful of them were currently sitting around Colin's giant dining room table putting a dent in that assignment.

Allison's phone beeped. It took her five minutes to find it under all the articles she'd spread out before her.

"You should really invest in a laptop," Ethan said.

"I prefer my desktop, thanks," she ground out. Her fingers strangled her phone, yet another text from her mother staring back at her.

MOM: Your father said you haven't checked in on him once. He's been home for almost two weeks.

Allison was tired of the guilt. And of her mother not respecting her decisions regarding her father. She jabbed out a response so violently that two of her pens rolled off the side of the table from the movement. Then she silenced her phone and threw it in her purse.

Colin arched an eyebrow from the seat beside her.

"Maybe I should have applied to schools a little farther away from Maine than Rhode Island," she muttered. Over his shoulder, she could see Ned the suit of armor, the empty gaze of his faceguard surveilling them like a medieval version of Big Brother.

"Your mom again?"

Allison nodded. "I bet Stanford's nice this time of year." Or Siberia. Or Narnia. Maybe Middle Earth or Wonderland. Camelot. Anywhere that wasn't within cell tower service.

"I got in there," Ethan announced to no one. He didn't bother to look up from his laptop.

Link stopped typing long enough to glance at him. "For undergrad?"

Windbag shook his head. "Grad program. I was accepted to all eight schools I applied to: Harvard, Brown, UCal Berkeley, Stanford, Princeton, Yale, Claymore, Northwestern." He ticked each one off on his fingers.

Colin flinched and began to rustle through his notes, his hands restless and jerky.

Allison couldn't imagine how he must be feeling, given that Ethan's list had her questioning the validity of her own small set of acceptances from Claymore, Tufts, and Boston College.

Reaching under the table, she gave his knee a squeeze. She would have preferred a soft kiss to his temple (forehead kisses were the height of reassuring gestures), but they hadn't told anyone in their cohort they were dating. They hadn't even said those words out loud to each other.

He kept his gaze locked on whatever article he was pretending to read, oblivious to her touch.

"I chose Claymore because of Isha Behi. Though UCal Berkeley was practically begging me to join them." Ethan spoke with the plainness of reading a grocery list, prompting Allison to glance around for a proper projectile. This guy had a superiority complex the size of Texas.

As if Ethan's gloating had summoned him, Captain Pepper Jack materialized onto the table. Swaying his large orange haunches, he meandered across, stopping to knock each piece of paper or pen he passed out of his way. When he reached Ethan, the cat plopped down on his copy of *Nicholas Nickleby* and began to lazily gnaw on a corner. His one eye tracked Windbag, challenging him to say more as the tip of his tail wicked the tabletop.

Colin shoved up from his seat. The legs squealed loudly against the floor. "Here, let me get him. He was supposed to be locked in my bedroom."

Hoisting the cat under his arm (and deliberately, Allison guessed, knocking Ethan's book to the floor in the process), he headed, not toward his room, but to the kitchen.

Allison made an excuse about refreshing her already full glass of water and hurried after him. She forgot her drink on the table.

Colin stood staring out the window, his fingers gripping the edge of the large farmer's sink. At his feet, Captain Pepper Jack wrestled with a pouch of catnip.

"Hey," she said quietly. "You okay?"

He cleared his throat, his already angular shoulders sharpening as his back went taut. "Just dealing with the cat."

"He's not in the sink."

Colin only went more rigid.

Moving beside him, Allison laid a hand on the small of his back. She tried to angle her face into his line of vision, but he glanced away, forcing her to use the window's reflection to read his expression. "If this is about Ethan, he's an assbag. We know this."

"Yup." The muscles in his jaw flexed as Colin threw open the drawer beside the sink. Silverware rattled like there was an earthquake. He grabbed a handful, which he then shoved into Allison's hands.

Spoons, forks, and knives spiked out in all directions. "While we're in here, let's get that cake I bought."

"Colin." It felt like she was trying to communicate with him through a wall of glass.

His hard gaze stung as it fell on her face. "I don't want to talk about this. Especially not with them here."

Allison had to fight off a flinch. This was the former Colin. Back at Brown, when he was upset, he always closed down like this. Shut her out. Found a way to ramp up the competition between them to avoid the heavy stuff.

She turned away, cradling the silverware to her chest. She'd only taken a step before he caught her arm.

"It's the same stuff that always eats at me," he said. "The insecurity. The fear I don't belong here. Twenty-five rejections and one acceptance. Not exactly Ethan's odds. And I'm sure everyone else is the same. Link probably got into ten schools." He shook his head. "I'm sure you did, too."

That shadow of the old Colin dissolved, leaving behind the man she now knew. The one for whom she'd fallen so hard, who opened his mouth and told her what he was thinking.

"I absolutely did not," she said. "And where people got in doesn't matter. We're all at Claymore, and we *belong* here."

He pushed at the bridge of his glasses, nodding. "I know. I know. This lecture for Wendy is just getting under my skin." He pulled his lips tight. "Sorry. I know we're not supposed to be talking about that."

Allison took his hand and squeezed it. "We can if you need to." She meant it, too, no matter how nice it had been the last few days not to obsess over all the reasons why Colin could still snag this mentorship with Wendy right out from under her. It was like they were no longer competing. They could just . . . be . . . together.

He shook his head as if rattling out his thoughts. "I'm good." To prove it, he gently tugged her toward him, and, cupping her neck with his free hand, drew her face to his.

Silverware crashed at their feet as Allison freed her hands to loop them around his neck. For a second, she forgot their classmates were in the other room. There was only Colin and her, only the dance of his fingers across her back, his tongue in her mouth, the sharp smell of his hair gel in her nose.

She stumbled back, back, back, until her spine pressed against the cool door of the refrigerator.

Colin fisted her shirt in his hands, stretching it against her chest as if he meant to tear it from her shoulders. His mouth was hard against hers. Like if he kissed her deeply enough, he could banish every bad thought in his head.

She wanted to be that powerful for him, and she kissed him back as if she could be.

Without thinking, her hand drifted across the front of his jeans. He moaned into her mouth, an invitation to increase the pressure, but then Allison heard the worst possible sound.

Ethan's voice. Approaching. Closer and closer. "Colin, do you have any actual alcohol in this house?"

They didn't have time to separate, or collect themselves, before Ethan was there, framed in the doorway, his mouth hanging open. Allison fussed with her hair while Colin shrugged his cardigan back over his shoulders.

"What were you two—"

"Nothing," they insisted in unison.

That seemed to be the last piece of evidence Ethan needed. Pivoting, he strode back toward the dining room, Allison and Colin on his heels, hissing his name. As soon as he was in sight of Mandy and Link, Ethan flicked a hand over his shoulder. "Well, they're fucking," he announced. Tasteless and with absolutely no affect, as usual.

Allison's heart drummed as she glanced, wide-eyed, at Colin. Now everyone would know. They'd be scrutinized endlessly. Watched like some sort of teen soap opera. It would be too much pressure, like their rivalry. They'd implode under it before they even figured out what they were.

Her mouth moved in protest, but she couldn't find the words to deny it. She didn't want to pretend that what she and Colin had didn't exist. Though he'd gone white under his freckles, the set of his jaw suggested he felt the same.

Before either of them could defend themselves, Mandy laughed. "Of course they are." She grinned widely at Allison as if they shared a secret joke.

Link, too, was nodding. "You two have been hate-flirting since the first day of classes. I'm honestly surprised it took this long."

Allison gaped at them. For the longest time, *she* hadn't realized how she felt about Colin. How had the rest of them already known?

"It's . . . more than that." Colin moved to Allison's side and braided his fingers in hers. "Right?" A whisper only for her. The uncertainty in his hazel eyes turned Allison's heart to putty. His doubt was comforting. It reminded her that they were treading this path together. Stepping over their old footprints to find a new way.

"Right. We're . . ." She wanted to be the one to say it, to etch them in stone. "Together."

Colin brought her hand to his lips. "So together."

Mandy beamed. "Even better."

They sat down, and shoving aside their homework, recounted for their friends how they'd met at Brown, and how they'd reconnected over the last month. The whole time, Allison couldn't help but feel like Mandy's words were right, even if she hadn't meant them quite that way.

Because things with Colin and Allison, were, without a doubt, so much better.

Chapter 30

For a month every year, the Wetlands Trail at the Roger Williams Zoo became a veritable jack-o'-lantern wonderland. Glowing grins and eyes were carved into pumpkins of all shapes and sizes: some leering, some cackling, some almost friendly. Others boasted artistic renderings of everything from famous movie scenes to portraits of celebrities, fictional characters, and even landscapes. They were balanced on tree branches, stacked along fence posts, trailed across the roofs of any available structure, lined up on the borders of the paths. Basically, anywhere a pumpkin could fit, there would be one, until their yellow dancing light dashed out even the glow of the moon and stars.

Allison's hand was woven with Colin's, and she tightened her grip as she drew him toward a cluster of pumpkins that bore the likenesses of sea creatures. Leaning forward to inspect the Loch Ness Monster, she let out a happy sigh. "I just love this place."

She'd been attending the Jack-O-Lantern Spectacular every year since she was a freshman at Brown. Halloween was already her favorite time of year, but the intricacy of the carved pumpkins and their sheer number made this particular spot feel a little more magical than anywhere else.

With Colin's presentation only ten days away, Allison had suggested a night out. They both needed a break from school stress, and since Halloween fell on a Friday this year, there seemed no more perfect way to spend All Hallows' Eve.

Colin stood next to her, admiring a nearby kraken. He kissed her temple as he gestured toward the pumpkin. "Look at the details in this thing's tentacles. I can't even draw on paper and these people are engraving gourds with masterpieces, using nothing but cutlery."

"They probably start with pencils," Allison quipped.

He narrowed his eyes. The lenses of his glasses winked in the wafting candlelight. "Don't ruin my illusions."

He kissed her again, this time a light flutter of his lips at the base of her jaw that made her heart dance. That mouth of his was a menace in every way.

As they stepped back on the trail, a group of little kids in superhero costumes ran by screaming with candy-filled bags slapping against their legs. It had rained for much of the day, and they stampeded in puddle after puddle, spraying torrents of water all over the path. Allison smoothed a few drops of water off the front of her striped chiffon shirt. (It might have been a mistake to wear something dry-clean-only to a rain-soaked zoo, but they were on a date, and she would dress like it, damnit.)

She watched the kids disappear around the corner. "I guess we wouldn't have looked so out of place if we'd worn costumes."

Colin huffed. "I *did*." He plucked at the front of the T-shirt beneath his burgundy cardigan, a giant red cross on a white background, the insignia of the Knights Templar.

"A T-shirt is not a costume."

"You made me leave the sword and shield in the car."

He'd shown up at her house with a plastic sword not even the width of his gangly arm, the strap of its matching shield hanging in the crook of his elbow like a purse. He'd looked like a babysitter playing dress-up in his charges' wardrobe. "I was offended by your lack of effort," she said.

He snorted. "I'll make sure to forge my own armor next time."

Allison jammed her hands on her hips. "Considering I spent most of my formative years devouring any bodice-ripper romance with a knight on the cover, and now study their predecessors for a living, I feel like it's the least you could do." She didn't dare admit how many daydreams she'd had about being swept off her feet onto the back of a steed by a hot, gallant knight.

He sketched a bow. "I swear, milady, the next time I dare to don armor, it will be authentic."

Satisfied (and also slightly distracted by the image of Colin conjured by his promise), she looped her arm in his. Though it had only been two weeks since their trip to Maine, everything between them felt so natural. As if they'd been together—the word sent a happy shiver through Allison ever since they'd said it out loud—for years, not days. Not that they were falling into old patterns, but rather finding new ones that had always been there, waiting and unused.

For a while, they walked along in a companionable silence broken only by the occasional stolen kiss or admiration for a particularly striking pumpkin. Finally, they rounded the last bend of the trail and joined the line for the snack bar. The smell of starchy fries and sweet fried dough dusted in sugar overwhelmed Allison's senses. She'd been so busy earlier working on her PowerPoint for her presentation for Wendy that she'd forgotten to eat lunch, and her stomach was beginning to revolt.

She was studying the menu above the order window when she heard the distinct tenor of a most unwelcomed voice.

Cole. A few groups ahead of them. Laughing loudly.

Allison spun around, putting her back to him. Her heart was in her throat and throbbing too hard for her to swallow. A few hours ago she'd had to kick him out of recitation for being disruptive, and he was the last person she wanted to run into right now. Especially with Colin, who still thought her classes were going great.

She grabbed his hand and led him out of line. "We forgot to walk by the elephants," she said. "I love them. They're like oversized, hairless dogs. And they have those giant ears." Words were rushing out of her mouth at the same pace as her racing heart. Cole could not see her. She had no idea what she'd say to him outside the confines of a room where she had any kind of authority. And then Colin would have questions, and she'd have to lie. Or tell him the truth. Neither was an acceptable option.

"They also smell terrible," Colin pointed out, gazing longingly over his shoulder at the snack bar.

She ignored him and tugged a little harder on his arm. "Come on. The faster we get there, the faster we get back."

"Or, hear me out, we could eat first, *then* see the elephants."

"Colin." Her eyes cut over his shoulder. Cole and his friends had their food and were heading in their direction.

Allison hurried her steps. Behind her, she could hear Colin's feet as he jogged to keep up.

There was the aoudad enclosure. And the red river hog beyond it. The African elephant exhibit was around the next corner. It had high walls and lots of viewing areas. Plenty of places she could hide until Cole was gone.

They were a few steps from safety when Colin jerked her to a stop. She faced him, already pointing over her shoulder. "It's ri—"

The rest of her sentence died in her throat as she realized they were too late. Cole and his friends were grouped around the hog enclosure. The only barrier left between them was a chain-link fence. He was going to see her. What would he do? What if he brought up how she'd gotten mad today and removed him from class? She was certain Colin had never lost his temper in a classroom. He'd probably never even had a student interrupt him. How would he believe she was a good teacher if he knew she'd dealt with all that and more?

Allison did the only thing she could think of. She rushed at Colin and swung her arms around his neck. In her mind, it looked sponta-

neous. Passionate. Romantic. They'd kiss under the stars as the swaying light from the jack-o'-lantern candles danced around them.

In reality, her aim was as bad as always, and her nose collided with
his cheek. An unattractive grunt heaved from her lips.

And that was all before Colin lost his balance, dumping them
both into the very large, very muddy puddle behind him.

The water was cold and slimy and some of it splashed across her
face and into her hair. More seeped through the thin layer of her shirt
and smeared over her jeans.

Colin sat motionless beside her, his long legs splayed in front
of him like a stringless puppet. Pinocchio come to life. His mouth
opened and closed, but no words came out.

Allison searched out Cole from between the few onlookers that
wandered by. One or two took pictures. Others laughed. No one
helped. Her stomach sank when she caught the back of his Red Sox
jacket disappearing down a different trail.

Of course Cole had gone the other way. He hadn't even noticed
her.

"What was that?" Colin painted mud across his face as he tried to
clear his vision.

A blush attacked Allison's cheeks. She'd forced them to take a
mud bath for nothing. "I wanted to see the elephants." Warily, she
climbed to her feet.

"And make out in front of them?" Colin rose too and began to
wring out the cuffs of his sweater. Droplets broke the surface of the
puddle like rain.

"I felt inspired," she deadpanned pathetically.

"Allison."

Sighing, she kicked at a loose stone. They weren't supposed to talk
about anything related to Wendy's class. That was the whole reason
they were doing so well. No competition. No need to cut each other
down. This also meant that she hadn't had to lie to him in weeks. The

thought of doing it again summoned a lump to her throat. One she couldn't bring herself to push past.

"Cole's here." A cold wind cut across the open path, and Allison wrapped her soggy arms around herself as if that might help.

"From Wendy's class?"

She nodded. "And my recitation."

Colin's eyes narrowed. "And you don't want him to know we're together?" he said carefully.

"No." Allison took a few steps toward him. "I want everyone to know we're together. I didn't want Cole to see *me*."

"Why?"

Her shoulders slumped. She didn't want to say it.

He spoke her name softly in that way that uncoiled her muscles and loosened her joints. This time, it unraveled the words from her mouth, too.

"I'm not a good teacher."

His head tilted. "What do you mean? Of course you are."

He reached for her hands, but she stuffed them behind her back. She couldn't touch him right now. She was too embarrassed.

"I haven't been honest about how my recitations are going." She leaned against the nearby fence. "I'm having a really hard time getting my students to talk. Some of them, like Cole, don't even listen to me. I don't know what I'm doing wrong. Maybe I don't know how to come up with good discussion questions or they don't trust me or I'm not interesting or . . ." She shrugged uselessly. Allison could list every reason she'd collected for why she was failing at teaching, but none of that would erase her lies. Her stomach clenched. "I just can't do it."

She'd never struggled so hard with anything. When she stood up in front of her students, watching half of them text on their phones or do homework on their laptops, others scribbling listlessly, all her confidence dissolved. It was like the smart, self-assured version of herself fell away, nothing but a facade. Over the last few weeks, she'd begun to doubt the parts of herself that she'd always loved most, and she worried, now that Colin knew the truth, he'd start to doubt them, too. "Those first few weeks, we were so competitive. I couldn't let you think I wasn't good enough, so I lied." She fisted her hands and dug them into her thighs. "Then, after things with us . . . changed, I'd hoped that I'd get better and turn it all into truth." Which still hadn't happened. Allison sometimes worried it never would.

Colin folded his arms over his chest, and his mouth pulled tight. "Why are you telling me now?"

It was not the question Allison had expected. Her mouth was gummy with nerves, and it seemed to take forever to find her answer. "Because we . . ." She cleared her throat. "We . . . *you,* deserve honesty."

"You could have told me."

Maybe that was true after their trip from Maine. But not before. Before, he would have taken any advantage he could get.

Or was that the old Colin? Their past was such a quagmire Allison struggled to know when exactly he'd become the man standing before her. The one she could love enough to break her all over again if she let him. "I'm telling you now," she said.

His thin throat bobbed against a swallow, and his eyes pinned her in place. He seemed, not angry, but stormy. As if he didn't know what to do. "Allison."

She leaned forward, shivering in her wet clothes.

"I . . ." He removed his glasses and wiped the lenses with a dry spot on his T-shirt. "I understand why you felt like you had to lie. But that was the old us." He took her hand and brought her knuckles to his lips the way he always did.

Her eyes widened as she anticipated the warm brush of his breath across her cold skin. She felt open, vulnerable, the last of the lies she was hiding fallen away. Nothing stood between them now. "And that's not us anymore."

He kissed her knuckles, then her palm. She felt his smile against her skin. "Definitely not." A smile of her own blossomed on her lips in return.

Wendy's mentorship would have been enough to tear them apart back at Brown. Allison's loss of the Rising Star Award had proven that. But this version of them was built of something stronger. She was sure it could weather anything. Hurricanes. Tornadoes. Grad school.

Whatever happened after their presentations, whatever Wendy decided, they'd get through it. As a team, not as rivals. As long as they were together, they'd be okay.

Allison pressed herself into Colin's side. The arm he stretched across her shoulders was solid and true.

Pulling her close, he said, "Let's get a hot chocolate or something. Those elephants look warmer than us."

Chapter 31

The upbeat chorus of an old song about doing the twist crooned from the speakers of Colin's car radio as he navigated through Providence's endless one-way streets. He bopped his head this way and that along with the tune. A smile had not left his mouth since he'd picked Allison up.

She couldn't understand his calm. Their presentations were days away, the workload for the semester was ramping up, and the encroaching burnout had Allison about ready to crawl out of her skin. Whether she was in class or not, there was always something she *could* be working on: getting ahead on the readings, grading student work, doing more research for her presentation. Her time never felt like her own. And on the rare occasion when she gave herself a day off, she wasted most of it worrying about how long it would take her to make up for the time she was losing.

Which was exactly what she was doing now as she watched the glow of busy restaurants and crowded stores blur by.

"Where are we going?" What Allison actually wanted to know was how his presentation prep was going and how the hell he wasn't freaking out. But they'd made a promise to leave all aspects of Wendy's class—including the stress—out of their relationship, and she wouldn't violate that, no matter how curious she was.

So, instead, she fixated on whatever this surprise was. Colin had said to wear a dress, and they were in an older part of the city she had never visited. They'd already eaten dinner. She had no idea what they were about to do.

Colin mimed zipping his mouth, then tossing a key out the window. "You have seen a zipper, right? They don't have keys."

With a sigh, he reached for the window as if retrieving the key, spun it a few times at the corner of his mouth, and chucked it outside once more.

Allison snorted. "I'm pretty sure you turned that enough times that you unlocked it again."

"I hate you," he insisted, but the gentle brightness in his eyes and the smile on his lips said the opposite.

After another few minutes, Colin slowed the car to parallel park next to a small store front. The sign above it read *Katrina's School of Dance*. Switching off the engine, he beamed at Allison. "I think it's time we learn something besides the Cowboy Hustle."

Her mouth fell open. "Are you serious?" Dance lessons, especially ones they were destined to be incredibly bad at, seemed like the last thing they had time for right now.

Colin pressed a hand gently to her knee. She hadn't realized how erratically she was bouncing it until he touched her. Man, she really was stressed out. "I think it would do us both some good to focus on something else. Even if it's just for an hour." Had she been like this all week and she hadn't even noticed? So much so that Colin felt like he needed to find a remedy?

Her eyes swept back toward the dance studio. "Sure, but we could have gone to a movie." Or better yet, gotten drunk or had sex (or, ideally, both). Something that would literally alter the chemicals of her brain and flip the panicked part off.

Unbuckling his seatbelt, Colin popped open his door. "I figured we needed something a little more active." Before he climbed out, he took her hand and brought her knuckles to his mouth in that way that always left Allison boneless and loose. "Besides, that night we line-danced was . . ." With a shake of his head, he kissed her hand again.

Epic? Magical? Unforgettable? She wanted him to fill in the blank, but he only brushed his lips a third time to her fingers and then urged her to follow him inside.

A sudden surge of emotion caught in Allison's chest. Whenever she thought of that night, she remembered how well they'd gotten along. Not only laughing and having fun, but working in tandem, as a team, Colin relying on his memory to know what came next, Allison keeping them in rhythm. It reminded her that, if they'd been smart enough to get out of their own way, they could have had something special, even back then. These last two years didn't have to have been wasted.

Is that why Colin wanted to revisit that night? Was this his way of showing her they were a good team? That no matter what happened after this week, whatever Wendy decided, they could remain that way if they chose to? If they decided it was worth the work.

As she stepped through the doorway of the dance studio in his wake, Allison realized that, every day, she became more sure that it was.

For the next hour, a very patient, very kind Katrina did her best to guide the two least graceful people on earth through a simple waltz and a beginner's samba.

Though there were a few crushed toes in the process, Allison and Colin managed to pick up most of the waltz's box step.

The samba was another story. The music was too quick and staccato, and the routine too intricate, with partner work that extended far beyond holding each other's hands at the correct height. Allison struggled not to collapse into giggles whenever Colin had to gyrate his hips, and she fell every time they tried to perform a dip.

There were a few counts in the middle of the dance, though, that they'd been able to master. Some cha-cha steps that transitioned into a series of hip rolls followed by Colin leading Allison in a twirl. Mostly, they fumbled around for an hour like newly born calves who didn't understand their legs, but when they danced those moves, Allison felt competent. Sexy, even.

For the last fifteen minutes, Katrina left them alone on the floor to practice. As soon as she shut her office door, Colin drew Allison closer, so their thighs brushed and their hips met as they swayed with the cha-cha. When they stepped into the hip roll, Allison thrust her backside firmly against his groin. His hands grasped at her waist like he couldn't hold her tight enough.

Colin burrowed his face into that sensitive spot between her shoulder and her neck. "I think we need to try that step again." His breath rushed hot across her skin.

"You mean this one?" Allison's voice was husky, half lost to the desire starting to burn at her center. She rocked her body against his. Almost like they were reenacting that first night they met, only with a completely different ending.

She had to swallow a gasp as his hands sketched hot paths up and down her thighs, his thumb venturing a little higher beneath her skirt's hem each time.

The five-minute drive back to Allison's was torture. Her body throbbed with want as Colin traced circles around her knee-cap with his thumb. She was seconds from grabbing his hand and shoving it between her legs when he pulled the car into her driveway.

Though all she wanted to do was sprint for the house, she waited as he came around to open her door. Cradling her face in his hands, he guided her mouth to his as he eased her up from the seat.

The kiss was hungry and alive, their mouths open, tongues pushing against each other as their limbs did the same.

There was no way they were making it all the way upstairs to her bedroom, but there was a table just inside the front door, beneath the stairs. Allison slid up on it as Colin wrestled off his pants. She was so worked up, so primed and ready, that she almost broke apart the moment he was inside her.

As they gripped each other with a need that left them frenzied, a sense of closeness overwhelmed Allison. Colin's arms felt like home, a promise of safety, even as her heart thudded like she'd just embarked somewhere new and unknown that she'd been dying to see.

An hour—and a second round—later, they lay in Allison's bed, a re-run of some crime investigation show murmuring in the background as the TV's soft glow spread over the twisted sheets, and their equally tangled limbs.

Colin curled a strand of Allison's hair around his fingers as she pillowed her head on his shoulder.

"So," he said softly. "Tell me the latest with your mom."

Allison sat up with a screech, clutching a sheet to her bare chest. "Don't bring up my mother when I'm naked."

He laughed. "Sorry." It took a second of coaxing (and quite a few soft kisses) to convince her to lie back down. "But since I've already summoned her, are things better? Has Mrs. Avery stopped bringing up your father constantly?"

With as much petulance as she could muster, Allison said, "You can call my mother Cassandra."

Colin held his hands up. "Oh no. Maybe when we're married, but until then, all significant others' parents are strictly Mr. and Mrs. or the gender-neutral equivalent."

Allison choked, flipping over on her stomach so she could see his face more clearly. Her bare legs kicked behind her in glee. "When we're what?"

His face flushed right up to the tips of his ears. He tried to pull a pillow over his head but she knocked it away. "I didn't . . . not like you and me, us . . . just, in general—the general royal we. I won't call anyone's parents by their first name until they're officially my in-laws. That's it. All I meant."

A harried Colin Benjamin was Allison's favorite toy. "We haven't even discussed if I *want* to get married," she said. "Have you been planning on kids too? Because I'm definitely not having any of those."

Colin covered his face with a sheet this time. "I didn't mean *us,*" he insisted, his voice muffled by the fabric.

"What's my wedding dress going to look like? Where will the wedding be? Do you have a *binder*? Can I see it?"

For the second time tonight, Colin said, "I hate you," with more affection in his voice than Allison could stand.

She laughed. "You *loooovvvveee* me."

Jerking the sheet down, he gazed at her with wide eyes. The corners of his lips wavered, his face more serious than she'd ever seen it. When he spoke, Allison could barely hear him over the TV. "What if I did?"

This time, it was her fumbling for words. "What?"

"Would that be so strange?"

She studied his face. Was this a joke? She was afraid to answer until she was sure. Because the truth was, those words had wanted to sneak their way out of Allison's mouth a few times now.

She'd already loved him once. Doing it again was easy.

"Are you being serious?" They were both angled forward, that invisible thread that bound them yanking tight.

"Allison." The intensity in his gaze pinned her in place. "I can't *fall* in love with you. I'm already there. I never stopped."

Her whole body went slack, the words so unexpected they snapped every bit of her restraint. Letting her sheet fall away, she eased up until they were face-to-face and brought her mouth down to his.

"I love you, too," she whispered against his lips.

Chapter 32

Two nights later, Allison sat on Mandy's couch, shaking her phone as if a text might rattle out of it.

Except for a Jed update from her mother, it hadn't made a sound all day. She'd checked the volume twice, switched the power on and off, and even disconnected and reconnected the Wi-Fi, but nothing seemed to be wrong. It was simply that no one (more specifically, Colin) was responding. Her *good morning* text sat on the chat screen, lonely and abandoned.

Mandy furrowed her brow as she glanced up from her cross-stitch pattern. "I don't think it works like a Polaroid picture."

"Did you know that's a myth?" The needle she'd stabbed into her Aida fabric jabbed Allison's thumb, making her grimace. She really needed to get a thimble. Or stop crafting with sharp objects when she was under duress.

"What is?"

"That you have to shake a Polaroid. OutKast was lying to a whole generation of listeners." Colin had told her that. Allison's stomach clenched.

Mandy pursed her lips. "Good to know. I'll add it to the vault."

She tapped her temple. "But seriously, what are you doing with your phone? You've been hounding it since dinner."

Allison set down her fabric and slouched deeper into Mandy's very soft, very cozy sofa. "I haven't heard from Colin at all today."

And not much since Monday. They'd been curled up together in Allison's bed, still breathless from post-I-love-you sex when Colin's aunt called. Allison couldn't hear what she'd said but Colin had turned to winter right in front of her: skin white as snow beneath glasses the color of holly berry. He was already pulling on his pants as he'd hung up. "They need my help with Charlie."

Allison had risen to her feet too, scrounging for her bra in the dark room. "Is everything okay?"

"I don't know." He was focused on picking up his belongings, shoving them all in his backpack.

Allison threw open her closet. "What should I bring?"

"For what?"

"Well, I'm coming, right?"

Colin reached out and squeezed her hand. "Not tonight. It's late. He's not himself at night. Sometimes, he's mean. I don't want you to see him like that."

Allison's stomach had dropped, a door slammed in her face. "Keep me updated, then?"

"Of course." The half kiss he'd forced to her temple as he rushed for the stairs wasn't the most reassuring.

That was the last time Allison had seen him, and, except for a few brief texts yesterday, the last time she'd talked to him.

"Huh. Weird. He wasn't in Victorian Lit, was he?" Mandy observed.

"He's missed all his classes this week." At this point, Allison wasn't sure if he'd be there for his lecture in Wendy's class tomorrow. "Something's up with his grandfather."

Mandy set her fabric aside. "Shit. What's going on?"

As Colin's girlfriend, Allison should know the answer to this. She should be privy to all of his stressors the way he was with hers. She should be *with* him right now, bringing everyone food, getting him to rest, whatever he needed. But all she could do was shrug. "I know he's got dementia but this seemed like something else. He didn't tell me much."

"Ah, he's one of those."

Allison narrowed her eyes. "One of what?"

"One of those people who refuses to let anyone help."

Colin 1.0 had certainly been that way.

Mandy grabbed a peanut butter cookie off the plate on the coffee table. "My ex-boyfriend was like that. He'd disappear anytime something was going on. Getting him to talk was like chipping at titanium with a plastic spoon."

Allison thought back to Colin's swift reply Monday night when she'd asked to go with him. And to all his curt, vague texts since. She was definitely being shut out.

"Is that what broke you two up?"

"Nah. He cheated on me."

"I'll curse him."

Mandy laughed. "I broke all his expensive Star Wars toys. I figure that's curse enough." She folded half the cookie into her small mouth. "Honestly, though. It was for the best. We'd dated for most of college and I think things between us had mostly fizzled but we didn't know how to end it."

"So, he went nuclear?"

"Basically."

"Fuck him." Mandy deserved better. Allison stabbed at her fabric again. "I'd say I'd have Colin set you up with a friend, but at this rate, it would end up being Ethan."

Mandy's cackle echoed against the ceiling. "I mean, theoretically he's hot, but his personality ruins it. Can you imagine having sex with him?"

"God, no."

"He'd probably bring a textbook along."

"Or correct your grammar while you talked dirty," Allison said.

"I need you to have fewer clothing on," Mandy mumbled in a faux-seductive whisper.

"Less clothing," Allison deadpanned.

They both dissolved into a fit of giggles.

By the time Allison gathered her stuff to head home half an hour later, her abs hurt from laughing and, finally, for a few minutes, she stopped worrying about Colin's silence.

The living room of Allison's house looked as if a fabric store had exploded.

The couch was half-covered in pink, yellow, and white stripes, and half-draped in a mulberry silk. Cotton in a creamy ivory puddled in the seat of the armchair, its back wearing gray crushed velvet like a cape. Scraps in a cascade of shades and textures spotted the floor and area rug, fashion confetti. And at the center of the room, a dress form held court, blocking the television.

On it was a black dress spotted with large sunflowers, sleeveless with knotting at the chest over a small peekaboo hole. Beneath its metal legs, Monty snoozed, little bows of fabric tied around each of his paws.

"Soph?" Allison set her stuff down on the floor and glanced around. The room was quiet except for the low hum of the TV and Monty's little scritches against the floor as he ran in his sleep.

Things with Allison and Sophie had been tense since their talk about Colin, though on the rare occasions they were both home, they pretended otherwise.

Feet drummed the stairs. "Hey." Black fabric was thrown over Sophie's head, more bunched in her arms, making her resemble a nun.

"You've outgrown your room, huh?" Allison joked.

Something clouded Sophie's face. "Yeah. Sorry. I have to get a ton of stuff done before the weekend." As she swept by, Allison's nose filled with Sophie's cinnamon scent. "I have an interview in Boston."

She might as well have shoved Excalibur through Allison's insides. "That's great!" She tried hard to sound excited. "With whom?"

"Kisses and Hugs. They're a relatively up-and-coming plus-sized label. Eric's friends with one of their lead designers, and he gave them my sketches. They called me."

Allison's eyes widened. "The Viking has connections?"

"I know he can be a Neanderthal, but he's fun. And he's a model so he knows *everyone*."

Allison swallowed hard against the burn of loneliness that crawled up her throat. "It sounds like a fantastic opportunity." She knelt in front of Monty and pulled the floppy animal into her lap. At least her puppy wouldn't outgrow her. Allison had all the food.

Sophie watched her, fussing with the yard of mulberry silk. "Would you have time to model some things for me tomorrow?"

Allison's head snapped her way. "Really?"

"I'll be bringing the garments, obviously, but it's always great to be able to show them on an actual body, too. And you're an excellent model."

She recognized the olive branch Sophie was extending, but the pettier, pretzel-levels-of-salty part of Allison didn't want to do anything to help her friend leave her. An inner battle of biblical proportions commenced.

"How long do you think it would take? I have a big presentation in my TA class next week." That was the truth, at least. Whether Colin showed up for his own lecture tomorrow or not, Allison's would happen next week. She needed to review it at least three more times and give it some final tweaks.

Sophie frowned. "I thought we could make a night of it. Just the two of us. Order Chinese and Thai"—a long-standing tradition for them, since they could never decide which they wanted more—"watch swoony movies."

Allison pressed her hands to her center, trying to quell the ache blooming there. It sounded perfect. Exactly what they needed.

"But we can make it quick if you're too busy with school and Colin and whatever—"

"I'm not." Allison's voice squeaked.

"What did he do?"

The harshness in Sophie's tone pulled Allison's gaze to her face. "What?"

"I know that voice. The Colin-was-a-dick voice."

Allison set Monty back in his bed of fabric beneath the dress form and rose to her feet. "He's just got a lot going on and has been a little distant."

Sophie surprised her by saying nothing. She only nodded.

Rubbing her palms against her legs, Allison made some excuse about craving her pajamas and headed for the stairs. Her mind was already writing a new WCS list.

WCS FOR YOUR BOYFRIEND IGNORING YOU DURING A CRISIS

1. He finds your presence stressful, not calming.

2. There's someone else he'd rather be leaning on.

3.

"Allison?" Sophie stood in the doorway.

"Yeah?"

"I just want what's best for you."

Allison swallowed. "Even if it's him?"

Sophie's mouth puckered like she'd eaten an entire lemon, but she nodded. "I'm not going anywhere, even if I leave. You know that, right?" Her jaw trembled, like she was afraid of how Allison might respond. "Brain twins forever."

Tears burned Allison's eyes, and she failed to blink them away.

"You know I want all the good things for you, right?" It was true, even if it hurt. Even if it meant everything had to change.

A smile tipped Sophie's lips. A few tears of her own stole down her round cheeks. "We're going to be great. Both of us."

Allison wanted so badly to believe her.

By the time she got to her room, her phone was already in her hand.

Allison Avery: I wish you'd talk to me about whatever is going on.

She needed to stop keeping things in, to stop swallowing stuff down to avoid rocking the boat. If she'd told Sophie how she was feeling, if she'd spoken up about Colin, they wouldn't have lost so much time together. And maybe, if Allison had opened up to Jed when she was younger, she wouldn't have all these unresolved issues eating at her now.

She didn't want Colin to be another item on the list of silences that hurt her.

She jumped when her phone buzzed in her hand.

Unknown Number: I know I've sucked the past few days. I'm sorry.

Allison Avery: What can I do?

Unknown Number: Bring your pom-poms tomorrow.

Allison Avery: You're going to do your lecture?

Unknown Number: Of course.

Allison Avery: I thought maybe you weren't up for it.

Unknown Number: It's more important than ever.

Allison Avery: What does that mean?

Unknown Number: I'll tell you about it tomorrow. I promise. After I
get this lecture off my plate, I'll tell you everything.

His words were cryptic. Ominous even. But at least he was talking.

Allison Avery: Okay.

Unknown Number: I love you.

Unknown Number: So much.

Allison Avery: I love you, too.

Tossing her phone on the bed, Allison dragged her laptop toward
her. When you wanted answers, tomorrow could feel like an eternity,
and too many thoughts were spinning through her head.

There was only one way to quiet that storm.

Feed it something else.

Clicking open her presentation, she stared at the first slide for
what felt like the hundredth time.

Beauty Is a Beast.

Chapter 33

It was a truth universally acknowledged that the acquisition of a Ph.D. resulted in a total loss of one's ability to properly manage electronics.

Allison observed this hypothesis in play as Wendy and Colin hustled around the front of the lecture hall jabbing the buttons on the control panel and poking at Colin's computer, all while waving at the projector as if it were powered by a motion sensor.

"I swear this thing is vindictive. I called it archaic last week and now it refuses to function." Wendy's bracelets (thick onyx cuffs this time) clacked over her head.

"Everything's plugged in, right?" Allison called from her seat. She'd offered assistance twice, only to have Colin practically shove her off the dais. It must be some presentation he had cued up because he hadn't been able to sit still since he'd rushed into the room a few minutes ago, his pale forehead a swimming pool of sweat.

This isn't about you, Allison reiterated to herself for what felt like the fiftieth time. *He's nervous.* After this, they'd talk like he promised and everything would go back to normal. Crisis averted. Hill climbed. Enemy dueled.

"Obviously, everything's plugged in," Colin replied in a huff.

"So then what's that?" Allison gestured to an HDMI cable flailing against the side of the podium.

"Shit." With a sheepish grin, he jammed the plug into his adapter and the gigantic screen behind him burst into brightness. Captain Pepper Jack, larger than life as he perched on the back of a worn sofa, surveyed the class with his typical apathy.

Returning to their table, Colin wrestled a notebook out of his bag and began flicking through it. The loose pages rattled against his trembling hands.

"Hey." Allison grabbed at the front of his cardigan. It was a gun-steel-gray cable knit with a hole in the left pocket he'd had forever. She remembered it vividly because he'd worn it the day he broke up with her. Then, she'd thought it was the ugliest article of clothing in existence, but now she appreciated how it broadened his shoulders and lured the green from his eyes. "Take a breath," she urged.

He started at her touch.

She pulled her hands back into her lap. "Is this about Charlie? Did something happen?"

Colin's gaze honed in on what Allison could see was an empty page in front of him. "No. No. Nothing like that." He swallowed. "I'm just ready for this to be over."

"You're going to be great. Your recitation students love you, re-member?" *Unlike mine,* Allison's tone said. She was surprised by how much she liked that he'd understand the subtext. No more secrets. *"I love you."*

He shook his head. There was so much gel in his hair that it didn't move. Nothing soothed Colin's nerves like styling products. "Talking the whole time, though? With Wendy here? I don't know this stuff well enough to do that."

Allison frowned. "Of course you do," she said. "You've done the work. It'll be there for you when you need it."

His sharp Adam's apple bobbed with another hard swallow. He

was chewing on the inside of his lip. She tried to take his hand, but he was a step out of reach.

Rubbing his eyes under his frames, Colin finally focused on her. "What if . . . what if today doesn't go as planned?"

"What do you mean?"

He closed his eyes, his shoulders pushing back, bracing for something. Was he worried about tanking this? Or about what would happen if his presentation was so good he won the mentorship?

Allison would be disappointed. And a little pissed. But if Colin earned the spot by his own merit, then she couldn't hold that against him.

For the first time, she truly let herself consider what it would mean if he won. It would suck. It would hurt something fierce. But unlike with the Rising Star, they'd get through it together, not let it tear them apart. She believed that with her whole heart.

"We'll be okay? No matter what happens today?" It was almost a plea.

Allison angled across the desk and caught his hand. "We'll be okay," she promised. "Always."

He closed his eyes like he was meditating. Or letting her words absorb into his skin. When he looked at her again, his gaze was a black hole, sucking in everything else around them. There was only the smell of hair product and soap and the way his presence pinned Allison in place like ink dried to a piece of parchment and the drum of her heart in every bit of her when he was this close.

He brought her knuckles to his mouth as he'd done a million times before, and yet somehow it was charged with something different.

His kiss was a forest, and Allison a little red-cloaked girl. His lips a candied cabin, and she lost and starving. She wasn't sure she wanted to be found.

Wendy cleared her throat, and Colin dropped Allison's hand as if he'd been yanked away.

"You've got this," she whispered as he turned back to the dais.

Hopefully, her words could break through the pressure he was putting on himself. Everything about graduate school was already amped up and urgent. Every time they spoke in class, every paper they wrote, every breath they took on this campus felt capable of tipping the scales. One perfect presentation could lead to a career-defining mentorship, while one off day, one bad paper, could be the difference between ABD (all but dissertation) status or a terminal MA (and dismissal from the program). No wonder Colin looked like he'd spent too long crammed in a waffle iron. He had no other options if Claymore didn't work out.

He shuffled his way toward the podium as Wendy called the class to order and introduced Colin. Some of the students clapped, a few others cheered.

Allison's insides twisted but she clamped down her jealousy. Colin had the right to be good at something.

His eyes settled on her as he cued up his monitor. His lips crimped up at the corners, as if the sight of her fortified him. She shook her fist in the air, a subtle sportsball cheer.

As the projector screen lit up and Colin's display bled into focus, Allison tried to guess what kind of image he'd use on the title page. Knowing him, he'd find something grossly pornographic to shock people. A really bawdy piece of medieval art or some NSFW cartoon. Maybe a still right out of a modern porno.

Even with all those guesses, what appeared made Allison's heart halt.

The cover photo was of a beauty pageant. Seven women graced the stage. Six of them, three on each side, were beautifully coifed, their hair styled to shine, sleek satin dresses hugging their curves, diamonds raining off their skin. Only the woman at the center wore a crown, a bouquet of roses clutched to her chest. Unlike the others, her dress was ragged and full of holes, her makeup smeared. Bald patches on her scalp peeked out from under her elaborate bun, and her skin was torn and bloody. Her eyes were black holes, her teeth bared and dripping with dark fluid.

Across the top, an elegant script read: *Beauty Is a Beast.*

Allison was on her feet and out the door before Colin began to speak.

Chapter 34

Unknown Number: Where did you go? [deleted]

Unknown Number: I was going to explain everything after the lecture, remember? I meant it when I promised you that. [deleted]

Unknown Number: Allison. Please talk to me. [deleted]

Unknown Number. I love you. [deleted]

Allison Avery: Leave me alone.

Chapter 35

"For, though myself be a ful vicious man, A moral tale yet I yow telle kan," or Why Colin Benjamin is a lying, swindling assbag and does not deserve a mentorship

1. He plagiarized. One of the academic mortal sins. Fraud is the eighth circle of hell in *The Inferno*.

2. He slept with Allison solely to steal her work. He actively manipulated her with this sole intent. He should be cloned and placed in that eighth circle twice.

3. Did he actually get into Claymore on his own . . . ?

Allison typed furiously into the open email window.

Had this been Colin's plan all along? Lull her into complacency? Build her trust by admitting his (probably false) failures? Convince her to do the same? Trick her into falling for him all over again so that he could steal her (clearly superior) presentation and win the mentorship? He was Rumpelstiltskin meets Mr. Hyde meets the Artful Dodger. Plus, a little bit of Marlowe's Faustus and Milton's Satan tossed in for good measure. A trickster. A demon. A cheat.

And like a fool, she'd trusted him. She should have known better. This time, though, he wouldn't win. She'd renew her focus. Dig in deeper. Slaughter him intellectually until he was nothing but a bloody pulp.

It was what she should have been doing all along.

"This is low, even by his standards." Sophie was pacing Allison's room, a piece of red licorice hanging from her mouth. Monty pranced in her wake, nipping at her heels. The clothes Allison was going to model for Sophie's interview were draped over the bed, except for the sailor dress, which Allison had thrown on for the extra confidence boost (it hugged all her best curves perfectly because Sophie was a fashion genius). "You're going to nail him to the floor, right?"

Allison smoothed down the dress's collar, the way its edges accentuated her cleavage feeling like its own kind of revenge. She'd beat Colin *and* look good doing it. Double whammy.

"I'm writing the email now." Wendy would appreciate Allison's quote from "The Pardoner's Prologue," and she was bound to be every bit as disgusted by Colin's theft as Allison was.

That presentation had been her best work. She'd been mulling over her analysis of beauty in medieval romance for years. She'd never come up with something to match it, not in four days. Maybe not ever.

She had no choice. She had to tell Wendy everything.

Sophie yanked the licorice from her mouth and flailed it around for emphasis. "Let her know they need to act fast. I want him expelled before I kill him."

Allison snorted. Her pulse felt like it was directing her fingertips as they clacked against the keys. No matter how fast they flew, they couldn't keep up with the angry thoughts roiling like a stormy sea through her head.

She had to focus on this presentation, on school, on the thing she could fix, because if Allison let her mind drift toward the ache at her center, she'd fall apart.

She would *not* fall apart. Not for him. Not for anyone.

She swiped her knuckles at her burning eyes and kept typing. She was adding the final letters to her signature when someone called her name.

It sounded muffled, like a voice yelling through a phone. Or from somewhere far away. Both she and Sophie were on their feet the next time they heard it.

Allison's bedroom window faced the street. Throwing it open, she hung her head out to see past the porch's overhang.

Colin stood on the sidewalk, still dressed in that awful cardigan, the gel on his head still shiny and sleek. He'd exploded her whole world, and he didn't even have a hair out of place. It only made her hate him more.

"What are you doing here?" Allison dipped her voice low so he'd have to strain to hear her.

Shielding his glasses from the sun, he gazed up. "You aren't answering my texts."

"I don't want to talk to you."

"Please. You have to."

"I definitely do not." Allison stepped away and began to close the window.

"Fuck off, Colin," Sophie yelled from behind her.

"Allison, please." Colin sat on the ground and crossed his arms over his chest. "I'm not leaving until you talk to me."

He was stubborn enough to mean it, and Allison would never figure out what to do about her own presentation with fucking Colin Benjamin (thief, liar, asshole) sitting out there lurking.

Slamming the window shut, she stalked toward the stairs. "I'll be back."

"Give him hell, girl," Sophie declared.

Allison's heart rammed in her chest, but she did her best to appear completely calm, nonplussed even, as she stepped out onto the porch. Silently thanking Sophie for the dress, she pushed back her shoulders and stared Colin down.

He jumped to his feet. She could imagine his knobby bones rattling beneath his skin. Any other day, the way his eyes slipped over her body would have made her shiver, but today she felt only rage. This dress was for *her*, and her alone.

"Thank you—"

"You have two minutes." Allison folded her arms.

He sighed and dragged a hand through his hair, finally mussing it. "I'm sorry. I thought . . . I thought changing my topic would level the playing field. Put us on the same page. It—"

"Bullshit." Allison's fists were cement. Heavy and dangerous. She clenched them at her sides. "We're so far from on the same page. If I present my work Tuesday, it will look like I copied you. I've been planning that lecture for weeks. On an idea I've been building on for years. Now I have *nothing*." She stomped down the porch steps until they were at eye level. "Be honest. Were you only pretending to be conflicted about your topic so I'd share mine?"

She was shaking, all the words she couldn't hold back pinging small cracks into her bones, forging fault lines she'd never fill. "How far back does this little ruse of yours go?" It was a struggle not to yell, but she wouldn't give him her anger. She wouldn't give him anything anymore. "Was anything between us ever real? Or have you been using me from the start, some insurance to guarantee you'd win?"

"No. That's not—Allison." Her name wasn't a sacred word. It was an entreaty. His jaw quivered.

But he'd ripped too many holes in her. There was nothing left. He'd taken the parts that Allison loved best—her ideas, her interpretative skills, her close readings—and used them against her. She was already a bad teacher. Now she'd look like a bad scholar, too.

So she found some weapons to fight back. "Maybe you don't belong in grad school if you can't come up with your own ideas."

He jerked as if she'd pelted him with something. His hands flitted at his sides. Sick hummingbirds. Dying butterflies. Searching for a final resting place. His mouth opened but nothing came out.

What if it was true? What if he'd been lying when he said his aunt had no role in his acceptance? If he'd stoop low enough to take Allison's ideas, who's to say he wouldn't force his way into grad school by whatever means necessary? His drive knew no limits. "Maybe that's because your aunt did get you into this program."

Colin's jaw was slack enough to catch flies. "You know she didn't."

"I don't know anything." Allison eased herself back up the stairs. The door felt a million miles away. "And I certainly don't know you. Because the guy I thought I was dating"—she stopped, stared him down—"who I thought I *loved,* would not have shown up in the sweater he wore when he dumped me two years ago to give a presentation he'd *stolen* from me. To win a mentorship I have been working toward for half a decade."

She couldn't reach him if she stretched her arms, but he was still too close. Anywhere on this block, in this city, this state, this hemisphere, on this *planet,* was too close.

"I don't want to see you again." She turned away as she said it. "Don't come back."

Every piece of Allison was full of lead. Deadened and numb. Somehow, though, she made it into the house. Back to her room.

Sophie's eyes followed her quietly as Allison dropped down at her computer. The searing anger that had inspired the first draft of her email to Wendy had been extinguished, replaced by a sadness so heavy it threatened to pull her right through the floor.

With fingers that could barely move, she revised her note to her professor and sent it off, then burst into tears.

Chapter 36

Mei bustled through the doorway of the English Department office, a steaming bowl cradled in a paper towel.

She dropped it to her desk like it burned. "Hey. Allison, do you need something?"

Allison had practically run from the library to Haber Hall after her recitations to find Wendy's office still dark. Which was what happened when you were half an hour early.

"I'm just waiting for Wendy." Her finger tapping against the desktop, Allison peeked again through the doorway, as if her professor might have been beamed into her office via spaceship.

Her phone vibrated in her pocket, but Allison didn't bother to check it. It would no doubt be Colin. Again. He didn't seem to know when to stop. If he thought this was going to be one of those situations where persistence would win the day, he was in for a rude awakening.

She should block his number, but Allison wanted to wait until she'd spoken to Wendy, so she could witness Colin's demise firsthand. She'd decided, rather than explaining it all in an email, to ask Wendy to meet in person to talk about what had happened.

Sitting at her desk, Mei stirred her meal—it smelled like rice and pork and deliciousness—with a spoon. "You look like my daughter when she needs to confess something." Her mouth curved into a grin. "Did you play with my makeup?"

Even as her hands crushed into fists, Allison laughed. "It's nothing."

"It doesn't look like nothing. Spill."

Maybe Mei would be a good outside perspective. Talking to her might help organize Allison's thoughts ahead of her meeting. She sighed. "Have you ever had someone copy your work?"

Mei's eyebrows dipped. "Like you say something in class and one of your classmates takes it and turns it into a paper?"

"Something like that." Allison couldn't bring herself to admit it was a far more flagrant offense.

"I have. My second year here. And it's a pretty terrible feeling. When I started this program, I had these rosy ideas about what graduate school would be. Everyone sitting around sharing their thoughts, learning to grow as scholars together. And there's plenty of times when it is like that."

It was a relief to hear that Allison hadn't been alone in her lofty expectations.

Giving her bowl another stir, Mei took a bite, chewing thoughtfully. "But academia is shrinking and the job market is a ghost town and everything about this world feels precarious. There's so much pressure, and that encourages people to make bad decisions."

That seemed like a charitable way of framing intellectual theft. But even as she seethed with anger, Allison couldn't ignore how much stress Colin was under. Wanting to make his family proud, all the self-doubt that came with so much rejection, this chance that felt like his only one, it had to be crushing. Not that any of that gave him the right to appropriate her work. Allison didn't have to forgive him just because he might have had a reasonable motivation.

He'd betrayed her. She hadn't set up this meeting to understand his choices. She was here to fix things for *her*. "What did you do about it?" she asked. "Did you confront them? Go to your professor?"

Allison still wasn't sure how much she wanted to tell Wendy. Of course, she'd explain that "Beauty Is a Beast" had been her lecture topic. But should she mention her suspicions about Colin's aunt? Should she explain how Colin had manipulated her?

Mei shook her head. "I came up with something else."

Allison startled. Say nothing? That seemed more in Colin's interest than hers. "But what if it was your best idea? What if you'd thought about it for a really long time?"

Mei slid open her top drawer and retrieved a small dish of wrapped caramels. She offered it to Allison. "This is my anxiety stash. Let it melt on your tongue. No chewing. It will help you calm down."

Allison did as she was told, though it went against everything she believed in. She was one of those people who cracked her teeth into a lozenge or a lollipop as soon as it hit her mouth. Candy was for chewing, not taking a bath in your saliva.

The caramel was sweet and buttery with a hint of salt. With all her focus on keeping her teeth in line, her heartbeat slowed.

Mei nodded as if she could see it. "We're made of more than one idea. If you had one great one, you'll have another. But hold this next one a little closer to your vest." She pushed another caramel toward Allison. "And get yourself an anxiety stash. Your dissertation will thank you."

If Allison ever got there.

Keeping what Colin had done a secret felt weak and wrong. As if, like Jed, he was stomping all over her. But Mei was right. If Allison spent all her energy fighting to hold on to her argument, she might never have the space to form another.

She was a library, full of stories and words and definitions. And her brain was a seamstress, with fingers as agile as Sophie's, stitching them all together into new designs and formations.

Allison didn't need to take Colin down to win. Her best revenge would be to earn that mentorship all on her own.

Most of Allison's meetings with Wendy Frances had taken place over meals, so this was the first time she'd spent more than a minute in her office.

Somehow, her professor had managed to achieve a cottage-core aesthetic in the tiny space. Her desk spanned one entire wall, the reclaimed-wood slats aged to shades of gray and blueish brown. A square platter lined with sea glass sat off to one side and held tiny succulent pots that served as file holders, and the two small lanterns beside Allison cradled a handful of pens and pencils. All the lamps were draped with scarves to dim the harsh fluorescent lights.

Wendy settled into a paisley armchair, while Allison took what looked to be a straight-backed chair from an old dining set. Her eyes strayed to the nearby windowsill, which displayed a photo of Wendy embracing a dark-haired woman in front of a garden so vibrant and fertile it could have burst out of a storybook. Beside it was a picture of two cats curled on a chair, one lithe with a coat of gray and white, the other a hearty tuxedo.

"My girls," Wendy said, nodding to the image. "Gwen and Dave." She pointed to the tuxedo cat.

Allison laughed. "Dave?"

Wendy's bangles (rose gold today) jingled against her own amused reaction. "It was the name the shelter gave her, and I love the message it sends. Names are a construct just like gender is."

"It's perfect."

Wendy drew a file folder from between two of her succulent pots and pulled a legal pad from it. Flipping to the first clean page, she crossed her legs and sat forward, giving Allison her full attention. She smelled like a bakery, vanilla and sugar and comfort.

Allison's slamming heart eased a little in response. Being around her professor closed some of the cracks Colin had splintered into her bones.

"So, tell me what I can help you with." Wendy's blond waves were swept off her face, and she had the lightest dusting of mauve eyeshadow over her gray-blue eyes. Her long-sleeved floral shirt resembled the kind of fancy, intricate wallpaper you'd see in mansions that got photographed for magazines. "I can't wait to see what you'll teach us next week."

Her words were genuine, and, like a spell working against a curse, they broke Allison's indecision. Her professor didn't want to hear about the ideas Allison couldn't use (because Colin had stolen them); she wanted to see Allison's mind at work. And nothing she confessed about Colin and his betrayal would show that. At least not the good parts.

She cleared her throat. "I was originally going to work with Chaucer, but as I was rereading Malory for class this weekend, I was struck by the parallels between Igraine and Elaine of Corbin." According to legend, Igraine conceived King Arthur when Uther Pendragon, a rival king, used magic to appear to her as her own husband. Elaine tricked Sir Lancelot into bed with similar means, disguising herself as Queen Guinevere. Yet Uther has been depicted as a hero, while Elaine has been construed as corruptive and dangerous. Women always took the fall for men's egos. Colin had taught Allison that lesson twice now.

Wendy's pen began scratching against her paper, as if Allison had said something worth writing down.

Maybe she had. She was more than one idea. She was an infinite cascade of them, and she let her words rain down, let them form shapes and angles that made meaning, that took stories and cracked them open to show what was inside.

"I think I'd like to discuss how Malory's *Le Morte d'Arthur*—as exemplary of a lot of other medieval romances and legends—vilifies female desire."

Narrowing her eyes at her notes, Wendy smiled. "This piggybacks onto Colin's presentation in effective ways. Did you two plan that?"

Anger jabbed like thorns in Allison's stomach. "In a manner of speaking," she muttered. If planning it meant that both presentations were Allison's.

But Wendy's comments also sparked an idea. Behind Allison's eyes, it exploded like an incandescent firework. Maybe she could take this new idea and intersect it with her old one. Then she could demonstrate to Wendy not only that, as a teacher, she would scaffold ideas well and build upon concepts, but that she could conceptualize analytical readings that extended beyond one or two texts to consider the field more broadly—exactly what she'd need to do for her dissertation.

Her body fizzed. She could do this. She'd create a new presentation by Tuesday. A *better* one. Fuck Colin. She'd win against *herself*—a far more worthy opponent any day.

Pulling her phone from her pocket, she asked, "Do you mind if I make some notes quickly?"

"Of course." Wendy turned to her computer.

Glancing down, Allison gaped at her lock screen. There were a handful of texts from Colin, which she swiped away. But there were also two missed calls from her mother.

It had to be more Jed updates. Allison had stopped responding to her mom's texts, so she'd taken to calling instead.

Her father was home from the hospital. Allison didn't need to know any more than that. Clearing the calls, she typed a few lines of notes into a blank email.

Her phone buzzed with her mom's number again. Allison hit *ignore* and kept typing. Except, a second later, Cleo's face appeared on her screen.

Wendy peered at her. "That seems important. Maybe you should answer it."

"It can wait." Allison tried to finish the sentence she was writing but her mother called again, stealing the screen. She groaned.

"Allison. It's okay. Take it."

With a sigh, she stepped into the hall. Clearly, she'd inherited her stubborn streak from her mother. "Hey, Ma." Allison tried her best not to sound as irritated as she felt. "I'm in the middle of a meeting with a professor. I'll call—"

"Allison." Her mom's voice was scratchy. "You need to come home."

Allison shook her head at no one. "I can't. I have a *huge* presentation Tuesday. I need to spend all weekend finishing it."

"Allison, it's your father."

This again. For fuck's sake. Allison was tired of Jed taking up every bit of space in her life. She certainly didn't take up any in his. "Let me guess. He isn't listening to the doctor's recommendations and now he's back in AFib and needs to be zapped again. I've read up on this, Ma. People can live a long time with AFib. I don't need to come home every time he has a little issue."

"Allison. Honey." Her mother's voice was too soft. Too patient.

Allison's stomach dropped to her feet.

"I don't know how to say this. Your father. He's . . . he's dead."

Chapter 37

Allison's eyes burned with the ghosts of her tears. It had been five hours since her mother's call, and she'd yet to feel anything.

Like a zombie, she'd shambled back into Wendy's office. She couldn't remember what she'd told her professor, but the echo of the woman's warm hug and the kindness in her voice clung to Allison's skin as she drove toward Maine.

The texts she'd sent to Sophie and Mandy were a stranger's words. The steering wheel Allison gripped was in someone else's hands. Monty nudged his cool nose against her arm in another dimension, another version of her rubbing his head. An unfamiliar heart drilled against a ribcage that wasn't Allison's. She was no one, nowhere, floating away as her life streamed before her.

What kind of person was she that Colin could turn her into a tangle of emotions but her father *died* and she felt nothing?

She swiped a bead of cold sweat off her face. She shouldn't be thinking about Colin right now. He didn't deserve any space in her head.

Jed had died. He was *gone*.

When she pulled her car into the driveway beside her mother's

SUV, Allison dropped her head to her steering wheel. She couldn't do this. Jed. Colin. Any of it.

It was all too much.

Monty huffed a small whine. He tried to balance his tiny front paws on the back of Allison's seat so he could lick her face, but only managed to tumble to the floor. The laugh that erupted out of her had jagged edges, but at least it got her moving.

Her mom and Cleo were waiting by the front door.

Her mother opened her arms. Her face was red and streaked with tears. Seeing it churned Allison's stomach. She should look like that. Her body should be a map of her pain. She'd lost a parent. One of the worst losses imaginable.

But Allison was blank. Vacant. Stripped bare.

Her mother smelled like bread and flowers and *home* as Allison stepped into her embrace. Her throat clogged. Who knew you could choke on nothing?

Her arms tightened. "I'm so sorry, sweetie."

For what? Jed's death or Allison's inability to feel it? She cleared her throat. "What happened?"

Releasing her, her mother picked up Allison's overnight bag and deposited it by the stairs. Then, with the sigh of a person who'd never truly known rest, she dropped into her favorite reclining chair. "He stopped taking his meds as soon as he left the hospital. He had a heart attack. Alone. Paula found him when she stopped by with groceries."

Allison pressed her hand to her mouth. It was awful, to die alone like that, but also so like Jed. He'd never wanted the burden of another person's presence. Everyone and their feelings were too much of a hassle. Too dramatic.

But if you kept pushing everyone away, they would stop coming back. Allison had come too close to learning that with Sophie. She clutched her phone against her palm as if that might tether her permanently to her best friend, no matter where she ended up.

She lowered herself to the couch. For a while, the dogs' playful growls as they tussled on the carpet were the only sounds.

The reclining chair creaked with her mom's movement. "We can talk about it, you know," she said.

"Talk about what?" Allison hugged a pillow to her chest.

"Whatever you're feeling."

"What if I'm not feeling anything?"

Her mother shook her head, her lips a frustrated line. "Of course you are. Your father just died."

"That's the thing, though." Allison crushed the pillow's cream cable knit between her fingers. "I know he was important to you, but he was in my life like the walls of this house are." Her eyes flit around the living room. "Always there, but I feel no attachment to them."

"Honey—"

"No. Maybe that's not the right metaphor." Allison studied the ceiling fan. One of the blades was bent at an angle with a crease like a fault line through the metal, a victim of Allison's attempt in sixth grade to learn to dribble a basketball in the house. Jed had never fixed it, even though he'd bought her the ball. "To start moving that heavy body," he'd said. The house retained as many scars from him as Allison did. "Maybe he was more like a mirror that kept forcing me to see my body the way he did."

Her mom sighed. "He wasn't perfect."

"No. He was awful." Allison tossed the pillow to her feet. "Why can't you admit that?"

Her mother's gaze fell to her lap, and her jaw began to tremble. "Because I don't want to believe that I could love someone who was truly awful."

Allison's chest cracked open. Her mother was too generous to believe that someone had no good in them. She'd love a scorpion as it stung her. She couldn't control that any more than Allison could will her own feelings into existence.

And after what had happened with Colin yesterday, she knew a little about not seeing the person you love clearly. The frustration she'd been nursing toward her mother melted away.

Crossing the room, Allison folded herself onto the floor beside the recliner, her head falling against her mom's arm. "I know I'm supposed to, but I don't love Jed, Ma. I can't. I'm not like you. I don't have endless stores of love to offer people. I can't give it away so easily."

She'd done so with Colin, twice, and she was emptier for it. The places in Allison's heart open for others shrank every time it broke, like a plate never glued back together exactly the right way. If she wasn't careful, eventually, there would be no room left.

The chair squeaked quietly as her mother rocked back and forth, and both dogs perked up their ears.

Allison caught her mother's gaze. "I need you to let me feel what I feel about this, without any guilt. Even if what I feel is nothing. This is my relationship to navigate. And it should have always been. All those calls telling me to visit, and to be in touch, and how he needs me, they hurt because I couldn't do it. It was as if my feelings toward him were wrong."

Closing her eyes, her mother waited a long moment before responding. "I'm sorry, honey. That was never my intent. I just didn't want you to have regrets when he was gone. I know what that's like from your grandma—it eats away at you."

"But you and grandma fought. You felt too much, maybe. Jed and I never had that." They'd never had anything. "So all that guilt about not being there for him kept reminding me of everything we weren't." Allison settled a hand over her heart. Its beat thrummed against her palm. Maybe her numbness was its own kind of grief, as if emptiness were the only way to mourn something that never existed.

Her mother's hand came to rest on Allison's head. "I'm sorry I couldn't see that," she said. "You're an adult. I need to listen more and parent less."

With a small grin, Allison muttered, "I like that plan."

Her mother snorted. "Well, while we're on the subject, maybe you could parent me a little less, too?"

"What does that mean?"

"Stop paying my bills."

"They were late. I wanted to help."

Her mom took her hand. "I don't need you to do that. I've been getting by your whole life. I'll keep getting by."

Emotion bubbled in Allison's stomach. "But you're my mother. I need to take care of you." Her voice cracked. A single tear slipped down Allison's cheek.

Her mother swiped away one from her own eyes. "Someday, maybe. But not yet. I promise to tell you when I need you. In the meantime, I can't be worried about you worrying about me. Got it?" Her mom's soft voice lacked authority. Not that she'd ever needed it for Allison. The two of them had always been a team. It felt good to be finding their way back to that.

Allison did her best to sound like the mopey teenager she never was. "Fine."

Smiling, her mother pushed herself from her chair. "Now I'm going to make some tea and pop some cookies in the oven so we can cue up *Steel Magnolias* and give ourselves a good cry."

And cry they did.

By the time Allison lugged her snoozing puppy upstairs, she was hollowed out from sobbing. Two of her wet tissues were still crumpled in her hand, and the cookies and tea she'd choked down had formed a rock in her stomach.

None of it had been for Jed, but the release was cathartic, nonetheless. It cleared her out, culling back some of the numbness to make room for other things. Allison had always teased her mother for this need to treat sadness with more sadness, but maybe there was something to it.

After a quick shower, she lay in bed, waiting for the exhaustion wringing her muscles to reach her brain. In an effort to avoid thinking about Colin, Allison ran through her new ideas for her lecture. Wendy had told her they'd reschedule when Allison returned to campus, but she just wanted it to be over. Until she gave her presentation, Wendy couldn't make her choice, and the longer it took Wendy to decide between them, the longer Allison remained tied to Colin.

She needed that slate clean.

Kicking off her blankets, Allison ransacked her room for supplies. Her old copy of Malory's *Le Morte d'Arthur* was buried at the back of her closet. In the bottom of her old white desk were leftover supplies from her word wall: a bunch of black Sharpies held together with an old hair elastic and stacks of neon sticky notes. Tucked away in her nightstand she unearthed her barely functioning tablet from high school.

Over the next few hours, Allison fashioned her presentation from academic scraps, like a kindergartener working on an art project. She pulled research from articles on Claymore's library databases and typed up passages from Malory into the Notes app on the tablet. With the sticky notes, Allison made a low-tech version of PowerPoint slides, complete with stick-figure drawings and scribbly fonts.

The end result was nothing like the polished lecture sitting on her computer back in Providence. There were no fancy backgrounds or elaborate lettering, no high-resolution stock photos. No adorable clip art. No selections from Chaucer underlined and annotated with PowerPoint animations.

In some ways, though, this felt like a more honest representation of Allison's teaching. It wasn't shiny or professional. It wasn't very good. But she was trying. That had to be enough for now.

The sun was starting to crawl its way up from the horizon as she set up her phone to record. She was too tired to cover the bags under her eyes or the splotches of red still bright on her face from crying. She didn't bother to change out of her "Shut Up, I'm Reading" T-shirt.

But for the next hour, Allison filmed herself giving that lecture with her raw, cracking voice, aiming the camera at her makeshift slides as needed and pointing to her dog-eared copy of Malory to demonstrate some close reading.

As the video converted, she clicked open her Claymore email. Inside were a dozen condolences, from her cohort and a few from students. She opened the first one.

Hey, Prof A. It sucks your dad died. I hope you're okay. I promise not to be a dick next class. Cole

Allison had thought she'd been wrung dry, but new tears dripped into her lap. Her hands were shaking as she uploaded the video to an email and addressed it to Wendy.

Her finger hovered over the send button. It was late (or early, depending on how one looked at it) and Allison was wrecked. Could she be trusted to make big decisions right now? What if sending this was a mistake? What if not waiting cost her the advisee position and the trip? What if Allison's haste only proved to Wendy that she wasn't Ph.D. material?

For once, Allison couldn't bring herself to care. Perfection required more energy than she had left. In some ways, it had been that need to be perfect that had gotten her into this mess in the first place.

She hit send.

Submitting her lecture was a door she could slam shut. With it, her competition with Colin came to an end. It was in Wendy's hands now.

And with nothing left to fight for, Allison could shut the door on Colin, too.

Chapter 38

Sophie Andrade: I am getting in the car.

Allison Avery: To drive to Boston for your interview.

Sophie Andrade: Nope, headed farther north.

Allison Avery: SOPHIA ROSA ANDRADE. TURN THE CAR AROUND.

Allison Avery: Also stop texting and driving.

Sophie Andrade: I haven't left yet. I'm sitting in the driveway.

Allison Avery: Set your GPS for Kisses and Hugs in Boston.

Sophie Andrade: I won't abandon you like that.

Allison Avery: And I won't hold you back from your dreams.

Allison Avery: And all the awesome free clothes I'm going to get out of you fulfilling your dreams.

Allison Avery: Come when you're done, okay?

Sophie Andrade: ♥

––––––––––––––––

Unknown Number: I caught Sophie at your place as she was leaving. She told me about your father. [deleted]

Unknown Number: Are you okay? [deleted]

Unknown Number: What can I do? [deleted]

Unknown Number: You can ignore me all you need to but I'm not disappearing. [deleted]

––––––––––––––––

Mandy Garcia: I think Ethan drinks cologne.

Mandy Garcia: I've been sitting with him in this car for almost two hours, and I swear it's seeping out of his pores like alcohol. Link is practically gagging in the back seat.

Mandy Garcia: You will also not be shocked to discover that Ethan is a talk-radio person. NO MUSIC. AT ALL.

Mandy Garcia: And he goes the precise speed limit. Not a mile above or below.

Mandy Garcia: This is the last time I let him drive anywhere.

Dear Allison,

My thoughts are with you and your family at this difficult time. The loss of a parent is a particularly fathomless grief for which there is little sage advice beyond to mourn as needed and as feels best for you. No one but you can understand the shape and feel of this loss and however you are dealing with it is an acceptable response, no matter how nonsensical it might appear to others.

When I lost my mother two years ago, I planted a new seed each time I felt like crying. As you might imagine, my garden is rather full. But each of these new lives feels like they have a tiny speck of her spirit in them, and with each new sprout that flourishes, a small mending stitch finds its way to my heart.

I reviewed your video and shared it with the class today. We were all delighted by the ways in which you adapted to the lack of resources at your disposal. You did a fantastic job organizing your ideas and presenting them to the class, and the students responded with an abundance of curiosity at the interpretations you offered. I also think Malory would have appreciated your stick figure renderings of his characters. ;) Especially Lancelot and his lofty . . . sword.

Should there be anything I can do for you, please don't hesitate to let me know.

Take care,

Wendy

Chapter 39

Jed's wake had begun half an hour ago, and already Allison felt as if she'd shaken hands with a million strangers.

She swallowed against the gritty dryness of her mouth as another middle-aged couple knelt before her father's closed casket and folded their hands in prayer. Sweat left a chalky residue in her palms, and Allison rubbed them against the sides of her black tights.

Her glance drifted to the back of the room, where her cohort and Sophie sat in a clump. They'd been the first group through the doors, and after a huddle around Allison by the casket, they'd stationed themselves in the corner, one of them coming by every few minutes to check on her.

An affectionate warmth hummed beneath the iceberg of numbness rooted in Allison's chest. She hadn't been prepared for everyone to be so supportive and wonderful.

Her only wish was that the presence of her friends didn't make Colin's absence so conspicuous.

Colin.

She shoved his name from her mind. She couldn't think about him. Or how he should be here, holding her hand, as he had been barely a month ago when this had all begun.

She hated how everything was ending at once. It might have been poetic, but it was not justice.

A rivulet of moisture slithered down her back. This funeral home was too hot. Allison wanted to shrug out of her cardigan but the goddess neckline of her dress didn't seem appropriate for the somber setting. The heat mixed with the heavy perfume of the countless flower arrangements caught like a thick fog in her throat.

Someone had worked hard to make the space seem cozy with soft and well-worn sofas, sunny yellow paint, and knit throw pillows in inviting shades of green. Yet Allison wasn't comforted by the decor. Instead, she felt like her muscles had been attached to her bones all wrong. She wanted to run screaming from the room, rip out her tight bun, and let her hair stream behind her as she dashed for the trees.

The ash-blond woman kneeling in front of Jed's casket made the sign of the cross, and Allison tensed. Everything about this wake was so performative. Jed wasn't a practicing Catholic. He'd specifically asked for no church service in his will. Just a wake and a quick burial. Then burgers and beers at the house of Paula's son. Allison would be skipping that. And maybe the burial, too. She didn't need to see her father lowered into the ground to know he was gone. For her, he'd never really been there to begin with.

The couple stood, and Allison and her mother straightened their backs, ready for another round of small talk with someone else whose name Allison would forget before they'd finished introducing themselves.

As Jed's only biological child, Allison had been placed first in line for condolences with her mother beside her for support. Paula and her son sat in the first row of seats facing the casket. Neither of them had spoken to Allison.

She preferred it that way.

The blond woman sniffled as she reached for Allison's hands. "You've got to be Jed's daughter."

Allison forced a smile. "Allison."

"I'm Nancy, your father's secretary. I recognize your picture from his desk."

That was new information. Allison hadn't been to her father's office since she was in high school, but she didn't recall anything there besides a signed baseball and his precious beer cap display. She also didn't recognize Nancy.

The woman clung to Allison's hand and patted her knuckles. "He used to talk about you all the time."

Allison choked. "He what?"

Nancy smiled sadly, assuming she was overcome with emotion. "Just before he went into the hospital, he was telling me that you were a teacher. In college. He said it's not easy to do. Most people never get into those programs." Not exactly accurate, but more than Allison had thought Jed understood about her life.

Her gaze flicked to her mother, who gave her a small shrug. Clearly, this was news to her as well. "I'm still in school," she said to Nancy, "but hopefully someday I'll teach in college."

Nancy tapped her cheek as she turned away. "I hope you know your father was proud of you." With that, she moved down the line.

Allison's attention drifted to the casket. Her eyes burned. Hearing Jed described this way, as someone who could have maybe loved his daughter, only made him more of a stranger.

She wished Nancy had never said anything. Or that she hadn't heard it.

More sweat pooled down Allison's back. Her body was starting to develop that parched, sandy feeling that accompanies a bad hangover. She moistened her lips and tried to swallow what little saliva still existed in her mouth. She needed water. And a snack. Something to give her blood sugar a jolt. There should be food at these things. And more chairs. And open fucking windows. Somehow, it seemed as if twenty more people had beamed into the space, sucking up what little air was left.

When Allison died, she was going to ask people to stay home and read their favorite book instead of subjecting her loved ones to this misery.

She was attempting to rescue her mascara from another onslaught of perspiration when she caught sight of a familiar face cresting the front of the line.

Wendy Frances tightened the gray shawl thrown over her black sheath dress as she approached the casket. The swirls of flying birds embroidered on the thin fabric seemed to spread their soaring wings wider with the motion. Her stack of black ceramic bangles slid down her arm as she kneeled.

Allison's hands began to shake. What was her professor doing here? Providence was a good four-hour drive from Stonington without midweek traffic. She couldn't possibly have made that trip to spend half an hour at the wake of a man she'd never met.

Had Wendy made her decision? Had she chosen Colin? Did she drive all this way to let Allison down gently?

Smoothing the front of her dress, Allison braced herself. If that was the case, *good*. She'd be thrilled to get that issue resolved, too. After the emotional train wreck the last few days had been, her pain receptors were shot. She'd barely feel the news if she received it now. Then she could truly put this whole mess of a semester (and Colin with it) behind her.

And smash that rearview mirror to smithereens.

Wendy turned from the casket and faced Allison, her arms opened wide.

"What are you doing here?" Allison mumbled as she let her teacher embrace her.

"I had to pay my respects and see how you were holding up." Stepping back, Wendy's gray-blue eyes surveyed her, as if Allison's feelings might be scrawled across her skin. Or pinned there with sticky notes like her old word wall.

"I'm okay. My relationship with my father was . . . fraught."

"That doesn't make it any easier. Harder in some ways, I suspect."

Allison shrugged and nodded at the same time, like the mess she was.

Wendy folded her hands in front of her. "I also hoped that maybe I could offer a small spot of sunshine in all this"—she glanced around them—"rain."

Allison's heart seized. Did that mean . . .

Wendy reached into the large leather tote on her shoulder and produced a stack of papers jammed within a brand-new copy of *The Mabinogion*. Allison's knees felt as if they'd cracked at the joints. That shiny black cover with its crisp white font might have been the most beautiful thing she'd ever seen.

Wendy offered her the bundle. "This is the paperwork you'll need to fill out for the trip to Wales in January. And a copy of *The Mabinogion*, in case you don't have one. I'm truly looking forward to working with you."

Allison only knew she'd accepted the book because she could see it gripped in her hands. She'd lost feeling in her extremities. "I won?"

Wendy's blond curls bounced as she chuckled. "*Won* isn't the word I'd use. You earned the spot. On the trip, and as my advisee."

"And Colin?" Allison hated to let his name touch her lips but she couldn't stop herself from asking. He'd be devastated, even if he hadn't deserved to win. And poor Charlie would probably keep forgetting, forcing Colin to experience this rejection over and over. Against her will, her heart squeezed in sympathy.

"Colin's presentation on the Wife of Bath and Dame Ragnell—"

Allison startled. "Wait. His what? He didn't talk about 'The Knight's Tale' and *Erec et Enide*?"

Wendy shook her head, the large silver hoops in her ears getting tangled in her hair. "He used two loathly lady tales to consider how medieval romance makes female bodies monstrous."

This time, Allison's knees did give out. Thankfully, there was a chair behind her.

The world spun as she dropped down into it.

There were no loathly lady tales in Allison's original presentation. "So, he didn't make an argument about how beauty disrupts chivalric masculinity?"

"No. He focused on the texts' treatment of femininity." Wendy lowered herself to the nearby couch. "What's this about?"

Allison's stomach lurched. Colin hadn't stolen anything but her title. And he'd taken the topic in a totally different direction. When he'd said they'd be on the same page, this must have been what he'd meant.

She'd been so quick to assume he'd plagiarized her. As if that was the only way he could properly compete.

Wendy said her name again, shaking Allison from her thoughts.

"From the title, I'd . . . I guess I misunderstood his argument."

"He told us you came up with the title, that it was a perfect fit for both your presentations."

Allison felt sick. "I wish I'd been able to see it."

Her professor smiled. "I know you and Colin have grown close. I hope this decision won't cause any undue tension. He's a smart young man and, when he returns from his leave of absence, we'll make sure he lands on his feet."

This whole conversation felt like an endless series of whiplash. Every time Allison got her grounding, Wendy said something else that sent her sprawling. "He's leaving?"

"For a time. He came to see me yesterday to let me know he was deferring his acceptance until next year. He said he plans to take the time to think more about what he wants to study."

"So, he took himself out of the running?"

Wendy chuckled. "Absolutely not. The first thing he asked when he sat down was who I was likely to choose."

None of this made any sense. Allison grabbed the arm of the chair as if that could bring her world back into balance.

"Do you know what he said when I told him?" Wendy asked.

Allison could only shake her head.

"That it was the right choice."

A tear slipped from Allison's eye, drawing a long, warm path down her cheek. Her head felt full of static. Colin was leaving. He hadn't plagiarized her. It was impossible to process any of this in the middle of her father's wake.

For now, she tucked it all away. She needed time to think, to order everything she'd learned into some sensible form.

Until then, she grasped tightly to her good news. Clutched it to her heart. Whatever had happened between her and Colin, Allison had *earned* this.

Wendy patted her hand. "You've proven to me again and again over the last few months that you share my passion for medieval literature, and I think our interests dovetail in ways that will allow us to learn from each other."

"But I'm a horrible teacher," Allison blurted out. She'd been so certain for so long that this would keep Wendy from ever choosing her.

Her professor let out another good-natured laugh. "I was never looking for perfection. Besides, I'm not sure I believe that's true." She gave Allison's hand a squeeze. "And even if it is, you'll get better. You'll grow."

Grow. Allison liked the sound of that.

She was tired of always striving to be the best. *Best* had been something she'd wanted for Jed's sake. To make him care. To prove him wrong. And it hadn't gotten her anywhere.

Best was what she and Colin had tried to be. It had only pushed them apart.

Maybe, instead, she'd aim for *better*. Because better meant there was always more to learn.

Chapter 40

"I'm going to be next door for a bit, but you kids eat up. It's been a long day."

Allison's mother set a stack of pizza boxes on the coffee table, waving away money as Sophie, Link, and Ethan tried to pay her. Cleo, who was right on her heels, toppled Link onto the couch in her haste to reach the cardboard tower. Her nose sniffed the air frantically.

The scene sent Sophie and Mandy into a fit of laughter from their spots on the floor.

The aroma of garlic and cheese filled Allison's nose and summoned a growl from her stomach. The wake had felt so long she couldn't remember when she'd last eaten.

They'd been back at her house for almost an hour, and Allison had yet to find the energy to go upstairs and change. Her tights stuck to her legs, and her feet ached from her shoes, and her bare shoulders were cold without her cardigan. Shivering, she wrapped a throw blanket around herself, fighting off the urge to take a nap.

In front of her, her friends threw open the boxes and dug in, their voices a low, comforting rumble in a house that had been too quiet for the past five days. Allison closed her eyes. Their presence was like sinking into a well-worn couch or opening a favorite book. It was the feeling of Chaucer's iambic pentameter rolling off her tongue.

No longer did she feel alone or left behind. Sophie had been right. All this time, while Allison feared her best friend's life was changing, growing without her, the same had been happening to her. Even if Sophie got that job in Boston, even if she left, she wouldn't be abandoning Allison. And Allison would be far from on her own.

As she watched them, her mind played back over her conversation with Wendy. For the rest of the wake, Allison hadn't been able to stop dwelling on what her teacher had said about Colin. No doubt she'd contributed to the pressure he was under that had caused him to doubt his original topic. Allison had been so insecure about herself as a teacher that she couldn't resist flaunting all her strengths. She'd known it bothered him. And for so long, that's exactly why she'd done it.

Yes, he'd made the choice to change his presentation to something closer to hers, but Allison had helped push him off that cliff.

Pulling her phone from her pocket, she brushed a thumb over the screen and started a new message.

> Allison Avery: Why didn't you tell me you talked about the loathly lady tales?

A moment later, the response dots popped up. Her heart danced with their blinking rhythm until they disappeared.

She dropped her head back against the sofa with a sigh.

"Are you okay?" Sophie was already standing up.

Allison waved her off. "I just . . ." She sighed again. She didn't have the bandwidth to hold on to secrets anymore. They'd never done her much good anyway. "You all saw Wendy Frances at the wake, right? She came to tell me that she'd chosen me for the research trip and advisee position."

Sophie clapped her hands. "That's great!"

"I know." Allison fussed with the hem of her dress. "Except, apparently, Colin's presentation wasn't quite as close to mine as I'd originally thought."

Mandy's eyebrows arched. "Oh?"

"He talked about beauty in medieval romance, but he took things in a completely different direction."

Link shrugged. "He still should have talked to you."

"Maybe." Allison tugged at the ends of her hair. "But I didn't really give him a chance. And now he's leaving."

Mandy offered her the pepperoni pizza, waiting with the top open like a jaw until Allison took a slice. "I guess his grandfather's really sick."

"His dementia's getting worse," Allison said.

Mandy shook her head. "No. He got diagnosed with pancreatic cancer. Stage 4."

"What?" Allison's stomach was in free fall. She jumped to her feet. How could he not tell her? His granddad was everything to him. He must be so lost. So afraid. The blanket tumbled from her shoulders as she searched around for her purse. "I need to go back to Providence."

Sophie draped the throw back over her and urged Allison to sit again. "I don't think he's there."

"How do you know?"

Sophie frowned. "He didn't come in, but I think he was at the wake. I'm pretty sure I saw his car. The same one he had at Brown, right? Silver Honda?" She spread open her empty palms when Allison nodded. "I was afraid if I told you and he didn't show his face, it would only hurt you more."

Allison slid deeper into the couch cushions. Poor Charlie, already dealing with so much, getting this new blow to his health that could only be complicated by his dementia. And Colin having to shoulder it all.

He'd driven four hours, only to be too afraid to face her. Allison had done that. She'd slammed the door. Thrown up the wall. Drawn conclusions without all the evidence. Colin might have been entirely to blame for their first ending. But Allison had played her part in this one.

She set her pizza aside, no longer hungry. Regret was a roiling pit of acid at her center.

Link handed her a bottle. "Brought this cider just for you."

Popping off the top, Allison raised it to her lips. If she couldn't eat her feelings, maybe she could drown them.

A burst of apple coated her tongue. It was only as she swallowed that she noticed the label.

Third Chance Cider.

Chapter 41

The doorbell startled Allison awake.

She would have sworn she'd just fallen asleep, but when she cracked her eyes open, the house was almost dark.

The dogs barked from the couch as the bell sounded again, both too lazy to investigate.

Groaning, Allison dragged herself to her knees and peeked out through the curtain. The streetlamp illuminated the driveway, empty except for her car, now that her friends had headed home. A noise like the banging of an aluminum trash can echoed from the porch, its source obscured by the angle of the window.

Muttering under her breath, she shuffled to the foyer. Though the clock on the wall read nine, the house was quiet, which meant her mom was still at their neighbor's. Allison took a swig from the last cider Link had left behind before throwing open the front door.

The bottle hit the floor with a *thud*.

Colin stood on the porch. His back was to her as he stared out at the street, but she'd know that lanky frame anywhere.

Even when it was buried under an ill-fitting suit of armor.

A pauldron hung off his left shoulder as if its strap had snapped, the other secured so close to his neck the metal seemed to be biting into his skin. Belts hugged bracers too loose to cuff his wrists, and the armor's chest piece stopped above his navel and was clamped to his body with layer after layer of silver duct tape (over, of course, a burnt orange cardigan). The helmet hadn't fit flush on his face, so his chin hung out the bottom, the faceguard balanced precariously on his maroon glasses. He'd completed the bizarre ensemble with leg plates taped over a pair of dark skinny jeans and some black Chucks.

"Colin?"

With a rattle that sounded like pots slamming together, he faced her.

"What are you . . ." Allison didn't know how to finish her question. There were too many things to ask.

"For the record, men in the Middle Ages were considerably smaller than the average man now." His hands smoothed the front of the chest piece as if that might put things in order.

The many dents in the helm and plates suggested he'd used a hammer to get them on. "Is that . . . Ned?"

He cleared his throat. "It is."

"Why? What? How?" Allison couldn't make sense of anything. Not with him standing here looking like *this*. Not with her heartbeat slamming in her chest.

He was here. She hadn't chased him too far away.

The armor clanked as he shifted from foot to foot, a heavy metal symphony. "You wouldn't talk to me. And the texts weren't helping. I had to *do* something. I needed to show you I was sorry. To make clear how much you matter to me."

"And you thought murdering Ned would do it?"

Colin tipped his head and the faceguard dropped lower, knocking his glasses to the porch. Watching him try to retrieve them was almost worth the emotional price of admission to this performance.

After another enjoyable minute, Allison saved him from his misery.

He poked himself in the eyes twice fitting the glasses back on his face.

"I'm not really into LARPing so I'm not sure what you're doing."

Colin coughed, then cleared his throat again. "I just—I thought maybe if I could be the thing you love, speak your language, then I could make you understand."

Even as they were expressed by this uncanny love child of the White Knight from *Through the Looking Glass* and Don Quixote, his words were beautiful.

"Colin."

He held up a hand to quiet her.

With a series of clumsy percussions, he extracted a piece of paper from his pocket. Only he (and maybe Ethan) would come to an apology with a pre-written speech.

But when he shook open the note, Allison saw it wasn't an outline. Instead, scribbles filled the page, upside down, sideways, perpendicular, in that barely legible scratch he called handwriting.

"And ther seyde oones a clerk in two vers,/What is bettre than gold? Jaspre./What is bettre than jaspre? Wisedoom./And what is better than wisedoom? Womman./And what is bettre than a good womman? Nothyng." He stumbled over the pronunciation, missing half the syllables and spoiling the rhythm. Still, the words sang to her.

"'The Tale of Melibee,'" Allison whispered.

Color bled into his cheeks, but his hazel eyes remained honed on his script. "'Thus, in this hevene he gan him to delyte,/And ther-with-al a thousand tyme hir kiste;/That, what to done, for Ioye unnethe he wiste."

"*Troilus and Criseyde.*"

He turned the page over, ready to start anew. Allison reached out. She was careful to catch the paper in her fingers and not his hand. "What is this? Every love quote in Chaucer?"

Beneath all the armor, Colin's Adam's apple bobbed. His hands trembled against the thin paper. "If these aren't right, I'll find a better one—"

"Colin."

"Oonly the sighte of hire whom that I serve,/Though that I nevere hir grace may deserve,/Wolde han suffised right ynough for me./'O deere cosyn Palamon,' quod he,/'Thyn is the victorie of this aventure./ Ful blisfully in prison maistow dure—/In prison? Certes nay, but in paradys!'"

A passage from "The Knight's Tale." The one they'd disagreed about all those weeks ago in Wendy's class.

"This is incredibly romantic—"

"I never got to tell you how I really felt about those lines." He crumpled the paper in his fist, his gaze as erratic as his flitting hands. "It reminds me of us. All the ways that love is messy and imperfect, and yet still so powerful. Like we've always been."

Tears stung Allison's eyes, and her heart stuttered against her ribs. When he started to recite another, she grabbed his hand this time.

"Colin, we should talk. Without the helmet and the cheat sheet. And maybe inside? Where we're not freezing?"

He shook beneath her hand. She had to tug him forward to get him to move.

As he stumbled inside, the clang of his armor summoned the dogs. Cleo and Monty raced across the wood floor and flung themselves at him. The momentum sent him crashing to the floor.

Allison laughed for what felt like the first time in a week, and an ache followed in its wake, settling in her insides. She missed how much Colin made her laugh. How much they laughed *together*.

"This was not your brightest idea," she said as she knelt beside him. With a lot of tugging and noise that drove the dogs batty enough for Allison to lock them away, they freed his legs from the armor.

"Possibly not." His voice echoed in the helmet as they both wrestled it off his head.

Allison cradled it in her lap.

"I shouldn't have used a topic so close to yours."

"Why didn't you tell me about Charlie?"

They spoke at the same time, their words tumbling over each other's. With a shy laugh, each encouraged the other to go first. It took them a second to find a rhythm.

Allison moved the helmet's faceguard up and down, the steel whispering with each movement. "Mandy told me about Charlie. I could have helped. I could have been there for you."

Colin's hair, sans gel, flopped over his forehead as he rubbed at his temples. "You know how you handle stress by planning and overplanning and planning more for all those plans?"

"Yes." Except, she'd planned in five hundred different ways for this moment. Made countless WCS lists. Not one had accounted for Colin showing up in a suit of armor quoting Chaucer.

"I handle stress by shutting down. I don't deal with things. I get myopic and focus on one thing and ignore everything else. And I let that one thing be that fucking lecture. And I spiraled and spiraled about it until I was sure my topic was garbage and I would never get the advisee spot or the research trip and Charlie would die before I had anything to show him that would make him proud."

He was talking fast and breathing faster, as if he was seconds from hyperventilating. One of his hands was braced to the wood floor, and she laid her fingers gently over it. "Hey," she whispered.

He didn't move. His eyes dropped to their hands like the sight of their skin meeting was something sacred and rare. "I swear I didn't steal your ideas. And I gave you credit for the title. You always talked so eloquently about how women are represented in romance that it was clear your idea was more compelling. It inspired me. I wanted to add to it. But it still wasn't mine." He shook his head, his hair falling over his glasses. "I didn't even do it justice. I slapped that whole thing together at three in the morning on Thursday. I should have given my own. It would have been better."

Allison gripped his fingers. "Colin. You're every bit as smart as me. And a hundred times more charismatic." She sighed. "It's my fault you don't feel that way."

"Of course it's not."

"I kept competing with you. Trying to show I was better, since I felt so shitty as a teacher." She dropped her head into her free hand, trying to ignore the circles Colin's thumb was feathering across her wrist. Her skin set aflame like she was a stick and his hands the flint. "And then I didn't give you the space to tell me what had happened and immediately assumed the worst of you."

"You know Jane didn't get me into Claymore, right?" He tightened his jaw, clearly afraid of the answer.

"I know. I think I just wanted something to make myself feel better. Like the idea that you didn't get in on your own somehow made what I thought you'd done more predictable. I felt so duped."

He shimmied straighter, the loose pauldron thundering against his chest plate. "I haven't exactly had the best track record with us. I don't blame you for your assumptions."

"They were still awful. And now Wendy said you're leaving? Is it because she chose me?"

His smile was as broken as his armor. "Of course not."

"But you wanted this."

When his eyes found hers, they were glassy. "I don't think I actually did." He clutched her hand to the chest piece. Allison didn't pull away. Part of her wished he'd bring it to his lips. As if that simple gesture might fix things. "I chose medieval lit because of Charlie. And because of you. I wanted to feel close to the people who meant something to me. I wanted him to be proud. I wanted you to think I was worthy of you."

"Colin—"

He shook his head, quieting her. "But I lost me in the process. I think stepping away while I take care of him will help me to find that again."

Without meaning to, Allison shifted closer, so her knee met Colin's hip. Her elbow kissed his. He was forever a magnet pulling her to him, her gravity endlessly caught in his orbit.

"I want to be there every minute he has left. That's my focus for now." A tear slipped down his freckled cheek.

Allison caught it with a knuckle. "It sounds like you've got everything figured out."

"There's still one big piece missing."

"Oh?" Her muscles trembled. Her skin zinged like it had three times as many nerves.

She knew what he was hinting at. And she already had her answer.

They'd both made mistakes. They'd handled this competition all wrong. But since he'd driven her to Maine, and maybe even before that, they'd been a true team, nothing like their first time together. And they'd made mistakes as a team. She wanted to believe they could fix them the same way.

"Can we try again?" His eyes caught hers. Pinned Allison in place. "I'll do it right this time. I swear."

She smiled. "The rule of threes, right?"

"I was so wrong that day I broke up with you at Brown. My life never could have started by leaving you behind. It began the day you walked . . . or . . . I guess danced . . . into it."

Allison tossed his helmet aside and started tugging at his chest piece. "I think it's time to get you out of this."

"Before my jousting pole rises?"

Cackling, she slapped his arm. She'd hardly made any progress on the four hundred layers of tape he'd used when he swept her up into his arms.

And for the first time in her life, Allison Avery kissed a knight.

Acknowledgments

The journey from the day that I first got the idea for *The Make-Up Test* to this moment as I sit writing acknowledgments for its publication has been the most wild, unexpected, *wonderful* adventure, and that adventure has been far from solitary. I am so grateful to everyone who has supported me along the way.

To my agent, Katelyn Detweiler, who is a superhero and the best book champion, thank you for that YES at the exact moment my heart needed it. You completely changed my life. I never thought I'd be so lucky as to find someone who sees me as a writer as clearly as you do, and I would be lost without your unwavering support and enthusiasm, and your keen ability to always help me find the right path for a story. Thank you for the constant bursts of creativity, for your willingness to read (and get excited about) every random pitch I send you, and for answering my endless barrage of questions. You are truly the best publishing partner I could ask for.

To my editor extraordinaire, Sarah Grill, what do I even say? Allison and Sophie call themselves "brain twins," and sometimes I think maybe you and I have some of that magic. From the beginning, you have understood and supported my approach to fat rep, celebrated the parade of animals I cram into my books, and appreciated every nerdy literary joke I planted in *The Make-Up Test*. You see straight into the heart of this story and have helped me to make it shine so much brighter. I'm so grateful for your enthusiasm, for your support for my vision, for how hard you've championed this book, and for letting me keep just a *few* lines of Middle English in there. Thank you for being such a wonderful guide and teammate on this publishing journey.

To my critique partner and friend Rosiee Thor, thank you for screaming so loudly about the first half-formed pitch for *The Make-Up Test* that I sent you and for all your thoughtful responses to its earliest draft. This book would not exist without you.

To *The Make-Up Test*'s earliest reader, Auriane Desombre, thank you for being so excited to read my very messy first draft and for loving Allison and Colin even as I was still trying to figure them out. Your enthusiasm helped make this book happen.

To Courtney Kae, Renée Reynolds, and Sam Eaton, my very first writer friends and critique partners, thank you for your love and support and for somehow finding the time to read everything I write. Your friendships keep me going, and I cherish all our chats. Renée—thank you for the LaBeouff memes; even if I didn't want them, I needed them. Sam—thank you for taffy and for constant animal pics and for just getting it, even when I'm a mess. Courtney—thank you for hot chocolate and Jax memes and all the laughs, and for loving every unreadable draft I throw at you and seeing what it could be. Your faith in me means everything. You have no idea how thrilled I am to be on this debut journey with you.

To Annette Christie, founding member of TATAF and the best of friends, quite frankly, I don't know what I'd do without you. Thank you for always inspiring me, encouraging me, and giving me a safe place to voice all my worries. Thank you also for answering every one of my publishing questions with patience and good humor. You are truly talented and tenacious. Your drive and focus keep me driven and focused, and I can't wait to see what comes next for us both, and to celebrate it together!

To Leanne Schwartz, thank for your friendship and support and for all those sprints in 2020. You kept me motivated and helped me get this book off the ground.

To my writing buddies, who inspire me every day—Kelsey Rodkey, Greg Andree, Karen McManus, Lindsay Hess, Kara Seal, and Caryn Greenwald—thank you for making this whole writing thing a lot less lonely.

To my fellow 2022 debuts, WE DID IT! I am so thrilled to cheer for every one of you and read all your amazing books!

I am so grateful to everyone who read *The Make-Up Test* early. Your feedback and enthusiasm mean so much. Thank you (in no particular order because I love you all) Kelly DeVos, Ashley Schumacher, Emily Thiede, Kate Dylan, Jessica James, Ava Wilder, Samantha Markum, M. K. Lobb, Amanda Quain, Kara McDowell, Jackie O'Dell, Katie DeLuca, Sarah Glenn Marsh, Mike Lasagna, Danielle LaMontagne, and Mom, of course.

I am also so grateful to the writers who took the time to write such wonderful blurbs for *The Make-Up Test*. Thank you Ali Hazelwood, Jodi Picoult, Denise Williams, Jen DeLuca, Rachel Lynn Solomon, Hannah Whitten, Lillie Vale, Sonia Hartl, Annette Christie, and Jesse Q. Sutanto.

My biggest thanks to the team at St. Martin's Press—Kejana Ayala, Meghan Harrington, Marissa Sangiacomo, Anne Marie Tallberg, Omar Chapa, Hannah Jones, Laurie Henderson, and Gail Friedman. *The Make-Up Test* would not be the book it is today without all of your help and support. A special thanks to my copy editor, Laura Starrett, for catching all those mistakes my eyes could no longer see! I appreciate your feedback so much.

I am so in love with the cover for *The Make-Up Test* and so grateful to Vi-An Nguyen and Olga Grlic at SMP for such a perfect visual introduction to my book. I could not have captured Allison and Colin better if I had tried myself.

I would not have had the inspiration for this grad school romcom without my own experiences in graduate school at Tufts University and the wonderful friends I made there—Jackie, Sara, Andy, Anne, Kristina, Caroline, Laurel, Claudia, and Nathan. I am also so grateful for the guidance and mentorship of my dissertation adviser, John Fyler, who helped instill in me my love of Chaucer.

I would not have a Ph.D. in medieval literature or be an English professor if it were not for Wendy Peek and Frances Restuccia, both of whom encouraged my love of literary analysis and my aspirations to teach. Wendy, thank you for introducing me to the books that would change the course of my life and for inspiring me to be the most fun, most supportive teacher I can be. I am so glad that after all these years, we're still in touch. Frances, thank you for instilling in me a love of literary theory and for making me believe I was a strong, critical thinker with something worth saying. Wendy Frances was inspired by you both and I hope you feel she did you justice.

This book is as much about teaching as it is about being a student, and I am so thankful to all of my students, who help me to grow and learn as an instructor every day.

It's probably weird to thank your dogs in your acknowledgments but here we are. Murray, my muffin man, I miss you every day. Thank you for coming on this decade-long writing journey with me, for listening intently to every line I read out loud to you, and for snuggles during all my writing sessions. Tucker and Dale, my wild beasts, the excellent ears crew, you were curled up by my side when I got the call that *The Make-Up Test* would be published. Thank you for making me get up from my computer for walks, for reminding me when it's time to take a break (or a nap!), and for all the cuddles and love. I can't wait to write more books with you at my side (or in my lap).

Thank you to all my friends and family who have always supported and believed in me—my siblings and siblings-in-law, Jon, Melissa, Suzy, Andrew, Tim, and Astrid; my in-laws, Mike and Kathy (we miss you every day, Mom H, I wish you could have been here to see this happen); my aunts and uncles, Richard, Janine, Denny, Shirley, Linda, Uncle Ed, and the whole LaMontagne clan (there are too many of you to list!); my cousins (who are basically my siblings), Kevin, Christine, Danielle, Katie, and Sam; my nieces and nephews, Callie, Abby, Brody, AJ, and Lincoln; my grandparents (I miss you every day), Roger, Helen, Lucille, and Joseph; my amazing friends and colleagues, Lindsay, Melisa, Katie, Matt, Jackie, Meghan, Eli, Eric, Courtney, Julie, Yuan, Josh, Alexis, Zak, Chris, Tom, and Elisabeth. I love you all. Thank you for everything.

Mom: thank you doesn't even begin to cover my gratitude for you and all you've done for me. I would never have realized my dreams of being an author if you hadn't always taken my aspirations seriously. I believe in myself because you always believed in me. You like to joke that you want to be like me when you grow up, but I hope you know the feeling is mutual. You are the strongest, bravest, kindest person I know. My admiration for you has no bounds. Neither does my love.

Kevin: thank you for being a true partner and my best friend. You have always believed in my desire to write and never once doubted for a second that I would be published. That unwavering faith keeps me going on those days where it would be easier to give up. I'm so grateful for every laugh, every inside joke, every sleepy evening on the couch watching TV, every video game we die horribly in together, every lively conversation, every comfortable silence, every minute with you. Thank you for all the clean dishes and clothes, all the meals, all the times you've kept the house from falling apart so I could write. I hope you know, if I write good love stories, it's because you showed me they exist and gave me the best one of all.

Finally, thank you to every reader who picks up this book. I hope you find what you need in it.

About the Author

Jenny L. Howe first started scribbling stories into black-and-white composition notebooks with neon pink pens when she was in junior high and never really stopped. In college, she decided to turn her love of books into a career by pursuing a Ph.D. in literature, where she spent the next few years studying bizarre and entertaining medieval romances. Now, as a professor, she teaches courses in college writing, literature, and children's media. When she's not writing and teaching, Jenny spends her time buried under puzzle pieces, cross-stitching her favorite characters, and taking too many pictures of her rescue dogs, Tucker and Dale. *The Make-Up Test* is her debut novel.